THIS ISN'T EVERYTHING YOU ARE

THIS ISN'T EVERYTHING YOU ARE

J MARIE RUNDQUIST

This is a work of fiction. Names, characters, places (with the exception of trademarked locales), and incidents are fictitious and the product of the author's imagination. Any resemblance to actual people, living or dead, is coincidental.

Any trademarked companies, products, or locales mentioned in this work of fiction belong to their respective trademark holders. Trademarks used in this work of fiction are used in an editorial fashion and do not represent specific interest, opinion, or endorsement by the author.

Copyright © 2024 by J. Marie Rundquist in collaboration with Book, Ink

All rights reserved.

No part of this book may be reproduced in any form or by any electronic or mechanical means, including information storage and retrieval systems, without written permission from the author, except for the use of brief quotations in a book review.

ISBN: 978-1-7379287-4-4 (eBook)

ISBN: 978-1-7379287-3-7 (Paperback)

Library of Congress Control Number: 2024921840

For all K-12 paraprofessionals. Your connections with our children are transformational.

ALSO BY J MARIE RUNDQUIST

All I'm Asking

As Though You Were Mine

CONTENT WARNING

This story is about the close relationship between Lizzie and her brother, Justin. Justin is autistic and while that is certainly *not* the warning, it did prompt me to give my sensitivity/authenticity readers a heads up on specific scenes in this story, and so I want to make you aware of them, too, because no one can ever know all that everyone has experienced and might find challenging or triggering.

The prologue includes an abusive scene between Justin–age eight–and his mom.

There is some bullying language in the Justin chapters while he is at work. And if you're familiar with The Office, the bullying includes pranks similar to what Jim pulled on Dwight.

Both characters (Justin and Lizzie) experience trauma moments throughout the story that call back a car accident they were in when they were young.

Always, dear reader, take care of yourself. If you cannot read a scene, a chapter, or even this book because you need to protect yourself, then stop reading. Always choose yourself first.

<3, J. Marie

PROLOGUE

Mommy is in Fun mode, which is usually how she is when Daddy and Justin aren't home. Except today is a snow day and Justin doesn't have school. Beth is happy because even though she and Issy and Mommy play lots of games and do a lot of make-believe in their house-turned-into-Magic Graham Castle while Justin goes to school, Beth likes when he comes home to be king.

Justin is a great king. He knows all the right things to say and how to walk with super importance while wearing the crown they made and his blankie as a cape. He makes good rules and treats all the subjects fairly in the kingdom. Mommy and Issy aren't always as happy because Mommy says they have enough rules in the house from Daddy, except Beth thinks Justin's rules are good ones. They have to talk with nice words and not call anyone names that make them feel bad.

Justin says everyone in their kingdom, including all of those who live in the castle, must act with courtesy. Beth and Issy love this, saying they already curtsy all the time, and then show off their graceful curtsies. Mommy laughs at them and does her own curtsy.

Justin frowns and shakes his finger at her. "No laughing, Mommy. IssyBeth's only four and they don't understand." IssyBeth is the name Justin uses for Beth and Issy together, since they are twins.

Mommy's laugh turns into anger so quickly it scares Beth. "Put that finger away. You don't get to boss me around."

Beth's eyes grow wide and her palms already go up to cover her ears, even as Issy chimes in. "Yeah! No bossing Mommy. Or me and Beth! We're *princesses.*"

Justin screams the moment Mommy turns him around and spanks him, then yells at him to go to his room. Justin thrashes and he hits Mommy. Mommy and Issy yell louder and Mommy wraps her hand around Justin's wrist and drags him across the floor to his room. She slams the door and slides the deadbolt into place. The screams continue, although now muffled slightly by the distance and the closed door. Justin pounds at the door and rattles the doorknob, and this doesn't ease Beth's anxiety any more than when he was out in the living room.

Beth races to hers and Issy's bedroom to find her bear, the one with the "E" on it for Elizabeth. When the screaming stops, she comes out of her room, and Mommy lets her go inside Justin's room. Justin sits on the floor, rocking and pulling at his hair. Beth rushes to Justin and throws her arms around him, hugging him as tightly as she can. Beth is the only one Justin allows to hug him without asking him first. He doesn't hug her back, but sinks his face into Beth's shoulder, and he takes in gasps of air with his cries until eventually the tears dry up and his breathing calms.

Beth finds Justin's favorite stuffed dog, the one with the softest fur on it, and together, they sit on the floor, snuggling their stuffed animals.

The rest of the day goes by quietly with a movie, and later they play outside. There is so much snow that each step has them falling down and laughing as they push themselves up to try again.

Mommy has started dinner by the time they come inside, but then the phone rings, and Mommy says, "Again?" as she leans against the stove. "Fine." She tosses the phone across the counter and it clatters against the wall. She follows this up with turning off the oven and the stove burners and throwing the pans into the sink. Justin winces and covers his ears, but stays calm.

"Put your boots and coats back on, kids. We're going out to eat. Justin, you choose where we go."

Putting coats, hats, mittens, and boots back on is a chore, since everything is still wet from their time outside, but eventually, they are ready and get into the car. Justin behind Mommy's seat, Beth in the middle, then Issy behind the passenger seat. Justin double checks they all have their seatbelts on. "Mommy, is your seatbelt on?"

"Of course it is."

"I didn't hear the click!"

Mommy sighs, but unfastens her seatbelt, invites Justin to stand and lean over the front seat while she refastens it so he can both see and hear the click. She waits for Justin to sit back again, fasten his seatbelt, and say, "Ready!" Beth hears him breathe out in relief and finally they are on their way.

It's snowing again, and Beth hopes tomorrow will be a snow day, too, so Justin will be home once more. She'll make it so they play together all day in his room so Issy and Mommy can't get mad at him. They'll play games, read stories, and draw. She's already smiling, thinking about this plan.

The car swerves as they make a turn and Beth's stomach swoops like they are on one of the kiddie roller coasters at the mall.

"Do that again, Mommy!" Issy laughs.

"You have to slow down!" Justin says at the same time.

"Hush, both of you!" Mommy yells, turning off the radio. The snow comes down harder now and seems to fly straight at them. It's hard to see out the front window, but not so bad out of Beth's and Issy's window. Justin's right hand grips the handle of Beth's car seat and his left hand squeezes his own thigh. Beth decides they should play a game since everyone's gone quiet.

"I'm sorry, kids," Mommy says. "I'm going to turn around. I can't see anything in this storm." She looks back at Justin.

Justin nods. "It's okay, Mo—"

A horn blares loud and long. Beth screams as Mommy pulls the steering wheel and suddenly they are going faster. They lurch forward, spin, and Issy screams, too, as the car heads down an embankment, straight towards the not yet frozen river. Beth looks to Justin, as though he can stop what is happening.

They hit the water, hard, and Beth sees nothing more.

1

LIZZIE

The apartment I was moving into was a step up from my last one. The improvements included an elevator, an underground heated garage, and a dishwasher. The furniture was nicer, the carpet divine, and it was quiet.

Except none of it was mine.

When you lost your job because you fucked up, then had to work two part-time, minimum wage jobs and still couldn't make rent for your own place, then you accepted—with grace—your brother's offer to move in with him. A few friends had futons and airbeds available for me, but they were only short-term fixes and couch-hopping didn't appeal to me. The only other realistic option was to move back home with my moms who lived in the next state over, which I'd been primed to do with a total lack of enthusiasm before Justin invited me to stay in his spare bedroom.

Living with my moms wouldn't have been a bad thing except I'd already hibernated with them for nearly a month right after everything went down with my job and I wanted to prove to them and myself that I could be independent. Was living with my brother tangential to moving in with our moms? Somehow, siblings banding together felt separate from sheltering under my parents' wings.

I heaved a sigh and dropped an overstuffed box onto the stack in front of Justin's apartment. One unit over, the door opened and I looked up to see someone about my age dressed for a morning workout. They were tall and broad-shouldered with a small beard on their chin. They wore a white, long-sleeved moisture-wicking shirt with green polka dots that contrasted their dark skin, along with magenta running pants. One green and one pink scrunchy held their hair in two puffs and as they slipped their phone into an armband, I noted a light blue French manicure. Though I'd never met them in person, Justin had talked about his newer neighbor who'd moved in a few months ago and how they'd become friends.

"That's a pretty deep sigh you've got going there," they said.

"Moving."

"JT's sister, yeah?" They held out their hand. "I'm Reign."

"I'm Bet—" I stopped, suddenly realizing that a new place and empty spaces might be just the opening I needed.

"Bet...ter than sliced bread? Bet...ting on help with those boxes? A major gamble, by the way. I'm a wildcard when it comes to helping with moving."

I shrugged. "I was going to say 'I'm Betsy,' but I'm not altogether sure I want to be her anymore."

I hadn't really meant to say that out loud, though I'd been thinking it for weeks. Reign's smile turned into a full-on grin and they tilted their head away a tiny bit as a gleam of mischief took over in their eyes. I was in for it now.

"Please tell me your full name is Elizabeth. There are so many ways we can go from there. Unless, of course, you're looking for something entirely different. Then the possibilities are endless."

"It's Elizabeth."

They clenched a hand into a mini, tight-chested fist pump.

"Yes. Okay, I will help you haul up the rest of your stuff if you will let me help you choose a new identity."

"Deal."

The elevator at the end of the hall dinged and out came Justin, pushing a two-wheeled hand truck stacked high with boxes because that's how we rolled. I hauled boxes by hand while he got the easy wheels. Whatever. He was already doing me a big favor.

He wheeled up to us. "I see you've met Reign. I'm surprised it took until your second trip up here for it to happen."

"I've even coerced them into helping us move in all my stuff."

Justin snorted. "I'm sure coercion had no part in it. Reign knows everyone in the building and helps whether or not you want them to."

"And you know absolutely no one," I countered.

"Correct."

"He knows me!" Reign said.

"Reluctantly," Justin said.

I smiled, knowing that wasn't true. I'm sure Justin didn't make it easy for Reign at the beginning, but the two were certainly friends now. I was glad. Justin didn't need many friends, but he definitely needed *a* friend.

"Aw, did you hear that?" Reign teased. "It's an outright declaration of love."

Ignoring Reign, Justin took off his boots, unlocked the door to his apartment, and told me to wait while he made sure his cat, Crash, didn't escape. "I'll lock her in my bedroom so she doesn't get underfoot. Remember to take off your boots before bringing the boxes inside."

"JT, I get it that you normally want the shoes off thing inside the apartment," I said. "But do we seriously have to take them on and off again each time? It'll double our time and work."

"Yes," was all he said as he slipped inside.

"Between the clear sidewalk, the short hall to the elevator, and this hall, our boots are clean enough, don't you think?" I said this to the door, but it was Reign behind me who answered.

"You make a fair point, but also, look at your Docs."

I did, and groaned at the dripping mess they still were. Maybe the sidewalk wasn't completely free of snow and slush. This was why no one should move at the end of January in Minnesota. Messy and stupidly cold.

"Fine."

As soon as we dropped off the load of boxes inside, put our boots back on, and waited for Reign to change out their running shoes for boots, Reign didn't waste further time on the new identity part of the deal. They talked about options while we all headed down the stairwell.

"Betsy is clearly a name for a happy-go-lucky, blond, four-year-old girl."

"Well, I think I was closer to blond when I was that age." But it had been a long time since I'd considered myself as "happy-go-lucky." I was four-years-old when everything went horribly wrong, although from about five-years-old to thirteen was as close to care-free as I'd ever been. The next sixteen years carried a few more burdens.

"What about Ellie?" Reign asked next.

"Been there, done that."

"What is happening here?" Justin asked as we exited the building—into a blast of frigid air—and approached the small U-Haul truck. Only a few items remained since we'd already transferred most of my stuff from my old apartment to a self-storage garage. I only needed bedroom furniture, as Justin's spare room had been a studio and office for him before. He did some photography as a hobby. Displacing his creative space dropped an extra layer of guilt over the other coat of shame that brought me into this situation.

"We're choosing a new name and identity for your sister! One of my favorite things."

I caught Justin glancing my way, and though his expression was unreadable, I guessed at his thinking. *Again?* Whatever Reign thought of it, Justin and I both knew better. This wasn't the first time I'd reinvented myself.

Reign pressed on, unbothered by Justin's lack of response. "Eliza? Lisa? You do sort of look like a Lisa." They said this with a lackluster shrug as they helped Justin maneuver a mattress out of the truck.

I eyed the bed frame and determined I could handle the two short ends on my own. "Why do I feel like that's not a compliment?"

"To be honest, and I bet I can be honest with you ... oh, what about Bette?" They slipped their head around the mattress to look at me as they traveled backwards, then said, "Nah. Anyway, if this guy is your brother, then I'm betting you're good with honesty, or at least used to honesty—"

"Skip to the end," Justin cut in.

"Right. Well, it's the hair."

I suddenly regretted choosing to wear a headband-style ear covering instead of a full winter hat. My hair was a nondescript dark blond, straighter than straight—by design. I didn't have much body, but there was enough wave that I had to work at keeping it to the sleek lines. It was, in fact, the complete opposite of Reign's dark head of free-floating puffs.

"What do you mean? What's wrong with my hair?"

"Too straight. Wrong color."

"Straight is the fashion." At least, it was among all the so-called friends I had at my ex-job. I was an ex-everything. Ex-friend. Ex-staff member. Ex-lease-holder. Ex-Betsy. Why not "ex" out my hair, too?

We paused at the elevator and I let one end of the bed frame rest on the floor as I pressed the UP button. Justin and Reign, as though to show off their overwhelming strength compared to mine, waited, the mattress still balanced along their arms and chest. It wasn't like I didn't get any exercise, but it didn't match Justin's intense swimming regimen and whatever Reign did.

"Nope," Reign said again. "Straight and nondescript is the thing for Lisas and Lulus and Lauras, and other white girls who have no imagination. If you want a new identity, you'll need a name that will inspire new hair, too."

The elevator doors opened, and as we finagled our way inside the small space with our large items, I smiled inwardly about Reign's assessment regarding the lack of imagination. They'd already described over half of the teaching staff at my ex-school. I had been the interesting one. I had become the "I have a gay friend!" friend. They loved my earlobe gauges and eyebrow piercings. I may have had boring hair now, but when I'd come into the job, I'd had a shorter cut with streaks of blue in it. I'd blown into my new special ed para position with confidence and conviction. There was some kind of saying about leaving things better than you found them. I'd destroyed that completely.

"Elsbeth?" Reign suggested.

"No," Justin said. The ding of the elevator reaching floor three added the ring of finality.

"No?"

"No."

"Agreed," I said. Justin's contribution surprised me. He'd never engaged with any of my name changes in the past. Then again, it hadn't ever been a group effort. It was a fresh experience to have someone help find the new me. With the way each of my prior identities failed, maybe the community venture was what I needed to get it right.

We got to Justin's door, set our furniture down, and removed our boots, which unfortunately hadn't been an exaggeration of mine to say we'd take twice as long because neither Reign nor I were wearing boots that were easily toed off and slipped back on again. Doc Martens for me and ASOS for them. Justin also worried someone might wander into his apartment uninvited, and he locked the door each time we left. He once again told us to wait while he sequestered Crash in his room before we carried in these two items.

"Wait, you let her out again before we left for this next trip? Can't you keep her in your room for the next hour while until we finish bringing everything in?" I asked.

"I don't want her to think she's being abandoned or punished."

I stifled the urge to push back, to argue that the amount of time his cat, of all animals, spent locked away—and likely sleeping—was negligible and wouldn't affect her at all. Or that the back and forth might not only confuse her, but also extend how long it would take us to complete the remainder of our work. His insistence upon the routine was for him, not Crash, and so I let it go and merely nodded in support.

Justin was attached to routine more like twist ties than zip ties. Sometimes things loosened behind a twist tie, but you could always release something or re-secure it with slight effort. Having me move in was like cutting the zip tie of his inner sanctuary and everything spilling out in an unpredictable mess. JT—a nickname bestowed upon Justin by our cousin, Hugh—and I had always been close since the early days of living with our moms. Our moms who were actually our aunts Lysianne and Mac. They took us in when our dad dropped us off at their doorstep twenty-five years ago after a car accident had claimed the lives of our mother and sister. I was four and Justin was eight. We couldn't ask for better parents than Mama LiLi and Mama Mac, yet Justin and I became our everything to each other.

Until I became Betsy three years ago.

I'd inhabited the names and identities of Beth, Liz, and Ellie over the years, continually searching for a better version of myself, and when I started my new position with Meadowfields Elementary, something possessed me to change myself yet again. I'd gone through a best friend breakup a few months before—a wreckage of my own creation—which pushed me into an eddy of self-recrimination. When the principal introduced me during an all-staff meeting, "You can call me Betsy" spilled out of my mouth and the new "me" was born. That "me" was a mistake. As Betsy, I'd allowed the swirling vortex in my mind to push me into becoming a person I didn't like very well. As Betsy, I'd slipped away from Justin, my moms, and the friends who had offered me couches despite the rarely returned texts.

As Betsy, I'd almost gotten a child killed.

Obviously, being left to my own devices for reinvention no longer created successful results. During the next round of re-lacing our boots, locking the door, fetching the next set of furniture and boxes, unlacing our boots, unlocking the door, re-locking up Crash, and reminding myself that fratricide was a felony—Reign had tossed out Liz, Lizbeth, Beth, E-Beth—*wtf*—, Bettina, and Betty.

Justin didn't offer another opinion about names, but his hand paused on the door lock when he heard "Beth." I quickly and quietly said, "No, I don't think so." Reign had moved on without noticing a thing. "Beth" had been my original nickname until high school, when I shifted over to "Liz." Middle school had been a shit show and I couldn't shed "Beth" fast enough. Justin had been irritated until I reminded him that he let me and Hugh call him JT and there wasn't even a logical reason for it. Justin's middle name was Anthony and our last name was Gramsie.

"Are you sure you don't want to branch out to an entirely different name?" Reign asked.

In truth, I wasn't sure. A brand new name held a lot of appeal. However, their next suggestion pinged inside of me.

"Wait, you vetoed Liz, but what about Lizzie? Lizzies are fun without being the immature Betsy or pretentious Elizabeth."

"Yes, that's the one," I said. "Does it match the hair?"

"Oh lord, no," they said. "Lizzies need curl. And a new color. I'm thinking red."

I turned to my brother. "JT? What do you think?"

He shrugged. "I like Beth."

His tone was so gentle, so different from his direct and often interpreted as brusque manner, I almost capitulated for how it pierced into my heart. I didn't know who Beth was anymore, and I'm not sure I ever knew. Lizzie sounded like someone I could handle, an identity I could achieve and mold me into the person my friends, and more importantly, my brother, deserved once again.

"Lizzie it is, Reign. Let's make it happen."

2

JUSTIN

Neither Lizzie nor Justin enjoys driving in the snow, given the traumatic accident from when they were young, but for Justin, even a winter day with roads in good condition can prove uncomfortable—too many moving variables. However, sometimes it calms him after more stressful days at work, but this is only because of the routes he chooses.

The most direct route home from work is via the highway, although it's not always the fastest way. During the winter months, like now, he puts even more effort into avoiding the highway. Mostly, he selects back roads because they give him ideas for his photography, which is the primary reason it calms him. It's an idea he and his therapist came up with during one of his bi-monthly visits. With the help of AI, on Sundays he plans out six different routes—the one extra for in case something unexpected occurs such as construction or an accident or weather inconveniences—and throughout the week he stars the routes he likes best.

Calm is what Justin seeks because work today was unusually stressful. He's a software analyst at All Choice Care, an intermediary health plan provider. They are still a relatively small business, so while acting as troubleshooter for employees isn't in his job description, some days he has to fill in for their usual tech support person. It was a little too much "peopling" today, as Reign would call it.

Justin pulls over to the side of the road when he spies an interesting subject for a photo shoot. A large branch, snapped and peeling away from a tree with snow and ice clinging to splinters and offshoots of the limb rests close enough to the street that he could probably do a few zoom shots right from the warmth of his heated seat. Except that feels like "phoning it in," an expression his boss, Caleb, uses to describe Justin's colleagues from time to time.

He keeps the car running as he pops open his trunk and gets out of the driver's seat to pull his camera from a lockbox. The sun is disappearing quickly, so he adjusts the shutter speed accordingly to increase light exposure. When he approaches the branch, however, his eye catches on a spill of some sort, part on the sidewalk and part on the shoveled snow next to it. It doesn't look like de-icing fluid or dog pee. An energy or electrolytes drink, probably. Then he squats at the edge of the corner curb cut and takes a few rapid shots at varying focal lengths before zooming in close, already fascinated by the spectrum of green hues along different parts of the pavement and the uneven icy edges of it both suspended and blended into the adjacent snow bank. This is the unique photo subject he likes.

Ground photos make up a lot of his collection. Nature patterns capture most people's interest, and while he completely understands why, those patterns, when studied regularly, have a predictability. Justin appreciates the unpredictability of the ground. Footprints, bike tracks, animal prints, and weather all impact different ground surfaces in myriad ways. Kind of like people, except the ground does its own thing and doesn't expect anything from him.

Unlike some of his co-workers.

Today's stress had been more than simply all the "peopling." Though still a challenge, Justin's grown much better at face-to-face interactions as he becomes more experienced with age. Facial expressions and tone of voice aren't always obvious to him, but at least they exist along with body language, of which he continually studied. Email exchanges usually work best, except for sarcasm and obscure emojis. So when a colleague writes to thank him for fixing the printer—which is even further away from his job description than occasionally helping other employees with their computer software—followed by a laughing-crying emoji, and he writes back with "You're welcome" only to find out the colleague is angry and frustrated because the printer still isn't working, the whole thing is maddening and exhausting.

It turns out he was supposed to decode sarcasm in the guy's email from his use of the emoji. What did that ridiculous emoji mean if not "dying laughing" like someone once told him when he finally asked? Sarcasm is one of his least favorite forms of expression. His boss, a former programmer, always surrounded his sarcastic statements in emails to him with sarcasm tags. In an email last week about the company potluck lunch, he wrote to Justin, "<sarcasm> I bet you'll be bringing salsa because I know how much you love tomatoes! </sarcasm>." Justin rarely figures out the best reply, but "Haha!" usually does the trick.

He likes his boss, Caleb. Caleb and also Claire from HR are his two favorite people in the entire company. They haven't worked at All Choice Care as long as Justin has, but he feels the most comfortable around them.

Returning his thoughts to the photo subject in front of him, Justin snaps a few more photos of the richly textured drink spill, then drives home, calmer and content after the creative respite. He turns onto his apartment complex's driveway, circles through the parking lot, spots Bet—Lizzie's car, and then continues on to enter the underground garage and to his assigned space.

As he walks into his apartment and sets his bag down on the oblong table next to the door, Crash trots out of Justin's bedroom, meowing in greeting. She stops at his feet and waits patiently while he carefully removes his shoes, puts them on the shoe rack, and hangs up his coat in the closet. She looks up at him expectantly, then stands on her haunches, front paws raised up. He smiles and squats down to pick her up. Her paws wrap around his neck with a satisfying purr, and he hugs her in return, massaging her head and petting her splotchy, calico-patterned fur.

"I saw her for about two seconds today, which was enough for her to hiss at me, turn her back, and saunter off," Lizzie calls out from the kitchen. "It's the only time she assures me she is a real cat and not a dog in disguise."

Justin laughs and nuzzles into Crash. "She'll come around eventually. I mean, she did walk away and leave you be instead of staring you down. That's progress."

Crash is the love of his life. For years, Lizzie worked at him to get a pet. Justin kept refusing. Too much work. Too noisy. A few months ago, Justin came upon Crash in the apartment parking garage, skulking near his car, thin with fur matted in spots. He recoiled when she glided between and around his legs, rubbing up against him. He might have kicked out at her from an uncontrolled defense mechanism if he hadn't also heard her sweet meow and the extremely satisfying purr emanating from her.

Her purr had an almost immediate effect on him. The next day she showed up again and then jumped up on the hood of his car, lost her footing, then comically scrabbled away at the surface, looking for purchase for her claws before Justin caught her just as she was about to slide off the edge. The purr returned, as did Justin's draw to her.

He'd texted Lizzie a photo of him and Crash a few days later, knowing Lizzie would gloat with her "I told you so's," but he didn't mind. He adores Crash and Crash adores him. She's a welcome sight when he comes home to an empty apartment. She listens to him spill out the many complaints he's had to bottle up throughout the day without telling him what he should have said or done.

Justin sets Crash back down on the floor and joins Lizzie in the kitchen. Crash follows and leaps up to the counter.

"Oh, sure," Lizzie eyes Crash warily. "Now you're willing to be in my presence." Crash releases a low, warning growl and Lizzie gives her the finger.

"Hey now," Justin intercedes. "Bet--," he starts, then catches himself and continues, "Lizzie, Crash, you're family. Be nice."

Lizzie smiles, reassuring Justin that she doesn't hold any real animosity towards Crash nor him for his slip-up for her new name. She finishes seasoning the tilapia filets and slides the tray into the oven. "Thanks for adapting," she tosses over her shoulder, "I know you don't love my continual name changes."

"It doesn't matter if I like, love, or hate them. How you want to be called is your choice."

Justin studies her, and she lets him for a moment before she turns to wet a sponge and wipe down the counter. Though he wants to ask her questions, he refrains because she kept her responses short. When it comes to studying facial expressions and body language, hers—and once upon a time, Hugh's—are ones he knows best. Now, her body language gives nothing away and when she does this, he's learned he'll get very few answers. He'll need to wait.

His sister does this—this name change thing. Her full name is Elizabeth and when they were growing up, she went by Beth. When she was seventeen, she came to the breakfast table one Sunday morning and declared to him and their moms that starting that day, she would be Liz. A few years later, after Hugh died, she used Ellie, and when she started her most recent job at Meadowfields, she changed over to Betsy. It's like she's hoping a new name will transform her into a new person.

"Lizzie" is as close as she's gotten to sounding like "Issy." He's unsure what this means or how he feels about it. He just wants her to be happy with who she is, no matter who she was before. Betsy—Lizzie—is the best person he knows. He can't let her remember how things were. He made a promise.

Without realizing it, Lizzie saves him from a rapid spiral into a memory-induced panic attack by pushing plates and silverware into his hands. "Here, dinner's almost ready. Can you set the table?"

"I have to change out of my work clothes."

"Okay. Go change and then set the table." She shoos him away and opens the oven to flip the fish.

When he returns, Lizzie has organized everything on the counter for him to grab and transfer to the table. Memories tug at him once more and he attempts levity to help tamp down his irritation and their insistence on resurfacing unexpectedly. "I appreciate the organization, but I'm not one of your kids. I obviously don't need help with how to prepare our table for dinner."

She stares at the line of dishes and food. From left to right: two plates (stacked), two forks on top of two napkins folded in half, two glasses (one in front of the other), salt and pepper (arranged like the glasses), the plate of broiled fish, a bowl of brown rice, a bowl of roasted Brussel sprouts, a carton of oat milk. "I didn't even realize I'd done that. I'm sorry."

When Justin and Lizzie were kids, they'd set and cleared the table a bit like this. Lizzie would hand him things from the cupboard and he would bring them to the table. Every once in a while they would switch roles, but it messed with their system and upset him and ultimately everyone else, too.

Wondering how irritated she might get, Justin tests her tolerance now in his own act of defiance. He grabs one of each dish—and only the pepper, not salt, just for good measure—and arranges them on the table. He briefly considers putting everything down disordered, such as the plate at his spot and the glass at hers, but he's had enough disorder for today. He doesn't need to add to it.

"Oh my god. You are so obnoxious," she says, laughing. He smiles in return, feeling victorious. "Point taken," she adds and grabs two of the dishes of food as he reaches for the remaining plate, fork, napkin, and glass before taking care of the rest of the items.

"It's my job," he says.

Lizzie sits and waits for him to finish transferring the items. "Reign and I were talking, and they asked about what happened at Meadowfields. I guess I had those kids on my mind and channeled my old self when setting everything up."

"Your old self. Betsy."

"Yes. My new self, Lizzie, will definitely be better. She'll save up some money and start looking for a new job completely different from what she used to do."

"I'd say selling cigarettes at the Gas-n-Guzzle is pretty different already." Justin sips his oat milk, not entirely intending the comment as a joke, even though Lizzie rolls her eyes at him.

"Yeah, true. Except, I mean I'll purposely find something permanently new instead of these filler jobs." She brings her arm to her nose and inhales. "A career that won't leave my clothing forever smelling slightly of gasoline, no matter how long I let them soak in the washer."

"Hot water and vinegar," Justin says. "I searched online for you and everyone said the same thing. Soak it in equal parts water and vinegar, but the water needs to be super hot."

"Oh, yeah? Awesome. I'll try that. Anyway. I like Reign. I can see why you like them so well."

Justin nods, then asks, "You don't want to teach anymore?"

"What? Oh. Well. I don't know. I was never a teacher, anyway."

This is Justin's fault, but he sets that aside and analyzes his role here. He needs more information, and it's been a tricky business getting Lizzie to open up recently. The accident with one of her students has flattened her in a way he hasn't seen before. She used to be more open with her thoughts and feelings. Now she's closed up tight. He imagines her as one of their software codes at work when something, somewhere has changed to make a single line of code break. He knows what caused the break, but where exactly is the broken code within Lizzie?

"You can stop analyzing me," Lizzie says. "I made some stupid decisions and almost got a kid killed. Pretty straightforward."

"It wasn't your fault."

"Wasn't it? How do you know?"

This response stops him short. He thought he knew because that's what Mama LiLi and Mama Mac told him, but Lizzie hasn't ever told him the full story.

"Are you saying our moms only told me what they thought I wanted to hear?" he asks.

Lizzie shrugs and looks only at her food as she carefully portions out a bite of fish to go with a forkful of rice.

Justin has always assumed Lizzie was unfairly accused of negligence, but now he examines more than the story from their moms. He considers the past year, especially, when Lizzie—well, *Betsy*—had reminded him too frequently of Issy. Issy, the twin sister to Lizzie who died in a car accident almost twenty-five years ago along with their biological mother. Issy, who more often than not, didn't like bossy and inflexible Justin.

Lizzie, who has always been his very best friend, had seen and called him less and less over the past year, and her text responses held long gaps and short answers. When they'd have dinner together, her answers to his questions would be short, lacking in any true information. Sometimes, she'd have a story about her colleagues—her friends—that didn't make them sound very kind, and he'd asked why she would hang out with them outside of work. "They're predictable," was all she'd said. While he didn't think this was a trait she'd normally appreciated—she didn't always love it about him—he'd understood it.

"There you're getting it," Lizzie breaks into his thoughts. "Betsy was a bitch. You don't know anything at all about what she was capable of. Best to be happy I'm Lizzie now."

He has nothing to say to that, and they continue the rest of their meal in silence.

3

LIZZIE

Walking into "Every Day Beauty, Everyone" flooded me with warm, calming vibes. People with big hair, no hair, colors, curls, and all the hairstyling accessories. Most importantly, smiles and laughter. So much laughter. The environment allowed me to take deep, cleansing breaths. I'd let my guard down and relaxed in clubs, theaters, coffee shops, and corners meant for me and all of my LGBTQ+ friends and family, but this place transcended them all. It bridged knowing I was in a safe space with the certainty I was safe among *everyone*.

I'd found my new salon and had no intention of sharing it with any of the "friends" I'd made at my current jobs or would make at future ones. They weren't worth...*this*.

Reign assured me that walking in without an appointment would be okay, except the salon was busy, so I told the receptionist I could come back another day. He smiled. "It's no problem. We have several stylists available for walk-ins." He tapped away with his full spread of ringed fingers and thumb on the tablet in front of him. Some fingers had multiple bands. I glanced at my own hands and imagined more jewelry on them, then reached up to touch my ears. One kid I used to work with at Meadowfields had the urge to pull at all varieties of dangling items. I'd stopped wearing anything other than my small, solid lobe gauges and my hoop nose ring. I'd forgotten that I could bring back the hoops, the danglers, the chains, and everything in between. I plotted out wardrobe changes as ring-guy waved at me to follow him.

"Nuria's open. I'll take you back."

Nuria's salon space spewed silver and gold with the mirror amplifying the shine. I almost needed sunglasses. Mobiles in gleaming gold and silver spiraled down from hooks arcing away from the wall. Silver bow ties specked with blue sparkles adorned jars of combs and scissors—and even those items were gold. It was ... a lot. And yet I also kind of dug it. I thanked ring-guy and sat in the swivel chair.

Where my stylist's station exuded glam, the one to the left embraced a homey warmth. Photos framed the entire perimeter of the mirror. Laughing, happy smiles. Upon closer inspection, almost all of them shared one woman's image, and when I saw the message at the top of the mirror written in swooping strokes with permanent marker, I understood a little better. "For Ellie—always and forever." A memorial of sorts. I gazed back at my station and resisted holding up my hand to block the glare from all the glitz. I must not have masked my expression enough, though, since a woman sitting in the stylist chair of the Ellie station laughed.

"There's still time to back out," she said, the edge of her hand perpendicular to her mouth, as though in conspiracy with me.

"Hush, Melly-Belle," her stylist chided, cuffing her playfully on the arm.

"Oh my god, Corrina. Can you cut it out with that elementary school nickname?" She turned to me and said, "It's just Mel."

"Well, I said 'Belle' instead of 'Belly.' That should count for something." Corrina shifted her attention to me. "By the way, don't you worry. I know the sparkle is a bit much, but Nuria's the best. You're in excellent hands."

"No lie," Mel said. "Corrina's mom has Nuria do her hair, and if she likes Nuria, you know she's the real deal."

Corrina snorted. "I'll say. Getting my mother to set foot in this part of town? Nuria is a miracle worker."

I pulled on the ends of my hair to fan it out and then let it flop down from my fingertips. "Reign says I need a miracle. Not a fan of straight, I guess."

"Few of us here are," Mel laughed. I grinned at the joke. Yep, this was definitely my new salon.

"It's not the style, babe," another woman said, joining us. "It's the color. Although I won't lie to you, your face could also do without the boring white-girl spaghetti strands."

She threaded her fingers through my hair, and I knew this must be Nuria. And Nuria was not some bouncy young upstart with wedge shoes and gold lamé leather pants. Instead, she was tall, dark, smooth, and had curves everywhere. Her skin was a warm sepia, and her high cheekbones accented her golden-brown eyes. She wore yoga-style pants with a simple black tank that revealed beautiful, strong shoulders. Then there was her hair. It fell—and really, it looked like a waterfall—in waves down to the middle of her back in silver, gold, and black. She was gorgeous, and I heated in response.

Throughout my life, I'd landed pretty firmly in the aromantic camp with no ambiguity. However, I glided along the ace spectrum and when attraction occasionally hit, it hit hard, though often short-lived. It was usually a one-and-done encounter.

Let's go clubbing it, my body whispered. Only the whisper was so soft, all Nuria actually heard was, "Reign suggested red curls."

"Hmm," Nuria murmured while coiling a few strands of hair around her fingers and rested her hands along my cheek. "Reign doesn't really know what they're talking about. Let's let them stick to their forte of fitness, yeah?"

"They were right in that I needed a change," I replied. "I need to be someone new."

Nuria raised her eyebrows. "And who is that someone?"

"You tell me." I shrugged and raised my hands to wiggle my fingers through the air. "Dive into my hair and make the magic happen."

She smiled and trailed a finger down my cheek as she released the coiled hair. "Outright red, no, but I think an auburn. Let me grab a cape for you. We'll wash that hair and see what we have to work with regarding any kind of curl." She walked away, and I heard a snicker next to me.

"Wow," Mel said. "Is this where you normally pick up women?"

"It might be now. She is *hot*. Is she single?"

"Perpetually so."

"Think I have a chance?"

"Oh yes," Corrina said. "She's got some interest. She may as well have purred while fingering your hair."

Mel's mouth dropped while I laughed in appreciation at the innuendo.

"Plenty of time for fingering later," Nuria said, returning with my cape along with the best hearing and timing ever. Corrina whooped in laughter. I owed Reign a cake for introducing this place to me. I'd never had so much fun getting a haircut. Looking at the past year, I was hard-pressed to remember when I'd last had any carefree fun at all.

Nuria pulled an album out of a drawer—the exterior façade covered in gold contact paper with sparkly rainbow flecks—and flipped through until she found her chosen pages. She turned to grab a wheeled stool and sat next to me to share the album.

"Remember to look at color, not style, right now. If there's anything you love or hate, I'll either honor those choices or I'll convince you you're wrong."

I smiled. She reminded me of one of my students from a few years ago, before Meadowfields, who daily gave me clear, unsolicited opinions about my appearance. My earring count was asymmetrical and made me look lopsided. If I'm going to have a blue stripe on one side of my head, then the other side should also be blue, not pink.

The album was different from the stock books I'd seen in other hair salons. This one had real people in them, with the salon in the background, including Nuria's gold bomb station. They all looked so happy. Bits of jealousy poked at me from different angles. I told myself I'd be happy, too, with the new look coming my way.

Nuria's hand landed gently on one of mine. "You're flipping through without pause. Are you sure you want to do color?"

"One hundred percent sure." No lie, but she was right. I hadn't really been studying color or style. I'd only seen the poses and expressions I longed to replicate.

"Do you trust me?" Nuria's hand still rested on mine as I turned my head to meet her gaze. I scoped her amazing, shimmering waves before returning to her eyes. The answer was obvious.

"I do."

She scooped the book away from me with a confident nod. "I'll be right back."

She left, presumably to do her mixing magic as she prepped the "trust me" color. I pulled my phone out to waste time in my most destructive way: stalked the Meadowfields Elementary website, read all the weekly newsletters, and scoured the internet for my name. Well, my old name. Basically, remind myself of everything I'd lost, including an entire career.

"Lizzie!"

I popped my head up from my screen to see Reign in the

mirror. They were standing behind me with a huge smile. I smiled back. "Hey!"

"You came!"

"Oh, she hasn't come yet," Mel said, eliciting a giggle from Corrina as she snipped away. "But in a few more minutes? It is *so* Nuria." And so me, apparently. I'd forgotten Mel was still there.

Reign nodded. "She's the perfect slut, it's true."

I laughed. "If that's all it is, then we'll be well-suited."

"She's not going to break your heart?"

"Nope. Aro all the way, baby."

Reign nodded again with approval. "Stop by to see me after you're all re-christened here. We'll set up our fitness plan."

I groaned. "I don't know if I was *actually* serious about doing that." I'd bumped into them in the hall earlier in the week and mistakenly mentioned how maybe doing some sort of couch-to-5k might be fun. I'd used the word "fun." Justin had a rigorous swimming workout during the week with a change-up on the weekends for other things like strength-training or other equipment-based cardio, but I don't know if he considered it *fun*, exactly. It was therapeutic, which made it necessary, not necessarily enjoyable.

On the other hand, I used to run and appreciated its cathartic, restorative value. With the therapy aspect on my mind combined with how for Reign, it seemed joyful, I'd let the thoughts slip out of my mouth and now Reign was ready to run with it. Literally, of course.

"Well then, we'll make jokes as we do it. Funny fitness. Byeeee!" They waved, did a little bounce, and headed back to the funny fitness area.

"They have got to stop doing that 'bye' thing," Nuria said, rolling over with her tray of dye and foil strips. "They sound ridiculous."

"My brother says Reign started doing it purposely to annoy

him. I think someone at his workplace says it every day before she leaves."

"Tell your brother he's created a monster. Reign does it all the time here now, too."

I laughed because Reign looked and sounded pretty goofy, except for the cute bounce. I liked the little bounce.

Nuria put on gloves and combed through my hair. "So, you need to be someone new. Breakup?"

"Kind of."

"Girl, on-again-off-again is no way to go."

I laughed at this blunt response from a woman I only met ten minutes ago. "Rude."

She smiled and brushed on the dye to the first section of my hair.

"Permanent breakup, just not from a romantic relationship. It was a split between me and my job."

"Time to show the world, then, the new magic of Lizzie."

"Magic. Yes. I like that."

"Magic like Willow? Or do you lean towards Tara?"

Well, the *Buffy* reference sealed the deal. Nuria and I were destined to meet and become friends. Hopefully with some benefits since her touch was still sending electricity through me, but I'd be okay with only the binge-watching of *Buffy, the Vampire Slayer* side of our partnership. "How about the looks of Willow with the 'good witch' vibe of Tara?"

Nuria's knuckles touched my chin gently, an indication for me to turn my head towards her. "Just a smidge," she said. Then added as she combed some strands over a sheet of foil. "Not a fan of Season Six Willow?"

I shrugged, not willing to give up the truth of how I wasn't always the nicest person as Betsy of Meadowfields Elementary. Tara's character didn't care what others thought of her and she didn't have a mean or snobby bone in her body. Lizzie of Astros and Gas-n-Guzzle needed to be better and more like Tara's character. Nicer. *Kinder*.

"Hard to like someone who is high on anything, really, let alone high on magic," I agreed, remembering my moms and I dissecting Willow's "addiction" to magic. Justin watched with us, too, equally invested with plenty of outrage over Tara's death. He had tons of thoughts about all the different ways they could have handled her character.

Given those thoughts and our creative play when we were kids, I wondered if Justin wrote in his spare time. He was so creative with his photography—simultaneously beautiful and technically fascinating—but his imagination held a similar creative weight. The characters we played during our childhood days often had stricter guidelines than I liked. (Why can't I be invisible *and* gigantic? I'd ask. *You just can't. That's not who that character is.*) The world-building and plot line of our stories? Top-notch. It's probably why I put up with playing a character he made me think I created all on my own. Years later, I realized it was smooth maneuvering on his part.

Nuria and I chatted away about TV and then podcasts—she followed true crime, I was all about behind-the-scenes for music and music history—and then she set me aside to wait out the dye as she took another customer. I watched, fascinated, as she shaved intricate patterns around his head. She was an artist. Briefly, I considered shearing all my hair down to the scalp in favor of her razor skills. She caught my eye at one point and winked when I raised my eyebrows and mouthed, "wow."

When she returned to me, I said, "I understand the sparkly color scheme of your station now. You make people shine."

Nuria laughed, a beautiful, deep throated sound. "I *help* people shine. I can't make it happen, but I can help showcase what's inside."

I offered a noncommittal noise and asked about the overflow of gold and silver.

"Corrina—the owner—is all about theme."

I darted my eyes over to the next stall, empty now, the two women having slipped away earlier without me noticing.

"Her space, you can see, is all about love and memory. Although, her stall doesn't really count since she's not an official stylist. She just uses that space for Mel, who you met, and a few other friends. It's mostly a way to enjoy the vibe of this place instead of being stuck in her office. She often sits in the chair herself with her laptop to work."

"The vibe here is absolutely perfect," I said. "I don't blame her."

"It is, isn't it? Anyway, we've got a retro jazz-type station, a Paris one, a *Steel Magnolias* southern theme, a rainbow cliché, and so on. Mine is glitter and glitz. I want my clients to feel like a million bucks. Okay, let's rinse and wash."

We headed over to the sinks and didn't speak for a few minutes while she rinsed out the dye and washed my hair. I closed my eyes, relaxing further into the cooling strokes of water all over my scalp, followed by warmer temperatures and Nuria's fingers massaging my head during the wash and condition.

Afterwards, she squeezed out the extra water, toweled my head down, then we headed back to her station.

"What do you think?" She swiveled my chair around and removed the towel. "Does this space make you feel like a million dollars?" She combed my newly colored hair to prepare for the cut. Though a little difficult to imagine the color of my hair while wet, I already saw the rich tones of the tawny shade of red.

"Well, watching you make magic with my hair in this space gives me a glam vibe."

Nuria's first snip resulted in a chunk of damp hair descending down the front of my cape. I don't have especially thick hair, but getting rid of a good two or three inches of length gave me breathing room, like the top button on a pair of jeans at the end of the day, releasing some pressure.

She laughed as more hair slid down the front of my cape. "Good enough. I find all this shine a bit overwhelming at times, myself. I'll tell you a secret, though." Our eyes met in the mirror's reflection and her expression turned mischievous. I reveled in the anticipatory moment, ready for the juicy gossip. She leaned in to whisper in my ear, "None of it's real."

My laughter yanked my head away from her at this unexpected response. "No, really?" I said, trying to paste on a shocked face. "But it looks like twenty-four karat gold!"

She grinned. "Right? I mean, who could guess that the gold bars underneath my implement jars are only cardboard boxes wrapped in gold paper?"

"Oh my god, I thought they were genuine!"

"Nope, all fake."

By now we were both laughing so hard, tears in my eyes made everything glitter and shine even more. Nuria handed me a tissue to blot away the tears before they could create eyeliner streaks down my cheeks. I hadn't laughed like that in a long time and it felt so good.

"Thank you for that," I said.

"See? A million bucks."

"A million bucks." I nodded.

4
JUSTIN

"I'm thinking about promoting you," Caleb says.

He and Justin sit in Caleb's office, drinking tea and coffee respectively, having their morning meeting during which they review the daily error reports and team requests.

Justin sets his tumbler down on the desk and types some notes on the spreadsheet. "Well, there's no reason not to keep thinking about it if that's how you want to spend your time."

Justin has declined two promotions from All Choice Care in the past five years. Not because he doesn't want a better or higher-paying position; rather, the offers did not, in fact, fit into the definition of "promotion." One offer was as a help desk manager which by Justin's figuring, would have been a *de*motion. The sole responsibility of the help desk manager is to route web-based tickets to their proper queues. Perhaps All Choice thought the title of "manager" implied a more advanced role since his current position includes the word "associate." Semantics within All Choice Care's organizational structure often present nonsensical ways to inaccurately represent skill sets.

Justin is an associate software design analyst. He studies

their systems for optimization while also testing and assisting with software design. Without him and the two other analysts, the company would fall apart. It's not ego behind this assessment; it's logic. The backbone of their company relies on the software engineering team.

The second opportunity was an invitation to interview for a senior customer service representative. Again, the term "senior" to mean some kind of higher, better position. As though they don't recognize his current role involves more skill and experience. As though they assume he won't see through their attempts to lure him into a potential pay cut, or more strategically, a layoff.

It's not that they're not aware he's good at his job. They know he's the best on the team. They also know he earns more than most anyone else at the company who isn't in a directorial position or above. So when Caleb talks of promotion, Justin has no compulsion to find out more. He likes what he does well enough. The work no longer carries the same challenge or variety it used to, although Caleb has had a good hand in changing the status quo in the past couple of years.

Caleb swivels towards his desk. "I'm serious, Justin. I'm not talking about any of those bullshit positions HR's been trying to force you into."

"What position wouldn't be a bullshit one?"

"Mine."

Several thoughts and emotions fly through Justin. First, he briefly looks at Caleb's chair, because he can't stop his brain from going to the literal and direct meaning of "mine" and "position." Second, he realizes Caleb obviously means his position in the company, Project Manager. Third, he wonders how this affects Caleb, which triggers a key emotion: anxiety. Justin likes his supervisor, and anxiety already seeps in about losing someone who has made it worthwhile to stay with All Choice, made it so Justin enjoys coming in to the office instead of working remotely, which he generally prefers if given the option. He trusts Caleb and likes having a work friend. Claire in HR is great, too, but with her office on the other side of the building, they mostly only see each other during lunch.

Justin instinctually touches his jawline, slightly roughened with stubble. He shaves at night instead of the morning to ensure this stubble, which acts as a natural calming texture for him to access without looking weird. Coupled with his anxiety over Caleb leaving is a spark of excitement, which causes more apprehension because he doesn't want to be excited about losing Caleb. He twirls his hand in order to stroke his jaw down to his chin and focuses on his breathing.

"Why are you only thinking about it?" Justin asks.

"I used 'thinking' as a way to edge us into this conversation. What I mean is I *want* to promote you if you want to apply for this position."

Justin looks back down at the spreadsheet on his laptop display and wipes away those two minutes he'd let himself believe what Caleb almost sold him before hearing the words, "apply for this position." This must have been Caleb trying a long joke on him. How disappointing.

"Good one, Caleb. Not very funny, but you had me going there."

"Wait, why do you think I'm joking?"

Justin closes his laptop, no longer able to concentrate on the document in front of him. "Apply? Interview? You know HR won't even let me get past the first round."

"Trudy and her HR don't have the final say. Nihal says I can hire whoever I want. He knows I want to hire you and fully approves."

All Choice Care hired Nihal Mishra, VP of Technology Operations, about six months ago. Justin met the new VP once, about a week after Nihal started. He insisted upon everyone calling him by his first name, and it's about all Justin knows about Nihal. It's about all Justin knows about this promotion, too.

"So, you're leaving All Choice?"

"Leaving? No, I'm—oh, now I get it. Sorry, man, I forgot to tell you about my own promotion! I'm going to be the org's new Systems Management Director."

"Is that a position we have here?"

Caleb grins—there's no misunderstanding the huge smile on his face and his excitement. "It is! Nihal created it with me in mind, but I said I wouldn't move into the new role until we had my position filled and the new guy trained and comfortable within it."

"Or new woman," Justin says, then adds, "or new person."

Caleb shakes his head. "No. Guy. You, Justin. You're the guy. I'm promoting you and only you for Project Manager."

"But you said I have to apply. What if someone better applies?"

"HR just wants you to update your resume in case they have to prove your qualifications. I've already got a letter of support ready to go. It's a hoop."

"A hoop."

"Yeah, you know, like in dog shows, how—"

"I know what you mean by hoop."

Caleb nods. "You'll be great in this position. Shane and Austin are good at their job, but you are exceptional, and I've seen how you work a problem with them when they snag on something. You see the big picture and show them how to revamp code within the whole framework like I would do."

"I'd be Shane and Austin's supervisor."

"You would."

Justin has never been in charge of people. Wait, no. There was that one time during his second year with All Choice when they assigned him an intern. Back when everything happened with his cousin, Hugh. Justin hadn't been able to cope at work.

They never assigned him another intern after that. Or even asked if he'd like one. Not that they'd consulted him about the original one, either.

He'd enjoyed working with the intern at the beginning. There was a different kind of satisfaction in guiding someone else, teaching them practical skills around code and evaluation within a real software environment. Lizzie has frequently told Justin he'd make a good teacher, but he's never been able to imagine reaching any level of comfort level in a building full of chaos, even if it's what Lizzie calls "structured" chaos.

Shane and Austin are decent enough to work with most of the time. Occasionally, Justin misses some kind of joke or other nonverbal communication between them, and then they treat Justin like he's an idiot, but Justin learned how to walk away from that sort of behavior towards the end of his high school years. Mr. Jones, his high school photography teacher, and his sister taught him that. Shane and Austin keep to themselves and do their job without making things difficult for Justin. Usually.

As though Caleb reads Justin's mind, he says, "Look, I'm not saying the transition from peer to supervisor will be a piece of cake. But you're already the team leader, whether or not you have that as an official title. Also, I'll train you in this role and we'll figure out together the best way for you to manage those guys. And you'll also have a direct hand at hiring your replacement."

Justin's never hired anyone before or been part of an interview team. "I get to decide?"

Caleb grins and leans forward. "Barring anything weird HR finds during their part of the reference check, absolutely."

"When is this all happening?"

Though feeling cautious about this new opportunity, Justin affords a slight smile when Caleb gives him an "attaboy" fist to the shoulder. "As soon as you submit your updated resume and letter of interest. Let me take a look at your materials before you give them to HR, yeah?"

Part of Justin ruffles at the idea of having to show Caleb his letter like it's a school assignment, but then he acknowledges the wisdom. Caleb is looking out for him and besides, Justin has well learned as a programmer the necessity of an extra set of eyes.

What appeals to Justin most about this promotion is exactly what Caleb mentioned. Managing the big picture of their software systems. Analyzing the cascading effects of their updates and anticipating the kinds of testing they need to incorporate as they implement the upgrades and enhancements. Developing new methods for their code to adapt to changing specs and mapping out plans for significant changes to their software, or even different software altogether.

Caleb is one of the few people at All Choice who sees Justin as a whole person. Shane—or maybe it was Austin—honestly, Justin rarely distinguishes their separation since their behaviors appear interchangeable—once made a crack about their shock to find out Justin was human after they'd heard him laughing with Caleb. Justin had briefly considered trying out a joke in return, but rapidly lost confidence in pulling it off and simply walked away while erasing the interaction from his mind to avoid an emotional response.

Already, confidence leaks away upon remembering these kinds of interactions. Caleb says Justin acts unofficially as team leader, but what if his effectiveness as a leader results only from Caleb supervising all the work? Shane and Austin follow Justin's lead because they assume it's all coming from Caleb.

As Justin walks back to his cubicle, he overhears Shane say to Austin, "I moved almost everything on his desk over to the right about an inch. Do you think he'll say anything?"

Suddenly, Justin is back in middle school. The prank is asinine and harmless, but he doesn't know what he's supposed to do with it. He's not sure if Shane and Austin have done it as a friendly joke or as jerks. And if it's a friendly joke, is he supposed to pull a prank on them in return? Because he definitely doesn't want to engage in juvenile antics. Can't they interact with him like professional adults?

He stares at his desk to find every object is, indeed, shifted to the right. If he had not overheard Shane talking about it, it might have taken him a while to notice. It's the pencil marks next to each item that give it away. He doesn't want to say anything. He'd far prefer to sit and get to work. However, the markings rankle him and if he is truly to be their supervisor, he should try a new approach.

"I'm not sure how this activity was meant to be entertaining," Justin says. "But I'm sure I'm not going to waste my time cleaning away all the markings you made on my desk."

"What? No way," Shane says, walking over to look over Justin's cubicle wall.

"I told you!" Austin shouts over without turning away from his monitor and continues typing. What, exactly, Austin had told Shane remains a mystery to Justin.

"I was running out of time and couldn't erase all the marks," Shane said.

"Well, I guess you have time now, then," Justin tells him.

"Seriously?"

"Yes. I'll work at your desk until you're done fixing mine."

"It was a joke."

"If you say so." Justin walks over to Shane's desk, sets his laptop down atop papers with careful effort not to disturb them, and sits down to work.

"I told you!" Austin calls out again, still not revealing the mystery of what he told Shane. Justin no longer cares.

A chat message chimes in from Caleb.

Perfectly handled. You're going to do great in the Project Manager role.

5

LIZZIE

"Lizzie," Justin said when I got home, "it's so pretty."
The soft tone caught me off guard. I would have thought he was pretending for politeness, except his fake courtesy usually came through flat. "Pretty? I was hoping for sexy."

"Gross."

"Or alluring," I added.

"Magnetic."

"Seductive," I countered.

"Appealing."

"Sultry."

"Attractive."

I grinned at his refusal to move in the direction I tried to take him with our synonym game and then touched the soft wisps around my ear. "I'll definitely accept attractive. And pretty. Thank you."

"It's way better than you used to wear it. That limp straight thing wasn't flattering at all."

He could build me up and then yank me right down again. I'm sure he meant the comment about my old hair as a comparison compliment, and I took it as one except the part about it not having been flattering. Justin's not one for double meaning and yet I felt the sting in my interpretation, knowing how unattractive my behaviors had been. Could Lizzie be pretty on the inside, too?

Nuria said she didn't make people shine, but not only did she give my hair a coppery auburn shade with shorter, lighter curls, but we had a date for later in the evening. I'd casually dropped the idea after she'd finished up the cut and style and she scooped it right up. A night out dancing and drinking with a blazing hot woman like Nuria absolutely would bring out my glow.

I sunk into the couch and put my feet up on the table. Crash, who lay sprawled across Justin's lap, raised her head and hissed.

"Good girl," Justin said.

I scowled at Crash. She narrowed her eyes at me, clearly signaling her plans to murder me in my sleep one of these nights if I didn't remember to shut my bedroom door all the way. I sighed and put my booted feet back on the floor and when I unlaced them and kicked them off, I groaned at Justin's expression of disapproval.

"You and Crash make a formidable team," I said, bringing my boots to my allotted mat by the door.

"We definitely see eye-to-eye, don't we, sweet thing?" Crash meowed in adoring agreement, a sound I'd yet to elicit from her. She was all screeches, hisses, and yowls towards me. And, "sweet thing"? Crash and Justin's relationship would be disturbing if it wasn't also kind of adorable.

"Grab a towel and clean up the mess you tracked in, too," Justin added, immediately making me want to retract my "adorable" thoughts.

I did as he asked and then stomped back to the couch in defiance, although socked feet on thick, soft carpet didn't make nearly as satisfying a statement as I'd hoped. Damn. Justin's apartment was nice. I should think about IT for my next career.

"Have you ever done a workout routine with Reign?" I asked, thinking about another positive feature of Justin's place. The building included a fitness room like I'd seen in hotels.

"Reign's all about running, which I hate. They've suggested some strength training routines for me, though."

"I stopped to see Reign after my hair appointment and they've got a mega program ready for me. I'm going to die, aren't I?"

"Yep."

Back in middle school I ran sprints for track—and long jump, although I'm not sure why I kept doing that event since I consistently placed in the bottom third in the groupings—and the farthest I ran for training was probably two miles. I preferred the longer distances, and my coaches recommended I try cross-country. I took it up during high school and while I never won any awards for it, I'd run fast enough to help our team. However, I didn't really care about that aspect. I'd discovered I enjoyed the individual freedom of it, the time to do something for myself, an activity uniquely mine.

Like so much in my life in the past few years, I'd fallen away from running. I figured Reign could help me get back into solid form. They could act as both a taskmaster and a cheerleader. Plus, running would give me something to do. I used to spend a lot of spare time creating activities and mini-lessons for my students when I worked with them one-on-one. Justin exercised daily, but also had his photography. Our moms still played tennis together regularly. Somehow, I needed to figure out my new life. Part of me didn't mind the simplicity of Astros and Gas-n-Guzzle work with their straightforward routine. They were pretty decent distractions, but the rest of the time? All I had was the field trip accident at Meadowfields playing on a loop in my head.

"Swimming is better," Justin said.

"Why? Just because you prefer it?"

"No. It is objectively better exercise. It offers a full-body workout and is low impact."

"It requires a gym membership, and I can't afford that right now." It wasn't the real reason I didn't want to do it, but it was an accurate enough one to move Justin away from this conversational path.

"I can get you a referral discount."

"It's still an extra monthly expense I can't take on. Evidence: I moved in with you."

"True. I can help with—"

"JT. I don't want to swim."

"Okay."

We'd both held a healthy fear of swimming when we were younger, which was a natural trauma response to surviving a car accident into a river. Justin overcame it by pushing himself into the water and becoming a master swimmer. I never fully conquered the fear, but it was more than that. A memory—or rather an imprint of one, as so many of my memories were from before the accident—clung to me every time I got into a pool. An impression of missing an essential piece of myself. Wading into the deep end and kicking into nothingness created a hole inside me, a route to drowning, both physically and emotionally.

I'd spent my life attempting to fill that hole with ballast, and yet I bobbed, still not finding the right amount or the right kind of balance to keep me afloat.

I took a deep breath and slowly exhaled my agitation.

Justin stopped petting Crash, and she reached a paw out to Justin's hand to nudge it back to her. Justin acquiesced and the wretched animal stretched out in annoying, happy contentment as she purred louder with the belly scratch. The scene would have been irritating if that purr weren't so ridiculously calming.

"Are we eating dinner together tonight?" I asked.

"Do you want to?"

"I have a date, but it's not until later. Want me to cook?"

"No. It's my turn. We have ingredients for homemade pizza. Sound good?"

Pure music to my ears. Justin's pizza was amazing. "Um, your pizza *always* sounds good. I'm salivating already."

"Help chop vegetables?"

"You got it."

Having to move out of my own place and into my brother's obviously didn't fall into my ideal life plan. Most people have their parents to lean back on, and I'd considered moving out to Madison, Wisconsin, with our moms. They'd offered, of course. Mac had pressed hard for me to stay with them and figure things out. She'd always held a little guilt for having moved them away from Minneapolis for a job opportunity a few years ago, and the temptation had tugged at me to leave Minnesota and begin somewhere fresh.

Two things kept me in Minneapolis. One, I didn't know what "fresh" looked like. What did it mean to start over? Should I seek a new career entirely? Go back to school? Or keep doing the same job, only in a new state? Since I didn't have those answers, working two jobs requiring no prior experience looked the same in Minnesota as it did anywhere. Which led to the second thing: my brother.

When our moms asked if I wanted to stay with them for a while, it was before I discovered I couldn't afford to live in my place for much longer. Even with the two jobs, I still had to rely on my savings, which were depleting rapidly as the account already held little. In a phone conversation a few weeks ago, I'd confessed to Justin my financial situation, and he'd said, "I have an extra bedroom I never use. You should move in with me. Rent-free."

"You don't have to do that," I'd told him. "Mama LiLi and Mama Mac said I could come stay with them until I regain my bearings."

"I'm not offering to be nice. It's practical."

"Do you *want* me to live with you, though?"

"Would I offer if I didn't?"

It was an odd question for him, which should have signaled something right away about his sincerity. "You might."

"You know I wouldn't."

I'd smiled, catching myself. Of course he wouldn't. This was Justin. "Okay. I'll move into that spare bedroom."

"Good, because I want you to. Mostly, I don't want you to move all the way to Madison."

I hadn't wanted to go to Madison, either. And it was funny, Justin saying he wasn't offering to be nice since telling me he *wanted* me to move in, "nice" was exactly what he was. To my knowledge, he'd never fully figured out when he should say the white lie "polite" things or when he shouldn't say anything at all. Or maybe he had, but didn't care. Either way, I had always appreciated knowing what Justin thought without any filters.

"LiLi's kindergarten students can chop tomatoes better than you," Justin said now as we prepped dinner.

Okay, well, maybe I didn't appreciate *every* unfiltered thought from Justin.

"No, they can't," I said. "I've seen how five-year-olds cut things. What's wrong with how I'm cutting them?"

"You're mashing them to bits. Here," he grabbed a knife from the block and passed it to me, handle side out. "You need a longer, serrated-edge, for one. Then put the tomato on its side like this." He rolled a tomato, its stem facing to the right. He gestured with his hand in a flat-palmed vertical motion. "Make even slices, then cut the slices into strips, then strips again the other way."

"Thanks."

"You're welcome." He plunged his hands back into his bowl of flour to mix in warm water for a soft dough. He added in garlic, oregano, and a little extra salt, all part of his special, mouth-watering pizza recipe. I almost cut myself daydreaming about how good it would taste fresh from the oven.

"Caleb offered me a promotion today."

I kept chopping away at the vegetables, working at keeping casual about this news. I was aware of the sham offers he'd received in the past. I'd encouraged him to quit after the most recent "offer," but he said he liked his current position well enough and each time he turned down an offer, he also asked for a raise. Considering the higher-scale apartment he'd moved into a couple of years ago, I guessed he knew what he was doing.

"Yeah? Like a real promotion? Or just a new excuse for you to ask for another raise?"

He tossed the rolled out circle of dough into the air. I didn't know how he did it. I watched a YouTube video and tried it once on my own. The dough tore in half almost right away on the upward toss. "A real one. He's offering me his job because he's been promoted."

"JT! That's awesome!"

A hint of a smile crossed his expression as he nodded while slathering tomato sauce over the crust and then sprinkling some red pepper flakes on it. "Yeah. Caleb said he'd mentor me to help with the transition. Austin and Shane are twits, but Caleb said I've already been leading the team, so it shouldn't be too major of a shift."

"Twits?" I asked, laughing. "You sound extremely generous. Aren't they more like assholes?"

"Well, yes. Sometimes. Mostly they're juvenile. Shane's last job was with Domino's. All Choice is his first professional role. And Austin worked in the profession before this, but it was a remote position with some start-up company. I don't think Caleb did much to train them."

Justin had been working with All Choice Care for about five years, and if I remembered correctly, Shane and Austin started a couple of years ago. Training or not, the maturity factor should have kicked in by now. Or at least had them emulating Justin as a professional.

"Are they trainable now?" I asked. "Or will your first action as their supervisor be to fire them?"

"I can't fire them. Or not yet, anyway. Not until I hire someone to replace me." Justin put the pizza into the oven. After setting a timer, he added, "Caleb said I'd have hiring power, but he didn't mention firing power. I hadn't considered that I'd have equal authority to let employees go, too."

"When do you start?"

"Caleb suggested in a couple of weeks."

"Are you nervous?"

The last time Justin managed people had been a disaster—his word, not mine—but it hadn't really been his fault. Our cousin—and Justin's best friend—Hugh had died, and it had sent Justin into a downward spiral. It had resulted in an "all hands on deck" kind of situation in our family.

"A little," Justin said as he wiped down the countertops. "But it's different this time. I didn't realize how important it was to have someone recognize my ability to do more. Caleb sees me."

"That's great, JT," I said. "And a long time coming. I'm really excited for you."

I was, too. Justin's entire life had been a struggle to prove he was more than a label. Autism was a part of him, but it should never have set him apart because of it. Justin was a huge reason for why I went in to the special education field and had the job I used to have.

Of course, he was also responsible for why I didn't have the career I planned to have. I didn't blame him for needing help after Hugh died, but helping him through the turmoil and breakdown meant I dropped everything else. I had been finishing up my second-to-last term of college and was to do my student-teaching internship during that next semester, the final step along with licensing exams to become a certified teacher.

Instead, I didn't return. I'd earned enough credits for a degree, but I couldn't find my way to finish the licensure after helping Justin get back on his feet again.

Mac and LiLi had tried to talk me into finishing all my licensure requirements, but I'd been full of excuses. I didn't have my PCA job anymore and didn't have enough savings to live off of for a semester. I lost too much time needed for studying for the exams. I was too late to get a placement in a local school. None of these excuses were acceptable to our moms. They'd help me financially. LiLi would help me study. They were certain getting a manageable placement would not be an issue.

And so I'd said I wasn't sure if I still wanted to be a teacher.

I wasn't certain if my last excuse had been a lie, even though I'd only said it to get our moms to back off, but it worked. I wasn't an "all hands on deck" situation, and so they let me be, not understanding that I was lost. That I had been lost for most of my life, continually trying to be "the good one."

But how could they know? Only two people knew I was never meant to be Elizabeth, and one of them died in the car accident twenty-five years ago.

6
JUSTIN

Of all Justin's routines, his swimming regimen remains the most rigid. He came to it late, having spent many years deathly afraid of full immersion in a large body of water. Baths weren't always so great, either, and he knows some of LiLi and Mac's greatest challenges when he and Lizzie started living with them had been bathing him, since water on his head initiated countless screaming fits from him as well as bruises and scratches for everyone.

They'd never questioned his fear of drowning, even if all of their methods dropped the chances of it down to virtually nothing. They tried numerous calming activities. They'd used the hottest water he could stand to counteract the bone-cold chill his body involuntarily experienced as soon as the threat of bathing presented itself. They'd limited the hair washing to only once a week and modified showers twice a week. They'd soothed and reassured him after each forceful session. He joined them in wanting it all to work. He simply couldn't do it.

Four weeks in, they stopped trying to wash his hair. At least, in the traditional way. Instead, they wet a towel in hot water, wrung out the excess, then massaged his head with it. Gradually, they added some shampoo to the process. He doesn't know if his hair was ever fully clean during that time, but he remembers feeling safe. And so much calmer.

Eventually, of course, he came around to showers. It was years, though, before he got into a pool, and many years after that before stepping foot in a lake. Despite living in the "Land of 10,000 Lakes," Justin still avoids getting on boats. The boundary-less expanse of uncertain depths of water gives him chills. His therapist tells him it's a natural response and reminds him it's okay not to conquer this particular fear. Understanding the fear and accepting it is healthy.

And understand it, he does. It was one of the primary motivating factors to become the strong swimmer he is today. That and the unexpected therapeutic power of it. He swims five days a week, a fast, steady rhythm of the front crawl. He sets his water bottle at the shallow side of his lane, walks around to the deep end, dives in. Does thirty—and a half—laps. Takes a break for water. Finishes out his mile with thirty more laps and completes the workout in thirty minutes.

Swimming clears his mind and helps him expend the nervous energy he generates through worrying about all the social interactions he'll need to navigate. Fundamentally, he knows he'll manage fine. The anxiety lies in the anticipation of the one unknown situation he'll misread or misunderstand because even though he can't predict *what* will happen, he can guarantee *something* will.

"How can you guarantee what you can't predict?" Lizzie had asked him once.

"Unpredictability is predictable," he'd replied.

"Sounds to me like you are looking for anxiety. A self-fulfilling prophecy."

"I don't believe in prophecies. Also, I can't see into the future."

Lizzie had rolled her eyes. "You are so annoying."

He'd smiled. Lizzie only told him he was annoying when she understood his jokes, even the dumb ones.

Justin's therapist, Alonso, agrees with Lizzie about the self-fulfilling prophecy idea, but at least Alonso recognizes the pattern that Justin's anxiety follows.

Today, Justin dives into the deep end of the pool like every other day. The temperature is cooler than usual. It spikes his heart rate for a moment, so he ramps up the speed of his warm-up laps, which then leads to a pace far higher than necessary. It's frenetic, as though he is back in the freezing cold water all those years ago and he forces himself to take an unscheduled break in order to regain his equilibrium.

He reaches for his water bottle and gulps down water before listening to his inner voice to slow down. He stops and breathes in through his nose slowly, then expels the air. After doing this again, calm returns. He doesn't know why the cooler water acts as a trigger today. It hasn't happened in over a year. Something to bring up with Alonso next month.

"Mind if I share your lane?"

Justin looks up, relieved the guy who asks isn't asking him, but the person one lane over. He's about to turn back into his routine when he hears a woman say, "Actually, no, I'm sorry, but I'd rather—" and Justin sees the guy slide into the water without having waited for the response.

"What the hell?" the woman says. "I said no."

The guy laughs, and Justin has to tell himself *not* to punch him.

"I didn't think you were really going to say I couldn't," the guy says, pulling his goggles down over his eyes.

"Well, I did," the woman says. "And you're still not listening. Get out of my lane."

Direct. Justin appreciates her response. He waits a beat longer to make sure the guy leaves.

"You don't have to be a bitch."

"I'm not even close to being a bitch, and yet you've reached full on asshole."

The guy turns and raises the rope to duck under and into Justin's lane. Justin's desire to punch the guy escalates. Already this douchebag disrupted Justin's routine by causing a scene with the woman next to him, and now he's pushing in on him.

"No. I don't share a lane," he tells the douchebag. Justin knows protocol says he's supposed to accommodate other swimmers when needed. This isn't the first time he's annoyed others with his refusal, yet this specific douchebag rankles him more than usual with the forceful and entitled attitude.

"What the fuck, asshole."

Justin shrugs. "No, I'm being a bitch." After all, it's what the douchebag called the woman. Why shouldn't he use the same epithet for Justin?

"Ha ha," douchebag says in a way Justin guesses isn't a genuine laugh. "Are you gay or something?"

"Something, but really, have you seen how bitches protect their pups? Get out of my lane. Your interruption of my workout is messing up my whole day."

"You're serious."

And people think Justin is the one who misses cues. Both he and the woman had made clear, unequivocal statements. Justin opts to wait the guy out, unwilling to consume more energy by repeating himself. It's also the best option to help Justin focus on calming himself down.

The guy shakes his head and climbs out of the pool tossing a "fuck you" over his shoulder to Justin.

"You should be so lucky," Justin replies and hears the woman snicker. She says something, but now that the douchebag's gone, Justin is already submerged and pushing off the wall to restart his messed up workout. He should have taken a beat longer to do a couple of meditative deep breaths first, but he doesn't have time. He'll just have to make do with salvaging what he has left of his thirty minutes, which is down to fifteen thanks to the rough start and the douchebag.

One, two, three, breathe. One, two, three, breathe. His pacing gradually returns. He focuses on the strokes, the flips, and the pushes off the wall until the douchebag disappears. Eventually, the chill of the water dissipates, and the memories slip back down into the deepest watery depths.

7

LIZZIE

One of the most entertaining parts of my job at Astros is watching customers try to manage the "all-in-one" drink machine. Somewhere some comedian has surely included this bit in their routine. I pulled out my phone and zoomed in on the back of a forty-something-year-old man holding his cup under the fountain spigot. He leaned heavily into pushing the touch screen icon that chooses the drink for him, not realizing that the "pour" button was right below the screen. As soon as he put his entire palm on the screen, I snipped some of the recording and texted it to Justin.

His reply came quickly. *"One-stop shop for palm-reading and peach-vanilla Fanta."*

I choked back a laugh as I slipped the phone into my pocket and helped the poor fellow out.

"Here you go," I offered, pointing to the big silver button. "The touchscreen is for choosing. The rest is mechanical."

"Oh, duh," he muttered. "I thought it was broken, but instead I was just an idiot."

"Nah," I reassured him, "people get confused by this all the time."

The buzz in my pocket pulled me away again. It was a picture of Kate Winslet's hand on a steamed window of the car in the movie *Titanic*. *"Or maybe he was going for this to commune with his lime-cherry-root beer."*

Another text followed. This one of a bloody palm print on a mirror from some horror film. *"Or he was leaving his last message to the world by saying how much he wanted his coke-Kool-aid."*

Gross, Justin.

Then the next text of an upside down palm print turned into an elephant. *"He was going to flip over the drink machine after imprinting."*

And there I'd gone and done it—vaulted my brother into a palm print vortex, which made me smile. We used to exchange these kinds of text threads all the time. Scrolling up through past texts, my interactions with Justin's thought trails were few. A tiny ache hit my heart, and I googled a photo of someone pushing on a "pull" door and sent it off to him. After that, though, I shut off all sound and vibrate alerts because if I didn't, I'd be distracted by at least a dozen more similar texts.

I wiped down two more tables and as I returned to the counter, I saw movement at the entrance. I regretted my return as soon as I recognized one of the people in the pair of customers. If only I'd gotten a list of where each of my former colleagues lived so that I'd have applied for jobs outside of each of those cities.

Moving to Wisconsin would have solved that problem. Instead, I was stuck here at 9:00 p.m. on a Wednesday night with no backup because we weren't busy enough for more than me, the cook in back, and the manager who sat in the office all shift playing Candy Crush.

"Hello, and welcome to Astros! How can I help you tonight?" Overly enthusiastic greeting? Check. I mean honestly, I've never given a "welcome" to anyone here.

Surprise flitted across Carrie's expression so fast, I wasn't sure it was real. I'd have been surprised to see her behind the counter at a place like this, too.

"Hey, Betsy," she said, trying for casual. "I didn't know you worked here." She might have succeeded but for that line. I might have succeeded too, had her use of my old name not taken me back to the moments of my principal telling me, "Betsy, let's get real, here."

Where did Carrie-the-ex-friend-who-threw-me-under-the-bus *think* I'd be working? Another school in the district? Oh, wait, no, because she's the one who agreed with Tad Carlisle, the principal who "got real" with me. Maybe she assumed I wouldn't be working at all, that she'd had the power to keep me from *all* jobs, whether or not they involved children.

"Yep," I answered.

A fantastic awkward pause followed before the other woman caught up to her. It was Ashley, fourth grade teacher and another ex-friend. As it turned out, she was only ever a work friend. The distinction never clearer than after the accident.

"Betsy! Wow." She was fast, but not fast enough for me to miss the wide eyes and the big "O" that her mouth formed before shifting into an expression of fake cheer and concern. "How've you been?"

"Oh, you know." I gave the slightest of shrugs, leaving her to any meaning she wanted behind my short, vague response.

"Right, right," Ashley replied, nodding. What she thought she knew was a mystery. "So, this is kind of surprising to see you here. Have you always worked at Astros?"

"Well, um, no," I said, unsure of what else to add. Carrie hid behind her phone.

"I mean," Ashley stumbled, "obviously you didn't always *only* work here. I just thought, well, maybe you'd always had this as a second job. Paras don't get paid that much, do they?"

We'd been friends for two years. Did she imagine I'd hidden a second job from her all that time?

"I did fine when I still worked for the district. This is a new job." *Please don't let her ever be in the same neighborhood as my Gas-n-Guzzle.* I didn't know if I could bear her compounded patronization.

"Right."

She appeared poised to extend this unnecessary and awkward conversation, so I jumped to business. "What can I get for you?"

"Oh!" She looked around, as though suddenly surprised by her surroundings and the need to tell me what she wanted instead of expecting me to guess. "A veggie personal pan with a Diet Coke." As I punched in the items, she slid in with an afterthought, "please."

Carrie placed her order—no "please" from her, which matched her track record—and when I handed her the receipt, her eyes knit together. "Are you, like, borrowing someone's shirt or something?"

"What?"

"Your name tag. It says 'Lizzie'."

I unpinned the tag and flipped it around. "If I'd forgotten my shirt, I wouldn't wear someone else's name tag."

"Except it says 'Lizzie'."

"Well, that *is* my name." Yep. This was what I was doing. Moonlighting and gaslighting.

"No, it's not. It's Betsy."

I glanced at her with a slight tilt of my head and a raised brow. "I think I know my own name."

She stared at me, uncertain about what was happening. "You've gone by 'Betsy' for as long as I've known you."

"Have I, though? Because my name is Lizzie."

"For fuck's sake, you *told* us to call you Betsy."

I couldn't deny enjoying her annoyance. Carrie was the first colleague to turn her back on me and she deserved a tiny bit of pushback. "When did I do that?"

Ashley, who hadn't stepped aside with her cup yet, caught my eye, then twisted her face away. Her upper lip curled down under her lower lip, a tell of hers I recognized as I'd seen it frequently when kids would say something with an innuendo only she and I would infer. She was trying not to laugh.

Carrie stared at me. I stared back. Her lips pressed together before her stare turned into a glare. "Bitch."

"No." I held the receipt she hadn't taken, yet. "It's *Lizzie*. Lizzie."

"We'll take our orders to go." She spun away without taking the paper.

Yes, Carrie. Indeed you will. The pleasure would be all mine to pack up their food in boxes and foil tins and avoid serving them at their table. To get them out of my space as fast as possible.

Once upon a time, Carrie had been a special education paraprofessional like me. We shared ideas with each other about how to coach our students with skill-building activities. I helped her with her classwork, especially the child psychology courses, and covered for her when she had to leave early from work so she could grab a quick dinner on her way to a night class.

She left for a semester to complete her student teaching in a different district. When she came back for the last three weeks of the school year, she was suddenly the expert on everything. One of our special ed teachers retired at the end of the year and our principal hired Carrie to replace her. After that, she became someone I no longer recognized.

The special ed teachers and paras usually worked as a team. We understood our support roles and the special ed teachers appreciated the close relationship we paras had with the students and therefore encouraged our input. We worked together on solutions when new, challenging behaviors arose. They trusted us to use effective strategies with our students both in and out of the classroom. I was lucky. Not all schools valued their paras like the team at Meadowfields did.

Well, valued them to a certain point, anyway.

Carrie in her new role as teacher changed into one like I'd worked with before at another school. Condescending and "taught" me how to work with kids I'd been working with for two years already. She monitored my arrival time, breaks, and where I was throughout the day. She was bossy, which seems a childish word to use, but accurate because while we paras take direction from teachers because they're the leads in students' education, the teachers are our not our bosses. And it wasn't only me, she scrutinized. Her hyper vigilance of our behavior was a muttered complaint among all of us paras on the team.

Over the past school year, I often ate lunch with the fourth grade teachers. Carrie's schedule didn't match with mine. But one afternoon she joined us after a morning workshop. It felt good having Carrie drop her guard for a bit. I liked seeing the Carrie I used to know. The one who had a great sense of humor and smiled. We got to talking of funny stories about our kids. Sweet things students say. *Cute* stories.

"Remember the closet?" Carrie had said, and I'd shook my head, not from lack of memory, but as a reminder of how much I did not want to remember it. I was positive she'd understood it. I was shooting daggers at her from my eyes when she continued, anyway.

Chase, a first grade student, was a kid we couldn't let out of our sight. He often ran away and when he did, many things could happen. Once he hid in a cabinet and it took us twenty minutes to find him. Other times he climbed bookshelves or desks or tables. He didn't do it to cause problems—we had other kids who tested us for attention. Rather, Chase had an enormous curiosity with no patience to find out what he needed to know. So, when he inadvertently locked me in a closet, it wasn't because he was upset with me or because he was trying to "get away" with something.

The door to the storage closet, where I intended to grab a small whiteboard and markers, didn't stay open on its own, so I had Chase stand and lean against it, figuring it gave him a purpose. He struggled with having little to do for longer than thirty seconds. Not surprisingly, some idea tickled his brain, and before I could process the change, the door clicked shut, locking me inside within complete darkness.

It wouldn't have been so bad, except I had a deep fear of the dark along with feeling trapped, and both had hit me simultaneously. Though able to use my flashlight from my phone, I had no signal, and I plunged into a tight barrel of panic I'd only experienced a handful of times before. When it happens, my body temperature drops—at least it feels like it does—and my heart races out of control.

I'd tried very hard to keep it together. I counted down, but kept losing my place. I counted up, which worked better. It worked enough for me to pound on the door and call out Chase's name as though he would answer. As though he were still anywhere near the door. I pounded harder as breathing became more difficult and made worse by my sobbing.

Of all people to hear my shouts, it was Di, our district Special Ed director, who was visiting our school that day. After a few minutes, I recovered and embarrassment set in. Except Di hadn't dismissed my reaction. She'd sat with me and put a hand on my back to help steady my shaking. When she found out what had happened, she was livid. Bad enough that I had gotten stuck, but what if it had been one of our students?

The district fixed the door and light switch two weeks later.

"That kid," one of the other fourth-grade teachers had said of Chase after listening to Carrie's less-than-empathetic story about the closet, "is *so* difficult, I've heard. I hope I don't have to deal with him next year."

"Oh, we can make sure Ava gets him, don't worry," Ashley had said. "She's always willing to take those kids."

"Those" kids. It was then that either Carrie or I should have said something. When Carrie only laughed and nodded, I'd looked down at my half-eaten sandwich and let it pass. Chase was one of the sweetest and most inquisitive of kids, and I'd left him out in the cold by saying nothing.

This was why I was currently serving pizza. I hadn't deserved to be with "those" kids. Our kids.

When I called out the order for Ashley, she approached the counter and accepted hers and Carrie's bags. "Your hair's really pretty," she said. "And Lizzie suits you."

"Thanks."

"Take care, Lizzie."

I didn't answer because I didn't know if I cared enough about her or Carrie to wish them well, especially since Ashley was as guilty as I was about what happened on the field trip that resulted in one our students getting hit by a car.

But I guess it didn't matter as much to her since the student was one of "those" kids.

8

JUSTIN

Justin sets his water bottle down at the shallow end of lane three, his preferred lane. He heads to the other end of the pool, dives in and moves through his warm-up laps, relieved the water temperature and his heart rate remain in the expected range, allowing him to return to his routine. Right-left-right-breathe. Left-right-left-breathe.

He pauses at his halfway mark to drink some water.

"Hey, thanks for yesterday, by the way."

Justin looks towards the voice. It's the woman who'd dealt with the douchebag. At least he assumes so since he hadn't gotten a good look at her before.

"You're welcome," he responds automatically. A couple seconds later it occurs to him he's not sure what he did to earn her thanks. Before he can ask, she speaks again.

"I'm Amelia."

He nods in greeting, takes another swallow of his water, and prepares to finish the second half of his workout.

"And you are?"

"Oh," he replies, pushing down some of the agitation caused by this interruption. "I'm Justin."

He used to swim at the YMCA, but people kept striking up conversations with him and being annoyingly friendly. It's not that he doesn't appreciate friendliness. Rather, he didn't join a gym for socialization. Within a month, he switched to Go Hard Fitness, where he could be an asshole like everyone else. It was a relief to have people ignore him or tell him to fuck off when he refused to share a lane or he rode the stationary bicycle for too long.

Swimming is meant to be a solitary activity. His daily therapy. Now here is another person trying to make conversation with him for the second day in a row and he feels his own "fuck off" ready to slip through his lips in spite of the woman's smile.

It's a nice smile. Not too big like Joe at the front desk, where you might think a big smile means friendly, but then words come out of his mouth and tell you otherwise. Not so small that he can't figure out if she is feeling something different from what he can guess. It was unbelievable how often the too-small smile shows up on people's faces. Yesterday, after he told Jake from the account management department at work to clear his browser cache, he used one of those too-small smiles. What did it mean? Was he laughing at him? Happy he helped him? Angry at him, but trying not to show it? Not paying attention to him at all and thinking about something else?

Turned out, it was more like angry. Or sarcastic—another tone he doesn't have a firm grasp on, even after thirty-three years. "I don't have any idea what that means, Justin," he said to him. "Just fix it for me."

He nodded, appreciating the direct request, and "fixed" it. Although he was pretty sure it wouldn't fix Jake's soft porn problem.

Then Bella did the small smile as he left their cubicle enclave, saying she'd love fixing him, "anytime you need, babe, and anywhere."

Or how about when Will—

"Justin? Hello?"

The woman in the next lane pulls him away from his thoughts, reminding him of why he doesn't like conversation during his swimming time. He is now even further off his schedule.

"Right. What?"

There is the nice smile again. "Do you have any tips for how to do that flip-thing at each end of the pool?" she asked.

"YouTube. Search terms: swim flip turn tutorial." He answers, then pushes off to re-boot his workout. He's well aware his answer is abrupt, incomplete, and rude, but if he doesn't curtail the conversation, he will lose all focus and he'll waste yet another morning's therapy, which will screw up the rest of his day. More people will be irritated with him at work than usual. If he's going to be in charge of things, he has to have his head on straight. He submitted his updated resume yesterday and Caleb said Justin should be ready to start in his new position on Monday, four days from now.

Right-left-right-breathe. Left-right-left-breathe. Right-left-right-breathe. Tuck, flip, land, push, twist.

He almost pauses mid-stroke when he realizes what he's just done. He hasn't focused on the mechanics of his flip turns in ages. He maps his strokes when he needs to find a calming rhythm, but the turn? It's become a single movement in his mind. His brain and body taking a beat before matching the metronome again. Except now he remembers how many days he spent talking himself through those steps before it finally became a fluid transition.

He pushes through his remaining workout at a faster clip. If he finishes at his usual time, he can make up for his rudeness and give Amelia a couple more tips before he leaves and not mess up his schedule any more than it has been.

When he gets to the end, he hops onto the edge of the pool to sit and wait for Amelia to complete her lap. However, when she reaches the wall, she twists and pushes off without looking at him. When she approaches again, Justin waves to signal her, but she still does not see him and swims away to continue her workout. Or, Justin realizes, maybe she's ignoring him because he was an asshole earlier.

Fair.

He walks over to the door, where a few mini clipboards hang on hooks. He uses the string-attached whiteboard marker to write on the laminated swim routine form, "At the T: tuck, flip, land, push off, twist." He sets it next to Amelia's water bottle before hurrying off to shower and head out to work.

❄

JUSTIN STUDIES the woman through the glass window of the Panera Bread Cafe. She carries a tray with her order in one hand and grips a cane in the other. His fascination comes from when her bag falls from her shoulder, the one attached to the arm carrying the tray, and how smooth her motion is to balance her tray without spilling anything. She glides into the table flush with the window and he knows he should avert his gaze, to not stare.

She looks up, but he's not quick enough to look or move away. He never is, which gets him more than his fair share of glares, middle fingers, and "what the fuck is your problem?" questions. Possibly it *is* a fair share, except he figures there ought to be some sort of balance for how often others have stared at him for too long. And do rude comments and insults count in his favor to outbalance his inability to pull away his focus quicker?

A knock on the window catches him before he slips too deep into this social interaction analysis. To his horror, the woman with the cane grins and waves. Then she motions for him to come inside. He hasn't meant to stop here at all, and now he's stuck. Even more confusing is why he doesn't turn and walk away.

He feels drawn to her, and to his surprise, he walks inside and maneuvers his way to her table. Her eyes are wide, her skin a light brown, and her hair is a thick cascade of dark curls. It's her hair that gives him the most difficulty. He can't quite draw his eyes away from it.

"Justin!" She flutters her hands towards the chair opposite of her. "Do you work near here? What a fun coincidence to run into you!"

Is he supposed to know her? Why did he come inside? This is the precise kind of unanticipated situation that spikes his anxiety. Ninety percent of him wants to turn around and leave. Nine percent knows that might be rude. The remaining one percent says he can't, anyway. His anxiety, the fickle bastard, chooses fight over flight this time. His feet root into the floor.

"Do I know you?"

She laughs, then reaches up to pull her hair away from her face and into a tight bun. "Amelia? From the pool?"

He mentally puts a swim cap over her head and hits instant recognition. "Oh, right. I don't do well with faces out of context."

She does a brush-off wave and smiles. "Don't worry about it. Swim caps, goggles, and half our bodies under water all act as a pretty good disguise."

"How did you recognize me?"

"Oh, um." She looks away. "I might have sort of stalked you. A little bit." She turns her head back to him and raises her thumb and pointer finger to an inch apart. "But only a teeny, tiny bit. Once."

Justin furrows his brow, thinking about how she would do this.

"A couple of days ago, I got to Go Hard Fitness a few minutes later than usual," Amelia supplies. "You had just checked in at the front desk. I thought I recognized you as the guy from the pool, but then you walked away so fast."

Justin nods. He doesn't "dawdle." That's how Mac always describes it, anyway. He and Lizzie like to use the word "dawdle" in various contexts when they joke around with each other. Water takes too long to get hot? It's dawdling. Timer goes off and they don't open the oven within two seconds? Dawdling. Oversleep? Definitely dawdling. Get caught in his thoughts?

Shit. Dawdling. For real. Amelia's talking.

"—thinking I'd have to do some big, convoluted story for why I just hoped to verify because we said we'd meet up this morning and also because you'd left your lights on in your car and I wanted to catch you before you'd gotten too far ... except I didn't need to. The receptionist said 'yep' right away, and that was it."

"But the lights on my car turn off on their own," Justin says, realizing a beat too late she'd been describing a made-up story as a ruse to find out his name, which prompts more questions in his head.

"Well, that's a relief," Amelia says. "Because I was worried I'd have to give you a jump start later, and that would have made me late to work."

"True. And then I'd have wondered who you were and how you knew I needed the jump, you stalker."

Amelia laughs and Justin smiles, warmth filling him at knowing he is in on the joke. Her laugh is a step higher than her voice and he imagines it providing harmony with her speaking voice, which curls around him with its deep, rich tone.

"Do you want to join me for a bit?" Amelia asks.

"Oh, I—yes."

Except when he pulls out a chair to sit, he remembers he can't. He's forgotten why he'd been walking past Panera in the first place. How long has he been in here? How does he not know? He looks at his watch and breathes in relief. It's only been five minutes and yet as all the surrounding noises come back into focus—the conversation of the threesome to their right, the random video playing loudly from a phone (*where are the guy's Air Pods?*) by the guy to the left, the music from the restaurant speakers, and the pager buzzing and rattling on another table nearby—it's like waking from sleep in the middle of the night and not seeing the time on the clock yet. The not knowing whether you've been asleep for hours or only twenty minutes.

Yet he sits. Amelia wears her nice smile again, compelling him to her. He says, "I'm sorry for my rudeness this morning."

"Well, you made up for it by leaving the note behind." She shrugs. "Besides, you weren't wrong. It's not like I don't know how to use YouTube."

He nods in agreement. "I learn most things from YouTube. Or other articles on the internet. It's much faster than finding someone else and waiting through their over-explanation when I only need one specific piece of information."

"Like recipe posts that don't have 'jump to recipe' links at the top of them?"

"Yes." He leans forward ever so slightly, mindful not to get in her space. "Exactly like that. Everyone wants to tell me the story of how they learned the line of JavaScript code to set up an automated task. I wish people had 'jump to' links."

Amelia laughs and Justin's insides turn to goo. He knows there's a more precise description he'll come up with later to describe this feeling, but for now, "goo" will do.

"And escape keys! Sometimes you just need people to exit out from full screen, you know?" she says.

He nods and grins because he does know. He wishes he could press escape *and* minimize on Jake and Austin. He's about to offer another comparison when she takes a sip of her soup, reminding him of why he'd been passing by Panera.

He looks at his watch again as his phone buzzes. The text

from the Thai restaurant next door says his order is ready for pickup. "I have to go." He stands and pushes in his chair.

"See you Monday at the pool?"

As soon as he'd sat down ten minutes ago, he'd already factored extra time into his morning routine in order to arrive early at the pool, so yes, he will see her there. "Yes," he says and turns, then rushes off to grab his and Caleb's lunch.

9

LIZZIE

Aside from the insipid gasoline vapors and the resulting headaches, I enjoyed my second job at the Gas-n-Guzzle far more than Astros. The general manager was fair and easy to work for, customers were straightforward, and most important, my coworkers were solid. No one held any lofty ideals of being higher up a ladder than anyone else. We clocked in, did our jobs, and got along. It helped to have a supervisor who didn't expect us to do more than our hourly pay justified.

"Feel free to take your scheduled break on time, even if there are five customers in line," she'd told us. "We're a gas station with a convenience store, not a Michelin-starred restaurant."

I didn't know if her attitude was a reverse-psychology-kind of leadership strategy, or if she really didn't care. Whichever it was, it worked. While I'd already witnessed a half a dozen employees come and go at Astros in the past two months, most having ghosted, I'd yet to see that same changeover at the Gas-n-Guzzle.

It was refreshing to step into a job with predictability in how a shift would play out and then walk away without second thoughts about what might happen the next day. The idea of predictability made me think of Justin. He would hate this job, of course. He struggled as it was with the residual odors I brought home. Immersing himself in it for eight hours would overload his senses, not to mention having to deal with customers all day. But he'd appreciate the structural consistency of the work.

On Saturday mornings I worked with seventeen-year-old JoJo, who never complained about anything and who updated me about all the bits of her life every week. Her most recent news was about her future boyfriend. I loved how confident she was about this guy. They'd been friends for a long time, but she could tell they were meant to be more.

"We have these, you know, *moments* now that we didn't used to have. Like the other night while watching a movie together and our *fingers* touched while reaching for popcorn at the *same time*. We did those awkward, laughing apologies. And then we bumped fingers *again*, you know? For real, I think he *planned* it. We're just like one of those rom-coms. You know, the friends-to-lovers thing."

I tried not to wonder how much was all in her head and wishful thinking. I hoped it wasn't, that it wasn't her doing the finger bumping and him clueless. Romance wasn't for me, but I remembered high school and watched these exact scenarios play out with my friends. So much heartache. Unfortunately, I'd been the cause of heartache, too. Not on purpose. But then, JoJo's rom-com hero might convert to villain without realizing it, either.

High school had been a shit show of navigating my brand of queerness. I'd understood my lesbian identity early on—it helped to have lesbian mothers—but figuring out the aromanticism came later and the broad spectrum of my asexuality confused things even more. Mostly for other others who didn't see how I could be both on the asexual continuum *and* a lesbian. Like there were set rules for each letter of the rainbow alphabet.

I'd found myself pretending a lot. Pretending to want a relationship. Pretending I wanted all the hook-ups. I'd never set out to hurt anyone, yet I did, and in return, people hurt me by calling me a fake. An imposter.

So I changed my name. Used a new nickname variant of Elizabeth and went from being soft and meek Beth to the bolder, more self-reliant Liz. Liz didn't need anyone to relate to her. To understand her. She'd be fine going it alone.

It was a lie, of course. As was Ellie, later, and then Betsy. I wanted Lizzie to be real. To be true.

"And then he asked me if I did something different with my *hair*."

JoJo was still talking about her own personal rom-com and a rush of affection swept through me for her and her joyful hope.

"A few weeks ago I *experimented* with parting it on the other side and yeah, I mean, I've been doing this *new thing* for quite a while now, but still. He *noticed*. That's definitely a *sign*, don't you think?"

I turned my head a smidge and allowed a smile. I've never met JoJo's boyfriend-hopeful and only knew what she'd told me.

"It's always good when someone you like notices your hair," I said. "It means they're paying attention."

"Right?"

I announced to Pump Three that they were ready to gas up while JoJo rang up five Slim Jims and two giant cans of Monster Energy.

"So, what are you going to do about it?" I asked her.

She bit her lip and fingered the earrings in her right ear. "I mean, like, I don't know? Do you think I should do or say something?"

I was about to delve deeper into a romantic arena I'd always messed up myself, but suddenly all the air around me pushed onto my chest when I caught sight of a familiar winter hat and jacket. Had it been only the hat or the jacket, I might have breathed through the rising panic in the assurance of clothing coincidences because kids' winter gear doesn't vary all that much. However, I recognized that combination of stegosaurus hat and jacket because her mom special ordered it. Skylar spent many days never taking them off, a sense of protection from the world around her when she wore them, even if they didn't do their job successfully on one particular day.

Why were Skylar and her mother in this neighborhood? Why the fuck did people from that damn school keep showing up in places they shouldn't? I needed to get out of there, out of the line of sight, but my feet wouldn't move. Nor could I pull my gaze away from Skylar and the small, yet repaired tears on the jacket, caused by skidding along rough gravel.

"I want these Mommy!" Skylar's shout carried throughout the entire store. "They're pink!"

"Hush, Sky. Use your indoor voice."

"Skylar," Skylar yelled in the same loud and commanding tone. "*Not* Sky."

I still couldn't move, despite my desperate need to get out of there. Skylar's "outside voice" continued to pierce into me, though her words blurred as they slid through my consciousness. Children's shrieks and cries swirled with the visions of adults racing by her and a sea of winter hats as kids were ushered rapidly onto big yellow school busses.

No. I didn't want that memory in my head right now. *Fix this, Lizzie*. The panic pressed hard on my chest and the desperate need to breathe triggered something in my brain, reminding me of what to do.

I saw Skylar's bright pink stegosaurus winter hat.

I smelled gasoline. Endlessly wretched, nasty gasoline.

I felt...what? What did I feel? I reached for my face, calling to mind Justin's stubble, except my skin, of course, was smooth. I pushed myself into one of Justin's wordplay games and ran through synonyms of smooth. Soft, satiny, glossy.

I heard the rough, grating buzzer of the debit card reader, signaling the end of a transaction and for the customer to remove their card.

"Lizzie? Helloooo?" JoJo's lilting voice floated over to me, and I wondered how long she'd been calling my name.

I finally turned to JoJo and inhaled deeply, then slowly released it. "I'm going to check the restrooms."

"Didn't you just do that—"

"Yeah, I'm doing it again."

Skylar's voice pierced through once more. "Time to go!"

"*Skylar,* come back here this instant!"

I pushed through the swinging half-door to our enclosed cashier station. Panic threatened to rise up again when I saw Skylar running up the aisle, hand glossing along the shelf, knocking cereal and macaroni and cheese boxes every which way. As they crashed down to the floor, she screamed out, "Time to go, time to go! I want to use my outside voice!"

Though the primary panic attack had passed, I still breathed shallowly and resisted the urge to cover my ears as Skylar continued to shout in her favorite volume. I shot down a different aisle to get to the bathroom, but it was the wrong choice, as Skylar had already made her way down another one and rounded the corner, slamming right into me, cast first.

I grunted and stepped back from the force. Unfortunately, Skylar did the same, except she fell backward on her rear. Skylar's mother chose this moment to catch up with her daughter.

"Sky, this is what happens when—"

"Mommy," Skylar yelled at max volume level. "It's Miss Betsy!"

Shit.

Mrs. Larson looked at me and her expression darkened from frustration to pure malevolence. "*You.* Did you *push* her down?"

The fu—"What? No, of course not."

"What is wrong with you?"

Disbelief and shock rendered me speechless. Skylar, in the meantime, continued to shout my name to get my attention. She hopped and slapped both her arm with the cast and her unbroken one on my chest with each hop. My torso remembered this Skylar well. It was how she always used to try to get an adult's attention at the beginning of the school year.

As if Skylar's shouting and physical antics weren't enough, her mother continued to dress me down, saying something about adding this incident to their lawsuit. When one of Skylar's hops landed on my foot, I found my voice.

"Skylarasaurus," I said, and placed a gentle hand on her shoulder.

Skylar stopped jumping and slipped her free hand into mine and squeezed two times.

Despite everything, I smiled. "Yes, Skylar? What do you need?"

She tugged on my hand to invite me down to her level. I crouched down before her and with her inside voice, she said, "I miss you."

"I miss you, too."

"Sky, we're leaving," said Mrs. Larson, re-booting Skylar's volume control.

"Skylar!" Skylar yelled at the top of her lungs, making me wish I was not still crouched with my ears right next to her mouth.

"*Now*, Sky...lar." Mrs. Larson slipped her arms under Skylar's armpits and lifted her. I narrowly escaped a kick to the face as Skylar fought the action and proceeded to kick boxes of energy bars to the ground. I watched with anger and helplessness as Mrs. Larson forcibly removed Skylar from the store.

"Whoa," JoJo said. She sounded far away, instead of the cashier cage a few feet from me. "That was *a lot*."

I stood, a multitude of emotions flooding my insides. All of them making me sick.

"I have to go," I whispered. And then I fled.

※

THE FRONT DOOR OPENED, and I listened to Justin talk to Crash. The murmurs floated through the air with a vibe of relaxation and contentment. I suddenly wished the cat liked me. Having a little animal that was soft and emanating a soothing rumble cuddled up next to me sounded comforting. Instead, when I came home, she was nowhere to be seen, which was just as well. She would have hissed at me and stuffed me deeper into my depression.

I'd made it through the rest of my shift at the Gas-n-Guzzle after escaping to the bathroom with an attempt to do a "reset" as we used to do with students after meltdowns. It worked well enough for me to go on autopilot until I got home and crawled into my bed. I called in sick to Astros.

"Lizzie?" Justin knocked on my door.

"Yeah, c'mon in."

Justin came through the door holding Crash. She bolted from him after he took a few steps farther into my room. I gave her the finger underneath my covers.

"Did you just flip her off?" Justin asked.

Busted.

"She might warm up to you if you were actually nice to her."

"She started it. I *was* nice to her at first. She hissed, growled, and scratched at me in return."

Justin sat on my bed near my feet. "I guess she's like me, then."

"You do not hiss, growl, and scratch."

"Some people think I do." He shrugged. "Why are you home? Tonight's an Astros shift, isn't it?"

"Yes."

"Are you sick?"

"No."

"Did Astros fire you?"

Ouch. Jesus. Why would he jump to that conclusion? "Fuck off, JT."

"I'm sorry. I didn't ask to be mean."

"Okay." I didn't have it in me to care why he asked. Maybe he just assumed that was the new norm for his sister.

"Did you quit?"

I nearly told him to go away and let me be, but his comment about people thinking he hissed and growled stopped me. I sighed, flipped the covers off, and sat up. "No, but that would have been the better question to ask before the one about being fired. I called in sick, but it's because I had a shitty day at the gas station and didn't have the energy to put on a happy face for another job."

"I'm sorry about the order of my questions." He rubbed his jaw with his palm. "It's not like you to miss work. Are you okay? What happened at the gas station?"

I recapped the events with Skylar and her mom. I described the almost-panic attack I had upon the first moments of hearing and seeing Skylar. Justin nodded. He certainly understood anxiety episodes.

"Her mom looked at me with such loathing, and I couldn't blame her. All I could think of was Skylar in a heap on the parking lot pavement and her screaming." It hadn't been her normal yell like in the gas station, either. They were cries filled with pain. I put my hands over my face as I leaned forward on my knees.

"At the gas station, she told me she missed me," I said. "And rationally, I know she's okay. The broken arm will heal. When she's older, though, and realizes it was my fault she got hurt, will she still be so forgiving?"

"I used to take care of you," Justin said.

I didn't reply, as I wasn't sure where he was going with that sudden proclamation that seemed to have nothing to do with what I told him about the Skylar incident.

"I mean, before," he added.

I lifted my head. "Before when?"

"Before it was obvious that I wasn't like other kids."

I frowned at him. I never liked it when he said things to separate himself.

"What do you mean?" I asked.

"Mama would let me hold you and Issy when you were babies, and she told me that when you cried, you either needed a diaper change, to eat, or wanted to be held. So that's what I tried every time one of you cried. I thought I did a good job of taking care of you."

I smiled, imagining the effectiveness of a list to work through.

"Sometimes you'd cry for a really long time, but I still held you, even though you were so loud that I'd squeeze my eyes closed to shut out the noise."

"I think you still do that to me sometimes."

He cut a look towards me. "I did a good job."

"Yeah, I'm sure you did."

He reached up and started tugging on his hair.

"What happened?" I asked.

He hummed and yanked harder.

"Justin? Tell me. It's okay."

He sat on his hands. "I dropped you." His hum continued, and he rocked, struggling to keep his hands trapped. "You shrieked so loud. It scared me. I dropped you and covered my ears. Mama yelled over your crying, and then she slapped me."

My stomach clenched, and my fingers curled into fists. I remembered very little about our parents. I was only four when we lost our mom and sister and then only days later our dad after he dropped us off with Mac and LiLi and never looked back. The cruelty of our parents—well, our biological parents since in my heart, Mac and LiLi were our true parents—towards Justin came back swiftly and cut into me in a way I couldn't fully identify. I wanted to believe part of how I felt was an angry protectiveness, but that wasn't all of it. I pushed away the unnamed, creeping emotion and focused on the empathy and tenderness I had for him now.

I put my hand on his shoulder. "I'm sorry that happened. That's awful. I wish Mom had understood you better and loved you the way she should have."

He slowed his rocking and stopped humming. "She wasn't always like that. You know that since she loved you best."

"No, that was Issy."

Justin looked away. "Yes. Right."

Again, my memories were few and mostly came through as impressions. Our mother did have favorites. She laughed, and most of it was with Issy, but my mom also cried and yelled. I remembered less about our father, and almost all of what I remembered triggered shame and fear. Justin didn't like talking about him and said he wasn't around much.

"Would you trust me with your baby if you had one?" Justin asked.

Oh, Justin. "Of course."

"Even though I dropped you when you were a baby?"

"Obviously. You were only four when that happened. It's not like you threw me to the floor. It was an accident."

"So was what happened with Skylar. It was an accident."

"Except I wasn't four." I stood, walked a couple of steps away, turned and flung my arms out as though to showcase myself. "I'm twenty-nine. *And* I've had all the education, training, and experience. I should have known better. *Done* better."

"How? You've never talked about what happened, but I know how kids like me are. I've *been* Skylar, and you described how Skylar can be in a closed space let alone an open one after a full day completely out of her routine." He stood now, too, as though to even our positions. "And I know you. You did what you always do. You handled more than you should have been expected to and did the best you could under the circumstances."

He was right. I'd never told him about what happened and listening to his misplaced confidence in me made me doubt ever telling him. I couldn't face his judgement and subsequent disappointment.

"Maybe you can hold me now?" I asked. "I think I'd like to be held."

"Yeah."

I walked into his open arms and he wrapped them tightly around me in the same way I often did for him. It was familiar and safe. He was wrong. He'd never stopped taking care of me. He was my older brother, but I'd taken on the responsibility of helping him navigate a lot of social situations. I remembered other times, though, like when I fell off my bike and cut my knees. He knew all the right steps to clean and bandage the cuts. He didn't cover his ears when I cried louder when he applied antibiotic spray. Instead, he told me a story about two girls who became knights and grew up to be the best swords people in the queendom.

He was also the one to teach me how to ride a bike and not fall off. And he tutored me with my chemistry homework. And tried to get me interested in the technical aspects of photography, although that never caught on. I loved his photos, but I lacked the same passion for the aesthetic behind photography. I excelled at Instagram-worthy food photos and selfies.

And he gave me hugs when I needed them like he did now.

"Thank you, JT."

"You're going to be okay," he said, releasing me.

"Probably. Until then, I can help you make dinner."

"I wasn't expecting you, so I'm not sure I have enough ingredients."

I led us out of my bedroom and looked over my shoulder. "Fine. I'll watch you make dinner and order Door Dash for myself."

"I could do delivery instead, too. A deep-dish pizza from Astros sounds great."

He laughed as I flipped him off and for the first time that day, the first time in weeks, felt like I would somehow be okay after all.

10

JUSTIN

Justin sets his water down at lane three. As he walks around to the deep end, he notices Amelia attempt—poorly—a flip turn. He had arrived at the pool early, anticipating extra time for talking with Amelia. Now he considers cutting his workout short, too, in order to help teach Amelia the way he learned how to do the flip. Assuming she wants more help than he's already provided. He doesn't want to come across as a rude know-it-all. A mansplainer.

He dives in and does his warm-up laps, followed by the first half of his workout, the entire time his head full of scenarios for how to approach Amelia. When he takes his halfway point water break, Amelia is also at the shallow end, drinking water.

"Hey," she says.

"Hey, back."

She smiles. "Have you happened to notice my flip-turns?"

"I saw one when I came in."

"What did you think?"

"I thought, 'That attempt looks pretty terrible and she could definitely use some more pointers, but I'd better not say that without her asking, otherwise she'll know I'm a total asshole mansplainer.'"

She laughs, louder and longer than when she did at Panera yesterday and it's like his insides all move around like the pool water when everyone is in it, doing laps. Swishing and swirling, trying to reach a rhythm. If she is laughing at him, he's not sure he cares, even if the sensation closely resembles anxiety. He's experienced it before—once—and despite how things turned out as a result, he clings to this feeling again.

"My attempts have been a mess," she says. "I will happily take the mansplaining."

"Can it wait until after I finish my next set of laps?"

"Of course."

"Thanks," he says, and pushes off into the latter half of his workout. Adrenaline courses through him, resulting in a speed which normally would leave him winded. Today, however, it's exhilarating.

When he finishes his last lap, he crouches low into the water and chugs his water down as he waits for Amelia to reach the shallow end again. She is doing the backstroke with good form overall, although a little uneven. The backstroke is his own weakest stroke as he doesn't like not seeing exactly where he's headed. Logically, his brain calculates when to turn at each end of the pool. It's psychological. His anxiety kicks in at the anticipation.

He wonders what other exercising she does, if any. Swimming works for her, given the physical condition of her leg—or legs; he's not sure why she uses a cane outside of the pool. Certainly, most athletic options have adaptations. Before he dips into a thorough analysis of these possibilities, Amelia reaches the edge of the pool next to him.

"Hey," she says, slightly winded. "All set now?"

"Yes," he says. "Thank you for letting me finish up. The full workout within my routine helps me focus for the start of the day."

"Oh sure. I'm glad you were honest with me instead of trying to accommodate right away. People who feel rushed rarely explain things well, and I want to learn how to do this right."

Justin nods in approval. "This is what you need to do. First, you have to do a solid somersault in the water. I think that is mostly where it's not working out for you at the wall. Let's go a little deeper and you can try one out."

In their respective lanes, they wade a couple of feet in. Amelia tries a somersault, but immediately twists and comes up facing the opposite way she started.

"For now," Justin says, "we're not trying to flip around. We just want to perfect the somersault action. No twisting."

"Okay, I think I need more help with how to do that because to me, that was an amazing forward roll in the water."

"Uh," Justin says. He's not sure how direct he should be.

Amelia laughs. "I'm kidding! You're right. I did a somersault like an eight-year-old."

Justin signs in relief and smiles. "Yes, that's exactly what it was like."

Justin models with arms extended and chin tucked. Amelia continues with her attempts. Her rolls start a little skewed, but with each attempt, she comes closer to a perfect spin. It's between the fourth and fifth tries that Justin determines what is happening. Her left leg carries most of the power and work and he sees how she modifies her push off the floor to compensate and allow for a more balanced result.

"Wait," he says after her latest somersault. "I think we're spending too much time on the wrong step."

"What do you mean?"

"You're working too hard to have an even roll based upon jumping from your feet, right?"

"I guess? I mean, mostly just the one foot, of course."

"Exactly. But you don't need that push off power to start the flip when swimming. It comes from the tuck of your body. Our next step was going to be practicing while mid-swim, but we should have started with that." He frowns. "I'm sorry we wasted all this time."

"It wasn't wasted. I have a good foundation for how the roll should feel."

"Except."

"What is it?"

"I don't have any more time today to help. I need to get to work."

"Oh!" She lifts her goggles from her eyes to her forehead and looks up and around for the clock. "Me too. No worries. Where is the clock, anyway? Didn't it used to be on the south wall?"

Justin spots the large wall clock, now tilted to the side and resting on a chair with the clock hands showing three-seventeen. "There it is." He points to it.

"Wow, we missed almost an entire day to my somersault failures," Amelia says, then shakes her head and blows out air. "I am sooo fired."

"Worth it, though, right?" Justin goes along with the joke, because he's sure Amelia can't possibly believe it really is after three in the afternoon. But he also realizes he isn't entirely joking with the words because adjusting his workout schedule to fit this time in with her was enjoyable. There was an ease to how they communicated with one another, something that seldom happens with him.

"Hey!" Someone shouts from the end of the pool. "If you guys are just going to fuck around and talk instead of swim, maybe you could at least share a lane?"

Amelia turns and waves. "Sorry!" Then she ducks under water and pops back up in Justin's lane. Her response is so fast and unexpected, Justin barely has time to take a step back to avoid the close contact. His heart races when suddenly she is simply *there*. He could see what color her eyes were, if he were calm enough to try.

Amelia turns to watch the shouter sit at the shallow end of her former lane and make deliberate actions to move her lap counter, water bottle, and kickboard over to Justin's lane. She looks back at Justin again.

"So, no 'thank-you,' I guess. But then, I wouldn't expect it since he's the same jerk from a few days ago," she says.

Justin nods in acknowledgment. He'd already blocked out everything about the guy in his memory, as he often does about unpleasant events. Middle school and high school don't seem so bad anymore when you dismiss the worst parts of it.

"He's not wrong," Justin says. "At least not today."

"That tone, though. And the language." Her eyebrows crinkle together.

Ah, he thinks. *The tone.*

"I'll concede that using 'fuck' was rude," Justin says. "I'm considered a pretty rude person myself, but I do try to use polite language to offset it."

Amelia nods and Justin wishes her hair wasn't tucked into the swim cap because he'd like to see her hair move as she speaks.

"Good point," she says. "Not everyone is aware of their tone. Except for this guy." She pitches a thumb in his direction as he passes them with exorbitant splashing. "He's already proven to be a jerk."

Justin nods then whispers, "Fuck," as he glances at his watch. He's running later than expected. He hears Amelia laugh, and he looks up again to say, "That wasn't aimed at you. I'm mad at myself."

Amelia is still smiling. "I know. Go! I don't want you to be later on account of me. I'll see you tomorrow, right?"

He's already wading back to the edge of the pool as he waves and calls out, "Right! See you tomorrow."

11

LIZZIE

"Even Reign has not been so cruel as to suggest we run outside when it's this cold," I grumbled while getting out of Nuria's SUV in the parking lot for Lake Elmo Park Reserve.

Nuria laughed. "We're not doing this as a training workout. It's supposed to be for *fun*."

Suddenly aware of my downer attitude, I attempted a more conciliatory tone as I called to mind an earlier conversation we'd had. "And beauty."

"And beauty," she echoed.

We were going snowshoeing, something I hadn't done since an elementary school field trip to a nature center. Honestly, I looked forward to the hiking adventure with Nuria, in spite of my negativity, which stemmed from an exhausting week. The run-in with Skylar and her mom had capped it all off. But also, after a month in the two jobs, I still wasn't transitioning well to either of them. Three days per week my six o'clock a.m. gas station shift followed a closing shift at Astros where I didn't get out until eleven at night because of being perpetually understaffed. The formula of life for me equaled a trash bin, including the literal odor of it on my body.

Most of my time off went to fitness training with Reign or hanging out with Nuria. The alternative meant spending time by myself, which journeyed me through all my poor choices.

My night out with Nuria had not been one of those poor decisions. We'd spent a few hours heating it up on the dance floor, then came together like fire afterwards at her place.

It hadn't all been sex, though. We ended up talking late into the night, getting to know one another and stoking the embers of a new friendship.

At one point, Nuria had asked, "Tell me, Lizzie of gorgeous new hair, what are you most passionate about in life?"

"Relationships," I'd said, without a touch of irony in my voice.

She'd swatted at me. "Don't fuck with me! I thought we were on the same page with that?"

"We are," I'd insisted. "And yes, really, relationships. I don't mean romantic ones. I mean, how we all connect. Finding the threads people have in common to build empathy. Creating a sense of belonging."

It's why I became Lizzie, after all. Betsy hadn't successfully found those threads, choosing instead to keep the seams loose. As soon as the line was drawn, it severed the connections as though a ruler had been set down on that line and a razor blade run along it for good measure. Lizzie had found a way in with Reign, who then led her to Nuria.

Nuria had told me her passion was beauty. "And before you say anything, I do *not* simply mean external looks like hair and nails. I'm talking about things like that sound you made when I kissed you after dancing. Pure, beautiful pleasure. I could live in that sound. A child's laughter. A person in an expensive suit having a genuine conversation with someone sitting next to them who has holes in their shoes. Beautiful."

Snowshoeing in the woods, regardless of sub-freezing temperatures, also meant beauty, so here we were. I wrapped my blue-flecked, gray scarf around me, tucked it inside my jacket, then flattened my hair underneath my blue-knit cap with yellow bobbles.

"Is that one of Reign's creations?" Nuria asked.

"It is! The scarf, too." They didn't match, but I didn't care. I loved them both not only for their warmth and pretty patterns, but for the thoughtful gesture.

"Nice!" She pointed to her own black, cable-knit cap. "Mine too. I have three others at home."

"Three more?" I asked as we stepped off the pavement and near the entrance to the trail. We strapped ourselves into the snowshoes and I took a couple of steps to test them out.

"Well, before the hats, they did mittens and before that, scarves." She gestured towards the path for us to begin our hike. "*A lot* of scarves."

I laughed as I realized the reason for the mismatch. Reign likely gave me a scarf from their pile. I still loved it.

We hiked alongside each other on the wide, groomed path, chatting about Reign's knitting creations, favorite clothing items from our own closets that we looked forward to wearing each season, and favorite accessories. Eventually, we lapsed into silence, and that's when the "beauty" part appeared.

To say we walked in silence was a bit misleading because the crunch of ice-tipped snow beneath our snowshoes that had been there before grew unexpectedly louder. Later I heard other noises: an occasional bird called out, squirrels rustled along tree branches, and the high-pitched whistle of the wind pierced the quiet moments as well as through my eyelids. It *felt* like silence, though, and I had to force myself away from it. Uninvited memories and self-recriminations slipped in through the cracks of silence.

I looked up from my snowshoes and out upon the trail ahead

and the sparseness around us. Trees surrounded us, except unlike in the summer, I could see hundreds of feet off into the distance without the green leaves to fill out the branches and bushes. It suddenly felt like a wasteland and I searched for something to latch onto.

"What got you into hair styling?" I asked Nuria.

"The short answer? Spite."

I chuckled. "Well now I definitely need the long answer."

She nodded and smiled in acknowledgement. "When I was in high school, I lost a friend to AIDS. No one thinks that still happens, but it does. It was horrible."

She stopped and looked out towards an opening ahead of us. I took her mittened hand into my own and squeezed. It might not have been her first time telling this story, but I also understood that grief hit randomly and unexpectedly.

She squeezed back, and we continued hiking as she spoke again. "It made me want to do something to help, so I enrolled in a training program to become a Certified Nursing Assistant. My mom's a certified nurse practitioner and a couple of my siblings are also in medicine, so it wasn't a big surprise to anyone that I would do it. I volunteered to be placed at a clinic specializing in HIV-AIDS treatment. After I graduated, I enrolled with Metro State to begin my BSN program."

"BSN?"

"Bachelor of Science in Nursing," Nuria clarified. "My mom estaba la mar de contenta with my career choice. Completely over the moon. She would have been even happier, of course, had I had 'doctor' in my sights instead of 'nurse,' but anything was better than how I'd spent my time before going the nurse route."

"Which was how?"

"Gaming. And art."

"Wait, did you do all of those drawings hanging in your bedroom?"

"Most of them."

"They were amazing. You really *do* create magic."

She stopped, turned and leaned in to me, pulled down our scarves and kissed me. Her cheeks matched the chill of mine, but her lips transferred all warmth, and any part of me that might have still been cold now sizzled. God, she was so *hot*. I might actually sleep with her again after all.

"You're a sexy supporter," she said.

"You've uncovered my secret to getting laid."

"There are definitely worse ones."

"I still don't see how you got into hair styling," I said.

"Impatient much? You're the one who said you wanted to hear the long answer."

"Fine," I mock sighed. "We need to slow down hiking, though. I'm not that far into Reign's couch-to-5k training and you may have to use your nursing skills to revive me should I collapse."

"I think you're just fishing for some mouth-to-mouth resuscitation."

"Whatever works."

We came to a fork in the trail and she pointed left and then continued with her story. "I got through a year and a half of the nursing program and hated it. It was so dry and clinical. It's not like that was surprising, but I didn't realize how much energy it would leach away from me. Nursing is about helping people, sure, but even that aspect became overwhelming. I was still working at the HIV specialty clinic and while most patients were in for basic bloodwork and check-ins, there were all the stories behind them. Tu sabes. Kicked out of their homes. Violence perpetrated against them. Sex work to help make ends meet. It was all too much."

She was right. I knew the stories. My cousin Hugh was one of those stories. Not HIV-positive, but a victim of violence. He and his boyfriend were both attacked after leaving a club one night. His boyfriend survived. Hugh had not. The months following were some of the most painful ones of my life, which didn't come close to how devastating they hit Justin. Not only were we cousins, but he and Hugh were best friends. I was grateful for Reign in Justin's life. Justin was mostly a one-friend-at-time person, but he needed that one friend.

Nuria returned me to the present. "So I quit everything. My mom was furious—*is* furious still. I started at 'Everyday Beauty, Everyone' as a manicurist because of the art factor. But the art behind hairstyling drew me in and I needed money to pay off student loans and there you have it."

"What about studying art?"

She shrugged. "Maybe. Hey, let's go down this direction. Remember to turn and work your way down sideways for more stability and balance." Her tone shifted, and she closed the subject for today, which was okay. I didn't know what was next for me, either. LiLi said there wasn't any reason I couldn't go back to being a para, or better yet—her words—apply for licensure and teach. I didn't know if I could do it. Or more specifically, if I wanted to.

We scaled down the hill, me grabbing a tree here and there to help stay upright and Nuria practically skipping down. At the bottom, a few feet out, was a small lake. Big enough that a stone's throw wouldn't reach across, but not so big that it would take us more than an hour to get around it. Although weariness crept in, and going all the way around didn't sound like the best plan.

A few animal tracks disrupted the mostly glittering, smooth surface that reflected the sun. The wind cut through a little more sharply with fewer trees to interrupt it. Along the shoreline, brown sticks and old fall leaves stuck out, and among the animal tracks, icy snow tips, and the leafless shrubbery, I imagined Justin could capture some pretty cool close up, pattern-like opportunities for his photography.

"My favorite part of snowshoeing!" Nuria said. "Traveling across lakes. The closest thing to walking on water."

Wait. What? Go across the lake and not around it?

Nope. Which I apparently said out loud because Nuria asked, "Why not? It's completely safe by now. It was safe by mid-December."

While I was okay with swimming at a beach, I didn't like jumping in from a boat in the middle of the lake and I definitely didn't walk, skate, or, in this case, snowshoe on one.

I shook my head.

"C'mon," she cajoled and reached out for my hand. "I'll hang on to you. The snow and ice on this lake are so thick we won't even notice we're on a lake."

I was about to say, "why bother, then?" but a deep cold penetrated into me.

Quick! Get your seatbelt off. Please! I can't do it!

Justin can do anything. Why can't he help me? It's so cold. And the water. Why is there water in the car? Mommy! Mommy!

Take my hand and climb!

"Lizzie? Lizzie!"

The water slipped away and the fog of memory dissipated as I focused on Nuria's eyes, near mine and her mittened hands framing my face.

"I can't do it," I whispered in a ragged breath.

"Yeah. Okay. You're shaking. Are you shaking from cold? Or from whatever happened just now?"

"Cold. No. I don't know." I couldn't differentiate between the cold of the air and the cold brought back by my patchy memory.

"It's all right." She wrapped her arms around me as best she could, despite our snowshoes forcing some distance. "Let's head back, okay?"

I nodded, and as soon as I turned away from the lake, everything started working again. My feet, my breathing, and my brain. We climbed back up the way we came in silence, and once we reached the top and retraced our steps, I apologized.

"Where were you?" Nuria asked. "It's like a part of you left for a minute."

I didn't talk about my mom and my sister very often. In some ways, there wasn't much to tell since I was only four when the accident happened and I didn't have many memories before then. Only bits and pieces of a puzzle. Sometimes the pieces came together in a larger section. The rest remained isolated in their unsorted pile.

"I was in a car accident when I was four. Winter. We crashed into a river."

"*Oh*. Shit. That sounds terrifying."

I didn't say anything, but also figured I owed her a little more than what I gave her. Most of the time it was easier to not tell anyone about any of it. It happened so long ago and I couldn't answer all the questions people had. What happened? Were you close to your sister? Where was your dad? Where's your dad now? Nuria had already proven to be more discerning in our conversations, so I offered a bite-sized portion.

"Justin and I made it out. My mom and twin sister didn't."

"Oh, babe, I'm so sorry. Do you remember much of it? Or is the fear of the lake more of an emotional response?"

This was what I meant about more thoughtful interaction. Maybe it was the nurse's training that guided her to more astute observations. Or maybe it was pure Nuria.

"Kind of both? Like sometimes I think I remember what we were doing before we got in the car, but then I'll see myself wearing shorts and a tank top and playing outside on our swings, and I know that isn't right because the accident definitely took place in December. Just now, I thought of Justin trying to get me out of my booster seat and being so scared because Justin was scared."

"Trauma messes a lot with our memories, and you were only four. I'm not surprised it's all jumbled."

"That's pretty much what my therapist said." Back when I still saw her. A couple of years ago, I'd let it slip that I wasn't seeing her or any other therapist anymore, and Justin, along with both of our moms, had been quietly nudging me to return.

"Tell me about her," Nuria said.

"Who?"

"Your sister. Your mom. Either. Both."

Monica—my best friend before I'd messed up our friendship, and just before I became Betsy—was the only one who'd ever asked me to do the same as Nuria asked now. I'd never known how to talk about my sister. I'd never known who, exactly, I'd be talking about. And my mother? Well, that was complicated, too. I chose the option Nuria hadn't offered.

"Maybe next time."

12

JUSTIN

It's Justin's second day as Project Manager and he and Caleb are going to co-run their team meeting later in the morning. They already went over the agenda the day before and Caleb insists he'll really only be present for moral support. He's confident Justin will do fine on his own. Caleb had said the sooner they transition to Justin handling the team with him as their point of contact, the better off they'll all be.

He and Caleb will still have their morning check-ins, which Justin appreciates. Not only is it a useful grounding meeting for the day, but he enjoys Caleb's company. He's his boss and mentor, but they also get along well. A good work friendship.

Except today he discovers their check-in won't happen. There's an email from Caleb, sent at four o'clock that morning, saying his dad has had a stroke and Caleb won't be in for the rest of the week.

<<*I'm sorry to bale on you like this, but I know you'll understand and I also have no doubt you will do great on your own. Just remember that you know what you're doing and I never would have promoted you if I didn't believe you were the right person for the job.*

I'll text you when I have more information about my return. Hopefully it will be in the next week or so.

Cheers and good luck,

C>>

Well, Justin thinks, *here goes everything.* He smiles to himself as he uses this expression while his chest tightens. It's an expression he and his cousin, Hugh, had adopted and then subsequently used ridiculously often. It came about when they'd mused over why the phrase was "here goes nothing" when it felt like everything was on the line. It's only been recently that he's been able to say that phrase to himself without immediately imagining Hugh in a crumpled heap on the pavement in the recess of an alley. Justin's therapist suggests the memories might feel easier as he lets more of Reign into his life. As he opens himself to Reign's friendship, Justin remembers more than the pain of losing Hugh.

Justin leans in to the positive memory, which bolsters his confidence while prepping the agenda notes for the team meeting. He makes a couple of changes, given Caleb's absence, including project tasks that Caleb initially had in place. Justin's change will be a great way to show off his own vision for how things will get done.

When he walks into the conference room, Shane and Austin are already present. A promising sign.

"Good morning," he says, adding in a friendly nod to each of them.

"Hey, Justin," Austin says.

"Hey man," says Shane, "how's it hangin'?"

Justin knows full well how Shane hopes and expects he'll reply, and he decides not to "disappoint" him.

"It's hanging exactly how it's supposed to. How's yours hanging?"

Austin snorts.

Shane smirks. "Ready for action. Like always."

"I'm not sure what kind of action it's anticipating this morning. You might need to keep it in check," Justin says.

Shane shakes his head. "You get that I'm talking about di—"

"Jesus, Shane," Austin interrupts. "He definitely knows what you're talking about."

Justin turns on the display with the remote and mirrors his laptop screen onto it with the meeting agenda alongside the daily error report spreadsheet.

"Let's get started," Justin says.

"Where's Caleb?" Shane asks.

"Not here today. Family emergency."

"He okay?" Austin asks.

"He is," Justin says. "But his dad had a stroke."

"Shit, that sucks," Austin says at the same time that Shane asks, "So we're stuck with just you?"

"Yes," Justin replies. "We'll go over the main issues from the error report first, and then plan out a few enhancement tasks."

"Are those enhancement tasks approved by Caleb?" Shane asks.

"I approve them."

"I mean, no offense, man, but you've been in this position for like, two seconds. Are you sure you should be making these kinds of decisions by yourself already?"

Justin glances at Austin to see if he'll "go along" as he often does. Austin stares at his own keyboard with nothing to add.

It's what Justin assumed would happen, even if Caleb had more faith.

"I don't have to justify myself to either of you," Justin says. "This is my decision to make, and these two items have been on top of the All Choice Care employee request line for months and it's critical for us to address these requests."

In fact, Justin *had* cleared these task items with Caleb

already. Justin had wanted to tackle several other items simultaneously, but Caleb recommended easing in, especially since the team would now essentially be down to two people instead of three with Justin's promotion. But there is no way he will give Shane and Austin the satisfaction of this knowledge.

Both Shane and Austin agree—Shane with some kind of exaggerated reluctance, Austin with no comment at all—and they spend the remainder of the meeting mapping out a plan for each project. Justin is proud of himself for not dictating all the steps to them. He definitely knows how he would handle the code development, but he knows a good leader lets his employees figure out their own way, too. All things considered, Justin is pleased with how the meeting goes, despite how it started.

Of course, it wouldn't be an hour with Shane and Austin without overhearing Shane say in a loud whisper to Austin as they leave the conference room, "I can't believe we have to work for C3P-D-Bag Sheldon now."

"You'll get used to it," Justin says.

Shane keeps walking, but Austin stops and turns around. "Sorry, man. He's just comparing you—"

"I know the reference," Justin says. It's not the first time someone's compared him to the popular character from *The Big Bang Theory*, although it's a creative combination with *Star Wars* and a general insult.

"Yeah," Austin says. "Um, well, yeah. Anyway..." He turns around and continues on to his cubicle.

Justin sits again at the conference table, losing some of the sense of victory he felt only moments ago. Could he fire his employees on his second day of being their supervisor? Well, it really only needed to be one of them. Austin obviously wasn't a model of respect, but if he weren't around Shane all of the time, he might turn into someone more tolerable.

For as supportive as he is of Justin, Caleb has a blind spot concerning how others treat Justin. Shane has become more outwardly confrontational in his antics in the past weeks. Yet Caleb insists that Shane is good at his job and while yes, his behaviors are juvenile, they have no bearing on the work.

"He's contributing to a hostile work environment," Justin has said.

"Hostile? With childish pranks?"

"Harassment and intimidation," Justin countered.

Then Caleb had laughed. "It's a little teasing, Justin, which you usually shut down quite handily."

Justin shakes his head at the memory and considers the new situation where Shane's behavior now means insubordination. He makes a mental note to check in with Claire in HR to see a copy of Shane's contract and to find out what options he has. He really just wants to fire him. Without Caleb here to discourage him or imply that Justin was the immature one who couldn't handle a little "teasing," he realizes he might finally be able to do something about his own work environment.

The problem, however, is that the team used to be three people, including himself, and now it's down to two. Laying off Shane would mean Justin would have to fill in the gaps until they hire someone new—two new people, really, and even then, it would take time to train in the new person and bring them up to speed. Caleb has said Shane was a strong coding analyst, but at the time, Shane wasn't vital to the team. Regardless of his asshole attitude, Justin currently needs Shane, especially since he launched them on this new project.

Hiring someone new has become a top priority. He clicks into his email to send a message to Claire in order to set up an appointment, only to discover an inbox overflowing with new messages. He stares at all the bold type, his heart rate ticking a touch faster for a moment until his eye catches the sender of most of them: Salesforce, their CRM, or customer relationship management system. The day before, Caleb said he was working on getting things transferred over to Justin and the changeover has kicked in. He breathes easier and sets to work on analyzing his inbox to manage a filtering system to organize and prioritize messages coming in.

He'll have to figure out the Shane situation later.

13

LIZZIE

Thursdays were my one glorious day off from both jobs. It was nice to have a day mid-week to avoid crowds in stores and to have the apartment all to myself. To dawdle the day away to my heart's content.

Well, almost to myself. When she wasn't sleeping on one of the ridiculous number of beds and pillows Justin had scattered everywhere for her, Crash followed me to each room and kept her evil eye on me.

"Can I just say," I said to her as I traipsed into the kitchen at the beautiful late hour of nine in the morning, "I'm really not *that* bad. The attempt to be nice goes both ways."

She yawned.

I found a note on the fridge from Justin. *Leftover French toast is inside the fridge on the middle shelf. Mac's recipe. Reheat in the oven, uncovered, at 350 degrees for ten minutes. Confection sugar shaker is next to the toaster.* I smiled at his neat, even printing. He always used lined paper because he liked the guides to keep his lettering straight. I also smiled at his thoughtfulness.

Mama Mac was a chef, which was where Justin got all his cooking skills. I learned a few things, too, but I lacked the passion and patience to learn the fine details and science that would yield perfect results. Justin easily gravitated to both the art and science of cooking. He was talented in so many areas it was sometimes aggravating. I'd put all my energy into being good at one thing, and then I fucked it up.

While at Meadowfields Elementary, I'd initially clicked with Carrie, but when she transformed into aloof and Superior Teacher Carrie, I went adrift. I ended up latching on to a set of fourth-grade teachers known teasingly as the Triple As—Ashley, Amber, and Anabel. While not quite the warmest of people, they were outgoing. Plus, our ages and "single" relationship statuses connected us. I'd started eating lunch in the lounge at the same time as them and Anabel had asked me about my gauges.

"Do they hurt?"

"Not at all."

"How do they put them in?" Amber had asked next. "Like, do they have a giant piercing gun they use to make such a big hole?"

I'd laughed and explained the process of stretching over time. Their interest in me had been shallow curiosity, but it's what I thought I'd wanted. I'd lost my friendship with Monica, then later with Carrie. I didn't have it in me to try again. With the Triple As, I didn't have to. They were never going to be lifelong friends.

It was a mistake. Our relationship stayed on a surface level, but I also shied away from disrupting it because then I'd have no one. Except, I didn't like who I'd become around them. They'd make comments about our students, and I wouldn't do anything or say anything to stop them or redirect. On more challenging days, for example, Amber would complain about how hard it had been to get through lessons, even if Marco wasn't the only kid reacting to things. And on the good days, it would still come across as a complaint.

"Marco was *finally* paying attention for once." I'd nod and other times I might say, "He really liked being a part of the discussion on the rug today," but Amber's reaction would be unappreciative. I wouldn't challenge her. And I should have. I should have made it so Marco could take part in things more often instead of always taking the path of least resistance and pulling him out to work with him one-on-one. He loved being included in the group, even if he couldn't conform the way Amber expected him to.

I had been good at my job. "Had been" being the key words. I'd reverted to the person I'd never wanted to be. The one I'd been running from most of my life.

The oven chimed its pre-heated readiness at the same time my phone rang out the refrain of Kesha's "Woman," my ring tone associated with Mama Mac.

I swiped to answer and put the phone in speaker mode. "Hi Ma."

"Hey, baby. How are you doing?" Mac's warm voice filled the room. It always did, no matter what volume she used. I'd seen her in action at her restaurant. Her voice was strong and held authority, but it was never mean or screamy like I'd watched on reality cooking shows. She never yelled at home, either, but we definitely knew when she was angry or frustrated. Now, her calm, even temperament soothed me.

"I'm okay. Getting ready to reheat some of your special-recipe French toast JT left for me."

"Don't forget to cover it tightly with foil so it'll keep its moisture for how you like it."

"Already on it," I said, tearing the foil away from the box, draping it over the pan, and cinching it around the edges. I slid the pan into the oven and set the timer.

"That's my girl. Tell me all about how you're doing."

I took her off speaker and brought the phone with me to the living room. Crash followed me, jumped to the coffee table, and then sat with her tail curled around her paws as she stared at me. I resisted the urge to flip her off, trying once again the "nice" route, as though it made any difference at all to a cat.

"I hate my jobs, Ma. Not much else to tell beyond that."

"You have other options, of course."

"Not sure I don't hate those options, too."

"Do you mean that? Or is it only self-doubt and fear talking to you?"

My stomach tightened. "Can we not do this right now?"

Mac was silent for a moment, probably holding back a giant sigh. "All right," she said. "Things still going okay with Justin?"

"Yeah. I mean, we obviously irritate the hell out of each other sometimes, but it's been good. It probably helps that my night shifts at Astros prevent us from seeing each other too much."

Mac laughed. "I bet that's right, but I know he's been really happy with you there. He's missed you."

"Missed me? Where have I been?"

"I don't know, Elizabeth." She always called me by my full name. Even when I was little. "You tell me."

It was my turn to remain silent. My answer had been flippant, but I caught the implication. It's funny how your subconscious self knows when it needs to hide away who you are when you stop being who you are supposed to be. The more I'd let myself fall into the dark hole of Betsy, the less I talked to or saw Justin. We used to talk weekly, and we'd had a standing monthly dinner together that I'd cancelled more often.

I'd hidden from Mac and LiLi, too. When I went home after the accident at Meadowfields, I realized how much I missed them. Unconditional love made for a powerful healer, and while I hadn't returned from that visit at one hundred percent, I'd been well-mended. I thought I could handle returning to my job until Skylar's mom brought up charges against the district. While I had union support, my principal and my teacher colleagues turned their backs on me. Once upon a time, the other paras would have had my back. They remained sympathetic, but I had alienated them in my quest to be besties with the Triple As.

In answer to Mac's implied question of where I'd been, I went for the truth. "I don't know, Ma. I'm trying to figure that out."

"We're all here for you. You know that, right?"

I did, which was partly what made everything so painful. I'd had no right to cut myself off from them before, and now I had no right to depend on them to fix all that I'd broken.

"Yeah," I said. "I know."

Much to my relief, Mac changed subjects. "I've got a new sauce for you to try next time you make pasta."

"Yeah? And you're only going to share the recipe with me, right?"

She laughed. "You know I always give you the first crack at the sauces."

"You're my favorite."

"I love you, baby."

"I love you, too."

I hung up and eyed Crash, who remained on the coffee table staring at me, although she had relaxed into a loaf.

"That was Mama Mac," I told her. "I bet you like her and Mama LiLi, don't you?"

Crash merely blinked.

"Yep. It's just me, then?" The timer from the oven beeped, and I got up from the couch to grab my breakfast. The more I reflected on my life these days, the more I agreed with Crash's assessment.

❄

THOUGH JUSTIN WAS the better cook between us, I wasn't unskilled. Sauces were my specialty, and I took over as chef on my days off, with Justin as my sous. I pulled together the new spicy Alfredo sauce recipe that Mac sent me to go with our chicken fettuccine while Justin finished prepping the garlic bread for the oven as he shared his big news.

"I have a date tomorrow night."

I slowly added the cream to the pot on the stove, continually stirring, which served as a good distraction to help me keep casual about this new development. Justin hadn't been on a date in well over a year.

"Yeah? Are you trying out one of the dating apps again?"

"No. I don't think I ever want to go back to those. I met her while swimming. And then later at Panera."

"So, you've already had a date and this will be your second?"

"No, the Panera thing happened by accident. She saw me through the window."

No doubt her gaze naturally found him. My brother was stupidly good looking. His daily swims and weekend gym workouts made for a perfect body, and he had soft brown eyes that made both men and women all gooey.

He was confident while simultaneously socially awkward, and somehow this combination made women swoon. They thought, "This guy can take care of me, and look how adorable he is—I can *fix* him." Not my words. Justin said that some women have told him exactly this. Sure, Justin had some traits that could be challenging at times. We all did, obviously, but his didn't always fit inside the norms of "different." Instead, they called him "difficult" or "weird." And yeah, I got it. I wasn't so focused within my world that I didn't "see" autistic behaviors, except Justin was one of the best people I knew. He deserved someone who saw nothing to fix.

"She's pretty," he said. "Great, thick, curly dark hair. Her eyes are kind of close together and her eyebrows are bushy, but her smile is nice even if she seems to have a bit of acne she's covering with make-up—"

"JT. Stop. Seriously."

"What?"

"I don't care what she looks like, least of all when you're making a pro-con list of her physical attributes. What's her name?"

"Oh. Right. Amelia."

I held back my sigh. The way his voice softened at her name cut into me, knowing that getting the date was never the hard part. Maintaining a relationship after the women discovered that Justin didn't need fixing, was.

"She talks with her hands," he added.

I smiled at that. "Well, there's something in common, then. Is that why you said yes?"

"That's a bit presumptuous. I was the one who asked her out."

Whoa. My brother made the first move? "Wow. I kinda want to meet a woman special enough for you to pursue instead."

He didn't answer and remained oddly quiet as he spread garlic butter on the last piece of bread.

"I'm nervous," he said, finally. His voice dipped into a low hum.

Oh Justin. I turned off the heat under the sauce, then walked over to him. "Can I give you a hug?" He nodded, and I wrapped my arms around him, squeezing him tightly. "It's okay to be nervous."

His hum pulsed into me for almost a minute before fading into even breaths. I stepped away. "If you liked her well enough already to ask her out first, those are probably good instincts kicking in."

Justin stroked his jaw and nodded. "Maybe. It's been a long time, Lizzie. I don't remember how to do this."

"Invite Reign over as you get ready for the date tomorrow," I suggested. "They'll help you choose what to wear if you want, and together you can map through how each part of the date will go."

"Okay. Yeah. That's a good idea. Thanks."

"You'll do great, JT. It's one date. Just be—" I stopped even before his glare smothered me. He hated it when I used the "be yourself" advice. "A good listener," I finished with instead.

Justin snorted. "Nice save. And still decent advice." He handed me the pan of bread to put into the oven next to the one with roasting vegetables.

Justin set the table as I finished up with the sauce and final preparations. By the time we settled at the table, I reopened the dating conversation.

"Whatever happened between you and the last woman you were seeing? Callie? Or was it Annie?"

"Lily."

His tone flattened, and I took it for judgment of me for not remembering something I should have. What I did remember was that Lily was also autistic, and I'd been surprised he was finally dating someone who probably wouldn't need to fix him. Someone who would actually get to know and understand the real Justin. But I also realized I didn't know much about her. I'd never met her like I had for his past girlfriends.

Shit. It hit me in the chest as I remembered I'd canceled on him the night I was to meet her. I'd backed out in order to go "clubbing it" with the Triple As, which ended up being as vapid of a night as it sounded. I'd watched them get stupid drunk, and I'd considered doing the same after they began the kisses for drinks game. They'd ask men if they wanted to see two women kissing, and if so, they had to buy them a drink. I sat at the far end of the bar to stay away from the game and to wait it out until I could make sure they got safely in a Lyft at the end of the night.

"Lily," I confirmed to Justin. "It seemed like it was going well. Better than some of your past girlfriends."

"I don't want to talk about her."

"She was autistic, too?"

He glared at me. "If you don't have to talk about what happened with Skylar, then I don't have to talk about Lily."

Fair.

"You're right. I'm sorry." *I'm sorry I didn't learn more about Lily. I'm sorry I almost got a child killed. I'm sorry you have to take care of me now as though I'm a child myself. I'm sorry I'm still acting like a child.*

I changed tactics. "What about work? How's the new role going?"

"It's fine."

"That's it? Fine?"

"Yes."

I knew better than to push him. I aggravated him with my questioning about Lily, he was worried about his date with Amelia, and obviously something was going on at work, but it was only going to tip him over the edge if I pried more information out of him.

I looked at Crash, who sat on the back of the couch. She gave me a baleful look before jumping down and doing figure eights around Justin's legs, purring and rubbing her face against him. Justin lifted her into his lap, and she curled up. Justin's shoulders dropped away from his ears, where they'd been hugging since the moment I'd mentioned Lily.

We continued eating and talking about innocuous topics, then we cleaned up and separated to do our own things for the rest of the night.

14

JUSTIN

"What do you think?" Justin holds up a blue tie with gold stripes and a red tie with black cats. Crash sits on the dresser, tilts her head, and paws the red tie. Justin nods knowingly. "You're right. It was a silly question, wasn't it? You always choose this one. The only problem, though, is I just realized the shirt I like to wear with it is dirty."

A set of knocks on the front door causes Crash to sit up straighter, her ears perked. She knows the pattern. A single knock, a pause, a double knock, a pause, and then a five-tap rhythm. She meows at Justin, jumps down to the floor, and pauses at the bedroom door to stare back at Justin as if to ask, "Are you coming?" Of course, Justin follows as he knows the knock pattern also. They walk to the door together.

"Hey, Reign," Justin says after opening the door. He steps aside to let Reign enter and Crash weaves in and out of their legs, purring her own hello.

Reign smiles and reaches down to scratch Crash's head. "Hello, my lovely. It's good to see you, too. Have you been helping JT get ready?" Crash meows in response.

Justin holds up the ties for Reign to see. "We were discussing ties. Crash naturally likes the one with the cats."

The three of them head back into Justin's bedroom as Reign says, "Where are you taking Amelia?"

"We're meeting up at Red Robin."

"Seriously?"

"Yes."

"Then definitely no tie at all." Reign takes them from Justin's hand and returns them to their properly labeled places on Justin's tie rack.

Justin frowns. "But I want to look nice."

"No doubt," Reign says, eyeing the clothes hanging in Justin's closet—all organized according to type of clothing and color spectrum. "But have you ever been to a Red Robin?"

"No."

"Why are you taking her there? It doesn't seem like a place you'd choose."

"Amelia chose it," Justin says. "I wanted to take her to Chianti Grill, but she said she didn't want the pressure of going somewhere too fancy."

"And Red Robin was her alternative?"

"She said she's never been and has always wanted to try it."

"All right, all right," Reign says, nodding. "Giving the lady what she wants right away. That's a good thing. You looked up the restaurant, though, right?"

Justin had, of course, researched it and now guesses at Reign's point. "I'll be way overdressed." This is one reason why Lizzie suggested having Reign over to help him out. Justin doesn't normally gloss over details like what Reign pointed out. It's a sign of his level of nervousness. And if he is already so nervous he can't focus on the most basic information about the dress code of a restaurant, he worries about what kind of disaster the actual date might be.

An involuntary hum seeps out of him and he paces.

"Hey." Reign catches him before he pivots away from the closet, and they grip each of Justin's biceps firmly to keep him in place. "No, no, man. It's not like that, okay? I didn't mean you shouldn't dress sharp, you know?"

He doesn't know, which is true most of the time. And even if it isn't actually true, it *feels* true. He can go days without a single social mess-up and then stumble over one thing and the full string of perfect days unravels, highlighting all of his deficiencies at once.

Justin focuses on the silver spiral cone earring hanging from Reign's right earlobe and shakes his head. "I don't know at all. What do I wear?"

"I'm sorry, Justin," Reign says, releasing their grip. "I said 'you know' as a reflex. It's okay not knowing ... you know?"

Justin sees Reign's smile *and* the joke. He pushes at their shoulder to shove them away, but smiles at the same time. "Asshole."

Reign brings a curled hand to their mouth and laughs. "You good now? Ready to let me help?"

"Yeah."

"Cool. So even without a jacket, a tie for a date at Red Robin makes you come across too formal. Stiff."

"I am pretty stiff."

"You are decidedly *not* stiff. Or formal for that matter." Reign turns back to Justin's closet and flips through his shirts. "Needing clarity of communication and preferring structure are two of the most common personality traits in the world."

Justin is positive that Reign has no idea if those traits are the most common ones, but lets it go.

Reign pulls out three button-downs from the blue-hued section. "These are smart and classy as well as your sexiest color."

"I have a sexy color?"

"You do."

Justin smiles at this knowledge. He knows he's good looking. He has muscles from daily workouts and he's grown used to the messy hair style Lizzie taught him to do. She calls it "lightly tousled," but in his eyes, it's clearly a disordered style. A buzz cut would be far easier and more practical given his swimming regimen and yet, he has to admit, it's nice having people smile as a first impression. It sometimes softens the second impression.

It won't hurt to wear his sexy color tonight. He wants all the chances to win Amelia over. He points to the ocean blue shirt with white flecks. "Will that one work? It's my most comfortable one of those three."

"Oh yeah, definitely! Together with some nice pants or with jeans and a jacket? You will look delicious." Reign hands Justin the chosen shirt and carefully returns the other two to the closet, hanging them in proper order. "I'll wait for you out in the living room and then we'll double check hair and go over all the things for first date prep."

"Okay, thanks."

Reign closes the door behind them and, as Justin puts on the shirt and buttons it up, he looks at Crash.

"I didn't think I'd be so nervous, Crash. It's not like I haven't been on a date before."

Crash shifts from sitting down to a loaf position on the dresser and tilts her head to listen.

"There's just something about her. I feel different around her. It's like when Hugh told me about Max." Crash knows all about Hugh. Justin has told her all about how they were best friends until something happened. He hasn't shared with her about what happened, but it doesn't matter. The important part is how she understands his waves of sadness. Finding people—or animals in this case—who recognize not only that he has feelings but what they are is, as Reign would say, like finding a unicorn. Or, to land back in the real world, like happening upon a four-leaf clover.

Justin continues. "Hugh said he felt fireworks in his stomach when he first met Max."

Crash's eyes go wide, and Justin nods. "I know, that sounds really extreme and uncomfortable, but I think I understand what he means now. When I think of Amelia, it feels like a firework starts in my stomach, shoots up and then explodes into one of those colorful bursts inside my head."

He'd felt some of this with Lily, a woman he'd met through a dating app. She wasn't the first woman he'd dated who was also autistic, so it wasn't as though that was what had especially attracted him to her. Rather, it was how they shared so many specific interests. Wordplay. Math puzzles. Fantasy novels. Photography—although she preferred selfies to his "weird obsession with hair follicles." The sting had been her telling him when they broke up that she was going to go back to dating normal men.

Crash meows now as Justin tucks the end of his belt into the loophole of his black pants, then goes to the dresser to pull out a pair of socks. Crash rolls to her side, puts a paw on Justin's wrist, and licks the top of his hand. Justin rubs Crash's head. "Thanks for the reassurance, Crash." Crash purrs in reply.

He puts on socks and shoes and once he's ready, he walks out into the living room, seeking Reign's approval. Crash follows and rubs up against Justin's legs in solidarity, and even though it means he'll have to brush off the cat hair, he doesn't mind. It's a special kind of warmth to feel Crash's love this way.

Reign offers their own purr. "Mm, mm, mm. Yep, blue is one hundred percent your sexy color. Any chance you can lose the undershirt?"

"No."

Reign nods and walks over to Justin and lifts their hands to near Justin's ears. "One more thing. May I touch your hair?"

"Is it not tousled enough?"

Reign grins. "It has the perfect amount of 'tousle,' as usual. I just want to smooth a little around the ears. There. Appearance-wise, you are ready." They give Justin's chest two light taps. "What about emotionally? Where are you at?"

"I'm okay right now. It's between now and when I meet up with her that I'm worried about."

"Yeah, I hear you. I get pretty anxious myself when it's someone I really like or really want to like."

"How do you work through it?"

"Honestly?" Reign asks, then continues after a nod from Justin. "Sometimes I plan out conversation topics in my head. I've got a bunch of random questions like, 'What kinds of movies do you like to watch?' and 'What's the latest song you added to your favorites on Spotify?' and 'Dogs or cats?'"

Justin's eyes widen. "What if she says dogs?"

Crash jumps to the armrest on the couch and gives a meandering-pitched meow.

"Well, then you know," Reign says. "But you don't have to use my questions. We can come up with some that make sense for you."

"That 'dogs vs cats' one is pretty important, so I'm keeping that one. Maybe I can ask what she likes to do creatively? I like it when people find out I do photography because so many people assume I only like computers and numbers." He does like computers and numbers, only not for the stereotype orderliness or technicality of them. He was good at those aspects, but what he enjoyed was the creating side of code and the problem-solving to fix things or improve them.

"Yeah, that's a good one. And it will say a lot about you before you even talk about your photography. It will show her you want to really learn and know about her instead of only the superficial stuff."

"She uses a cane, and I really want to know why, but should I not ask about it?"

Reign sits, and Crash curls up in their lap. "I think you can definitely ask her, but wait until you're a couple of discussion topics in. Or if you need a different time indicator, wait until after you've started eating when your dinner order comes. Wait, Red Robin serves you your food at the table, right? You don't pick it up at a counter?"

"It's a full-service restaurant, yes. So, not until after the food arrives?"

"Yeah, it's a good time marker to keep in the back of your mind. You got this, JT."

"Thank you for helping me."

Crash rolls in Reign's lap to lie on her back and Reign gives her a full-on belly rub. Justin smiles as he thinks of how Crash and Lizzie still eye each other warily.

"Crash liked you right away, didn't she?" Justin asks.

"Oh yeah," Reign croons, dipping their head to nuzzle Crash. "We both know a good buddy when we see one."

"She's still pretty prickly around Lizzie."

Reign nods and asks, "Can you tell me your sister's story? It was kind of surprising when she suddenly wanted a new name instead of, well … the name you always used."

"Betsy?"

"So, it's not a dead name?"

"Oh. No," Justin says, realizing Reign's confusion. And honestly, Justin doesn't blame them. Lizzie's name changes, while always a variation of her given name, occur with a regular enough frequency to cause Justin's anxiety to spike. It takes everything in him to hide his emotions when he discovers the newest variation. But when he asks, she only says, "I just felt like changing it up."

This latest change to Lizzie prickles him the most. It's too close to the truth of who she is.

He's not sure how much to reveal to Reign about Lizzie. How much Lizzie would like to keep private, or what Lizzie herself should share of her own story to Reign, especially now that those two were becoming friends. Reign has been a really good friend—almost as good a friend as Hugh had been—and Justin wants to have that kind of friendship again. The kind where you can share feelings. He and Caleb talk about topics not related to work, but nothing serious. Caleb is his boss, after all. Not quite a friend, only friend-like.

And while he and Caleb have learned how to communicate with one another, Reign understands him. And in turn, Justin's beginning to understand Reign, too.

"Do you plan conversation topics for talking to my sister?"

Reign grins. "Busted. She's your sister and I know how important she is to you, so I don't want to mess that up."

Justin nods and reflects upon his conversation earlier with Lizzie. "She listened to you about her hair. And she's working with you for personal training. Seems like those are all good signs, right?"

Reign shrugs. "She's sizing me up. She's pretty protective of you, too."

"Because I'm autistic," Justin says with a sigh. "But I can take care of myself."

"Yeah, definitely that's part of it, but it's more than that. She feels safe with you. I can't tell you why I know this—I just sense it right now, I guess."

The prickliness returns and fills his chest and his hand automatically reaches to stroke his jaw. The word "safe" sinks to the bottom of his stomach and a chill creeps into him without warning. He stands up quickly and shakes out his limbs. He refuses to let a past promise surface and derail his date with someone he genuinely likes. He concentrates on how he's felt around Amelia and breathes deeply as warmth settles back into his body. He can do this.

"And now I'm stressing you out," Reign says, who lifts Crash from their lap, maintaining her curled position, and sets her on the cushion next to them. "You look amazing. You've got things to talk about. Amelia won't be able to *not* fall for you. And you can always shoot me a text if you need to, okay?"

Justin nods and joins in with their dap routine: back of the hand tap, side-positioned palm slap, followed by a fists-up bump. "Thanks for helping me out."

"You know I got you." Reign waves and slips out the door.

"*Cold, Justin. I'm cold!*"

"*I've got you —*" Justin snaps the memory shut. He *promised*. He will close that memory away again. *Why is it even coming up so often right now?* He picks up Crash and nuzzles her to his neck. He relaxes into her purr.

15

LIZZIE

Between two and three days per week, I worked both jobs, and it was kind of the worst, especially on days like today when both places were stupid busy. It didn't help that Chuck, the manager at Astros, did nothing except shout orders from his office while he pretended to study sales spreadsheets.

I worked at the counter and dining room. Anthony worked in the kitchen. Chuck worked the games on his phone. Anthony and I had an efficient system, but the unexpected rush just before closing time at nine-thirty put us behind and we didn't get out of the restaurant until after eleven. Add to that, the temperature had dropped significantly and my gloves were cold and stiff from being left in my car instead of warm and soft in my coat pockets. I spent the first half of the drive home with muscles sore from constant shivering.

When I got home, all I wanted was to fall into my bed and black out for the minuscule four hours I had until my alarm went off for my Gas-n-Guzzle shift. My new routine for entering the apartment was to take off my boots in the hall outside the apartment and put them on the tray inside in order to protect Justin's precious carpet that he neither chose nor owned.

When I entered the apartment, only the light from the hall offered a visual of the boot tray. A piercing screech followed the thud of my boots. Startled, I fell into the corner of the shelf, also positioned by the door. I cursed the bruising pain while catching a flash of calico fur whiz past me and out the door.

Fuck.

I stepped out in time to see a fluffed-out bit of a tail disappear around the corner at the end of the hall. I whispered another curse and trudged after her.

Except when I rounded the corner, she was nowhere in sight. My stomach knotted at the idea of Crash in the stairwell. If I missed her getting in there, she could be virtually anywhere.

I sped up my pace. I opened the door to the stairwell and quietly called out to Crash. A foolish endeavor, considering the hissing demon never responded to my calls under the best circumstances in Justin's apartment. Yet I heard a faint meow, and I slowly climbed the next flight of stairs.

"Crash?"

Nothing. I went up another half flight to the roof access door, which remained decidedly locked before heading back down, past my floor and to the next level down.

"Crash?"

Still nothing. Fifteen minutes had already passed, and I was down to three and a half hours of sleep before my Gas-n-Guzzle shift. Fucking cat. Fucking stupid jobs. Fuck me for being a coward and quitting my job at the school, which put me in this whole situation.

Justin would probably find Crash quickly, but I didn't have it in me to wake him up, which would start a chain reaction of behaviors that would all end badly.

I left the stairwell and leaned up against the wall next to the door. How long until I had no choice but to get Justin? Crash liked Reign pretty well. They might be awake and able to help.

I shot out a text to them, moved back into the stairwell where I heard the faint meow, and called out to Crash again.

My ears caught another meow, this one a little stronger.

"Where *are* you?" Once more, holding out an unreasonable hope that this cat nemesis would, for once, be amenable to letting me get near her.

Meow.

Louder. Maybe she wanted me to find her after all.

Wait. There. I didn't know how I missed it the first time. A loose metal panel to some sort of... electrical thing, maybe? My heart sped up at the potential danger. What if there were loose wires, too?

I knelt down and peered through the narrow opening in the wall. "Crash?" It was too dark to see anything, so I shone my phone's flashlight inside and caught two eyes glowing from the light.

Meow.

"Well, you got in there," I said. "Surely you can find your way out again."

She had the gall to hiss at me. *FFS.* My breathing shallowed into tight, rapid wheezes. I pulled away and sat back along the wall next to the panel. Normal intakes of air followed as I relaxed into the open environment of the stairwell and away from the dark, narrow space where Crash hid.

Why couldn't she just be on a fire escape or a window ledge? I stared at my phone, willing Reign to return my text. Probably I should call at this late hour instead of text. Was it late for Reign? I still didn't know them super well, regardless of our training sessions.

The brief adrenaline rush of fear I'd had at the wall panel entrance dissolved back into exhaustion. This next day was going to suck. I had to work both jobs again except on no sleep. I needed to find something else. I could search for PCA work with adults instead of children. Someone who might have fewer unpredictable behaviors that wouldn't contribute to me endangering their life.

My body was losing the fight against staying awake. Just as I was about to succumb to blissful oblivion, a voice startled me back.

"Lizzie? What are you doing here?"

"JT! What are *you* doing here?"

He frowned at me. "I'm obviously coming home from my date. What isn't clear is why you are slouched on the floor in the stairwell. Are you drunk?"

"That sounds like an infinitely better option than what's really happening here."

His date. I checked the time on my phone as though I wasn't already fully aware it was after midnight. It surprised me. Justin never stayed out this late, not even on weekends.

Did he? I didn't know his life and routines like I used to. Or maybe dating-Justin was different than working- or non-dating-Justin. I set aside those thoughts to concentrate on what I had to tell him and braced for his reaction.

"Try not to panic when I tell you this," I said, immediately realizing the idiocy of my words, but carried on. "Crash escaped from the apartment and she's stuck inside this maintenance panel thingy. I'm so sorry, JT. It was too dark to see, and she was right by the door and I banged into things which startled her and she ran out too fast for me to grab her, and I can't get her out because it's small and dark in there." Just saying the last bit made me catch my breath in anticipatory fear.

Justin was already crouching and pushing the panel over as I finished spilling out my confession.

"Hey, Crash," he said, his voice slipping into as tender a tone as I've ever heard him use. "Come on out, sweet kitty." It wasn't a significant pitch change, and most wouldn't notice it, but I did. And so did Crash, obviously, since she stepped right out to him with a meow. Justin scooped her up and loud purrs emanated from her as he stared at the floor next to me. I shrugged out of my coat and spread it out.

When he still didn't move, I sighed inwardly, not sure I had it in me to deal with a potential meltdown. "Whatever, JT. You don't have to join me down here. I'll muster the energy to get back to your apartment in a bit. I'm sorry about letting Crash escape." I closed my eyes again and rested my head against the corner of the walls.

Justin's shoulder brushed against mine as he settled in. "I was working it out, not refusing. There's a lot out of my comfort zone and routine going on here right now."

I recognized this. Bone deep fatigue made it harder for me to find the patience, though. "Good date, I'm guessing?" I murmured, my eyes still closed, relaxing into the warmth of my brother's nearness and the rumbling motor pouring out of Crash.

"Yeah. We talked for a long time. She's a pediatric physical therapist, and she shared some pretty cool stories about kids she's worked with. She knows a lot about swimming statistics. Did you know that Sarah Thomas, an American woman, has the record for the longest open water swim? 104.6 miles from Vermont to New York. It took her a little over sixty-seven hours."

I smiled and opened my eyes to look at Justin. "Was she trying to impress you? Because that's how you met? Swimming?"

"Oh," he said. He scratched Crash's neck, and she arched her head back in appreciation. "I don't know. She didn't say so, but do you think that's why she knew so much?"

"Possibly." I shrugged. "But maybe she really is in to all that stuff and that's why she also enjoys swimming."

"Or she researched in preparation," Justin suggested. "It's what I do."

"What did you research ahead of time for this date?"

"Mostly I scripted out questions to ask and questions she might ask me. I didn't do a good job, though. I didn't even think about researching swimming facts. Instead, I did what I probably shouldn't have, which was to look up all the reasons why she might use a cane."

My chuckle slipped out involuntarily. "Sorry, I didn't really mean to laugh, it's just, there are like a billion possibilities, right?"

"Obviously not a billion, but yes, too many to guess."

"Did you ask her about her cane?"

"No, but she told me about it later."

"And?" I asked, wondering why he didn't tell me more.

"And then we talked some more and left the restaurant at eleven-fifteen, when Amelia noticed the employees were cleaning everything up."

"No, I meant, and what did she tell you about the cane?" Although now I had additional questions about what happened between eleven-fifteen and twelve-thirty, which was about the time he came up the stairwell.

"I'm not sure if that's private or not. I'll text her tomorrow to find out if I can share that information."

Justin proved to me again how he was one of the best people I knew. He seriously drove me bonkers sometimes—the shoes and carpet issue part of the plethora of ways—but it was this courtesy, this utter respect he gave everyone, that summed him up. He could sound rude as fuck at times, yet rarely was it deliberate. It was honest and curious. I once read that if autistics ruled the world, wars would be fewer and shorter because they would say what they meant without subterfuge.

"I'm glad you came home when you did because I had no idea how I was going to get Crash out of that wall. I'm also surprised it didn't faze you about her being there."

Justin nodded. "She's done it before. I complained to the landlord about this loose panel. I don't know why they haven't fixed it yet. The first time I didn't handle it very well." He looked at me. "How far in did you get?"

"An inch? So that tells you how well I didn't handle it, either. Your date explains why Crash was hanging by so close to the door, though. She was obviously waiting for you."

"That's my good girl," Justin crooned, lifting Crash up to his face.

"I hate my jobs, JT. Is your company hiring?"

"We're looking for a new software analyst."

"You would hire me?"

"No, of course not. You're not at all qualified."

I almost asked why he told me about it before I realized he'd simply answered my question. "I don't know what to do."

"What about being a para? Or teaching?"

"That's not who I am anymore."

"It was never who you were. It's what you did."

"It's what Ellie and Betsy did."

Justin gave what I'd call a grimaced sigh. "Those and Lizzie are all names for you. What difference does it make what name you were using?"

Everything, I thought. But also, in spite of my efforts, nothing. "You wouldn't understand."

"How do you know? You never explain it to me. How can you say I'm incapable of understanding something when you don't give me a chance? You sound just like Mom and Is—" He stopped. Mom and who? *Mom*? Who exactly did he mean by *Mom*? We never called LiLi or Mac, "mom."

"Mom? As in *mom* mom and not Mama Mac and Mama LiLi? How can you say that? I'm not..." But then I trailed off because I didn't want to talk anymore about who I wasn't.

And then a memory burst into my head.

You wouldn't understand, Justin. Issy and Beth are like other kids. That's how normal kids act.

Yeah, Justin. We're normal *kids. Not like you.*

Oh, shit. What was that? Definitely not Mac or LiLi. Never them.

And what was that noise? *Fuck.* It was JT; he was banging his head—lightly, but still banging- against the wall and letting out a continual, low-keening moan.

All exhaustion melted away as I jumped into action. I shooed Crash out of Justin's lap as I started singing *Row, Row, Row Your Boat*. Then I used all my strength to cradle his head against my chest with one arm and then wrap my other arm and both of my legs around his arms and torso in my tightest embrace. Over and over again I quietly sang until finally, Justin calmed.

"I'm sorry, JT," I whispered as I released him. "That was a terrible thing for me to tell you. I'm sure you could understand. And me saying you couldn't is all part of why I'm trying to shed the name of Betsy."

"I can't do more tonight," he said, as though he didn't hear me. I understood. I was done for the night, too.

"Thank you for staying with Crash out here," he added as we both stood. "It means a lot to me that you tried to help her."

"She's your family, JT. I wouldn't abandon her."

The word "abandon" caused an unexpected frisson, and not the thrilling kind. Instead, it gave me a déjà vu of having abandoned someone else in the past. I closed the thought away and followed Justin back to the apartment.

16

JUSTIN

Amelia isn't at the pool Monday morning, and regardless of the many reasons why this might be, Justin's brain circles around her possible rejection of him. He focuses on his strokes, reminding himself to settle into his normal pace that will calm him.

Friday's date had gone exceedingly well. Talking with Amelia quickly became easy as they talked about movies, books, art, and animals. Thankfully, she likes cats. She said she likes all animals except for ferrets, who play far too chaotically for her tastes. He emphatically agreed, although he doesn't have any experience first-hand. But one of his colleagues has them and the stories make him prickly with discomfort about the mess and unpredictability.

Eventually he and Amelia discussed work, and he liked how it wasn't the driving force of their conversation. He considers what he told Lizzie in the stairwell about how her job is what she does, not who she is. Mac and LiLi have both pointed out that Lizzie is a bit lost right now and Justin is starting to see what they mean. It's the kind of thing Justin might sort out with Alonso, his therapist. As far as he knows, Lizzie doesn't have a therapist, although until she moved in with him last month, they hadn't talked as often as they used to. He knows Mac and LiLi have encouraged Lizzie many times to see someone. Justin has never pushed because he knows his sister. He's always known her as confident and self-aware.

Yet, he's recently realized that she has been changing her name as a way to reinvent herself. He used to assume she simply enjoyed trying out different nicknames, but back when Lizzie was moving into his place and Reign said they were choosing a new identity for Lizzie, his brain traveled to that day in the hospital. *Did she know?*

He flips and pushes off from the wall, mentally noting he is at the halfway point of his swim. He has to be hyperconscious about time today as he is interviewing new candidates for his old position and can't be late. He pushes himself to concentrate on each stroke and breath of his workout. It works for one length before he is thinking of Lizzie again.

He knows her. She doesn't think he does, but she forgets his ability to catalog everything. He disagrees with the idea behind people "not being themselves" because no matter what you do, you are always yourself. On the other hand, he sees the changes in Lizzie. She isn't someone else. Rather, she seems … muted. Less confident. Quieter.

He's made more slip-ups than he ever has before about that day in the hospital. He's never told anyone about it. Not Mac or LiLi. Not Hugh. Not Reign. Not even Alonso. For nearly twenty-five years he's packed it away so deep inside himself that he's almost forgotten about it. It just isn't important anymore.

Except what if it is? A lot about the early days with Mac and LiLi are a blur in his normally crystal-clear memory. He's learned, with help from Alonso, to live with the cloudiness of that time. He remembers Lizzie, though. He remembers Beth/Lizzie acting much the same as she is doing now. Her own shock and fear enveloped him, amplifying his difficulty with transitioning into their new environment.

As he finishes his final lap, a pang of realization shoots through him. Lizzie is *sad*. He can't help her with the identity thing, but he can do something to help her sadness. His heart lifts at his confidence in being able to fix something. It's a good feeling to counteract the other emotion fighting for control: dread. He gets out of the pool and clocks the empty lane next to him—a weird coincidence that Douchebag also isn't around to appreciate a lane of his own without confrontation.

He returns his thoughts to Amelia. Their date had gone well. He doesn't think this is a story he's telling himself. They both enjoyed their conversation, and she said "yes" when he asked to kiss her. And keep kissing her for all that time in his car before she finally got out and into her own to drive home. Then they exchanged texts throughout the weekend. Maybe he'd messed it up when he did what Lizzie called "going down the rabbit hole" with the text thread about misspelled tattoos. There were so many to choose from and he'd tried to only send her a few. But reviewing it now, it might have been twelve, which he had to admit was probably too many, even though she shared some in return. And she must not have meant it when she texted him last night with "See you tomorrow morning!" followed by a smile emoji.

It's not until after his shower and he's about to pocket his phone that he looks at it to count how many tattoo photos he sent, only to discover a new text this morning.

Ay, dios mio. Won't be at the pool after all this am. Forgot about early dr appt. Call you tonight?

His mood immediately shifts. He smiles and texts back.

I'll be done with dinner by 6:30pm, so you can call anytime between then and 9:30pm.

❄

AT THE CONFERENCE ROOM TABLE, he sits with Claire from HR and he breathes in a deep breath and slowly exhales. In spite of all the preparation, he remains nervous about the interview process. Though he would have preferred Caleb to help him conduct the interviews, Claire readily agreed when he asked her. She made one suggestion for a question to add and assured him he would do just fine.

Unfortunately, he let Shane get into his head. Shane who complained that since he is now the senior analyst, he should be able to sit in on the interviews. There was no way Justin was going to let that happen unless forced to do so. He'd checked in with Claire, who said he could have anyone he wanted on the interview team. He could do them on his own, though she didn't recommend it. So, Justin asked her.

"I mean, no offense, man," Shane had said with an obvious intent to offend. "But the guy should know he'll be working with people who are ... not as stiff."

If he hadn't been working with Shane for as long as he had, Justin might not have understood the juvenile word choice. Naturally, he understood immediately, and it made Justin's decision even more resolute to exclude Shane.

"Person, you mean," Justin had clarified.

"Huh?"

"You said the 'guy' should know, but I don't know any of their genders. And if I'm going by names only, then at least two of the three might be women. But they also might be non-binary. Or it's possible they have what I've assumed is a woman's name, but—"

"Jesus," Shane said. "Never mind, stiff. You'll just weird them out."

And the conversation only tumbled downhill from there with Justin having to say he was in charge and not Shane, so it wasn't Shane's decision. Justin had nearly expected Shane to retort with a "you're not the boss of me" comment to reflect the deterioration of a professional exchange into a sibling-style squabble.

And now here Justin is, doing a breathing exercise while worrying about how not to sound "stiff" or weird and pulling all his energy in to prepare for when he might miss a joke or process one of his misinterpretations out loud. Worrying about how to come across as "normal." "Normal" is not a word that bothers him anymore. His sister and Mama LiLi like to push for the fancy words of "neurodivergent," and while the term is accurate, it doesn't feel true. Shane and Austin already know he's neurodivergent and still they make it clear that he is also not normal.

Most days, he doesn't care about others' perceptions of his "abnormal" self. He mostly doesn't care today. Mostly. He cares enough today to have Claire help him.

"Ready?" Claire asks.

He nods as he stands and leaves the conference room to fetch the first candidate. Claire offered to do this part, but Justin doesn't want anyone feeling intimidated. Like he is too important to greet them on his own. In the small reception area of their wing of the technology operations sector he looks to their administrative assistant, Cassie—not a fan of his—who tips her head toward the man sitting in one of two chairs.

Justin, who probably knows better than most about reserving judgment during first impressions, forces himself to reread the man's resume in his mind to keep himself from the potentially erroneous conclusions that want to insert themselves.

The man wears faded jeans, a t-shirt, and a hoodie. He slouches with his legs outstretched and an elbow resting on the arm of the chair. He scrolls through his phone. On the plus side, Justin concedes, the jeans don't have holes or tears and the t-shirt has an XKCD cartoon, which Justin enjoys. It's a dramatic difference from Justin's own suit. Even with Shane and Austin's immaturity, they did still wear slacks and nice polos or other dress shirts vs jeans and t-shirts.

"Gavin?"

The man chuckles and at first, Justin guesses he is already laughing at him. Then he realizes Gavin hasn't heard him. He's laughing at something on his phone. Justin speaks louder.

"Gavin Smythe?"

Still nothing. Justin stands, uncertain what to do. He isn't going to yell. He stretches out a hand to wave in Gavin's direction. It isn't until a second later, after a crumpled ball of paper hits the hand holding the phone, that Gavin looks up.

"Idiot," Cassie mutters. Justin isn't sure if she's talking about him or Gavin, but there isn't time to dwell on it as Gavin puts away his phone and stands.

"Hey! Are we ready to roll?"

The rest of the interview continues in a similar fashion. Gavin's responses don't sound rude, exactly, yet he doesn't come across as interested, either.

After he steps out of the conference room Claire says, "So. No?"

Justin strokes his jaw. "His solution to the logic problem was quite innovative. A little messy, but impressive."

"Okay, but what about when he said," Claire mimes air quotes. "This is programming. Who's really talking to anyone long enough to have problems with them?"

This was Gavin's answer to Claire's extra question of "Tell us about a conflict or challenge you've had with a coworker and how you overcame it." She says you can learn a lot about a person in how they deal with conflict. Justin isn't sure how much her opinion would change of him if she were aware of his meltdowns. He's never had one here since he started working for All Choice and he hopes it will never happen. His one with Lizzie a few days ago was mild. His bigger worry is how quickly he got to that point. He's been detecting his threshold for unpredictability lowering in recent days. Bringing a new person into his team certainly won't help.

"I know you want to be fair and thorough," Claire continues. She puts her fingertips on her stomach. "But gut instinct. Is he right for this position?"

"No."

The next candidate is far better, but she won't be able to start for another month, which annoys Justin. Why did she apply if she couldn't start immediately, like the posting stipulated?

"To be fair," Claire tells him, "many corporate hirings take a glacial amount of time to push through. We're a little bit smaller and you're a bit more organized, so 'immediate hire' actually means what it sounds like."

The last candidate, Yasmin Arora, demonstrates the wisdom of Claire's added question.

"I once took a workshop about conflict management and it was pretty useful in a couple of situations," Yasmin says. "The idea is to remember that our reactions often reflect some other, deeper-rooted issue and to find that cause instead of assuming the worst." She describes a specific situation with a colleague. At the end she adds, "Although, to be completely honest, sometimes people are nothing more than jerks for no good reason and I basically tell them so."

Claire says on a personal level, she likes Yasmin's straightforward attitude.

"On a professional level, though," Claire says. "I'm worried I'll be fielding complaints based upon this 'jerks for no good reason' comment."

Justin understands her concerns, yet he points to his stomach and tells Claire, "She's the one."

Claire smiles. "Okay. Let me know when you've completed the reference calls—" Claire waves him off at his groan about this next step, "—and I'll get all the paperwork going on the assumption she'll accept your offer, because I think she will, based upon how your problem-solving code-programmy-thingy conversation went."

"Code programmy thingy?"

"Yeah, you know ... 'uncrumple the variable Python flux capacitor!' and 'Redo the gift package core!'"

Justin shakes his head. "You missed the most exciting part where we talked about positronic variants."

She laughs. "You're making that up, right?"

"I am."

"See? She's definitely going to accept your offer."

Justin heads back to his office, his mood light and confident, and he doesn't even offer Shane the satisfaction of a reaction to his ridiculous shout of "I call being team leader when the new guy starts!" as Justin walks by the cubicles, increasingly grateful for an office with four walls and a door.

17

LIZZIE

"Your. Stopwatch. Is. Wrong," I gasped out to Reign as I now lagged behind them instead of jogging alongside.

They turned around and did the backwards running thing as they said, with no gasping whatsoever, "C'mon Bette, only thirty more seconds to go for this cycle." Reign only called me "Bette" when trying to elevate me to a greatness far beyond my reach.

"Longest. Interval. Ever." God, I wanted to die. We were starting week four of Reign's personalized couch to 5k training, but what started out as a casual ease-in had rapidly transformed into an impossible running-to-walking ratio. This week added an additional two minutes to the running intervals, bringing it up to ten minutes on, two minutes off. The extra two minutes may as well have been twenty.

Reign sang a made-up song in a big voice that was supposed to be like Bette Midler. Only, they didn't know any of her songs, so it sounded more like Adele, if Adele were an adolescent boy. Reign's voice cracked all over.

"Oh. My. God." *Gasp. Gasp.* "Stop. That. Awful. Noise." Seriously, I could not do this for thirty more seconds.

Fortunately, they'd distracted me enough as thirty seconds

had passed and they announced it was walking time. I slowed to a shuffle.

"Nope, nope. A faster walk than that, Bette. You gotta keep that heart rate up for the next cycle."

The first couple of weeks hadn't been too bad. I'd been feeling good about keeping up the running intervals. It wasn't easy, but my body fell back into the familiar rhythm. Well, most of my body. My lungs weren't getting the memo. Reign helped, though, by distracting me with all of their stories. I was pretty sure most of them were made up, but then again, Reign was one of the best people-watchers. They'd create stories that absolutely could be true.

We'd quickly moved from the apartment complex exercise room to the community center indoor track because I couldn't figure out how to stay on the damn treadmill. My inability to maintain my equilibrium on the moving belt was embarrassing, but Reign didn't give it a second thought.

"Treadmills aren't for everyone," they'd said. "Besides, Everyday Beauty has a partnership with the community center. No membership fee when you're there working with me."

Working *for* Reign seemed a more accurate description. Reign kept trying to convince me to run outside, but dying by exercise *and* in the cold? No, thank you.

"Okay! Last running interval of the workout, Bette. Did you ever know that you're my hero?"

"Did you ever know that this workout might seriously make me barf all over you before we're done?" Starting up again wasn't as bad as I expected. That relief lasted nine seconds. By second ten, puking didn't sound too far-fetched.

Reign pivoted to my right to face forward once more and put their hand underneath one of mine in a gentle grasp. "Down at the edge of the water. See them?"

One half of the track had a glass wall with a view of the indoor water park. I saw two kids, a boy and a girl, both dark-haired and skin the light-brown color of playground sand, sitting in a crouch, heads nearly touching, hands on their own knees, staring at something along the zero depth edge of the pool. If I could have moved anything on my face, I would have smiled. And since my lips couldn't shape any words anymore—the running was impossibly hard—I grunted in acknowledgment.

"Brother and sister," Reign said in a tone I recognized to be a launch into one of their made-up stories. "They were watching a toy float by, but when they crouched down low like that, Brother leaned in to Sister and whispered, 'Mama says she doesn't have a favorite kid, that all three of us are the most special. But I do.'

"'You do what?' Sister whispered back." Reign's own voice had dropped to a whisper, too. All the ambient noise disappeared except my panting and the pounding beat of my heart in my ears.

"'Have a favorite. It's you. Other Sister is smart, but I like you best.'"

I gulped in and held a lungful of air as a random memory slammed into me.

I like you best, Beth. Beth is best. Beth is better than Issy.

Justin's words. How old were they when he spoke them?

Beth best bestie better, not bitter like iffy, irritable, Issy.

Swings. At the playground. The swings had been too high, and Justin had helped me onto one of them and pushed me.

"Gimme an underdog, Justin! I wanna go high!"

"No, no thank you with underdogs. I don't like them. You'll go higher if I just push you like this."

I'd agreed. Justin was smart. He usually knew what was best.

Beth is better than Issy.

I didn't like this memory at all. My chest constricted.

"Lizzie?" A tug on my fingertips snapped me back into the moment. Reign was a step ahead of me, studying my face. "You okay?"

I wasn't running. Or walking. I'd come to a complete stop with no consciousness of making that decision. "Yeah," I pushed out. "Weird memory came to me just now from your story about the kids."

"Are you going to share?"

"It brought back a time when Justin said something similar to me when we were kids."

"Justin asked you what worms tasted like?"

"What?"

Reign laughed, and I realized they had told more of the story, but I didn't hear it once I got hit by the memory. "C'mon, let's keep walking before you get all stiff."

"Sorry," I said. "I missed that part. Justin would probably never have asked me that, though. Too pukey-sounding." Kind of like how I felt right now. I breathed in deeply and exhaled in three staccato-like successions, as Reign had taught me. They rubbed their hands together for my inhale and mimicked my exhale pattern with rhythmic claps.

"What did Justin tell you when you were kids?"

I shook my head. The memory was already slipping away. It felt mixed-up in my brain, anyway. "Probably some drawn-out story he'd made up on the ride back from school. And then sometimes we'd act it out when he got home." Later, after we moved in to Mac and LiLi's house and I started school, we'd sit together on the bus and he'd tell me the stories out loud. Other times he wouldn't talk at all, which I hadn't liked. I felt left out.

"This couch-to-5k regimen sucks balls, by the way," I told them as we left the track and into a small, open area where Reign led me through some cool-down stretches.

"Some of us like balls."

"You can have them all."

Reign laughed. "You would have made it if you hadn't suddenly disappeared into the astral plane back there. You sure you're okay?"

"I disappeared into another universe because I had to escape this ball-sucking workout. I'm okay, though. It was just a harder interval jump today."

"Tomorrow will be easier," they said.

I grunted noncommittally, and then we focused on the stretches. When I'd started working at Meadowfields, I'd gradually traded in my running time in favor of yoga with the As, which might not have been a bad thing, except they couldn't stop talking. Or rather, whispering. Everyone at the studio hated us, and if I'd been deeper into the friendship with the As, I probably wouldn't have noticed and joined in on all the whispering. Instead, I stopped going and never picked running back up again. Or yoga.

Reign and I wrapped up our cool-down, put on our ten layers of winter gear—well, ten layers for me and one extra for Reign even though it was colder than the north pole outside—and headed down from the track and out to our cars.

"Two-thirty tomorrow?" they asked.

"Yep. Maybe I'll find energy in trying to outrun the gasoline fumes."

"Whatever works, Lizzie McGuire."

I gave them the finger in response to yet another nickname for me, but they didn't see it because they were already running away. Literally running because they were, as Justin had pointed out, a bit on the obsessive side. They had ridden with me in my car this morning to the community center, but now ran to work at the salon and spa, five miles away in sub-zero weather.

I did not have the same obsession about exercise and happily got in my car and out of the wind. I headed home, wondering how I would fill the rest of my empty morning and afternoon before my shift at Astros.

After a hot shower and my daily staring match with Crash, I hovered over recent text threads from a couple of friends, then hesitated. I'd been trying to reconnect with a few people and while it felt good to catch up with them, our schedules rarely meshed. Instead, I texted Nuria.

Me: *Coffee?*

Nuria: *Yes! 20 min at pc?*

New friends also felt good.

18

LIZZIE

"Can I ask you a question?" Nuria asked as we sipped from our giant mugs of coffee.

"Is it about how fast I ate that scone? Because yes, I was hungry, and it was delicious."

She laughed. "I mean, yeah, every time we have a meal together, I do wonder if your parents ever threatened to take your plate away if you didn't finish eating everything on it in three minutes or less. But no, it's not that."

She stared at the table and fiddled with her napkin. I pushed down any more jokes.

"What's up?" I asked.

"Is it normal for a kid to never want to play with other kids?"

I set down my mug and sat back in my chair. "How do you mean? Like they're afraid of other kids? Or anxious around them? Or they just have a really intense imagination and live inside of it?"

"No. My nephew, Sebastian, hardly interacts with his cousins. They'll be doing things with dinosaurs while he organizes all the blocks by shape and color. Or he'll go outside with everyone, and they'll all build a big snow fort together while he shuffles through the snow, making shapes or letters. It's like he's ... play-adjacent with them, if that makes sense."

I nodded. "It does. What else have you noticed about him that seems different than you might expect?"

She set the napkin aside and leaned into the table, pushing her coffee mug forward along with her. "He doesn't like loud or sudden noises. Like in rare moments when it's quieter, someone's phone will ring and he'll cover his ears as though fireworks went off. Of course, he definitely does not like fireworks, either. Sometimes he rocks and hums. Not a song. Just a low noise."

There were a lot of things that might be going on with Sebastian based upon what she shared so far. I guessed she already suspected what it all might mean. What I wasn't sure was how she felt about it.

"Are you worried about him?" I asked.

"Not exactly? I used to think it was because he's an only child, except he's around his cousins all the time and none of them seem to notice ... or care, I guess. But when I mentioned something to my sister, she got upset with me, saying he's just shy or that he's gifted and 'everyone' knows gifted kids don't always know how to interact with their peers who might not see things the same way."

"You're guessing autism, though?"

She extended a hand, palm up. I took it. "Yes," she breathed out in a kind of heavy relief. "I've been googling, you know? I want Paula—and Simon—to understand that autism isn't a bad thing."

I squeezed her hand, grateful my instinct about her was correct. These days I didn't always trust my inner voice. "Having him assessed can ensure he has the support for when he starts school, too."

"Exactly! Paula said he'd been having a hard time at daycare and she pulled him from it. She and Simon are still adjusting their schedules to make it work."

"I know you've been googling," I said and smiled to reassure I wasn't criticizing. "But I can direct you to some resources that you can show your sister. Ones with her worries and uncertainties in mind."

"That would be so great. I don't suppose you'd be interested in working with him a little? Paid, of course."

I narrowed my eyes at her. "You just said Paula wasn't on board with this unofficial diagnosis. Why would she suddenly agree to someone 'working' with him?"

"We-ell." She drew out the word, verifying my suspicions. "She's not exactly looking for a teacher or, what do you call it, a special assistant?"

"PCA—personal care assistant."

"Right. I don't think she knows a lot about that except in a medical, home health care sense, but she *is* searching for a nanny and I thought, maybe, because you also obviously like kids since you've worked in elementary schools, that you might rather do the nanny thing instead of Astros or the gas station. And you could teach him or train him kind of unobtrusively."

"Train him?" I sputtered out a light laugh. "What exactly do you think my job was? Teaching kids to fetch?"

Nuria dropped her head into her palms. "Ugh. No. I'm sorry. Terrible choice of words."

"It's okay, I get it." I did. She wasn't meaning to dehumanize her nephew. She really wanted to help him and his parents. During my PCA days, I saw the exhaustion some parents, and in one case grandparents, experienced. Autism Spectrum Disorder was called a spectrum for a reason. I'd worked with children who needed a lot of support—physically, mentally, and cognitively—and many others who simply wanted or needed guidance with how to navigate through the world around them.

Though Nuria didn't say her own observations of Sebastian

indicated having an especially challenging time with general development, the reference to the difficulties in daycare signaled something different. I had many guesses, but that's all they were. I'd need to give Sebastian an initial evaluation and—*wait*. What was I doing? I wasn't even *qualified* to conduct an evaluation and had never done one since that was reserved for the licensed teachers, and I'd only sat in on them twice. Honestly, given my recent track record, I wasn't qualified to do any of it.

"That's not who I am," I eventually answered.

"What's not who you are?"

"This..." I circled my hand around an empty space where I imagined knowledge to be. "Autism expert."

"You're not Temple Grandin?"

I smiled, even with my mild annoyance with this entire conversation. "Fucking Google."

Nuria's laugh dissipated the rest of my irritation and I shook my head at her.

"What about kids?" she asked next. "Do you still like kids?"

"Maybe."

"Cállate, pendeja. Of course you do."

"Fine, yes. Of course I still like kids."

She nodded. "And what about Astros? And the Gas-n-Guzzle? How do you feel about those places?"

"You are definitely trying to trick me into being some kind of undercover autism whisperer—which is absolutely not a thing, by the way—for Sebastian, because obviously, you know I am dying a slow death from both of those jobs."

Nuria put her hands up and waved them, palms out. "No. Forget the teaching part of it. Instead, be only the nanny. Part-time. For my amazing, sweet, smart nephew. It'll be good pay because both Paula and Simon are surgeons and make piles of money."

"I don't know if it's a good idea."

"Why not?"

Why not, indeed? I asked myself. Because clearly I wasn't competent around young children in terms of safety. Because parents were more unpredictable than their kids and could mess up your life. Because sometimes I said stupid, hurtful things to those parents, and that wouldn't be fair to Sebastian.

I twisted my now empty, giant mug in back-and-forth half circles as counterarguments seeped in around all the doubts. If I quit Astros, I'd have my nights back, which meant having more time with Justin and Nuria. I'd hang out with a little person who enjoyed doing his own thing and offer a kind of calm that didn't exist in my other jobs. I could prove to myself that one-on-one, maybe I really was capable of keeping him safe. And incognito or not, I had the knowledge and experience to help both Sebastian and his parents. Maybe I owed that to them. Maybe I owed it to myself.

"What are the hours?"

Nuria beamed. "Afternoons from three o'clock until six. It's kind of the worst time of day for him—"

"This is your sales pitch?"

"—*but*," she continued, fake glaring at me. "That's why they'll pay you well. Paula and Simon arranged their hours to tag team being home with Seb. Unfortunately, their schedules often overlap during the late afternoon and it would help them out a ton. I told you Seb is sweet and smart, right?"

"You did." I tried not to smile, but my lips quirked against the effort.

"He can read already and he's only just turned five. He loves rainbows and stories about pigs. You know how some kids can name all the dinosaurs? Seb can do that for all the different breeds of pigs. There's one called Metallica."

"Not really?"

"No, but it sounds like that and Seb likes to give me the side eye when I ask him about it while making pig noises as I rock out with my air guitar."

And now I couldn't hold back the smile or the laughter because she followed up with a demonstration of pig Metallica in what might have been a rendition of "Enter Sandman," though it was hard to tell. Pig snorts and grunts don't have much tonal range. I offered a squeal, and she threw her head back and cackled, which made me laugh harder.

"You're so ridiculous," I said, pushing out the words between wheezes as I got myself under control. "Why don't *you* be his nanny?"

The face she gave me and subsequent response of "Because I don't wanna" set me off into another fit of giggles. Her actions were so unexpected. I liked this silly side of Nuria. I didn't remember the last time I laughed with such abandon. Though my Triple A friends—well, *colleagues*—acted sillier sometimes with their students, they never seemed to let go of themselves away from the kids. So, neither did I.

With Carrie, we'd text each other funny gifs. Or we'd giggle over cute things students would say and do, or save treats for each other that others brought to share in the staff lounge since our lunch breaks were often later in the day. Ashley would ask me if I tried any of the brownies someone brought in and then express regret that they were all gone by the time I got there.

Obviously, it wasn't about saving food. It was more like none of that group of so-called friends *knew* me. Their texts to me were photos of people with outrageously large lobe-stretching gauges or various styles of belly button rings as they were insistent I should get a navel piercing to "complete my look." Sure, I had the extra piercings on my eyebrows, the nose ring, and the earlobe gauges, and when I first started at Meadowfields, I had blue highlights in my dark blond hair. At my last school, I'd fit right in, but Meadowfields seemed more homogenous.

One Monday, after a vacation break, one of the As, Amber, showed up to work with a tiny stud piercing in her nose. "What do you think?" she'd asked me.

"It looks good!" I'd replied. "What made you decide to get it?"

"You! I wanted to look more mysterious and unpredictable. Like people might have to guess whether or not I'm straight."

It was another reminder of how I was not so much the A's friend as I was their *lesbian* friend. And as I thought about it and compared everything to my friendship with Nuria—and Monica a few years earlier—it occurred to me that Amber and Ashley and Anabel wanted to impress me. If you were trying to impress someone, you ended up losing sight of making actual connections. As soon as I blurted "Call me Betsy" during new staff introductions when I started at Meadowfields, and then rattled off all my credentials, I'd already set the stage for myself at attempting to impress rather than connect.

Nuria was showing me how she did her own thing without worrying about what others thought, including her family. I wished I had the same option. Removing the pressure of coming in as teacher for Sebastian, the idea held some appeal. Definitely appealing enough to drop Astros.

"I guess it couldn't hurt to meet with Sebastian and his parents," I said.

"Yes!" Nuria pumped her fist and went back to her air guitar and sang an unknown tune to me with interspersed pig snorts. "Lizzie will be," *snort* "the best nanny," *snort* "just wait and see."

"I am so glad your passion is visual art and not music."

She grinned and pulled out her phone to text her sister while I held both hope and uncertainty in a tight grip, unsure of why I held them together. I crossed my fingers that they'd serve each other.

19

JUSTIN

In Justin's opinion, taking photos of snowflakes definitely falls into the cliché category, but winter in Minnesota is too long to ignore all the infinite snowflake patterns. Prints left behind by vehicles, people, and animals provide the most interesting patterns while also appealing to his curiosity about the amount of weight required to leave an imprint. Especially when freshly fallen snow from the day before is followed by a deep freeze. The surface just off the walking path near his apartment building has a fine sheen that appears as though one could glide along it with ice skates. And while it's sturdy enough for small birds and careful squirrels to land on and skitter across, Justin can still poke his thumb through the layer with little effort.

He does so with some regret as it only emphasizes how cold it is and the crunching sound it makes causes his throat to tighten. Breathing is already difficult enough with the frigid air. He's not a fan of winter, which is an unfortunate attitude living in a state where half the year is snow, cold, and ice.

"JT!" Reign's voice carries over to him, echoing as it bounces along with the wind against the trees and distant building walls. "Check this one out!"

Justin blinks and pulls his scarf—a Reign product made especially for Justin and his texture predilection—up over his mouth in an attempt to warm the air he breathes in. He remains impressed with the quality and thoughtfulness behind this gift from Reign. The deep blue yarn is from bamboo, and Reign used a basic, tiny knit pattern to minimize irritation. Justin likes it so much, he sends it to the dry cleaners to ensure it doesn't get wrecked in his washer.

He looks up to search for where, exactly, Reign's voice comes from. He squints into the bright reflections of sun from the icy snow, this brightness being the one redeeming feature of minus twenty-degree temperatures. The coldest days always seem to be the brightest. He heads over to where Reign stands, waving.

Reign is responsible for getting Justin outdoors more often this winter season. Reign *loves* winter. They talk about how much change happens even though people usually look at it as a time of hibernation, not realizing what is happening both inside and outside of the cave. "Think about it, JT," Reign would say. "Spring comes along and everyone feels fresh and new and ready to take on the world. But it's only because they've had the winter to rest and figure themselves out. That's when the change process really happens."

Winter has wrecked Justin's life more than once and Reign apparently wants to prove the season's merits in spite of past circumstances. Justin's therapist approves, stating that Justin can create a "new narrative" for himself surrounding winter. So he tries, for Reign's sake, for now. Maybe he'll try for himself somewhere down the road.

Justin appreciates the time to dip into his creative passion and to forget about work for a while. Yasmin doesn't start until the following week, and one of the two projects Justin initiated continues to run into obstacles. Between that and difficult communications with Shane, Justin is exhausted.

Traipsing around outside his apartment building in sub-zero

weather during a season he does not love proves surprisingly the better alternative to his current work situation. Reign knows this. Hence, they convince Justin to find something beautiful or fascinating without going beyond their backyard.

He joins Reign at a "No Parking" sign. "Take a look at this ice pattern," Reign says, pointing to the back of the metal sign pole.

Justin sees it right away and wonders how the zig zag of water had managed to weave around more than one of the holes instead of following the full rim of the machine-cut circle. He wants to trace the "s"-shaped trail of the ice, and without thinking, he takes off one of his gloves.

"JT! Stop!"

Too late. The initial warmth of his finger melts the tiniest bit of the ice and Justin's imperfect trace leads his finger quickly to the end of the pattern and on to the metal of the pole where his finger stops moving. *Fuck.* It's Winter 101: don't touch metal surfaces outside with your bare skin, and especially not with your tongue. Fortunately, he'd never done that. Yet here he is, putting all his energy into defying the panic response of yanking his hand back, although the temptation is high as his other fingers are already going numb from the cold. Yanking could lead to tearing away half the skin on his finger. *Breathe.*

"Oh shit, I can't believe you did that!" Reign cups their mittened hands around the pole and Justin's stuck finger. They lean in and exhale a deep breath of air over his finger and then spit several times until, with a jolt, his finger releases and Reign catches Justin's hand to hold him upright from the sudden jerk backward.

"Let's get that glove back on quick and then head inside," Reign says, taking off their own mittens to help Justin on with the glove. Justin feels like a three-year-old, but doesn't care because *fuck*, his hand is painfully cold, especially now with the moisture on it.

They hurry back to the closest entrance to their building, through the garage. As soon as the door latches closed behind them, Reign sheds their mittens, turns to take Justin's hand, removes the glove and then rubs their own on either side of his. Their hands move rapidly and Justin's hand tingles as blood circulates more freely again from the frictional warmth.

"It's good now," Justin says. He alternates between flexing and wiggling his fingers after Reign releases his hand. "Thank you."

They both stand in their same spots breathing heavily. Justin releases a low hum while systematically squeezing each icy finger with his slightly warmer one. Pinky, ring, middle, pointer, thumb. Pinky, ring, middle, pointer, thumb. Three rounds through and he's regulated himself, and when he looks up, he discovers Reign is also working through an anxiety episode.

"Count fives to twenty," he says to Reign while holding their hand.

"Five. Ten." Reign stops, their breathing still fast and irregular.

Justin brings Reign's hand to his jaw, helping them trace the rough stubble. "Keep going, Reign."

Reign starts again. "Five. Ten. Fifteen." They pause, then finish, "Twenty." Their breathing slows. Justin has only been with Reign once before when they've had an anxiety spike, but this is the first time Reign and Justin have been caught in one together.

"I need to wash my hands," Justin says. "I've got some stranger's spit on them and it's giving me the heebie jeebies." "Heebie jeebies" is Reign's expression, and not only does Justin like the sound of it, he's pretty sure using it with his comment right now will have the desired effect.

He's right. "Some *stranger*? That whole sentence just gave me the willies."

Justin scoffs as they walk through the garage and into the

building proper. "No *friend* of mine would ever think putting their own bodily fluids on my skin was a good idea. Talk about major screaming meemies."

"Hold up. I seem to remember that *friend* warning you to stop. It's not their fault—" Reign pauses to search on their phone, "—you suddenly have the jim jams about a teeny bit of saliva that saved you from losing all the skin from your finger."

Now Justin has his phone at the ready. The aforementioned pointer finger is still tender and so he uses his middle finger—first holding it up for Reign to see while he dramatically brings it down to his phone screen to scroll through the synonyms. "I would have figured it out. I was the picture of calm. *You're* the one who had all the hurry scurry."

Reign breaks into laughter first. The elevator door opens, and they race into it. "I'm hurry-scurrying in right now!"

"That's because you have ants in your pants!"

Reign laughs harder and jumps in place as though trying to free all the ants from their pants.

"You're giving me jittery whim whams watching you now!" Justin barely gets the words out before he, too, is laughing because though he has teased Reign for their frenetic-sounding laugh in the past, it has grown on him and he can't help but join in every time Reign starts up.

Reign is doubled over now and when Justin snorts, Reign grabs Justin's arm for balance as their maniacal laughter reaches a pitch of gasping silence.

"Can't. Breathe," Reign wheezes out. "Say. Something. Obnoxious."

"Your mom is the absolute worst." It's not a sucker punch. Rather, it's one of the few things Justin says on purpose when Reign needs him to pull them out of a moment because their mom? She really is the worst. When Reign came out years earlier as gay and then later non-binary, she disowned them. Though her actions mostly don't bother Reign anymore, they still harbored a lot of guilt for their parents' divorce not long afterwards. Justin can't quite work out the logic for this, yet also knows he doesn't need to.

The statement has an immediate effect. Reign drops their hold on Justin and remains hunched over, propping themself up with their hands on their knees. "Damn," they say, their breathing still labored. "It's amazing how well that works." They push back up to standing and continue, "It's also amazing that I almost wish you'd have stuck your tongue on that pole instead of just your finger."

"Asshole," Justin says. "You're lucky your lips didn't stick when you got close enough to spit. Speaking of your disgusting spit, why aren't we moving?"

The elevator doors open to the garage and a blonde-headed man wearing red plaid earmuffs, a red scarf, and a black peacoat with a rich leather messenger bag hanging over his shoulder waits. Reign immediately slings an arm around Justin's shoulders and pulls him in close.

"Hey, Brad," Reign says in a sing-song voice. Justin doesn't know what Reign is doing, but goes along and doesn't move away.

Brad stays on his side of the elevator. "Aren't you getting out?"

"Oops!" Reign continues in that same drippy tone. "We got, um, a little distracted I guess and somehow forgot to press the button. C'mon in and join us!"

Brad remains where he is. The doors start to close. No one makes a move to catch them.

"What a shame," Reign calls out with a wave. "I guess you can take the stairs."

The doors come together and Justin reaches out to press the button for four. He definitely does not want to see Brad again. He doesn't care if he ever sees any neighbors. They all think he's rude, which he probably is most of the time, though not always intentionally. It's all So. Much. Small talk. Reign, however, seems to love all of their neighbors, so this exchange feels off.

"I don't understand what just happened," he says.

"Did you see how Brad was looking at us?"

"No." In fact, Justin had detected everything but Brad's expression. And by the time he thought to look, the elevator doors were closing. "I noticed his messenger bag though, because it almost looks like new and mine is falling apart. I need to order a new one ASAP because a supervisor should appear more professional." At his unfortunate recall of work, Justin closes his eyes while reaching up to stroke his jaw.

The elevator chimes, the doors open, and Reign nudges him. "Hey, forget about work right now, right? I'm talking about asshole Brad."

"Right," Justin says, opening his eyes and walking out of the elevator with Reign and towards their apartments. "How was Brad looking at us?"

"Like we disgusted him. He doesn't approve of who I am or your sister and you, by proxy." Reign gives him a sidelong glance. "Well, he might just think you're rude as fuck."

Justin nods, now having a name for the face. "Oh, I'm definitely rude as fuck to him. He tosses his junk mail into the trash bin by the mailboxes, but misses half the time and never picks it up from the floor. He also bumps into me when getting his mail from the box. Lizzie says he's a closet gay who can't admit he's attracted to me."

"Whoa, what?" They stand in front of Justin's door. "Damn. She's probably right. How did I miss that? I guess I should be nicer to him."

"Why?"

"To be more sympathetic and understanding."

This, of course, is one reason Justin likes Reign so well. They have a never-ending amount of compassion. Lizzie has mentioned Brad's homophobic attitude before and then said,

"Fuck that guy. It's not our problem if he can't come to terms with who he is." Obviously, Justin agrees. He only has so much patience with people who can't find ways to be decent to others.

"You don't have to be the one who fixes him," Justin says. He unlocks his door and opens it enough for Crash to see him and cease her meowing from the past minute. She steps out and purrs, weaving her way in and out of both Justin's and Reign's legs.

"But I can stop taunting him and start just saying 'hi' again," Reign says while bending down to give Crash her much sought-after attention.

Justin opens his door wider to step inside and remove his boots and other winter gear. "Okay. I'm still going to avoid Brad though, like I do everyone else here."

Reign laughs. "Fair, JT. Do your own thing."

"Lizzie's making some kind of pasta dish tonight for dinner. Do you want to join us?"

Reign shakes their head. "Thanks, but I got some other stuff to take care of. Next time."

"Thanks for coming with me today to distract me from work."

"Always, my man. Always."

20

LIZZIE

The first thing I'd learned about Sebastian was that he did not like nicknames.

"Hello," I said, as I sat in a comfortable squat—*thank you, Reign*—to match Sebastian's height. "I'm Lizzie. You can call me Lizzie or you can call me Ms. Lizzie, if you want to be more formal."

He nodded and said nothing in return. I followed up with a question. "Are you Sebastian?"

Another nod.

"Do you want me to call you Sebastian? Or do you prefer Seb?"

"Sebastian, please. No thank you, Seb."

A light laugh came from Paula, behind me. "We call you Seb all the time, little man."

Sebastian shook his head. "No thank you, Seb. No thank you, little man. No thank you, buddy."

"What about 'kiddo'?" I asked, knowing this was a frequent one I used and already guessed the answer.

"No thank you, kiddo."

How often did we automatically shorten someone's name

when they didn't offer this option to us? I thought of all my trans friends who had family members who still called them by their dead names and how much that hurt them each time it happened. "Seb" and "Sky" might not be dead names, but if it hurt them every time someone used those shortened versions with them, then, for now at least, they may as well have been.

"Okay, I'm happy to meet you, Sebastian. What are you working on?"

He described his drawing about none other than the pigs Nuria mentioned.

One week after Nuria's and subsequently Paula's offer, I'd quit Astros and started nannying sweet Sebastian. I felt bad for my coworkers, but not enough to work an occasional shift to help out. The first day with Sebastian went well. He really was a great kid. Not that the transition wasn't challenging, because here we were at day two, and fifteen minutes into my time with him, he was screaming bloody murder, or at the very least third-degree assault, and he liked to run his arm along surfaces and walls and knock things down.

Based upon the plastic pen holders, cardboard coasters, and artificial plants, I wondered if this behavior was common. Paula, instead of leaving me to deal with Sebastian, kept trying to head him off and talk to him. I didn't blame her. It was stressful to see any child in these circumstances, let alone your own and hoping a person you'd only known for the sum total of six hours would do right by him.

Except, each time she stood directly in front of him and tried to stop him from knocking something down, Sebastian would open his mouth wider, tip his head up, and scream one notch louder. Paula's entire body flinched.

They carried on the failed communication pattern while I looked on, debating how best to insert myself, if at all. On the one hand, she was paying me to help. On the other hand, interrupting a mother-child interaction was tricky, and I didn't want to escalate Sebastian's behavior and get anyone hurt.

When he pivoted away from Paula, I found my opportunity. I put myself between him and a bookshelf, where he was heading next. Risky, but as far as I'd learned from Nuria, he wasn't a hitter. The idea was to interrupt and redirect, although I didn't have a plan for the redirection. Not yet knowing Sebastian well, I wasn't sure if this was a meltdown or a tantrum.

His movements didn't pause. He kept his arms out and his left one brushed right over my torso as he continued in what I now saw was a circular path. I cleared the surfaces near me so that when he returned, his arms would meet little-to-no resistance.

"Sebastian, it's okay," I said, my tone even and calm. "We're going to read a story next, just like we did yesterday."

I repeated these words as a mantra as Sebastian cycled around the room, yelling. Over the years, the length of time kids could devote to screaming, impressed me. I'd be exhausted after one minute. We approached minute twenty, and I wracked my brain on how to interrupt Sebastian's spiral. When I thought of the word, "interrupt," I landed on a possible solution. To Paula, in a lower voice, I asked, "Does he have a favorite toy that makes noise?"

Her expression brightened as she nodded. She slipped into the adjoining room and returned with a large, round, stuffed pink pig. She pressed a button and a succession of snorts and squeals came from it. I raised my eyebrows at the elaborate pattern of noises from a toy pig. She smiled and leaned in to talk into my ear, since Sebastian was still yelling. "Customizable. Seb—Sebastian said pigs do more than snort."

"Perfect. Press the button again and we'll see if it gets through to him as a recognizable sound he can process."

She did, and Sebastian's yell dropped to a loud hum. He continued pacing, though his arms had lowered and moved into flapping gestures closer to his body. Paula pressed the button again. "Está bien, amor," she said when the pig noises stopped. "Te amo, Sebastian."

Sebastian walked to his mother and reached for the pig. "Can I give you a hug?" Paula asked him. He shook his head and I could see how this hurt her. She looked at me and said, "I wish..."

I nodded, understanding. She wished she could snuggle with her child. Offer him gentle touches of affection that might have calmed others, but triggered him, instead. Justin had never been averse to affection, though he didn't love it in high doses and definitely preferred permission, or at the very least, warning. Honestly, I preferred permission, too.

"The kids at his daycare used to hug him or try to wrestle with him and the daycare provider said she couldn't control what the other kids did." Paula shook her head. "As though she's unable to teach them any self-control at all."

"If we can teach kids not to hit each other, then we can certainly teach them about hugs," I said.

"Exactly." She looked at Sebastian, who sat, rocking and holding his pig and pressing its button over and over again. "At one point he yelled when another kid pulled at him to play with something and Amanda said Sebastian couldn't come to her daycare anymore if he was going to scare the children."

"Good riddance," I said. "Not all daycares will be like that. I've heard from other families about providers who are very sensitive to the needs of kiddos like Sebastian."

"Well, he'll be starting school in the fall, so I think we'll try to make it work until then."

I sat next to Sebastian and felt a rush of warmth for him. He was so sweet in his self-soothing ritual. "Hey Sebastian." He didn't look up, but he also didn't press the pig's button again. "It's time for stories. We'll read two stories that you pick out. Then we'll have a snack. What's for snack today?"

"Goldfish and pepperoni."

"That's right. Goldfish and pepperoni. Then we'll get our snow gear on and play outside in the backyard. After that, we'll watch Peppa Pig. And then it will be time for dinner."

"Peppa Pig isn't a real pig, but I like watching her anyway."

"Me too. Ready for stories?"

He nodded, and we made it through the remaining two and a half hours without further incident. Of course, some kiddos I'd worked with needed far higher support needs than Sebastian. Some were nonverbal. Some had more violent meltdowns involving throwing items and kicking or biting. Many or most also had other issues they experienced, such as anxiety, like Justin, or learning challenges like dyslexia or similar reading comprehension disorders.

Still, I breathed easier knowing I didn't have to deal with several more hours of demanding families ordering pizzas they needed *right now*, late-arriving sports teams who left behind a mess worthy of their spectators in the stands, and a do-nothing boss who yelled at me for not working fast enough.

I would take five Sebastians screaming in my face over Chuck, the blowhard boss, any day. Sebastians and Skylars and Justins fell into their meltdowns due to a shutdown in processing. Chuck voluntarily chose asshole behavior.

When I thought I'd become a teacher, I hadn't planned on narrowing my focus on the ASD area. Special education covered so many exceptionalities, and while my brother had been the inspiration behind a special education license, I wanted more than my direct experience.

All my life, my moms told me what a wonderful teacher I would make. As a kindergarten teacher, LiLi naturally enjoyed the idea of leading me down the education path. Yet Mac also encouraged the career choice. It wasn't until I'd started college that I'd heard how my teachers, at open houses and conferences, frequently told my moms about how helpful I was with other students, especially with those who needed extra support.

I didn't remember doing much, and it wasn't me being modest or oblivious to my actions. It was more that I didn't think some teachers were aware of how much some of my classmates struggled. Usually, all I did was repeat directions or agree to be their field trip buddy. My experience with Justin and his observations of behaviors of other kids would come up in our conversations, and as I got older, it pushed me to advocate for my classmates.

I'm sure I could be a good teacher, yet I didn't know if I *wanted* to teach. Something I also learned from Justin was that being good at something didn't necessarily mean equally enjoying that same thing. I loved kids. But did I want to manage a classroom of them? Special education, while carrying a whole host of unique challenges, offered smaller groups of kids, which was a pretty lame reason to choose it.

When Hugh died and Justin's subsequent breakdown necessitated longer term support for him, I immediately jumped into that role. I had options for my school situation such as applying for class extensions or taking incompletes. Yet as Justin and I processed our initial grief together, I reassessed my career goals. They didn't include teaching. The problem remained that I also didn't know what I wanted instead. So I did the things I had experience with, and they had served me well enough. For a minute, I'd thought maybe I'd go back to school and complete what I needed for my license.

Then the accident with Skylar happened, and I knew I would never be a para again or become a teacher.

❋

WHEN I GOT BACK to Justin's apartment—probably I should have called it home at some point—it was past six-thirty and

Justin was still cooking dinner. He usually ate promptly at six. I'd told him he didn't need to change his schedule for me. I'd already upended his daily routine enough. It wasn't fair to push one of his core activities five days a week.

Crash trotted over to me, sat, and meowed as I hung up my coat. This was new. She had never willingly approached me before.

"Hey," I called out to Justin. "I thought we agreed you wouldn't change your schedule for me."

"I'm not. I'm behind today."

Crash meowed again. I wondered if she was trying to tell me something. I bent down towards her, although not too close as I didn't trust her not to claw my eyes out. "What's up with JT?" I reached out to pet her head, which was enough for her to give a screechy meow and race away.

"Yeah, that's what I thought," I muttered.

I slid into my slippers and met Justin at the kitchen counter.

"I made an extra sandwich for you."

My stomach rumbled with anticipation. BLTs. They were such a basic sandwich, yet Justin elevated them by using a spicy mayo and grilling the bread with butter and parmesan.

"Didn't we decide you also wouldn't worry about cooking for me?" He'd left me a plate yesterday. A rice and beans dish with peppers and onions.

"Yesterday's recipe made a lot even when scaled down. I'm happy to eat leftovers for lunch or dinner, but there was enough for you, too. Tonight might have been out of habit. Only last week you were still on your old schedule and it would be my turn to cook."

"That makes sense. Want help?"

"Add some butter to the corn, please. Then we'll be ready."

I drained the extra water from the pot with the corn and stirred in some butter. "You doing okay?" I asked.

I didn't know how often he worked late since I hadn't been

around because of my night shift at Astros Mondays, Wednesdays, and Fridays. Given the unusual mess in the kitchen, I'd guessed tonight was a little different.

The deep sigh he released gave me more evidence of his internal disarray. "Work has been challenging."

"Challenging in what ways?"

He transferred our sandwiches to plates as I closed and secured the twist tie to the bread bag, popped the lettuce into its container, and moved used utensils to the sink. Justin poured himself a glass of milk and I got myself some water and by the time we sat with our meal, he finally spoke again.

"Shane and Austin haven't been handling the extra workload very well. I've had to fix a lot of things they've worked on. Sometimes I'm still doing my old job besides the new one, and I'm simultaneously learning what, precisely, the new one *is*. Caleb gave me access to his files, but I'm not sure what they all mean. Are they notes? Systems I'm supposed to be managing? Or developing? I don't have any instructions on how my position should function and so I'm doing that 'making it up as I go' thing and I'm terrible at that."

His voice had turned mocking with the air quotes around "making it up as I go" and I had to suppress a laugh. I wasn't sure why he hated that expression, but he always scoffed at it. Considering what he said about being terrible at it, I better understood why. On a daily basis, he had to construct his actions and reactions for multiple scenarios throughout the day. "Making it up as he goes" was simply his life and not some occasional experience.

"You are better than most at making it up minute-by-minute, given your need for predictability," I said. "But I get what you're saying. The more guesswork you have, the more exhausting it is."

He nodded and went on. "I hired a new person to replace my open position, and she's a quick learner. Except I introduced her to Shane and Austin, and then Shane made an asinine comment about her qualifications. I told him Yasmin came in with higher qualifications and more experience than he had when he started at All Choice."

"Oh, I know that didn't go over well with that dude bro, did it?"

"No."

"Did you say it in front of Yasmin?"

"Yes."

I fist pumped. *Fuck yeah, that's my brother.* "JT, you're my hero."

He was still tense, but I also saw a small smile.

"And the emails." The smile disappeared as he continued his rant. "The number of emails I get every day is ridiculous. Most of them don't even apply to me. They come from the VP admins and are almost all 'reminders' and reminders of reminders for sales reps and claims processors. It's a colossal waste of time."

"Do you regret taking the promotion?"

A lilting tune emanating from Justin's pocket prevented him from answering.

"It's Amelia," he said as he pulled out his phone. "We always talk at seven, but I can—"

"Take the call, Justin. I'll clean up."

He didn't need convincing. His voice changed immediately into something softer and happier as he stood, grabbed his plate, and walked away, telling Amelia she was right on time. He paused at the entrance to his bedroom, waiting for Crash to follow him in before he shut the door, leaving me with an unexpected feeling of isolation.

I pulled out my phone and texted Nuria. *Should I get a pet?*

Nuria: *Only if it's a koala bear.*

Me: *I've heard koalas are kinda mean.*

Nuria: *Then definitely a koala. I'll help you pick one out this weekend.*

I laughed and imagined Justin's response to me coming home with an ornery koala, and then I grinned at the idea of my cranky koala facing off with crusty Crash. Who would win?

My phone buzzed with another text from Nuria. *Paula said you were really good with Sebastian today.*

Me: *Like you said, he's a great kid.*

Me: *Hey, wanna get a drink somewhere?*

Nuria: *Desperately, but can't. I'm busy getting lectured for the five hundredth time by my mom about going back to school for my nursing degree.*

Me: **throws life preserver**

Nuria: *ahhhh! I can't reach it! gtg talk later*

I cleared the table and cleaned the kitchen and Justin remained locked away in his room and I struggled to shake off my restless unease. I don't think I realized how much Astros, despite being the worst, at least distracted me. Maybe I could try Reign. We hadn't been hanging out socially, but it didn't mean we couldn't try it out.

I texted them. *u up?*

Reign: *gtfo*

I snort-laughed at the response.

Me: *lol jk*

Me: *can I come hang out with you?*

Reign: *JT choosing his new lady over his sister?*

Me: *…*

Reign: *lmao. Come over. I'm playing Never Yield.*

Until meeting Nuria, I hadn't been big on gaming, but it was growing on me and it definitely sounded better than endlessly scrolling TikTok and falling down the black hole of my future. I texted Justin to let him know where I was going, grabbed a bag of chips, and headed next door.

21

JUSTIN

Yasmin slips into the work at All Choice quickly and easily. Within a week, she has learned their systems and discerns the vision Justin has for the upgrades and optimization plans. She learns and adapts so swiftly that Justin worries she'll regret the choice due to lack of challenge. So he assigns her to a project he and Caleb talked about a couple of weeks before Justin's promotion. Caleb had called it a "back burner" idea. Justin sees the potential of moving it to the front burner with a programmer who immediately appreciates the value of it.

"Who will clean up the interface?" she asks. "I can do it, but it's not one of my strengths."

"Austin can," Justin says. "Shane, too, if needed."

Yasmin makes a noise that causes Justin to study her. He asks, "What does that noise mean? I can't tell from your expression."

"Sorry, it's nothing. How much time do you want allocated to this?"

Justin suspects the noise was not "nothing," but he honestly doesn't know what she meant by it and can only take her at face value. "Let's see how you do at fifty percent, with the other fifty percent supporting the daily error report and other current projects. We'll re-evaluate in a month."

One of Yasmin's references told Justin, "Maybe she speaks her mind too openly and not always diplomatically, but most people wouldn't be offended if she were a man in the same situations."

It was the most useful reference he'd talked to. The other two merely verified Yasmin's skills and accomplishments already listed on her resume. Justin knew any woman coming onto his team would need confidence to deal with Shane and Austin and probably himself, too, though in different ways. Openness and honesty are positive traits. "Not always diplomatic" doesn't bother Justin in the least. Justin often isn't diplomatic, either.

As Yasmin leaves his office and he wonders again about her inscrutable noise reaction to working with Shane and possibly Austin, Justin suddenly sees the problem with needing a new employee who *required* confidence to deal with his team. There was nothing wrong with desiring an employee to be confident, but it shouldn't be a survival skill like it has been for him. He didn't choose Shane or Austin as colleagues, but now Justin is in charge and it's up to him to figure out how to create a better working environment.

If Justin is being honest—and he almost always is—he has never felt like he was in a truly *friendly* working situation. Before he became their supervisor, he had picked up all the dropped pieces of projects. He hadn't minded it. What he had disliked was how, despite Caleb knowing full well that Justin did the clean-up work, Caleb never acknowledged it. Because they were a team.

If Caleb ever spoke to Shane and Austin about their performance, Justin's unaware of it. He understands not criticizing a colleague in public. However, he doesn't see the harm in praising someone. So far, Justin has seen little out of Shane or Austin to warrant undue praise and while they were appearing to make laudable progress on the one project, the execution was sloppy and rushed. They all ended up spending more time fixing the errors than creating and amplifying the new system.

Shane keeps pushing Justin to let them go live with the project, claiming it to be the fastest way to spot the errors. To Justin's surprise, Austin had agreed when Justin said unleashing an untested program was a foolish and unnecessary risk.

"This isn't some kind of winner-takes-all live coding event," Austin had said. "We're a tiny, start-up, supplemental health insurance company, not Meta or Google."

"Like you could even keep up with programmers there," Shane said.

"And you could?"

"Hell yeah," Shane said, and before his two ego-ballooning juveniles could take it further, Justin had shut it down and moved them on to the next item on his agenda.

Now, he does a web search for the question, "how do I create a positive working environment?" A job search site offers five suggestions. The first one is "provide a comprehensive onboarding process for new hires." Well, he's already failed the number one tip. He gave Yasmin a tour, introduced her to people she needs to know in the company, and got her account access set up. When he reviews the steps he's taken, he sees how it's not been thorough. He's done the very least of the process. He made a list of items Yasmin would need to get started, but didn't consider options like having her sit in on meetings with the other arms of the technology department, such as the web developers and network managers. She will want, no, *need* to understand the goals of All Choice and the ways it interfaces with both their external and internal audience.

He writes down the tip, noting that it's only been a week and there is still time to "comprehensively" onboard Yasmin. He reads the next tip. "Initiate a new round of ice-breaker and team-building activities." He groans, closes his laptop, and leans back in his chair. He loathes team-building activities and icebreakers even more. If this is what he's expected to do, he might as well resign right now, tell Caleb he made a mistake with promoting him.

There's a light knock on Justin's open door. "I'm not sure if that groan means I'm stopping in at the right time or the wrong time," says Nihal Mishra, All Choice's relatively new VP of Technology Operations. He's a tall, slender, and dark-skinned man with thick, wavy black hair. Justin has only met him once, about seven months ago, when Nihal was hired. He is Caleb's boss, and with Caleb on leave, Nihal is effectively Justin's direct supervisor, a connection Justin only makes this second, with no time to decide how he should respond, which leads him to an unfortunate, starkly honest reaction.

"Unexpected arrivals are always wrong," Justin says. He raises a hand, palm out, as a placating gesture to make up for the words he already knows should have stayed inside his head. "I'm sorry—"

Nihal's loud laughter interrupts Justin from saying more. "Caleb said you were direct and honest. You're right, it's unsettling when your super-boss drops by spontaneously."

"Super boss," Justin says. "Do you mean super as in 'amazing' or super as 'above'?"

Nihal leans back slightly and points "finger guns" at him. "Maybe both, yeah?"

"Just like Superman." Justin smiles.

"Yes!" Nihal's enthusiasm is loud and strong, and Justin's first instinct is that Nihal is being sarcastically excited and humoring Justin. He wants to be wrong, but if Caleb already talked about Justin, then it was probably some kind of "warning" about how to deal with him. He prepares to handle himself accordingly.

But Nihal sits in a chair opposite Justin at his desk and talks about how Superman does great things, is held to a higher standard, and flies above everyone. "Talk about all meanings of the word 'super,' right?"

Justin agrees and resists the urge to add on more words that make him delve into their roots and multiple contexts. Nihal *seems* like he could be interested, but Justin doesn't know this boss of his boss and chooses not to risk the rabbit hole. He has enough new interpersonal interactions going on right now to navigate.

"So, do you want to tell me what your groan was all about? How are things going, Justin?"

Two questions in a row that have different answers. Justin has never been a fan of this conversational format. It ends up being like an email where people end up only answering the first or last thing you asked and the other questions—numbered, obviously, if you are aiming for clear communication—get ignored entirely. Justin responds as he always does, with answers to both questions in the order given.

"Icebreaker and team-building activities. And with respect to your second question, I'd appreciate it if you could be more specific about what 'things' you are referring to."

"Direct! Yes!" Nihal gives a single clap, and Justin is struck again by the loud exuberance. "I love the request for specificity. It's been a while since I've been knee-deep in programming, but I wouldn't know how to answer a question like 'how's that code coming along?' I mean, which piece of code? What aspect of it?"

Justin has no idea if he's supposed to answer the non sequitur questions, nod in agreement, or ask a return question. He gives a slight nod.

"I want to know how you are feeling about your new position," Nihal says as he leans forward to rest his forearms on his thighs. "Are you happy in your new role? I realize the transition was sudden, what with Caleb's father and all. Do you have a good handle on what you're doing? What kinds of questions do you have? How can I help?"

Again with the string of questions. Justin runs a hand along the cover of his laptop while he processes all the questions and which one to answer. Probably the last one, based upon how the conversation has already gone.

"I did it again, didn't I?" Nihal says.

"Did what again?"

"Asked a whole bunch of vague questions. And too many of them, yeah?"

Since Nihal has commented on Justin's directness and honesty already, he says, "Yes. Do you want me to answer them all?"

Nihal shakes his head and smiles. "I don't even remember all the questions I asked. I do that. Get nervous when trying to get to know new people and I come across a little…"

"Loud?" Justin suggests.

Nihal laughs—loudly—and says, "Well, yes. In truth, I'm frequently loud, but louder and overzealous when trying to make a good impression."

Justin takes a deep breath in, then slowly releases it, along with the tension that has been building up in his neck and shoulders. "I understand. I don't always come across the way I'd like in new, social interactions, either."

"Let's start over then. Yes?"

"Yes."

❄

LATER, Justin and Amelia meet for lunch at All Square, a restaurant specializing in gourmet grilled cheese sandwiches, a place Mama Mac recommended a couple of years ago. Justin has been visiting it monthly ever since.

Justin recaps the story of Nihal dropping in and how they ended up restarting the entire conversation and turning it into something productive. "I thought he was going to be one of those guys who talks in nonsense circles about visualization and incoherent goals," Justin says.

"Hey," Amelia says. "Are you making fun of mindset strategies?"

"No. I'm criticizing all the flowery, 'woo woo' language about them and how often people say the words, but don't understand what they mean. I practice mindset work and use visualization techniques all day, every day. Except I call it preparing for all scenarios and my sister calls it scripting. They are much more concrete terms."

"That's a relief. I thought we were about to be on our last date."

Justin's chest immediately tightens and his heart races. He grips his soup spoon, and he places his other hand flat on the table to steady himself. A thought exists telling him she is kidding with him, but the possibility she isn't bulldozes over that thought and flattens it into the dirt and gravel of uncertainties.

"What?" His question comes out with an involuntary crack in his voice. He has barely shared how he uses visualization techniques all day when he has to access the one where he says or does something to chase someone away. Someone he likes too much. Yet he must always be prepared for it.

Amelia's hand slides over his on the table. Her beautiful, strong fingers, brown and with forest green polish painted on her short nails. "Justin," she says, and he forces his eyes up from her hand to her face. "I'm totally kidding. I mean, don't get me wrong, I would have had to set you straight, if necessary, but I definitely hope this is not our last date."

He closes his eyes and takes a deep breath in and out.

"Are you okay? Did my joke trigger something else?"

They've only been on two dates, four if you count their two lunches together. Justin's anxiety spike probably seems extreme for what Amelia likely considers some casual dating when he's already envisioned them in a relationship. He thought he'd learned not to jump to this conclusion too soon, except Amelia isn't like the other women he's dated.

He opens his eyes again to focus on Amelia's face. Her expression. Studies all the difficult but not impossible cues from it to understand. The eyebrows scrunched together. The slight downturn of her mouth. A tilt of her head. Her eyes steady on him. He knows, of course, these all reflect concern. In others it hasn't always been genuine, and somehow he's supposed to recognize this more from someone's eyes, a skill that remains elusive for him.

He can hear her tone and feel her touch, though. It isn't impatience, another reaction he's frequently heard within apparent concern. He takes a risk.

"Yes and no," he finally says. "I really like you and for a second, I worried you would break up with me, which might not make sense since you probably weren't thinking we were in a relationship, but I already feel like I'm there with you. So yes, the joke I didn't immediately catch triggered my anxiety." He takes another deep breath, leans back in his chair and sets down the spoon he still grips too tightly in his hand.

"Also," he continues before she can correct his assumption about them. "I'm sure you already guessed this about me, but I'm autistic, and I don't always catch jokes right away. I don't often point out my autism to people for many reasons, mostly because of wrong assumptions. Except I've discovered sometimes it's useful to get that out there so I can discover faster if I'm going to turn into a character in someone's mind instead of a real person—those are my therapist's words by the way—and this seems like a proper time to do it."

Her hand tightens around his and she smiles. "Thank you for trusting me with that, Justin. Thank you for trusting me with you. And we've been on four dates and talk every night, so yes, we are in a relationship."

"Our lunches count as dates?"

She laughs and shrugs. "That's how I've been counting them. I considered including the time you first sat with me at the Panera before you knew who I was, but we didn't exactly eat or drink together, so I'm not sure it qualifies."

"That was a chance encounter."

"Right! A random happenstance."

Every muscle—save for his heart, which squeezes with an emotion he is too afraid to name—relaxes as he counters with, "A lucky coincidence."

"A happy accident." She leans forward and grabs his other hand. "And I'm going to stop you from one-upping me right now because I have to get back to work."

He nods and they both stand to clean up their dishes. "Would you like to come to my place for dinner on Saturday?" Justin asks. "You can meet Lizzie, Reign, and Crash."

"I would love that."

They step outside and see a layer of fresh snow blanketing the sidewalks and cars with more still falling. Justin's anxiety spikes as it always does when he knows he has to drive while it snows.

"It's so pretty," Amelia coos.

Justin takes in a deep breath, exhales slowly, and tries to view the scene with her vision. It's a thin layer, not more than a quarter inch, and the falling snow is a light flurry.

Manageable, he thinks. Then he focuses on Amelia and her profile against the backdrop and agrees with her. *Pretty.* He meticulously clears the snow off of Amelia's car, kisses her through her open window—*heaven,* and then prepares his own car. Once it's ready, he sits in the driver's seat and checks the time. He will be late getting back. He takes two more deep breaths and maps out an alternate route to the office, one that accounts for avoiding busier streets with higher speed limits.

He's a good driver, but also cautious, especially during winter weather.

Another memory slams into him.

What's wrong with Mommy! Where's Beth? I'm so cold, Justin!

He breathes in again and swallows the memory. He breathes out and conjures the image of Amelia's face, her smile, and recalls her words.

"Yes, we are in a relationship."

He drives back to work.

22

LIZZIE

Nuria and I each sat on an Östanö chair opposite each other at a Doksta table in the dining section of Ikea, testing them out for comfort. Nuria was searching for a pair of chairs for her dining room table.

"Want to come to Justin's place tonight for dinner and be a buffer for me as we get to know his new girlfriend?" I asked.

"What will we be eating?"

I grinned. "Valid question. Some kind of vegetable and rice thing. JT's an amazing cook, so you can take this as a legit dinner invitation." I knew every detail of the menu because naturally, Justin talked it all out with me. Vegetable kebabs with some sort of special sauce and Nigerian jollof rice. Naan and homemade hummus as an appetizer. Key lime pie for dessert. He'd been making the pie when I got home from my Gas-n-Guzzle shift, a blend of sweet graham cracker crust and fresh lime already cleansing the gasoline fumes from my sinuses.

"I'm meeting up with Kat around ten," Nuria said. "But if you think it's enough time to let you get the lowdown on the girlfriend, then sure, I'm in."

Kat was someone Nuria had been seeing fairly steadily

before meeting me. When the woman at the salon said Nuria was "perpetually" single, she wasn't wrong. Nuria and Kat weren't a couple, but they weren't really *not* a couple, either. I met Kat once, and I liked her. She and Nuria hooked up through an app and clicked. Just like Nuria and I had also clicked, except Nuria wanted to share space and resources and it wouldn't surprise me if she and Kat ended up moving in together at some point.

I enjoyed living on my own. Preferred it, even. Moving in with my brother had been a forced financial situation, but regardless of all the annoyances we had with one another as siblings, navigating our relationship far outweighed rooming with someone you may or may not hook up with.

Back in college, my best friend Monica and I did everything together. We were ride-or-die friends until I completely ruined it by sleeping with her. She saw it as a turning point for her and I … did not. It was stupid. I *knew* I shouldn't have done it. I loved Monica, of course I did, and I loved her all the more for being straight with the bonus that I had no sexual attraction to her. It should have been a "safe" friendship.

It would have been had I listened to my inner voice when Monica told me she thought she might be bi and then asked if I'd be willing to have sex with her as an experiment. She wanted to try it out with someone she trusted, who wouldn't make her feel awkward or silly. I reminded her about how I felt about romantic relationships. She said she understood.

Turned out she didn't understand. After our "experimental" night together, things changed between us. Monica became overly affectionate with me and though we used to tell each other we loved one another, suddenly her tone shifted when she said it until finally, she confessed to being in love with me. I couldn't return the sentiment and we fought. Said terrible things to each other. Apologized the next day. And yet, Monica said it would be too hard to go back to only friendship and walked away.

I'd changed from Liz to Ellie while friends with Monica, and I'd loved being Ellie. Ellie had been loved and supported through change and loss.

Hindsight told me I might have lost Monica even had I not slept with her since her feelings toward me transformed into something else. Or maybe it could have gone another direction and I could have saved our friendship somehow. Regardless, I was grateful for the clear communication between me and Nuria *and* her relationship with Kat. I didn't need to act a certain way or hold anything back with Nuria. Parts of me were loosening up.

"Is this a traditional thing?" Nuria asked, bringing me back to the present. "Do women have to pass the sister test in order to court your brother?" She stood, signaling to me to follow as we proceeded to another dining room table and chair set.

No cushions on these chairs and sharp corners. I was Goldilocks. Too hard.

"No. I think he really likes her and just wants validation."

We moved to a third set-up. "Or maybe an assessment of how interested she really is in him. He doesn't have a great track record."

Reign was originally supposed to be the fourth person at the table, but they backed out earlier for an undisclosed reason, which caused some panic texts from Justin while I was at work. I had to let him spiral down on his own because I was working solo for part of my shift and we were crazy busy. By the time I called him on my break, he'd been an inch away from scrapping the whole plan and canceling on Amelia.

He'd been stuck on planning a meal for four and the balance at the table. Even after all our years together, it still surprised me when certain situations knocked him off his line of logic. He worked with hundreds of lines of code every day and figured out solutions with ease, yet this small adjustment triggered something. It gave me further proof about how much he liked Amelia. He really didn't want to mess this up.

"Well, then I've got Justin's back along with you," Nuria said. "Which these chairs definitely don't have for us."

"Right?" I said, shifting on the round seat of no sharp corners but not enough room for any standard-sized butt. "I'm afraid IKEA-chic is not in the cards for you."

Nuria sighed. "Yeah. I guess I'll have to drop some money on real furniture."

I shook my head. "Nope. Check out estate sales first. I bet you can find some great chairs that are still in decent shape."

"Good plan. You'll join me?"

I thought of how I used to spend my Saturday mornings. A select few of us from Meadowfields would drink coffee and eat amazing pastries and rolls at La Boulangerie Marguerite at around nine, and then later pick up a few things from Trader Joe's. Now I sold scratch cards and single-serving Frosted Flakes starting at five a.m. Estate sale hopping sounded like a decent bridge between then and now.

"I work on Saturday mornings, but I hear Fridays have more of the good stuff if we hit them early," I said.

"Perfect. Let's plan on next Friday. In the meantime, I'm going to run home and spruce myself up for our double date."

Frankly, I was happy Nuria had Kat and whomever else. The Triple As never got a handle on my aromantic nature, and I grew tired of correcting them or explaining myself to them. It was so much easier being around Nuria, Kat, Reign, and my brother. I knew Justin could have really used Reign tonight, but since he still had me, I was glad I'd have Nuria. I hoped we all would have Amelia after tonight, too.

23

JUSTIN

Reign is the first real friend Justin has had since Hugh died. Justin probably would have gone years longer without this kind of friendship had Reign not been so persistent. Justin, as a rule, does not like his neighbors. Mama LiLi always says "proximity doesn't automatically equal permanent pals," but Mac likes to tease both him and LiLi for their antisocial tendencies.

Aside from neighbors who are just plain assholes—experiences when growing up and stories from his moms recently—there's continual small talk. Justin is terrible at small talk. Nobody wants an honest answer to "how are you?" and if he is always expected to say "yep" to "Beautiful day, huh?" or "Cold enough for ya?" then he doesn't understand the point to any of the questions. He's willing to offer up a "hello" or "good morning" for courtesy's sake, and even says it first sometimes. All the rest is irritating and exhausting. For a brain like his, each day offers a pile-up of learned responses, rote reactions, and constant decision-making.

Reign, on the other hand, went straight to questions that

required specific, personalized answers. They first met in the mailbox foyer in May of last year.

"Hey, you live in 417, right?" they'd asked. "I moved in next door to you in 419 a couple of weeks ago."

Justin had only nodded. He knew someone had moved in based upon all the noise, but had never noticed who it was. Apparently, it was this person.

"I'm Reign. I use they-them pronouns."

Justin understood the importance of Reign's introduction. They wanted to know if they were safe with him as a neighbor. He nodded and gave a small smile. "Justin. He-him." And then, he'd decided on something he hadn't done since elementary school and had added on, "Autistic." He hadn't any idea why he suddenly felt compelled to do so. Something about Reign came across as open and genuine.

"Cool," Reign said, and then their eye caught on someone else. "Hey, stairs workout pal, how are you doing? Going up?"

Justin glimpsed a big smile from the woman and the two continued their conversation while Justin had slipped into the elevator. The next few times he and Reign had run into each other—mail foyer again, garage, in the hall outside each of their respective apartments—Reign asked more questions. How long he'd lived there. What he did for work. A recommendation for a mechanic. The mechanic question proved the tipping point from friendly—or possibly annoying, of course—neighbors to friends, as Justin had strong opinions about reliable and trustworthy mechanics.

Justin had ticked off his fingers every mechanic in the area, noting their strengths, weaknesses, star-ratings on Google and Yelp, and cleanliness at the customer service counter. Reign, instead of waving Justin off, had started bouncing and said, "My friend, this is amazingly helpful. But I need to take notes. Wanna come in for a bit?"

The invitation touched something inside Justin. Maybe it

was Reign's use of the word "friend," even though he didn't think they were actually friends. Or maybe it was Reign's bounce. While an excited, joyful action and not a nervous one, Justin felt a kinship with it. Later, upon learning Reign also experienced generalized anxiety, Justin's protective walls thinned, and he's been opening windows and doors to allow Reign in.

There's a lot they still don't know about each other, such as what causes Reign to disappear for a few days at a time, like they have now. Justin received a text from Reign earlier in the day, asking him to feed Annabelle, their betta fish. This means Reign left yesterday because while Reign usually feeds Annabelle twice daily, she stops eating for a bit when Reign leaves and tossing a pellet into her tank only mucks up her water. This is the third time Reign has gone out of town to some mysterious place. When Justin has asked, Reign has only said, "I needed to get away."

Justin lets himself in to Reign's apartment and scans the disarray. Reign is not especially tidy, so Justin always expects the stray water bottles, random piles of mail, and trails of discarded workout clothing.

It's worse than usual, though. Dishes with dried-on food stacked on the coffee table. Mail, both opened and unopened, scattered on the floor. A basket of laundry that appears to have been picked through with clothes half-in and half-out of it takes up part of the couch.

Justin's own anxiety amps up his need for orderliness. He usually goes into overdrive with deep cleaning and mapping out every minute of his day. It also means he misses important tasks because he gets so focused on the minutiae, he forgets why he has done certain things, such as leaving a gap in his calendar for the afternoon, which was meant to have been for taking care of loose ends of various projects at work, but his high-octane anxiety has filled that gap with new projects instead. Reign's anxiety must do the opposite. If there is one thing Justin understands well, it is the power of executive function control, and what he sees in Reign's apartment is a complete failure of that control.

He hopes Reign goes some place safe.

In the meantime, he focuses on the requested task of feeding Annabelle. He clears away debris from her previous, not fully eaten food pellet and drops a new one in. He decides to talk to her like he might with Crash. He's done his research on betta fish and learned how they are intelligent, have their own unique personalities, and often recognize their guardians. Annabelle darted behind a castle when Justin approached and while no longer completely hiding, she still darts from one structure to another inside her tank.

"Hello Miss Annabelle. Or should I call you Mx Annabelle?" Justin pauses in thought. He's pretty sure Reign has used "she" for her. "Well, I guess I don't have to use a title at all," he says to her. "I wanted to be polite."

He pulls over a chair from the dining area in order to sit in front of the tank. "What's going on with our friend, Reign, hm? I think there's more to their excuse of 'needing to get away.' What do you think? I'm a little worried about them."

As he talks, Annabelle swims out into the open area and glides by the glass as though to do a drive-by recon mission of Justin. She's a deep blue with a brilliant red tail. The textures of her tail and fin would make for great photos. Lately he's also been experimenting with editing software to blend different images together to show a pattern progression or sometimes, for fun, in ways to Picasso things up because the strange imagery stirs something inside of him.

"What do you and Reign do for some fun bonding?" Justin continues with his conversation with Annabelle. His eyes rove around a bit until they see a turntable. "Music! I bet you like that. The soundproofing in these walls is pretty good, but sometimes Reign plays their music rather loudly." Fortunately, it's not unpleasant music. Justin moves to the modern record player designed to mimic an original seventies-model turnstile. He flips through the albums in a standing rack that looks like it came right from a record store.

Reign has a mix of old, original vinyls and newly produced ones. Gloria Gaynor, Jackson 5, Earth, Wind, and Fire, and Judy Garland are some vintage albums Justin finds towards the back of the stack, but instead of pulling from the stack, he plays the album already on the turnstile. "Wary+Strange" from Amythyst Kiah.

The short first track of "Soapbox" doesn't do much for drawing Annabelle out, but the next song, "Black Myself" with the faster and harder beats has Annabelle bobbing and swimming about. Justin smiles in appreciation and the success buoys him to turn around and assess the chaos that is Reign's apartment. Justin has almost everything ready to go at his place for his small dinner party for Amelia and has a little time to take care of Reign. The question is whether it would be helpful for him to clean and straighten things up for Reign. If it were him, he might feel on edge knowing someone handled all his stuff without his permission.

However, he has always been grateful for his sister and his moms for what they did for him after Hugh died. He'd been unable to process the barrage of emotions that threatened to drown him, and managing his environment would have only compounded the effects and completely debilitated him. He knows what it cost Lizzie. He knows all the things he's been responsible for that have cost her. Inviting her to move in with him when she needed a place to stay had been a straightforward decision, but it also served as a small repayment.

Justin decides to tackle only the dishes. As he picks up stray silverware and glasses from the living room, he catches a glance at a haphazard stack of both opened and unopened mail. There are bills from an unfamiliar clinic in Stillwater and another from a hospital. None of them have Reign's name on them. Justin steps away quickly, guilt overcoming him, certain he's inadvertently glimpsed Reign's dead name and seen more than Reign would want Justin to know.

He has to take a deep breath in the kitchen in order to refocus on his task, one he is no longer certain he should be doing. Reign only asked him to feed the fish, not poke his nose into the rest of his business. Reign doesn't even trust Justin enough to tell him where they've been going, so why does Justin think he should do more than feed the fish?

He leaves the dishes and flees the apartment, leaving Amythyst Kiah to sing "Hangover Blues" to Annabelle and the secrets within.

24

LIZZIE

The evening started out rough. Amelia arrived a few minutes late, which had Justin—and me, if I was being honest—sure she was standing him up. I reminded him that for a lot of people, showing up a little later was polite. It allowed for the host to take care of any last minute or unexpected things.

"Not everyone is able or willing to time themselves as precisely as you are."

"I know," he said, his response fast and clipped.

He was nervous. Me stating the obvious to him didn't help. Nuria filling in for Reign also made him anxious. Justin met Nuria a couple of weeks ago, so it wasn't that he was specifically nervous about her. Rather, it was a change in the plan he had for the night. Justin had anticipated a higher comfort level, a predictability in how we would interact with him with only the uncertainty of how we would engage with Amelia. Now he had another wildcard.

Not only that, but Nuria was also running late. She called to say she was stuck behind a long backup on the highway due to an accident. Her maps app said she was at least thirty minutes out.

"Do you remember when we used to turn the bathroom into a spaceship?" I asked, pulling out the memory to distract him.

"The J.B. Galaxy Explorer."

"Yes! I was just now thinking about when we discovered Flusher." Justin mostly thought up the new planets or stars we "discovered." Sometimes, as in the case of Flusher, he allowed me to have some input. I'd wanted "Poopiter" because it sounded like "Jupiter" and our spaceship was the bathroom. At first he'd said "no, that's too obvious and gross," but I'd pushed back with how LiLi said he needed to work on considering other people's ideas. He'd relented and offered a variation, leading us to Flusher.

"That had been a tricky landing," Justin said.

I laughed. "Yeah, it involved a lot more twisting of knobs and the need to dim and brighten the lights repeatedly." That dimmer knob was probably our favorite thing in the bathroom. That and the chain to raise and lower the window blinds.

"I was thinking about how you turned on the shower while I checked the engine sensors."

"Oh, damn. I forgot about that part." I had turned the knob on the shower, assuming the water would flow out of the spigot. Instead, the shower lever, the one to pull up when you want the water to come through the shower head instead of the faucet, was still in the UP position, and water came shooting out and onto Justin. He'd screamed, I'd cried, Mac flew in, and then ... I couldn't quite retrieve the rest of the memory. Probably it was the end of that space journey.

"It turned out okay," Justin said. "You didn't know it would happen. We landed safely on Flusher."

"Are you so sure I didn't know? Seems like something obnoxious a younger sister would do."

He paused his pattern of repositioning the hummus tray and checking on the vegetable skewers in the oven. "Of course I am. I tried really hard to keep it together, but then you were so upset, crying and saying how sorry you were and that you didn't know, and unfortunately, that pushed me over the edge. The next thing I remember, you were hugging me as tight as your six-year-old arms could and singing 'Row, Row, Row Your Boat.' Same as you did the other night."

I calmed him down? "No, Mac did all that."

His phone rang, and by "ring" I mean it called out, in Reign's voice, "Front Door" in a poor imitation of James Earl Jones. All of Justin's ring tones for contacts were a voice recording of the contact calling. They used to all be in Justin's voice, but recently Reign had been hijacking the phone and having the actual contacts record their own names and any Reign couldn't get a hold of, they made up a voice.

"Hello?" Justin answered, not missing a beat with the ring tone. He paused for the return greeting, presumably from Amelia, then told her, "I'll buzz you in. Also, the carpet on our floor by the elevator is coming up a bit, so you'll want to watch your step there. Okay, I'm going to do the buzzer now."

Justin rubbed his jaw, then ran through his pattern to check everything one more time. He kept his phone in his hand, probably for the possibility that Amelia didn't get in and he would have to buzz her again.

"You might be thinking of the time we dropped the hand mirror, and you got cut," Justin said, returning to our conversation. "The blood triggered you. Mac had to hold you still while I cleaned you up and put the Band-Aid on."

The blood triggered you. "Trigger" wasn't the word he would have used back in those days, but it's a situation we both understand now. I'm still not good with blood, although it's not as traumatic for me anymore. Mostly anyway.

The knock on the door scattered away the jumbled memories. When Amelia came in, Justin's extra comment about the torn carpet by the elevator made more sense. Had Justin told me she used a cane? I couldn't remember, but as I thought about some of the minor adjustments to furniture placement he'd done earlier around the apartment—widened the distance between the coffee table and the couch and armchair on either side of it, boxed up any cat toys lying on the floor—it was all quintessential Justin. Ignorantly rude and socially clueless at times, but exceedingly thoughtful and courteous the rest of the time. A lot could be credited to how Mac and LiLi raised us, but even my muddied memories before those years showed me this about him.

Throughout my life I've had flashes of my mother and father ... and of my sister. I thought of them as emotional sensations and not actual memories. My stomach knotted when thinking of my father and my mother, and it brought about a confusing onslaught of both warm and cold feelings. I used to think the icy feelings were about the accident, but given my recent, more specific memories, I wasn't sure anymore. And if our parents weren't that great towards Justin, how had he escaped the lack of nurture?

Justin made the introductions as he took Amelia's coat, hat, and scarf, and afterwards, she immediately unzipped her boots. "The temperature has dropped quite a bit," she said as she positioned her boots neatly on Justin's tray by the door. "I'd had hope earlier today when it got close to freezing that we might finally break the subzero streak, but no such luck." She stepped up to Justin, placed a hand on the side of his face, then went on her tiptoes as he then bent his head to meet her kiss. It was one of the sweetest things I'd seen in a long time.

Following that was one of the most annoying things I'd ever seen. Crash wandered over, meowed like a *kitten*—a sound I had never heard from her—then wove in-between and around Amelia's ankles while purring. What a complete witch.

Crash was the witch, of course, and not Amelia as she cooed away and pet Crash without a single hiss, growl, or scratch from the cat.

"What magic do you possess?" I asked, full of suspicion. "Did you rub your hands in fish sauce before coming here?"

Amelia laughed, and I saw Justin smile in response to that laugh. He was a goner. I swallowed down the sudden lump in my throat, signaling my own nervousness about their relationship. I sent out a silent entreaty. *Please don't hurt him.*

"Whatever is for dinner smells amazing, and is this your homemade hummus that you told me about?" Amelia walked over to the peninsula counter that separated the dining area from the kitchen. "I'm famished, which is a word I've recently been wanting to use and tonight it finally feels right since I missed lunch today."

"Starved, undernourished," Justin said.

"Ravenous," Amelia countered.

"Peckish," Justin volleyed.

I almost joined in, except I enjoyed witnessing this dynamic between them.

"Hollow," Amelia continued with the game.

"Underfed."

"Voracious."

"Empty."

Amelia paused before saying with finality, "Hungry."

"Rapacious."

"I think she was done at 'hungry,' JT," I said.

"Oh," Amelia gave a playful huff. "He knows. He always gets the better of me in this game. I don't stand a chance unless I use my phone to google more options."

"He lets you do that?"

"No."

I laughed, and we dove into the hummus. "You're in for a treat with Justin's cooking and baking. He's making one of his recent specialties of jollof rice."

"I can't wait. One of your moms is a chef, right? Did the cooking genes get passed on to you, too?"

"She's passable," Justin said.

"Rude," I said. Justin's mouth quirked the slightest bit. I loved this playful side of him. Again, I sent out another plea into the universe that Amelia would treat my brother well. He didn't act like this with everyone. She was obviously something special. I only hoped she earned that special honor.

"It's true that Justin is definitely the better chef between the two of us, but I've done pretty well with some of my instincts."

"To be transparent," Amelia said, "I know you are good with fish, pasta, and sauces. Justin is partial to your honey garlic sauce with salmon."

"Yeah, it's passable, for sure," I said.

Justin's phone buzzed. "All Choice" came through in his own voice. His brow furrowed at the alert and without looking up, he said, "I have to take care of this," and went to his room. Not a good sign. Justin was working extra time at home more often than he used to. I hoped it only signaled his increased responsibility, but I also worried things weren't going very well. Based upon his erratic moods lately, I guessed the latter.

Amelia and I chatted on our own for a bit until the oven timer chimed. I wasn't sure which dish it was for, the rice or the vegetable skewers, or both. I didn't want to make the wrong choice since this was Justin's meal and he'd need it perfect for Amelia. His bedroom door was open, and I leaned in.

"Justin? The oven timer went off. What do you need me to do?"

"Flip the skewers. Reset the timer for ten minutes. Turn off the heat under the rice."

"Everything okay?"

He didn't answer, but I decided not to interrupt him again. One thing I understood about his job was that he had to concentrate on a lot of little details within a bunch of code. Taking his eyes off it often made it so he'd have to start over.

Amelia wandered the living room and studied the artwork on

the walls, much of it Justin's photographs. "Justin's photos are mesmerizing," she commented. She pointed to one above a lamp. "Is this a cracked windshield? Or maybe, given what he does, a cracked computer display?"

"It looks like glass, doesn't it?" I closed the oven and set the new timer. "It's part of a spider web. My favorite one is this one of a strawberry." I gestured to the splash of red above the sink. "I love how bright it is and those seeds that look like discs remind me of a *Star Trek* episode."

"Next Generation? The game with Wesley?"

"Yes! I would have been so easily addicted to that brain-washing game."

Amelia laughed. "Me too! Justin would be disgusted with me."

"Totally."

My phone buzzed with a text. *"I'm here, but there's no answer when I buzz to get in."*

That would be Justin, thoroughly absorbed in whatever problem he had to fix. *"I'll be right down."* I texted back.

When we re-entered the apartment, I could already tell that something had shifted. Justin had gone from anxious when Amelia was late, to a smoothed out relaxation once she arrived, and now I sensed a charged energy.

"I know you are willing to help, but I'm the host and I'm supposed to take care of everything." Justin moved about the kitchen with long, quick strides as he tossed items onto the counter.

"He-ey," I called out, trying to sound casual. "Nuria made it!"

"That's not how it has to work," Amelia replied to Justin, her tone calm. "Guests like me enjoy offering help and doing something to feel useful."

"There's not enough time to teach you what to do."

"I can chop. I can stir. I can put things into a bowl. I don't need to be *taught* anything." Amelia's voice was no longer as calm as it had been.

"Uh-oh," Nuria said quietly.

An accurate assessment. To me, the problem was obvious, but I'd been in Amelia's shoes before and definitely did not always handle it well. Justin hummed, and I moved to step in and mediate, which I knew I probably shouldn't do, except this dinner was important to him. He liked Amelia so much. Before I made it to the kitchen, though, Justin had closed his eyes and taken first one centering breath, and then another.

He opened his eyes and spoke. "You're right. I'm sorry. I didn't mean it like that. I was considering the full directions of the recipe rather than the meal as a whole."

Amelia nodded. "Thank you. That makes sense. How about while you make the sauce, I get the kabobs and rice ready for the table?"

As Amelia and Justin navigated around each other, Nuria sidled up next to me and whispered, "Were you about to insert yourself into the middle of a lover's quarrel?"

"It was more than a lover's—" I stopped and rolled my eyes at her single raised eyebrow, an exceptional skill of hers. "Fine. Yes. I was. And yes, it would have been a mistake."

"Interesting," she said.

"What does that mean?"

"All this time, and I never pegged you as a fixer."

I shrugged. "I don't think I am. It's just a deeply ingrained habit I have for my brother. Life was harder for him growing up, and I haven't always been the best sister."

Justin finished the sauce, Amelia got all the food transferred to serving dishes, and as we began filling our plates, the next shoe dropped.

Nuria held the small pitcher of the sauce and asked, "I can already tell there's turmeric in the rice, but what about the sauce?"

"Half a teaspoon, yes," Justin said.

She passed the pitcher on to me. "And the kabobs?"

"No, none on those."

"Perfect!"

"You don't like turmeric?" I asked.

"I'm allergic."

"Lizzie, you didn't tell me she had any allergies. Reign is only allergic to dairy."

I understood what Justin was telling me. He'd originally planned this meal with Reign in mind instead of Nuria. One more unscripted thing to deal with.

"I didn't think to—"

"I have nothing else prepared." Justin stroked his jaw as he looked at Nuria's forlorn plate with only a single kabob.

"All good!" Nuria reassured. "I didn't ask Lizzie for details, but since I'm lactose intolerant, I can still eat the kabobs and have some extra naan."

All Choice. All Choice. Another alert came from Justin's phone. He pulled it out as he backed his chair away from the table and stood.

"Again?" I asked.

"Yes." He read the message and reached around to grip the back of his neck as he started pacing, at first slowly, and then increasingly faster. "I don't understand what's going wrong," he muttered. He paced and hummed and moments later, his hand with the phone went to his head, tapping and then pounding.

Amelia stood and approached Justin. I opted to wait, to stop myself from interfering, because maybe she understood this part of Justin. Maybe she knew what to expect and do. It was one of the most difficult things I've done. The head pounding always gutted me. Years of therapy when he was younger helped him reduce the screaming and flailing, but it never stripped away everything.

Amelia's first mistake was to ask Justin what happened.

What was wrong? It was a common first reaction, so I didn't blame her for trying to figure out what was happening. Except he couldn't hear her or anyone else at this point. The hum was a strategy for him, a self-soother. Once he moved past that, it became increasingly difficult to catch him before hitting full meltdown.

In other words, it was already too late.

"Everything is falling apart," Justin kept saying, along with, "I don't understand."

"Justin," Amelia tried, louder, and then she reached out to touch him after he'd turned away. In a flash, I was out of my chair with hands up, squared at the elbows and blocking Justin's swinging arms from catching Amelia's face as he swiveled back in our direction.

"Best to step back." I tossed the warning over my shoulder to Amelia, hoping she'd listen without argument. To Justin, I tempered my voice, dropping into a gentle, soothing tone.

"You're okay, JT. It will be all right. You're okay."

I stepped away again to let him pace. He was still unapproachable.

"You're all right, JT. It will be okay."

After another minute or two, his pacing slowed, and he stopped repeating his own words. I asked him if I could touch him, and he nodded. He dropped his arms, and I wrapped my own around him, squeezing tightly. I sang. And because of last time in the stairwell, and because of memory, I once again sang *Row, Row, Row Your Boat*.

Maybe it sounded silly to choose a toddler song, but as Justin relaxed in my embrace and his hum joined in, ever so softly, with the tune, it didn't matter. Everyone and everything else faded away. I was six years old; he was ten.

He was my captain and I was his Number One, and we always landed safely, together.

25

JUSTIN

The pool is busy on Monday morning. The last lane, his least favorite, is the only one open. He sets his water bottle down at the shallow end and speeds his way around to the deep end before anyone tries to make contact with him about sharing his lane. He dives in and swims fast and hard without warmup. He knows it's unwise to delve in so quickly, but his mind and body are wound so tight, all he can think to do is to expel the energy as rapidly as possible.

The dinner he'd planned so carefully for Amelia the night before had turned into a fiasco. After his meltdown, he couldn't look at anyone, least of all Amelia. Lizzie and Nuria had done their best to salvage it, but he knows he ruined it and probably his relationship with Amelia.

Amelia.

It occurs to him he didn't search for her before diving in. He pushes the distraction away. He needs to clear his head for all that awaits him at the office. After rushing through dinner, he somehow saw Amelia to the door, but he was so distracted by work, he only remembers somewhere in it all, she'd said it was okay and so he'd moved on to tackling the programming problem right after closing the door. Later, Lizzie asked him what happened and when he explained that Shane took a project "live" before it was ready, she reminded him that Justin was the boss and that Shane should have to fix it.

She was right, except Shane ended up being unreachable. Justin had already taken the program offline, but damage had already occurred. The urge to rebuild it all last night was quelled by Lizzie, who talked him down from another anxiety attack and convinced him sleep and help from his team in the morning would fix the mess more efficiently. Again, she'd been right. With the program offline, he conceded that the urgency of the problem dissipated. He emailed the affected colleagues to prepare them in the morning, shut off his phone, and then meditated for over thirty minutes until he was calm enough to fall asleep.

He woke up feeling somewhat refreshed until his brain caught up. He'd flown into hyper drive, scripting every moment of his day and, so far, he is right on schedule, even accounting for the lack of warm-up, which he adjusts easily with extra laps.

When he pauses for his mid-workout break, Amelia waits for him, sitting on the deck with her legs dangling in the water. His heart speeds up.

"Hey, stranger," she says. "How come you're not answering your calls or returning my texts?"

He grunts in frustration. "I forgot to turn my phone back on from when I went to bed last night." He closes his eyes and works through two deep breaths to tamp the anxiety building from what else he's missed. He hates going into work blind, especially lately.

"Good for you for giving yourself some peace," Amelia says. "It's super busy here this morning. Mind if join you in this lane?"

"I do mind. I don't share a lane."

"Justin, really?" She fans her arm out across the rest of the pool. "There's nothing available. And it's me, not the douchebag."

He's losing time, and he doesn't understand why Amelia is asking him this question. "I don't share a lane. And now I'm running late. I have to get back to my workout." He turns, squats into the water, and pushes off.

By the time he finishes the lap, Amelia's legs are gone from the water and when he finishes his swim, he doesn't see her anywhere in the pool area.

26

LIZZIE

Aside from the fumes, which sadly, one got used to after a time, and the terrible early morning shift, I didn't mind working at the Gas-n-Guzzle. Management was decent. Co-workers weren't obnoxious, and it didn't have indecisive customers like at Astros. Or expectations of amazing service. They were mostly all "get in, get out" interactions, which provided exactly what I needed after the exhausting dinner the night before.

Nuria took it all in stride. Amelia also seemed to do the same. Justin apologized multiple times as we rushed through an awkward dinner. At one point, Amelia had taken a deep breath, put her hands on either side of his face and said, "It's okay." Justin had stopped apologizing, but I'm not sure he absorbed what she was trying to do, especially since he barely lifted his head to anyone the entire time. He'd seen Amelia to the door with an absentmindedness that reflected how the work issues pulled in all of his focus.

Was Amelia upset? Did she understand? I had no idea. I'd been tempted to follow her out, but Nuria anticipated my actions and reminded me that Justin and Amelia were grown-ups and this was a relationship issue they'd have to work out on their own.

I knew she was right. But she also hadn't seen Justin through my eyes and how "off" he'd acted for the past few weeks. Or how much he liked Amelia and deserved to have that happiness.

"MISS BETSY!"

A miniature body crashed into me unexpectedly inside our little cashier cubicle.

I looked down at the top of a knitted pink stegosaurus hat and two small arms—one still sporting a pink cast—around my hips.

I dropped my arm to return the hug while also taking deep breaths and wondering how quickly and safely I could extract myself before her mother started another lawsuit against me. Why was she here again? Surely her mom would never risk returning to this gas station with the daughter she assumed I was out to harm in any way I could.

"Skylar, what have we talked about with running away?"

I looked up from Skylar to the voice. With both relief and surprise, I discovered it wasn't her mom, but a former colleague of mine, Fiona. A para I used to work with at Meadowfields.

"I didn't run *away*," Skylar said. "I ran *to* Miss Betsy."

Fiona sighed. I smiled at her and said, "She's not all wrong."

"She's not all right, either," Fiona said, but also returned my smile. "Hi."

"Hi."

"Uh," another voice joined in. Lou, my co-worker, stood behind Fiona.

His single word and glance from Skylar to me was all I needed to understand his reticence. He was the opposite of my Saturday morning shift colleague, JoJo.

"Yeah, I know," I said, then gently loosened Skylar's grip from around my hips and crouched down to her eye-level. "It's good to see you, Miss Skylar, but people who don't work at the gas station aren't supposed to be in this area. If you go back and stay with Miss Fiona, I can still talk to you across the counter, okay?"

"Okay!" She raced out and dragged Fiona around to the customer side of the cash register and then told me, "I go to a new school now."

"Oh yeah? Do you like it?"

"Mr. Eddie is nice." She tugged on Fiona's hand. "I need my pop-it toy, please."

"Nicely asked, Skylar." Fiona pulled a rainbow-colored, dinosaur-shaped silicone bubble pop fidget from her bag. Skylar took it and paced back and forth, all focus on popping the bubbles one way and then the other.

"So, how've you been, Bet…" Fiona trailed off, and I saw her study my name tag. I've learned that more people than I ever realized actually pay attention to the name tags on random workers. "Lizzie?"

I nodded. "Yeah, I changed up my nickname. I needed something … different."

"Do you want me to have Skylar call you Lizzie?"

I never knew Fiona well. Our team generally worked by support-level clusters so while I almost always directly supported one or two students all day—Skylar, of course, being one of the two—Fiona helped with the Special Education teachers during small group instruction. I liked how she interacted with our kids. She'd also been one of the few people to offer support after the accident.

"No, it's okay. No need to confuse her." Skylar continued to pace and pop while chanting the names of all the different dinosaurs she had memorized. "She's at a new school?"

Fiona shrugged. "Yeah. You know how it is. It's hard to stick with someplace that has caused harm, right?"

I looked away, wondering if I misjudged Fiona after all.

Maybe Mrs. Larson sent her daughter and Fiona here to make sure I didn't forget that I was the one to harm Skylar.

Except, it had never been fair to blame the accident on me. At least not entirely on me. I faced Fiona again. "Why are you here?"

"Skylar missed you."

"But why are *you* here?"

"Oh," Fiona's face revealed understanding. "I've been working as a PCA for Skylar before and after school, and this gas station is on the way to Rockaway Elementary, Skylar's new school."

It shouldn't have bothered me that Fiona was working for the woman who hated me. Fiona hadn't been on the field trip or in any way involved with what happened. And Skylar was a great kid, so why shouldn't Fiona take advantage of the extra money? And when it came down to it, could I blame Mrs. Larson for her feelings towards me? Not really.

Yet it still stung.

"Well, that's—" I started.

"Look, I don't know if—" Fiona spoke at the same time.

I gestured for Fiona to speak first.

"In case you didn't know, Di really fought for you after they put you on leave. I mean, that girl *showed up*. She was in everyone's face from the superintendent all the way on down to all of us teachers. And then, after you resigned? She was livid about how you were forced out."

Di was the district's Elementary Education Special Education Director, and Meadowfields provided her primary office. She wasn't always there as she made frequent site visits to the other three elementary schools, but we got to see her more often because of it.

I imagined Di throwing down with the superintendent in the way she does with our principal and allowed a scant smile. She could always get away with the confrontations because she's been with the district forever. Given how little Meadowfields' principal cared about any of our special needs kids, Di challenged him a lot.

"I appreciate that," I said. I don't think it occurred to me that anyone had fought on my behalf. Someone in my corner. "But I wasn't forced out. I simply quit."

"Time to go!" For once, I was grateful for Skylar's penchant for sudden, high volumes. Skylar shoved her pop-it toy into Fiona's bag and grabbed her wrist with both of her hands. "Let's go-let's go-let's go."

"Well," Fiona said with a half- laugh. "I guess—"

"Yeah, I get it. Bye, Skylar!" I waved, but Skylar had forgotten all about me from the moment she had the pop-it toy in her hands and remained oblivious of me as my hand dropped away quickly and the glass door whooshed the cold air into my face.

27

JUSTIN

The rest of Justin's day moves rapidly from bad to worse.

His inbox overflows, although he expects the uptick and already has a system in place to triage the messages. Some colleagues affected by the errors react poorly and angrily and accuse Justin of incompetence. He doesn't expect this reaction, and it creates a bitter taste in his mouth to accept the accusations on behalf of his team.

Yasmin is witness to one of the in-person complaints—a couple of colleagues are irate enough to make a special trip to his office rather than email or call him—and says, "It isn't Jus—"

"I'm very sorry for the disruptions," Justin interrupts before Yasmin can finish.

"Disruption?" his colleague says. "It's going to take most of the morning to untangle which files have been affected!"

"Yes," Justin says. "That exemplifies the word 'disruption.' It's an interruption. A hindrance. An annoyance."

"A nuisance," Yasmin adds.

The colleague huffs and leaves, muttering something about Justin being an annoyance.

"Wow," Yasmin says.

"Yes," Justin replies. Of course, Justin has seen the colleague's haphazard file system and suspects it will be more than a nuisance, but he can't be blamed for his colleague's inefficiency.

He instructs Yasmin to work with the web development team to analyze how the program interfered with the user interface and to learn how best to integrate everything once it finally is ready to go live.

"Shane should have done that," Yasmin says.

"Yes." Shane should have done a lot of things. But Justin has also learned he should have done some different things, too. Nihal suggested that team-building didn't need to involve games and deep, personal feelings. People simply wanted a sense of belonging and a voice. Justin understood this and thought he had done this by entrusting the team with the new projects, except each of their activities on the projects had been siloed.

Justin's next realization had been that maybe Shane and Austin didn't possess the skills and knowledge for what he asked them to do. He'd set aside time to work with them and teach them. Austin had been open and willing. Shane had not.

Justin has patience. He would have kept at it, even for the man who made Justin's life difficult most days because Caleb likes Shane and isn't wrong about his potential. Yet Shane's choice to expressly defy Justin by going live with the project that caused all of their current problems make Justin's next decision necessary.

He steps to Shane's cubicle. "Good morning, Shane."

"S'up," Shane says, without looking at Justin.

"I'm taking you off special projects. Today I need you to focus on the daily error reports and—"

"What?"

"I'm taking you off—"

"Jesus, I heard you. You can't take me off special projects when I've been doing all the work for them!"

"Do you understand the depth of the problems our company is facing this morning because of your work?"

"Code breaks all the time. It's why we have this job, isn't it?"

"Of course," Justin says. "But the program you pushed out wasn't ready. I told you—"

"And you were wrong because you're a moronic robot. This is fucking bullshit."

Justin's hand moves to stroke his jawline. "I would prefer you not to use that kind of language in our work environment."

"And I would prefer you get out of my space right now."

Justin nods and as he leaves and passes by Austin's cubicle, Austin says in a low voice, "I'll calm him down."

Justin nods again. He walks into his office and closes the door behind him, hoping not to speak to anyone directly for a few minutes. And he doesn't, except his phone buzzes and it's a text from Amelia.

Maybe I don't "get" you all the time, but it doesn't excuse acting like an ass to me.

He paces and works through some deep breaths.

Another text, this time from Lizzie.

I won't be home for dinner tonight. Paula asked if I could stay later.

He replies, "*Amelia says I acted like an ass to her this morning.*"

Lizzie: *Is she right?*

Justin: *Probably.*

Lizzie: *Bring her dinner and talk it through with her in person.*

He exhales in relief. It's a good idea. He skips a reply to Lizzie and jumps to the thread with Amelia.

Justin: *You're right. I'm sorry. May I bring dinner over to your place tonight so we can talk about it?*

Amelia: *Yes, thanks.*

He hopes it's not a goodbye dinner.

28

JUSTIN AND LIZZIE

Justin

When Justin's phone rings just after midnight on Friday —well, Saturday morning technically—he almost turns it off in his half-sleep state, assuming it to be All Choice. He's truly had enough of that place. But then he hears Reign's voice and ridiculous laugh and suddenly Justin's mind snaps into focus and he sits up to answer it.

"Hello?"

There's no answer right away and Justin thinks it's an accidental dial until he hears a raspy breath.

"Reign?"

"JT." Reign's voice doesn't sound right at all.

"Are you okay?" Justin asks.

"No."

"Are you hurt?"

Justin hears a sound like a hiccupping breath in and he realizes Reign is crying.

"No," Reign struggles out. "It's..." More crying.

"What do you need?" Justin asks, his heart picking up speed and his stomach squeezing in on itself.

"Can you come get me?"

"Okay. Where are you?"

"At my mom's. In Faribault."

Justin very much wants to ask a lot of questions with the first being, *why?* The next being, *why didn't you tell me?* And then—Justin stops himself. He can ask questions later. Reign needs him now.

"Are you safe?" Justin asks.

"I think so."

Not the most reassuring answer. "Okay. Text me the address."

Justin leaves a note for Lizzie, heads down to the underground garage, and gets into his car. Except, when the garage door opens as he's ready to exit, he sees snow coming down. Hard. He tightens his grip on the steering wheel and grits his teeth in frustration with himself for not checking the weather first. He backs up again into his parking spot and considers what to do.

Justin will drive in snow storms if he has to, but only locally such as going home from work. Driving to work if Caleb insists. Never longer distances, like the one-hour trip ahead of him, and that one hour is with good road conditions. He has to help Reign, but anxiety is already ratcheting up.

He calls Lizzie.

❄

Lizzie

Justin was in the passenger seat of his SUV when I got down to the garage. I'd called in to Gas-n-Guzzle to say I wouldn't be in for my Saturday morning shift and my manager was another reason the gas station wasn't so bad. She never fussed or asked too many questions. She either knew I was calling in for good reason, or she simply didn't care.

I slid into the driver's seat. "You have an emergency kit, right?"

"Yes. Thank you for doing this."

I connected my phone to the SUV's Bluetooth and pulled up the map directions. "It's no problem. I'm glad I'm here to help."

I clicked my seatbelt. "I remember when you used to freak out about seatbelts. You needed to hear every single click."

His voice was quiet when he said, "I still prefer it."

I immediately regretted my comment. I hadn't been asleep long and the afternoon beforehand with Sebastian—and his parents—had been challenging. "I'm sorry. 'Freak out' was a poor choice of words."

"Let's just get going."

Exiting the garage, I understood Justin's anxiety. Not only was the snow coming down hard, but gusts of wind blew it all sideways. I was glad for Justin's heavier SUV instead of my smaller car as the next rush of wind blasted into the driver's side of the car like it wanted to reach inside and knock us over.

"Will it be like this the whole way down?" I asked.

Justin consulted his phone while I crept through the neighborhood streets towards the freeway entrance. I hoped the freeway would be slightly better since plows usually cleared those major thoroughfares first.

"The storm's not as bad farther south," Justin said. "They're not getting as much snow south of us, just wind and cold."

"Here's to hoping that's accurate."

"Do you want to turn back?"

I didn't harbor the same amount of fear and anxiety about driving in poor winter weather as Justin did, but I never chose to head out of town in a snowstorm, either. I entered the freeway and played "guess where the lanes are," and wondered how much ice lay beneath the sheet of snow. Already my body coiled tightly, and we'd only been on the road for ten minutes.

Except, in the queer community, we didn't turn back. We couldn't. Lives depended on us showing up for one another. If Reign called Justin in the middle of the night with a snowstorm going on, it was bad.

"No," I replied to Justin's question. "Just keep texting Reign every few minutes, okay?"

"Yeah."

With the current weather, we would surely double the normal commute time to the smaller, southern Minnesota city. The silver lining was that it was a straight shot down the freeway, and there might be less snow as we got closer. I gave Justin my phone.

"Can you find a playlist on my Spotify that you'll like?"

"What's your code?"

"Zero-three-zero-three."

"Hugh's birthday?" There was something in Justin's voice. A softness, but also ... maybe fear.

"Reign's going to be okay, JT. It's not the same situation."

❄

Justin

Justin scrolls through Lizzie's playlists and wavers between Indigo Girls and a list named "Covers." He's curious about the latter, which sounds like a much needed distraction. The first song to play is, coincidentally, the Indigo Girls singing a cover of "I Don't Want to Talk About It," which seems fitting because he doesn't want to talk about all the ways since Hugh's death that he worries about Lizzie or Reign when they go out to clubs or bars at night. He hopes Lizzie is right in saying it's a different situation for Reign, even though she has no idea what's going on. He doesn't know much, either.

"Reign's with their mom," he says.

"And I'm guessing that's bad," Lizzie says.

"Yes. She refuses to acknowledge them for who they are and calls them awful names."

"Then why—"

"I don't know."

A wind gust buffets against the car and Justin can feel the push as he looks to Lizzie's hands, tight on the steering wheel. Maybe it wasn't fair to have asked her to drive. He's the older brother. He should be able to handle it. Except he knows that if he is driving and something happens, he won't recover from it. He can't be the cause for anything happening to Lizzie.

He looks back over his text exchange with Reign. Reign's texts are short and incomplete, and despite Reign saying they are safe, Justin doesn't quite believe it. Reign is never so reticent. Everything about the situation is wrong.

"Have they told you anything at all about what's going on?" Lizzie asks, and he hears the modulated tone she uses when trying to be extra patient with him. He remembers that she's probably equally anxious about Reign.

"Their mom is sick. Reign's car won't start. They won't or can't talk so instead I'm getting short, sporadic texts that don't tell me anything."

"Be gentle with them, JT. They might be worried about judgement."

"I'm not…" he trails off. "Judgmental" is probably exactly how he's coming across in his texts to Reign.

"I know," Lizzie says.

"Do you have friends with awful parents?"

"Too many."

He considers their own parents … well, their original mom

and dad, and an overwhelming warmth for Mac and LiLi blankets him. Mac and LiLi have been the very best of parents.

"Mom and Dad probably wouldn't have been great either, to be honest," Lizzie adds.

The assessment hits him directly in the chest. It's as though she's read his mind. They hardly ever talk about their mom and dad, not only because it's a painful subject, but Justin has always assumed Lizzie remembers next to nothing about them. She was so much younger when the accident happened.

"Mom might have been okay," he says, although he's not sure it's true. He just knows his sister and his mom got along best in the family. "Plus, she liked you best."

"No, not me. She liked Isabel, best."

Justin takes in a deep breath and closes his eyes. *Does she really not know? Has he held this knowledge as a secret all this time, not realizing he is the sole keeper of it?* He's always assumed she has known and wanted to be who she is. But what if he's been wrong all of these years?

All the nickname changes start to make sense to him when he considers the possibility that she has never really known herself. The first time she declared a new name for herself—well, second, of course, she'd been starting high school. She wanted to be called Liz. He hadn't understood and LiLi had reminded him it was his sister's right to use the name she preferred.

It wasn't the concept of using a different name that confused him. It was the "why" behind the change, especially since it was so different from "Beth." When he asked her about it, she said, "'Liz' sounds like someone who is more sure of herself than 'Beth'" as though she weren't talking about herself. About actually *becoming* more confident rather than pretending the name was what worked the magic.

Lizzie keeps trying to "reinvent" herself, which he doesn't fully grasp how this works. People are always who they are. Just as Lizzie has always been who she is, regardless of the name she uses. Suddenly, he needs her to see this about herself.

"Lizzie," he says. Then, more emphatically, "*Issy*. That's you. *You're* Isabel. You've never been Elizabeth. You know this, right?"

❄

Lizzie

"What? Why would you say that?" He couldn't know, could he? And if he did, why didn't he say something years ago?

"Because it's true," he said.

I sucked in my breath, my mind racing in pace with my heart rate. I think Justin might have said something else, but I couldn't hear him. I put my focus on the road in front of me, full of black with white swirls. *No. No-no-no.* How could he know?

Except how could he not? Justin doesn't forget things.

He also doesn't lie.

But what did it mean if he thought … *knew* I wasn't who I've always said I was?

That he's wanted it to be true just as much as I thought he would. As much as I've wanted it to be true.

Daddy leans in close to her where she lies in the hospital bed. The memory comes swiftly and in sharp focus. One of the few moments I've held on to with any clarity.

"Which one are you?" he whispers.

"Silly Daddy. I'm Beth!"

It was a joke my sister and I used to play on our dad to try to fool him. Only, in retrospect, he'd never figured out the joke. He'd laugh, say, "oh yeah, right," and call us by our wrong names.

Daddy laughs in a way that doesn't sound funny and all she can hear is Justin crying and saying over and over, "She was supposed to be the good one. Why did she do that?"

She tries again with Daddy. *"I'm Beth! Such a silly daddy."*

I no longer remember if I wanted him to catch my joke or not. I didn't know what my four-year-old self was thinking except that maybe, in that moment, I wanted Justin to stop crying and be happy with the sister he was stuck with, and that was Beth.

"We're twins, Issy, which means we get to be best friends forever and ever."

❄

Justin

"No-no-no-no," Lizzie says again. Her breathing comes fast, and she's crying.

Both of Justin's hands fly to his jaw as he tries to lean forward in his seat to hide away from everything. His hands move to his hair as he rocks. He's not ready for this. He's had so little control in the past weeks, and he can't hold all the parts together anymore. Why did Reign have to disappear *now*? And why, of all places and times, does he bring up the truth about his sister in the car in the middle of a snowstorm? *Fuck winter,* Justin tells himself. *Fuck Reign's attempts to make me like it as much as they do. And fuck my therapist for going along with it.*

"No," Lizzie says, slamming her hand on the steering wheel, and Justin flinches at the force and gasps at the sudden speed surge. "You don't get to hide behind your autism this time." Her voice is a mix of tears and anger. "*I'm* the victim. My whole life I've been trying to live up to being 'The Good One' because that's what you said. 'She was supposed to be the good one.' It was supposed to be Beth you got to still have as a sister, not me."

He can't find words to tell her to slow down. He can't find the words to ask her what she means. He can't find any words. Only a buzzing noise filling his brain. He rocks and the buzzing gets louder, and it hits him that the buzzing is him. He squeezes his eyes shut and forces his hum into *Row, Row, Row Your Boat* because Lizzie's right. He has to be present for her and he can do this.

"You *are* the good one, Lizzie," he forces out, though he's not sure she can hear him when he is speaking into the floor while in his hunched over position. The wind blasts into the car again, overpowering the music and flattening his own hum into the mat beneath his feet. He pushes himself to a sitting position and another rush of wind batters into the car.

"Beth is better," Lizzie says. "Beth is better."

He swallows her words down and they mix inside his stomach and make him nauseated. Somehow, he's done this to her and he doesn't know how. *Why can't he remember? He always remembers everything.*

"Lizzie," he says. "Lizzie, please slow down." He takes a deep breath and slowly exhales. He wants to close his eyes, but he can't miss anything this time. He can keep them safe.

❄

Lizzie

Reign's ring tone from Justin's phone pulled me out of my haze of memories. I looked at the speedometer to find I was going sixty-five miles per hour in some of the worst storm conditions I'd ever driven in. *Shit.* I immediately lifted my foot from the gas pedal, then clamped my hands tight around the steering wheel as wind gusts rocked the SUV.

Beth wouldn't have said something so stupid as saying Justin was "hiding" behind his autism. Beth wouldn't be almost getting them killed on the highway right now. Beth wouldn't have almost gotten Skylar killed or yelled at Sebastian's mom like I had earlier in the day. Beth *was* better. Pretending to be her had never worked, since Icky Issy kept presenting herself in all her terrible glory.

Justin said, "You *are* the good one, Lizzie," but if he could lie about knowing who I was all these years, he could certainly have been lying about so many other things. Like wanting me to move in with him. Or pretending he didn't think Skylar's accident wasn't all my fault. Or having me believe that I've ever been the one to help him through a meltdown when he'd probably done it all on his own, like he did in the car minutes ago.

Maybe I had never really been his co-captain. Maybe it was all a way to push me into finally being "the good one."

"Lizzie, I'm sor—"

"No," I interrupted. "Don't. I don't believe you, anyway."

"Why no—Lizzie, watch out!"

I slammed on the brakes and screamed as we went spinning.

29

JUSTIN

Justin isn't the only one breathing heavily. He reaches for Lizzie's hand and squeezes it.

"Are you hurt?" Lizzie's voice quivers through the words.

"I'm okay. Are you okay?"

She shakes her head as she lets go of his hand, opens her door, and vomits. All the heat gets sucked out and replaced by the frigid air from outside. It quells his own roiling stomach and calms his mind quickly and unexpectedly.

They are facing the wrong direction on the side of the highway and Justin can see the marks on the road from the wild skid and spin they encountered after another car entered their lane without warning. He wonders if that car, too, is crunched up against the metal barrier that stopped them or if it had continued on, oblivious.

A semi truck whooshes by in the far lane and the SUV rocks slightly from the wind it creates. Justin grips his door handle.

He startles when someone knocks on his window and he sees a large figure and hears a muffled voice, "Are you okay?"

He looks to Lizzie for what to do or say. She's wiping her face with her gloves and not looking back at him.

The person outside is talking again and Justin rolls down the window.

"Jesus," the man says. "I saw what happened. It's a miracle you guys aren't crumpled or flipped over. Are you okay? I can help get you going again unless you need me to call an ambulance or something."

More cars pass them by from the far lane and Justin takes in their situation. They are angled against one of the metal barriers, likely also mired in a snowbank. Their front end is precariously close to the right lane. He peers over his shoulder to see a large pickup truck around fifty yards down, its flashers on and exhaust puffing steadily out of the tailpipe.

He looks to Lizzie again, who's shaking, then he turns back to the man. "We're physically okay, but I don't know if we're stuck in the snow or how we'll get turned around."

The man nods and hooks a thumb over his shoulder to his truck. "I've got a buddy with me who can help us look out for traffic once we push you out. We're about two hundred yards from an exit. I figure you can back your way up along the shoulder until then and have some space to turn around there."

"Thank you." Justin turns to Lizzie again. "Lizzie?"

She still doesn't look at him as she grips the steering wheel and puts the car in neutral. "Yeah. Okay."

Their roadside helpers make quick work of getting the SUV out of the snowbank. Lizzie, with the help of the pickup truck to guide with their taillights, reverses them along the shoulder and then turns around on the exit ramp. The pickup driver puts his arm out his window with a thumbs-up, which Lizzie returns in kind.

Yet, they don't move. They sit on the side of the exit ramp, the music off, wind still swirling around them, and the windshield wipers thumping back and forth. Thoughts, memories, and emotions fill up all parts of his mind and he works to sort through and prioritize them. Floating to the top are images of Amelia, even though he tells himself he should focus on Lizzie, first. And Reign.

Reign. Reign had been calling him right before the world went spinning. He pats his pockets and looks around him, then tamps down the bubbling panic as he turns on an overhead light to help him search for his phone. He breathes out the anxiety when he sees it on the floor near his left foot.

There's a voicemail alert and a few texts. The texts ask if Justin is okay and to please check in. Reign is sorry for making him and Lizzie come down. The next text says it would be okay if Lizzie and Justin turned back and Reign will figure out their car tomorrow. But when Justin listens to the voicemail on speaker so Lizzie can hear directly, he knows turning back is not something they can do.

"I can talk now because I'm in my car. It still won't start, but the gas station a mile away had those hand warmer things, so I bought a bunch and I'm using them for heat."

Lizzie puts the car in gear, and they get going again.

He texts Reign to keep their doors locked and also to assure them he and Lizzie are still en route. He lets himself draw on the comfort of Amelia's smile before approaching all that lays between him and Lizzie.

"Lizzie?"

"No."

"No, what?"

"No, I don't want to talk about it and no, that isn't my name, is it? Not anymore? Not ever?"

Justin clenches his teeth together, and his stomach tightens. He hates being shut down, and Lizzie's words from earlier come back to him. *You don't get to hide behind your autism this time. I'm the victim.* Her words are all wrong and cut into him in ways that bring him back to their mom—their biological mother. She used the same expression, "I'm the victim here," with Justin, numerous times. He knows he was a difficult child, yet years of therapy and finally adulthood have taught him how wrong it was for his mother to say that to him.

Only hours earlier, Justin would have assumed Lizzie's words resulted from anger and the upsetting instincts of self-preservation. Now, however, he isn't sure. She's cutting him off and he can't see her well enough to work out what she's feeling. Lizzie, whose body language and expressions he knows best of all, and she's cut him off from that, too.

Maybe she's right to do so. Because the more he thinks about the promise he made so many years ago, the more he remembers about that day and wonders if he's gotten it wrong. Yes, he knew his sister was really Isabel. He knew his dad could never tell the difference, so why would his dad extract a promise from Justin, especially since he didn't care about them and dumped them at his sister's door without a second thought?

The truth is that the promise wasn't to his dad; it was to himself. Issy insisted she was Beth, and Justin promised himself he wouldn't say anything because if he did, he would ruin everything again, like always.

The problem is that he's thirty-three now, not eight, and his adult brain understands all the many flaws behind that child promise. His father had always hated when Justin corrected or contradicted him. Justin's decision not to correct his dad was clearly self-preservation, and the days following the hospital were lost to Justin. He's frequently thought it odd that he can remember the accident, but can't remember the first few days of living with Mac and LiLi. Alonso says that for most, the accident would be what their brains hid from them, but for a kid like Justin, having his whole world change into something completely different was the more impactful trauma of the two incidents. He might never recover those days.

As Justin stares out into the snow-streaked road ahead

surrounded by a starless, moonless dark, he circles around the day in the hospital. The day Issy became Beth. Finally, he understands what he is missing.

"I didn't understand your joke," he says without preamble after their minutes of silence.

"I wasn't joking. I don't want to talk about it and I'm not really Lizzie. Or Betsy or Ellie, or Beth."

"No. I mean, your joke to Dad in the hospital. You and Issy … Beth used to tell him you were the other sister, and most of the time he'd believe you. And then he'd get it wrong, and you'd tell him he was wrong in the exact same way as when you told him the wrong thing." It had been exasperating. Justin didn't understand how their dad couldn't tell Issy-Beth apart. Justin always knew. The differences were obvious.

"I never understood the joke."

Lizzie doesn't respond, but after a few minutes, she asks, "Is Reign still okay?"

"Yes."

She nods. "How much farther?"

Somehow, in all the chaos, Lizzie's phone has disconnected from the Bluetooth. "Where's your phone?"

She shrugs. "Probably on the floor somewhere. It doesn't matter. We can use yours and listen to something you want."

It feels like a proverbial olive branch. An offering. A concession. A possible forgiveness. He enters the address into the maps app.

"Google says we'll arrive in thirty-three minutes."

He opens up his music app and searches for the Indigo Girls. "Kid Fears" plays and they drive the rest of the way with only folk guitars and wind gusts between them.

30

LIZZIE

By the time we got to Faribault, I was mentally and physically exhausted. It was a relief to finally reach Reign so that Justin and I could focus on helping them instead of the gulf of silence and the big lie between us.

We retrieved Reign from their car and found a 24-hour Denny's. Not only did we need the break before heading home again, but Reign hadn't eaten since lunchtime. When our food arrived, only I ate like I'd been starved for days. Likely anxiety still plagued Reign. Probably Justin, too, but I didn't dwell on him. He could deal with that on his own. However, the food in front of us gave Reign the strength to talk to us about what happened.

"My mom has cancer," Reign said. "I found out pretty quickly that she only told me about it because she needed help with the bills, but it had her talking to me, you know?"

It seemed like a shitty deal to me, given what Justin had said about Reign's mom, but I nodded, if only to keep them talking.

"It felt like things between us were getting a little better. Not a one-eighty change of heart or anything, but she'd asked me to come down to help, and she's my moms, you know? The last time we'd spoken before all of this she'd said I was a deluded, attention-seeking, abomination, so this seemed like progress."

Fucking hell. My heart hurt in all kinds of ways for Reign. I truly didn't understand how parents could be such assholes. I was no angel towards other adults—some of my recent issues at Meadowfields being a case-in-point—but to take out our poor behavior on our children was the abomination. Not Reign. Not Justin.

My memories of before being with Mac and LiLi are so few and more like impressions than fully developed photos or film. Justin had said that our mother liked me best, and he was right. With an unpleasant—and often mean—father and an unpredictable mother, I'd aimed to be an agreeable child for my parents so that the meanness wouldn't come at me. Justin kept doing and saying the wrong things and I never understood why, since he was older and supposed to "know better."

This realization spiked into my gut and suddenly I plunged into deep shame for essentially blaming my brother for having autism. Or for not "playing along." No wonder Justin always liked Beth best of all of us.

"And this week had been going really well," Reign continued. "We were watching TV and movies together. Joking around. She let me do her nails and hair and I thought..." Their voice broke at the end and I held one of Reign's hands and Justin followed suit with their other hand.

Reign took a deep breath and squeezed our hands in appreciation before releasing the hold and drawing away again. "Her boyfriend came over earlier today, or I guess it's yesterday or whatever, and he's a piece of work. He wrecked everything my mom and I had been building. He yelled at her. She yelled back. He yelled at me for being there and for babying my mom, and she didn't defend me even a little bit. And I guessed I'd just stay out of their way for a while. I left for a run and when I came back, Dwayne had locked me out.

Neither one of them came to the door to talk to me or let me in."

"Why didn't you call me then?" Justin asked.

"I don't know. I didn't think the lockout would last so long and my bags were inside, including my wallet. I ran to the closest fast-food restaurant to hang out and figure out what to do. Just before ten o'clock, my mom finally texted me back and said all my stuff was on the front steps and I should come and get it before Dwayne put it all in the trash. I went back and still she wouldn't let me in and went back to calling me names. And then my car wouldn't start and I was stuck, JT. Stuck in all the ways, you know?"

Reign looked at Justin, and he nodded. In some ways, he and Reign couldn't be more different from one another, but the exchange I saw made it clear they were alike in all the ways that mattered.

"Any idea what's wrong with your car?" I asked.

Reign shrugged. "Probably the battery. I've had to get it jumped a couple of times in the past few weeks."

"Well, that's easy enough for us to take care of, right, JT?"

"Do you feel safe going back to your mom's house so we can do the jump start?" Justin asked. "Because Li..." He trailed off, likely wondering whether or not to use my name. I held my breath for a moment as I looked away before breathing back out and finishing the thought.

"We can go do it while you wait here."

Reign looked to Justin, then me, then back to Justin. "Uh," they said. "What's going on between you two?"

"Nothing," I said. "We should just get going."

An unwelcome heaviness from the past few hours rolled in and pressed upon my chest. The faster we got moving, the less likely the weight would have a chance to settle inside me. I thought I'd been finally figuring my life out and shedding the guilt and blame for Skylar's accident and now it was all unraveling again. I wanted to focus on getting Reign out of this awful place and home safe. I needed something to go right, and taking Reign away from the toxic situation with their mom was the only right thing for now.

Reign opted to come with us to jump their car. Mindful of the late hour, the cold temperature, and of the unpredictability of the boyfriend—whose car wasn't in the driveway, but Reign didn't know where the guy was or when he'd return—we popped hoods and jumped Reign's car. I was relieved it started up because I hadn't relished the idea of leaving their car behind or waiting for a tow truck that may or may not have come at three-thirty in the morning.

Justin and I stood between the two cars and I took in his awkward fidgeting. The winter gear interfered with his usual techniques for dealing with uncertain situations and emotions so instead he twisted his hands at the wrist and rocked, ever-so-slightly, from side to side. We'd barely spoken to each other since spinning off the highway, and I didn't have any words for him now, either.

"Are you okay with—" he started.

"You should drive back with Reign," I said. "They shouldn't be alone right now." *And I needed to be.*

"Right. Lizzie? Are we okay?"

"I don't know." I got back inside the driver's side of his SUV, shut the door, and backed out of the driveway before he could reply or expect me to elaborate.

Though the snow and wind had died down, the road conditions were less than ideal. While jumpstarting Reign's car, there had been brief talk of getting a hotel for the rest of the night in order to wait for better roads in the daylight, but none of us wanted to spend any more time in that town than we had to. I didn't blame Reign for their urgency to get away. Justin might have had his own reasons, but for my part, I needed to get away from my brother.

Justin was the one who taught me that we should always be honest with each other from little things to big things. I told him when he acted like a jerk and he told me when I was being too stubborn. We always knew where we stood with one another. No pretending.

Yet practically our whole lives, we pretended about the biggest thing of all. And if Justin had been willing to go along with it for all that time, what did it mean for him to stop now?

It felt like punishment for something. Things had been finally coming together for me while his world was falling apart and maybe the point was to take me down with him. Rationally, I knew this wasn't it—and unfair, but I struggled all my life to be the worthy sister to have lived, to be someone others could point to and say, "I want to be like her."

Instead, I was a college dropout with no money, irresponsible with children, aimless, and foolishly believed changing my name would be all it took to change who I was. I remembered when Reign helped me choose my new name and Justin saying, "I like Beth."

Well, fuck him for telling me that without telling me he knew the truth, I thought. *And fuck him for not letting me be my true self.*

I didn't want to go back to his place, but I also didn't want to go to Nuria's.

I wanted to go home.

31

JUSTIN

Justin sleeps longer than he has in years. When he wakes up, Crash stands on his chest, staring down at him, as though to ask, "What happened to you?"

"I have a lot to tell you," Justin says. Crash settles into a loaf, ready to listen. Justin scratches her head. "But not yet."

Justin reaches for his phone. It's almost two o'clock in the afternoon, and he's slept through multiple calls and text messages. Most of them are from Amelia. Only two, thankfully, are from All Choice, and four more are from Reign.

Amelia's texts are mostly photos of some sketches. One is an eye. Another is a bicycle. The next is a math problem, which seems odd until he smiles upon figuring out all the images make up a rebus. Working out rebuses is not one of his strengths, but Amelia loves them and what he most appreciates is the effort into making one for him. Eye, bicycle, -B+L, sheep. He works it out when he figures out bicycle is actually bike. It all equals "I like you." He texts back a photo of his own eye, a symbol for a hiker, then -H+L, her own sketch of a ewe, then the number "2" to say, "I like you, too."

He breathes in deeply before reading the two texts from All

Choice and releases the air in relief to see they are only mass all-call reminder alerts about remote work communications in the event of a major winter storm.

Reign's texts are the most recent.

10:32 A.M.: Thank you for coming to get me. I love you, my friend.

11:18 A.M.: I made pumpkin muffins. Come on over.

11:45 A.M.: Yo, JT! Did I break you? Text or call me when you wake up.

Justin texts Reign to let them know he's now awake, then he looks to Crash. "Why aren't you yelling at me about eating? Did Liz—" He stops himself. What name is he supposed to use? She said Lizzie wasn't her name anymore, and he has always respected her name changes even when he didn't understand them. Which had been never until their conversation in the car, when it all made more sense.

Guilt and sadness crawl into him as he recalls her eyes before they started home in separate cars. He's seen the expression on her before. Most recently, after the incident at Meadowfields, but also there were moments when she supported him after Hugh's death. And back in the hospital after the accident that changed everything between them. She is lost.

When he and Reign helped his sister move in and decide on her new name of "Lizzie," Reign and his sister asked him what he thought of the new name. He'd said, "I like Beth." He'd meant he liked his sister as she was. As she'd always been. Her new names haven't changed the fundamental essence of who she is, nor has he wanted them to do so. Except those words, "I like Beth," were a mistake upon learning she'd been trying to live up to the ideal image of a ghost. A physical ache expands in his chest at how he's contributed to his sister's pain at not accepting all that makes her the best sibling he could ask for.

She's also angry with him and he isn't sure if he can help her find her way back to herself when he is responsible for leading her into the woods in the first place, but he can definitely make amends somehow. He hopes she will talk to him today.

He chats with Crash, talking through his plans and how he will make the day all about him and his sister.

"We'll binge-watch several episodes of *Charmed* before I make whatever she wants for dinner. Well, maybe not whatever she wants since we might not have all the ingredients, but we have everything needed for homemade pizza, which is probably what she'll choose. And then we'll talk about things because by then she'll be ready. She always says it's best to ease others into hard conversations instead of asking questions right away. Waiting and doing her favorites will show her I've been listening to her, won't it, Crash? And that I'm willing to do it again?"

Crash purrs and brushes her body along Justin's shin.

After Justin showers and dresses for the day, he leaves his bedroom and discovers an empty apartment. The door to his sister's room is open, but she's not in it. He looks to the front door and her boots and coat are also missing. He walks to the kitchen, sees fresh water and food for Crash and a note on the counter. All it says is "went home."

All of his hopeful and optimistic energy sinks down and leaks out of him. He needs a new script for the day, but can't think. He pulls his phone from his pocket and texts Reign.

I think I'd like one of your pumpkin muffins. Can you bring them over to my place?

32

LIZZIE

I spent the four and a half-hour drive to Madison trying not to think of anything at all. I listened to upbeat music because I didn't want to "reflect" or "analyze my feelings." I listened to David Sedaris tell me stories of his childhood and Samantha Irby reassure me that awkwardness doesn't escape anyone.

I'd almost driven straight to my moms' place from Faribault. Lack of sleep, poor road conditions, and the fact I was driving Justin's car were all reasons that stopped me. Instead, I went back to Justin's, slept for a few hours, texted Mac and LiLi, and packed a bag.

As I pulled into the driveway of my moms' house on the east side of the city, all my anger and self-doubt strained through my emotional sieve, leaving me with the swell of love and support I knew would wait for me inside. The drain beneath the sieve was clogged, but for now, not enough to push the sludge back up. For a moment, I wondered why, after quitting my job at Meadowfields, I hadn't accepted my moms' offer to move in with them instead of my brother.

Mac and LiLi had told me it would be an opportunity for a

fresh start. New state, a place to fully take some time for myself instead of taking on unreliable jobs simply to pay bills. They wanted to smooth the way for me. I'd been tempted. But then Justin made his own offer and for all that Mac and LiLi did to raise us as their own and create a safe and loving home, Justin and I were a refuge for one another. When I needed a playmate, Justin was there. When he had nightmares, I crawled into bed with him. When another kid at school wrecked my picture, Justin sat with me and helped me make a new, better one. When he came home from a bad day at school because other kids made fun of him, I snuck out cookies from the kitchen and watched *Redwall* with him. We've always had each other's backs. We were always *there* for each other.

But now? I couldn't assuage the doubts. Doubts behind Justin's motivation or deeply held desire that his refuge had been our sister. It's not that I saw our whole lives as a lie or that Justin didn't love me. Him hiding away the knowledge of who I was meant something, though. I wasn't sure I wanted to uncover what that something was.

I grabbed my bag, got out of the car, cursed the icy wind, and let myself in through the front door.

LiLi sat on the couch in the living room, legs stretched out on the cushions, a book in her lap and her head flopped forward with her chin touching the top of her chest. I closed the door behind me and called out a gentle, "Hey."

Her head popped up. "Oh, you made it safely. Thank goodness." Little did she know. I hadn't told her or Mac about the treacherous journey down to get Reign. Fortunately, the drive home had been blissfully uneventful.

As I toed off my boots and stripped off the many layers of outerwear, LiLi came to me and opened her arms. I walked into them with relief. I stood, locked in her embrace, initially in silence. Her greeting lacked expectation, which then released my tears. I'd been holding them back ever since Justin and I met up with Reign last night. I cried, and still LiLi said nothing more than words and sounds of comfort.

Finally, I breathed in slowly and deeply, then exhaled to reach a manageable calm as I pulled away.

"C'mon, sweetie," LiLi tugged at my hand. "Let's sit. Do you want some water or coffee? We have some hot chocolate if you'd rather."

"And cookies?" I asked, suddenly feeling as though I were eight years old.

"It just so happens I baked up some chocolate chip cookies earlier today. A text from a certain someone a few hours ago gave me the idea." She smiled and touched my cheek. "Hot chocolate?"

"Yes, please."

33

JUSTIN

"Well, shit," Reign says after Justin shares his and his sister's story. All of it from the accident twenty-five years ago to the accident last night. "So she *has* been using a dead name. In the most literal way possible."

It's true, though Justin hasn't ever considered it in that light. It emphasizes his intention to not use her current name or any of the other incarnations of it. He desperately wishes he could talk to her. He's texted her several times, knowing he is overdoing it, but he can't stop himself. He picks up his phone again and sends another one that has a close-up photo of Reign's knitting needle and the question, "Can you guess what this is?" He hopes it's better to send something random rather than all the information-seeking ones from earlier. "Are you okay?" "I'm sorry. Please call me." "When did you leave?" "Are you there, yet? Text me when you get there." "When are you coming home? I'll make us pizza."

"She said I kept repeating 'She was supposed to be the good one,' but I don't know what that means. Why would I say that? What does 'the good one' mean?"

"JT. How old were you at the time of the accident?"

"Eight."

Reign grabs a new color yarn and weaves it into their current knitting project of a cardigan. It's a thick yarn to create a chunky sweater that is exactly Reign's style. "Do you know what I remember about being eight?" Reign asks.

"No."

"I barely do, either. I loved playing with my stuffed tiger and sneaking into my mom's closet and trying on her high heels. That's about it. Your memory is legit top dog most of the time, but eight-years old and trauma? Who can say what kind of mess of words were coming out of your mouth?"

Justin picks up the ball of yarn Crash has been batting around the room and re-winds the unraveled yarn, working against the different game of Crash jumping and swatting at the moving string. He sets the ball down and Reign picks it up to throw it out for Crash again, undoing Justin's work. He glares.

"What?" Reign asks. "You have your game with Crash and I have mine with both of you."

Something tickles inside Justin's brain about this interaction. The barest glimmer of a memory of the back seat of the car with his sisters. It clouds up again and Justin grunts.

Reign laughs, as though Justin had been responding to their "game" comment. "I should get hypnotized," Justin says.

"Say what now?"

"Hypnotism can call back the memories I lost. I can find out why I said the words about Elizabeth being the 'good one'."

Reign sets down their needles. "Wait, you know you said *Elizabeth* was the good one?"

"No. That's why I should get hypnotized."

"My friend, no. That is not a good idea."

"Why not?"

"You barely remember everything that happened during the accident and right after it. I don't know if you realize how many gaps there were in your story. What if you meant it back then?

That Elizabeth was the sister you liked better? How does that help either of you?"

"It will be truthful," Justin says.

"Truthful then? Or truthful now? And maybe your sister is misremembering because she was four-years-old, JT. *Four*. Neither of you can say what actually happened that day."

"How can I fix things between us if I don't know what happened?"

Crash jumps into Justin's lap and puts her front paws on his chest. She purrs and rubs her face on his stubbled jaw.

"You can't," Reign says and picks up their knitting again. "Your sister has to figure herself out. No one else can do that for her."

❄

MAMA LILI'S text arrives shortly after Reign leaves. *Lizzie arrived safely.*

Justin: *Is she okay?*

Mama LiLi: *Is there anything you want to tell me?*

Justin hums in frustration at his mom's non-answer.

Justin: *Yes.*

Mama LiLi: *I'm listening when you're ready.*

Justin: *I know. But I can't.*

He's told Reign everything, so Justin isn't sure why he answers Mama LiLi this way, only that somehow, he knows LiLi and Mac should hear the story from his sister instead.

Mama LiLi: *I love you, sweetheart.*

Justin: *I love you, too.*

Reign's presence had kept Justin's anxiety at bay, but now, on his own again, the restless, fretful energy bubbles up and he channels as much of it as he can into catching up on his normal Saturday tasks such as cleaning and laundry until Amelia arrives for dinner.

He opens his door to invite her inside, and she greets him with a smile so beautiful he doesn't wait for her to step through the doorway before he cups her face in his hands and kisses her. Her lips are cool from the winter air, yet the kiss infuses warmth into him and offers a brief respite from the nervous anxiousness continuing to course through his body.

"Hey," Amelia says gently after the kiss and sets her gloved hand atop his. "You okay?"

"Not really," Justin says. "I'm really happy you're here now. And that you're staying tonight."

"Me too. Speaking of which..." She hands him her cane and then pulls the straps of both her duffel bag and purse up and over her head, then trades him her bags for her cane.

Her overnight stay partially contributes to his anxiety because while they've had sex, neither one has yet stayed the night at either of their places. So far, she's seen some of the worst parts of him and hasn't walked away. How much more will she accept? And, if he's being honest, how much more can he adapt? He hasn't dated anyone in almost a year and in the space of two months, he's gotten a promotion, his sister has moved in with him, and they've unboxed a secret he thought would be locked away forever. Maybe starting a relationship is too much.

He sets the idea aside because he doesn't want to process it. He's not sure he's ever liked a woman as much as he does Amelia. Processing that emotion is also something he'd rather not do. Instead, he brings Amelia's bag to his bedroom, then suggests they start dinner. They're making pizza, even though he knows his sister won't be back for it. On the slim chance she returns later that night, he wants the leftovers available for her.

He gets to work on the crust while Amelia prepares onions, peppers, and mushrooms. She tells him about a new patient she saw in the morning, an eight-year-old who'd slipped during her routine on the uneven bars.

"I had to ask her mother to leave because she kept yelling at her daughter to push harder and then at me for not having her daughter do more."

Justin adds water to the bowl with the flour mixture and gently kneads the sticky dough. "Is her mother a physical therapist, too?"

"No. So you can understand why I was frustrated with the situation. That kind of response from the parent often has me worried about the child."

"In what way?"

Amelia scoops up the thin red pepper strips, puts them into a bowl, then gets to work on slicing mushrooms. "I see a lot of child athletes and while most are dedicated and enthusiastic about their sport, some of them don't seem very happy. And I know what you're going to say next."

Oddly, though his line of thought always appears completely logical and obvious to him, most others don't think so. He doubts Amelia will be different. Yet he offers her a chance. "Do you?"

"You're going to say the ones who aren't happy are that way because they're in pain."

Indeed, this is very similar to what he was thinking. "You are almost correct. I was going to say that probably *all* of them are unhappy, but some are good at pretending."

She hip checks him and says, "I am totally correct, you stubborn nitpicker."

He smiles. "I'm a tenacious precisionist."

"Obstinate quibbler."

"Adamant perfectionist."

"Willful stickler."

"Indomitable literalist."

Amelia's eyebrows go up as her eyes get wide. "That is exactly what you are! I concede defeat since you have landed on the precise phrase for this conversation."

Justin nods and adds, "I never mean for it to be a competition." Hugh made up the synonym game back when they were both in high school. It came about when Hugh's mom had him complete hours of test prep for the SAT and ACT. He and Hugh enjoyed the wordplay, but they never deemed anyone a "winner" at it. When Justin's sister joked about allowing Amelia to use her phone, he didn't understand where she got the idea about any rules.

"Hmm," Amelia says, then nods. "Yeah, I guess that's true. I don't think I've ever heard you gloat about getting the last word. Although your brain holds a remarkable amount of words in it, so you do always win."

"But there's nothing to win."

"Justin, my sweet bear," Amelia looks at him and touches his arm and heat rushes through him at her touch, coupled with the new development of using a nickname endearment with him. "I know. Let's move on. Are you ready to tell me about what happened with Lizzie?"

It occurs to him that Amelia has done with him what his own plan had been for his sister. She's eased him into being ready to talk about the hard things. So he does. He gives her the same story he told Reign—leaving out the idea about hypnotism since Reign had solidly discarded it—and when he gets to the part about his sister and the "good one," his anxiety seizes, twisting his stomach, filling his lungs, and contracting his throat.

He steps back from the counter and paces, alternately pulling at his hair and punching his thighs. "It's all my fault. I always ruin things. Why did I let her call herself Beth? Why did I make that promise?"

Arms come from behind him and bind themselves tightly around his chest. He stops pacing, closes his eyes, and breathes deeply once. Twice. A third time. He hears Amelia murmuring against his back. "It's okay, Justin. It's not your fault. It's okay."

"Thank you," he tells her quietly, and she loosens her grip and moves around to face him, still keeping her arms around his torso. He frees his arms and embraces her, lets her heartbeat slow down with his.

He pulls away and asks, "How did you know to do that?"

She shrugs. "I saw Lizzie do it the night I came here for dinner that first time."

He nods. "We should talk more about you approaching me when I start to … freak out." He says the last part with hesitation, not liking the expression, but also recognizing it's what others more readily understand.

"Lizzie says it's not 'freaking out.' That this kind of thing is called a meltdown?"

Justin mulls over Amelia's apparent conversations with his sister, wondering when they've happened and why he's not aware of them. "You shouldn't use the name, 'Lizzie,' She doesn't think that's who she is anymore. And yes, I appreciate you learning about the difference. Most people don't see it or understand it."

She takes his hand and leads him out of the kitchen and onto the couch in the living room. Crash immediately jumps up and curls up on his lap as Amelia sculpts her legs into a pretzel next to him. She performs her own deep breath before saying, "I'm going to be brave here, and be completely honest with you about a couple of things, okay? Because I know you value honest and clear communication."

He nods and even though her statement is one hundred percent accurate, his relationship with Amelia remains tenuous. Her "complete honesty" might lead to her saying he has "too many issues" or he is "too intense" or "overly rigid and sensitive." He has inadvertently revealed more of his "issues" with Amelia than with any other woman he has dated, so logic tells him he's certainly pushed her away from pursuing this relationship anymore. He readies himself for the blow.

"Your meltdown when I was here with Nuria? It was alarming. I knew you lived with anxiety and that something was happening to ramp it up for you, but I didn't expect how quickly it happened and how extreme it was. It scared me because I didn't know if this was a common thing for you or not. The way your sister immediately jumped into action told me it might be an expected reaction for you, and I wondered if I was up to the challenge."

He looks away, no longer brave enough to take her rejection head on. Amelia places her hand on his face and gently turns it back to her.

"I'm not sure if I am, but I want to try because..." She pauses and takes another deep breath. "I really like you. Like, a lot."

Justin's heart rate rises and warmth floods through him. Her words set off fireworks in his brain and thoughts he's bottled up come pouring out. "I like you, too, Amelia. So much. Sometimes I'm scared by how much I like you and I was sure you were about to break up with me. Every time I see you and talk to you, everything around me is better. You're amazing."

Amelia embraces his face and kisses him and the affirmation of their affection for one another launches a deep need for her.

"Sorry, girl," Justin says to Crash as he removes her from his lap, and then pulls Amelia closer as their kisses become more fervent and his hands slip under her shirt.

The growl of his stomach interrupts them and Amelia laughs. "Maybe we should have dinner first."

"Normally, I would agree. But ... I can wait for dinner if you can."

Amelia straddles his lap and wraps her arms around his neck. "Dinner can definitely wait."

Justin's past companions may have thought he lived too rigidly, but they forgot about those ideas during sex, where he proved to be a relaxed and attentive lover. Now, with Amelia, however, they both give in to their urgent need. They shed their clothing and leave it in an abandoned heap. They make it to the bedroom and Justin has the presence of mind to pull back the comforter and sheets on his bed, and then they fall into it. Their lovemaking is fervent and breath-taking. Afterwards, they lie together on their backs, with Amelia's head resting on Justin's outstretched arm.

"Wow," Justin says.

"You got that right. Feel free to let yourself go like that more often."

He smiles, a giddiness dancing inside him. He knows he'll need to figure out what "more often" means to her since the term is too vague for him, but the sentiment settles in.

"Are you okay staying in bed for a little longer?" Amelia asks. "Or should we get back to making dinner?"

"I can lie here with you a little longer."

She turns and snuggles into him. "Good, because I'm hoping you'll tell me more about you and your sisters. Both of them."

The request surprises him less than he would have expected it to. No one has ever asked him to talk about his other sister and he realizes he wants to talk about her and about the three of them together. About when his sisters were babies, and he helped feed and change them and rock them to sleep. About reading them stories and playing Graham Cracker Kingdom. And about what he remembers about Elizabeth, the "real" Elizabeth.

He doesn't remember as much as he thought he would, which makes him think about Reign's words about age and memory. What's important, Justin realizes, is how he feels, and talking to Amelia about those moments and emotions from so long ago offers another arc to an incomplete circle. He almost feels whole.

34

LIZZIE

The only thing I'd revealed to LiLi the evening before was that I'd had a big fight with Justin. She'd let my silence go, and we'd had our hot chocolate and cookies followed up with a dinner of leftover lasagna and a movie before calling it a night.

By the end of a delicious brunch Mac prepared Sunday morning, neither she nor LiLi were having my silence any longer.

"Elizabeth, baby," Mac said, and I gave a small flinch at her use of the name—she'd always used the full name and I had never minded it until this moment—"You've been dancing around your troubles. How about letting us in now?"

"I don't know how. It feels too big."

"Well then, belch it out all at once. We'll piece it all together after it's all out there."

LiLi nodded in agreement. "No context. Just spill it. Better out than in."

I almost smiled at this. LiLi was a kindergarten teacher and has deal with more than her fair share of various kinds of "out."

"Belching it out," though, still daunted me. All my life I'd been running from the real me and chasing after a better version. Saying it out loud would strike down the illusion. *Pay no attention to that girl behind the curtain.*

But where had it gotten me? Failed friendships, trashed careers, and hurting innocent bystanders. Better out than in it was.

"I'm not really Lizzie. Or Elizabeth," I said, my voice shaking. "I mean, I never was. It's the wrong birth certificate. I'm Isabel. Elizabeth—Beth is the one..." I faltered and immediately Mac had one of my hands in hers and LiLi came over to sit next to me and put an arm around me and I finished, "Beth is the one who died in the accident. Not Isabel. Not me."

With the word "me," I broke down again. Saying "me" in conjunction with the name Isabel unlocked something. A jail cell where the secret, the true Isabel, had been caged for twenty-five years.

"Sweetie," LiLi said. "Why do you say that?"

"Because it's true."

"You were only four when you came to us," Mac said. "And it was after a highly traumatic experience. I can see why you might have something like that messing with your head, even now."

I pulled my hand away from Mac's and shook off LiLi's arm as I stood to pace. They thought I was simply misremembering. And, yeah, there was a lot I didn't have straight in my head. But not this. I remembered Justin saying the words over and over. *She was supposed to be the good one.* Then the nurses coming in to pull the curtain closed between our beds, and Justin suddenly drifting off. My adult self realized they likely sedated him. My dad came into the room later. I don't know where he'd been until then and when I thought back on everything now, as an adult...

"Elizabeth, baby—"

"Stop saying that name," I yelled. "I'm not Elizabeth. I'm trying to tell you—"

Mac came to me and laid her hands on my shoulders. "I just

want you to take a breath. You're talking fast and we can't understand what's going through your head."

"Come," LiLi said. "Sit down. Take some deep breaths."

Apparently, I'd been speaking all my jumbled thoughts out loud. I nodded, and Mac led me back to the table.

"We're listening," Mac said. "Breathe for a moment and start again."

I put my elbows on the table and rested my forehead on my palms. "I don't know how to start again. Saying all of that out loud ... it doesn't make any sense, does it? I mean, why do I think anything I remember about that day is real? Except Justin knows, too."

"Knows what, exactly?" LiLi asked.

I lifted my head. "What I've been telling you. That I'm Isabel, not Elizabeth. I've been pretending all my life to be Elizabeth—or at least some incarnation of her."

LiLi and Mac stared at one another, their expressions communicating a silent conversation.

"What is it?" I asked. "You're not going to tell me you knew this all along, too?"

"Liz—sweetheart, no. That's not it," LiLi said.

"I can't believe we missed all the clues," Mac said, shaking her head. "I'm so sorry, baby."

"I don't follow. What clues?"

Mac leaned back in her chair. "You have to understand, when Rod showed up at our door with you two, we'd had very little warning."

"I wouldn't call five hours warning at all, especially for what he ended up asking of us," LiLi added.

"True, but not only that, you kids were shell-shocked in different ways. Justin launched into a full meltdown thirty minutes after your daddy left and you were near catatonic."

"And we knew so little about you," LiLi said. "We'd only met you once, about a few months after you and your sister were born. Rod and I got into a fight, and both he and your mom told us we should never come back."

Mac and LiLi hardly ever talked about my mom and dad. I'd always had the impression they never met my mom and LiLi herself and told me that she and my dad—her brother—weren't on speaking terms. I sat at the kitchen table, making a birthday card for Justin one year and I asked if she ever made cards for her brother.

"I could pretend for you, but I won't," she'd said. "Your dad and I do not share words with one another. Of any kind."

I'd merely nodded. I may have been only eight or nine, but I held no young and innocent fondness for my dad. I didn't know about Justin, but I never brought up the topic of my dad because I didn't want anyone to suddenly decide he should be in our lives again, or that we should go back to him.

Only one other time did I ask after him. It was after I turned eighteen and no longer had to worry about being sent away.

"Have you ever heard from our father? Has he ever asked about us?" I'd asked LiLi.

She'd hesitated, then said, "Once. After your gran died, he asked if you both turned out all right. I told him you were the happiest I'd ever seen you and were well-loved. I also told him he'd better not think of interfering with that happiness."

As I came back from the memories, my dad saying, "I don't need this mess" popped into my head. My dad used that phrase anytime he didn't like how we behaved and I'd bet he said the same thing to LiLi at my gran's funeral.

"What did you fight about?" I asked, returning to LiLi's story about me and Justin arriving at her house. "Back when they told you both to not come back."

"Justin," LiLi said. "I had a student who I later learned was autistic, and while Mac and I were visiting at your house, Justin displayed so many of the same behaviors as my student, that I mentioned it to Rod and Emily. They didn't take it well."

I believed it. "I don't need this mess" had obviously manifested early. I wondered if my parents had listened to LiLi and gotten help earlier, whether things would have been any better for Justin. For all of us.

"When Rod dropped you off all those years ago, he pointed to you two and said, 'Beth and Justin. Emily and the other one didn't survive.' That's what he called your sister. 'The other one.'" LiLi's voice broke and Mac took her hand as LiLi continued. "It was such a devastating punch to the gut. Her precious little life reduced…"

Mac took up the story. "I want to be graceful and say your dad was in shock, but we don't have room for any more lies right now. The point we're trying to get to is that there were clues we dismissed so easily because those first several weeks were some of the most stressful and chaotic ones of our lives. You didn't always respond to your name right away, and Justin sometimes called you Issy, which seemed natural enough to mix up. And other times he would call you Izzibeth. Each time he did that, though, he punched at his head. It was heartbreaking."

An ache surrounded my heart. I heard a voice that was Justin's, yet not quite his voice since I couldn't pull up the full memory. *Want to play magic forest, Issy-Beth?*

"No," I said. "Not Izzibeth. Issy-Beth. Issy was my nickname. Justin put it together when he talked to or about both of us."

"Oh, love," Mac said to LiLi. "I hear it now, do you?"

LiLi breathed out a small, "Oh," and brought her hand to her mouth as she nodded.

"It makes so much sense now, especially since Justin spoke so clearly most of the time," Mac said. "We just assumed he was muddling your full name of Elizabeth."

Mac saying the name made me flinch again.

"Baby, I'm sorry. I didn't mean to hurt you with that."

"I know."

"And then there was the teddy bear," LiLi said. "In amongst

your things—because at least Rod packed up most of your possessions—were two teddy bears. One had an 'E' embroidered on it while the other had an 'I'. You latched on to the bear with the 'I' and we just assumed it reminded you of your sister. Mac," LiLi gasped. "What have we done?"

Mac put her arm around me and reached for LiLi's hand. "We didn't know." Her voice was low and thick. "I'm so sorry, baby. We didn't know."

LiLi released a quiet sob and soon we were all crying and holding each other as though everything had just happened. I cried for Mac and LiLi and their lives turned upside down for two deeply traumatized children they barely knew. I cried for my brother, who held onto a secret on top of his loss and struggles to find sense in his new world. He took so much responsibility to take care of me and protect me.

And for the first time that I could remember, I cried for my sister. For the giggles we no longer had at night when we were meant to be sleeping. For the forts we built and the green M&Ms I traded for her yellow ones. And for the things we never had—trading clothes, doing each other's hair, talking about girls and maybe boys, going to clubs together and going on double dates. Fighting, laughing, and crying together.

In the end, I also cried for Isabel. For Issy, who could never be whoever it was she was meant to be. And for all the times I kept trying to fit into a mold that should have been the same as Elizabeth's—we were identical and it should have been the same mold—I cried for myself.

35

JUSTIN

Justin still hasn't heard directly from his sister on Monday, and his morning swim starts out rough as he works out his anxiety. Even before she moved in with him, they texted each other every day, although during the last year those texts were short and without much substance. When she agreed to move in, however, their daily exchanges resumed with random facts or images about their day. Though he's been the more prolific one, she always responded.

What calms him about halfway through his workout is Amelia swimming in the lane next to him. Since the morning he rejected her suggestion of sharing a lane, he has spent considerable time thinking about if—how—he could swim in the same lane with her after all. The situation will arise again and he's concluded that they can try out a practice swim during a different time of day, outside of his morning routine he relies on. If they run into the scenario of not enough open lanes before then, their compromise is to split their time in the single lane.

He's allowing himself to have hope for his relationship with Amelia. After Hugh died, Justin lost his confidante in matters of his heart. His sister understands almost everything about him, and to say she doesn't understand his yearning for love isn't true and probably not fair. It isn't that he doesn't feel her full support in his hopes, but he isn't sure she fully grasps his need for love. Hugh did because he'd wanted and needed it for himself, too.

He misses Hugh.

Justin sluices through the sadness in his final laps and refocuses on the feeling he had when Amelia told him she really liked him. "Like a lot." The energy boosts him to the end of his workout. As he drinks down the rest of his water, he smiles at Amelia's clumsy flip at the opposite wall. She follows it up with clean, powerful strokes down the lane. He could spend all day watching her swim. Unfortunately, he looks at the time and sees he's dawdled for too long.

Amelia pauses at the end of the pool and glances at the clock. "My sweet bear, you gotta get going, don't you?"

His heart squeezes at the nickname and he wishes he had one for her. His penchant for words and their synonyms should help him, but he hasn't landed on anything that sounds right. "Yeah," he says. "See you tonight?"

She leans over the rope to give him a light, quick kiss. "I'll bring over some fresh ingredients for pizza."

He wants to tell her which specific items to get, but doesn't, knowing it's not something that has to matter. He can adapt.

His expression must convey his restraint, however, because Amelia says, "It's okay. Text me what you want. I'll add on if I see anything extra that appeals to me and put it on my side of the pizza."

He thanks her, but she doesn't hear it, as she's already streamlining into her next lap after pushing off the wall.

36

LIZZIE

Mac and LiLi offered to have me stay with them for a while until I figured things out. I might have taken them up on their offer if I didn't have the nanny job with Sebastian to return to.

My moms sandwiched me in a goodbye hug.

"What name would you like us to call you?" LiLi asked.

"I don't know," I said. "I've spent most of my life not knowing who I really am or want to be. Maybe it doesn't matter what name I choose."

"You know who you are and always have been," Mac said. "The right name will come to you when you embrace that."

I appreciated her confidence and hoped she was right.

I got in my car and texted Justin to let him know I was coming home. I waited a beat, expecting a rapid reply. When nothing came, I double-checked the time. He was probably driving to work. It was just as well. I wasn't ready to talk to him and by the time he got my text, he'd know I couldn't answer all his follow-up texts while I was driving.

The sun was bright, the skies were clear, the temperature was a balmy thirty-one degrees, practically shorts and t-shirt weather for a Minnesotan at the end of mid-winter. I popped on my sunglasses and got going, hoping the bright drive would keep me afloat as I had nothing except me and my thoughts to keep me company for the next four hours.

I'd learned a lot from my moms the day before, after we'd all recovered from our crying session. They pulled out a box of photos, paperwork, and other odds-n-ends. The photos were from their visit when my sister and I were babies. A couple of them included Justin. One photo had him holding one of us in his lap and giving us a bottle. Another had my sister and I lying on our backs on the floor with big smiles as Justin knelt over us with his hands at the side of his face, palms facing us. Peekaboo.

"It was so precious," Mac had said. "But then, because you were babies, one of you got overstimulated and started crying, which started the other one crying, and poor Justin just kept trying to make the game work. He didn't understand why it suddenly stopped bringing smiles. He would yell 'peekaboo' louder, which only made things worse."

It sounded exactly like Justin in all the ways. It made me smile until neither of them said anything else. "What happened next?" I'd asked.

"There was only two of us and three of you. LiLi and I grabbed you and your sister, which left Justin to your mother." I understood the problem. Already she'd not had the patience with him, his vulnerability misunderstood in the face of the far more acceptable vulnerability of a baby's cry.

"So many mistakes," LiLi said, grabbing Mac's hand.

My heart broke a little, as it always did when people pressed down on Justin. Not that Mac and LiLi did, which I'd been quick to reassure them. "You didn't know. And honestly, who knows how Justin would have reacted if you'd tried to work with him instead? He wasn't familiar with you yet."

"You might be right," Mac said. "By the time you came to us, at least his behaviors didn't surprise us. And despite your age difference, he relied on you then as much as he relies on you now. Listen to your heart, baby. It'll tell you everything about where you stand with him, no matter what you're trying to believe."

She hadn't mentioned how much I depended on him, too, though I think they both knew my reliance on Justin, especially given my choice to move in with him when I needed support.

I merged onto the freeway and took in Mac's words. *Listen to your heart.* I had four hours ahead of me to do a lot of listening.

37

JUSTIN

Relief ripples through him when he reads his sister's text after he pulls into the office park lot. He replies immediately.

Homemade pizza tonight?

Then he remembers Amelia is coming over, too.

Okay if Amelia joins us?

There's also leftover pizza in the refrigerator.

Neither Amelia nor I will be offended if you don't want her there tonight.

In case you wanted to talk.

It occurs to him she might not come home for dinner. Her text said she was coming home, but nothing about anything else at all.

Let me know if you'll be home for dinner.

I hope you are. I miss you.

He puts the phone to vibrate and pockets it to stop him from continuing. She's driving and shouldn't be distracted by his texts, plus he needs to get inside to his office. He breathes in a deep, calming breath and releases it slowly before getting out of his car. Work remains a hectic situation. He and his team, in cooperation with their network and web counterparts, fixed the initial mess, but code has a way of leaving stray marks. Errors pop up, some without any anticipation.

Claire from HR pulls in next to him as he locks his door, and he forces himself to wait so they can walk in together. He'd rather simply wave acknowledgement and keep walking in, but she commented once that people might "warm up" to him better—people in technology were intimidating, apparently—if he took a moment to walk in the building with them. It would be a lot easier if it didn't take everyone so long to do it.

Her cheerful enthusiasm when she joins him—after checking her face in the mirror, putting on gloves, grabbing her purse from the front seat, then opening the back door to grab another bag and a pair of shoes—balances out the impatient anxiety. She thanks him for waiting on her and they trade inane "how was your weekend" courtesies and as he holds the door open for her, she hits him with the first curveball piece of news.

"I got an email from Caleb. He's coming back to work later this week. That'll be nice to have a lighter workload again, won't it?"

Justin offers a noncommittal, "hmm," and pulls out his phone, wondering if he somehow missed a message from Caleb. He types in a search, in case he accidentally filed or trashed it, but there is nothing after the one telling him about going on leave. He's not sure why Caleb didn't contact him at the same time. He's also not certain why he isn't happy about the news.

He doesn't spend any more time thinking about Caleb's return, however, when Justin's hand slips on the knob of his office door. He stares at his palm and grunts in disgust. Petroleum jelly. *For fuck's sake.* He walks over to Shane's cubicle, finds it empty, then moves over to Austin's. He holds up his hand.

"Hey, boss," Austin smiles and waves. The careless greeting grates at Justin. He's certain Austin is mocking him and Justin's disappointment sinks deep into himself. He'd thought Austin was changing, distancing himself from Shane and welcoming the time Justin gave to guide and teach Austin. It's been years since Justin has felt like a fool.

"As your colleague, the practical jokes were annoying and petty. As your boss, they are completely unacceptable. Clean up the mess on my door immediately."

Austin's eyes go wide. "What?" He stands and looks closer at Justin's hand, then reaches behind him to grab a handful of tissues and gives them to Justin. "No, I didn't do this. I swear. I wouldn't—" he stops at Justin's glare, and mumbles, "I didn't do this, but yes, I'll take care of it."

As Austin strides away, Yasmin's head pops up from her cubicle and she rests her forearms along the top of the makeshift walls. "If it's any consolation, I don't think Austin had anything to do with this prank."

"Because he said he didn't do it?"

"I hope that's you asking a literal question instead of believing I'm that naïve. No, not because he said so. I don't think he and Shane are getting along with each other, and Austin comes away from meetings with you energized and focused. He stops by my desk and recaps what he learned and talks over what his next steps will be."

Justin nods. "Thank you."

"Yep," she says and sinks back down into her chair. "See you in thirty for our meeting."

※

SHANE ARRIVES LATE TO WORK, which wouldn't normally bother Justin much, except for the petroleum jelly prank and not enough time to confront Shane about it directly before their Monday morning meeting. The meeting accomplishes what it needs to, in spite of Shane inserting comments about how he would do things if he were back on the new project. Justin, Austin, and Yasmin all ignore most of the remarks until the end of the meeting when Shane brings up Caleb.

"I heard Caleb's coming back later this week. I can't wait until we can do things again the way they're supposed to be done."

"Is that why you acted like a twelve-year-old before you left yesterday?" Yasmin asks as she stands, readying to leave the conference room. "Because if that's what things are 'supposed' to be, then I'll be updating my resume."

"Nobody's stopping you from doing that anyway," Shane says.

Yasmin only shakes her head and walks away.

Shane hooks a thumb behind him and turns to Austin. "What's her problem?"

Austin also shakes his head. "You, man."

"Dude, what are—"

"Shane," Justin interrupts. "I'd like to talk with you for a moment."

"I'd rather go back to work."

"Let me clarify. Sit down again, please, and I will talk to you."

Shane rolls his eyes and mutters, "Literally everyone else in the world would recognize sarcasm and not respond with robot language."

"You mentioned Caleb returning, but your supervisor will still be me," Justin says.

"What's your point? I can still take my ideas to Caleb and he can let me do something about them. He can override you."

Shane's not wrong and Justin harbors a pocket of anxiety about the possible override of his authority and decisions. Shane may have technically caused the recent debacle, but all steps leading up to it are on Justin and, ultimately Justin's responsibility. Justin and Caleb have always worked well together, though, with Caleb trusting Justin's strategies.

"My point is that I will no longer tolerate childish behaviors such as practical jokes." Justin gives finger hooks for the air quotes around "practical." The descriptor is highly inaccurate. None of the replacement words for "practical" like "useful," "effective," or "sensible" fit all of the ridiculous and annoying things Shane and Austin have perpetrated.

"The pranks you have done have never been appropriate," Justin continues, "but they are even less so with our new roles. The pranks must stop."

"So, not only are new ideas not welcome, but we also can't have any fun because you don't have a sense of humor. Well, that's just great. Are we done talking? I've got error reports and other busywork a robot assigned to me."

Shane is already standing with his laptop and walks out of the conference room before Justin can respond. With Caleb coming back, at least Justin can get advice about how to handle Shane. To Justin's knowledge, Caleb was never a target for pranks, so possibly that problem is still in Justin's hands.

Justin gathers his laptop and coffee mug and leaves the room, too. He passes by his team's set of cubicles and fortunately, everyone is working peacefully. Once in his office, his phone buzzes. Relief and then disappointment fill him upon seeing his sister's text about going out with Nuria right after nannying. He'd planned on making pizza again when he'd still had the hope of preparing it with his sister. Making it without her no longer appeals to him.

He texts Amelia. *Is it okay if I have dinner with you at your place?*

Thankfully, her reply is immediate. She is between appointments. *Yes! We can still make pizza, but I also have ingredients for soup, which might be perfect for a snowy evening in.*

Snowy evening in. Dread crawls into him as he leaves his office to find a window. The snow falls in large, fluffy flakes and the temperature hovers right above freezing, which means the roads are more likely to be slushy instead of icy. He wants to cancel dinner with Amelia except he worries he's dictated too many of their plans lately and he's trying to show her he can adapt to her needs and wishes. He *wants* to adapt, and frustration bubbles inside him about how difficult it is.

I can do this, he thinks. The drive won't be as bad as it was when driving down to Faribault and if he leaves work on time, rush hour will keep travel slow. Amelia doesn't live far away and the best part will be seeing her at the end of the commute. He breathes in and out slowly and opens the weather app on his phone. The snow is expected to taper off by six o'clock. Already he's tamped down the anxiety and turns to go back to his office and focus on work.

"Worried about the snow melting in your joints and making you rusty?" Shane's voice calls out.

Justin doesn't offer any sign of recognition and keeps walking.

38

LIZZIE

I wasn't ready to talk to Justin. He was trying with me, and I didn't mean to hurt him or reject him. It wasn't about him. It was about me. And I should have told him that, but it was faster—easier—to put him off instead.

Thanks for pizza. I'm going to Nuria's after nannying today. Not sure what time I'll be home after that.

I closed my eyes and swallowed down guilt for my shallow-sounding text. While he was accustomed to me not replying to every question or comment he sent me via text, he'd fixate on my avoidance of his emotional pleas. Tomorrow. I'd be ready tomorrow.

I'd started with sun in Madison, but by the time I reached St. Paul, clouds filled the sky and a light snow flurried from those clouds. I trudged into the apartment building from my car and inwardly whined about the unending days of snow and cold. I looked at the stairwell, and then the elevator. Weariness tempted me to take the easy way up. Instead I turned to the stairs, chastising myself for balking at only four flights of steps.

I heard Reign's voice in my head saying training doesn't only happen for thirty minutes a day. "Getting fit is a mindset." I'd been trying to reinvent myself, but taking up running again had been more about returning to a "me" that only I saw. Running used to be the time to live inside myself and not worry about anyone else's expectations or fitting inside a box of who Liz-Ellie-Betsy-Lizzie should be. This time around, though, it felt a little more like I was running away from that inner me.

I needed to rethink the mindset.

Reign was locking up their apartment, carrying a large duffle when I reached Justin's door. They gave me a big grin when they saw me.

It was hard to resist. I smiled back. "Hey, Reign. Going somewhere?"

They looked down at their bag and nodded. "Yeah, I'm off to stay with my dad for a few days. I need to remember what unconditional love truly feels like."

"I think that's great. You deserve that."

"I do. Say, you're Justin's sister, right?"

I tilted my head at them, wondering at the question. Then I caught the wink and went along with the game. "Yeah, I moved in a couple of months ago. You must be Reign."

"That's me. I don't remember your name?"

I now understood the ruse as a re-creation of when we first met in this exact spot. "I'm not sure, yet. You seem like someone who could help me find one."

"Hmm, probably that's left best up to you, but I'd be happy to be a sounding board." They held out their hand. "It's great to meet you at last. Justin's told me so much about you."

"You, too."

I shook their hand, and they pulled me into a hug and whispered into my ear. "I can't wait to meet you again when I get back."

After wishing Reign well, I slipped inside the apartment and took a deep breath. Justin's place held a comforting sense of familiarity, and I appreciated the need for routine and predictability. A lot had happened in the past few days and for all the disorientation, Justin's home provided grounding.

I'd need it. In an hour I'd be heading out for my nannying job with Sebastian, and things had not gone well with the "hand-off" on Friday. I'd stayed later at Paula's request and tried to stick to as much dinner routine as possible with Sebastian, which might have gone better if there had been a plan for dinner at all. Sebastian and I had navigated it pretty well with basically repeating his afternoon snack and embellishing it with more of the food groups. I filled a muffin pan with different options, telling him to choose at least one thing from each row of the pan. He'd enjoyed carefully choosing and arranging the finger foods on his own partitioned plate.

Then Simon came home in a loud rush, dumping bags of takeout from a local Greek restaurant onto the table and then picking up the muffin pan, only to toss it unceremoniously across the kitchen counter, commenting that they didn't live in poverty. I hadn't time to even parse his interpretation of our meal set-up because the disruption and dismissal of Sebastian's dinner set off a chain of Sebastian crying, Simon criticizing me, and me trying to put myself as a wall between Simon and his son so that I could calm Sebastian down.

Simon had claimed "he could take it from there," so I left. I didn't know how things were going to go today. Sebastian and I would be fine. It was his parents I wasn't sure about.

I reheated the leftover pizza Justin had left for me and stood at the counter to eat while Crash sat on the other side, on top of the dining table, staring at me.

"Sebastian's parents are in denial," I told Crash, since no one else was around. She continued staring. How long could a cat go before they had to blink? "They've got this great kid, but keep pretending all of his character traits are a phase or attention-seeking. And he's five, so of course some things he does are for attention. The rest are all who he is. They've only got the one kid. I wish they saw all of Sebastian's potential and figured him out instead of putting the expectation on him to change."

Crash flicked her tail, and a flash of something like a blink happened with her eyes. She didn't settle in to listen to me like I'd seen her do with Justin, but nor did she growl, hiss, or run away. Tiny bits of progress.

Bite-sized changes were what Sebastian needed to survive in a neurotypical world, and his parents were the best people to offer a safe space to experiment and practice with those changes. First, they had to be willing to consider Sebastian's need. Their house reflected adaptations to Sebastian, except they all centered on reactions to his behaviors rather than encouraging his development.

I'd told Nuria I wasn't qualified to diagnose Sebastian, and it wasn't up to me to teach or change his parents. That remained true. My problem with all of my previous jobs had never been about my work with the kids. The issues came about from having to deal with the adults in the kids' lives. I had no patience with parents and teachers who refused to raise, support, and teach children instead of the *idea* of children.

When I left Meadowfields Elementary, it was due to my inability to tolerate the teachers complicit in Skylar's accident. I had taken much of the blame for it, and while the mantra of "it's nobody's fault—accidents happen" floated everywhere, the real truth was that we were all responsible, and I hadn't been quiet about it.

I cleaned up my dishes and bundled up once more to head out to Sebastian's house. Crash sauntered over and casually sat and stared at me again as I opened the door.

"Wish me luck," I told her.

39

JUSTIN

By late afternoon, Justin's anxiety remains a low hum in his gut. He's grateful for an office with a door, but wishes it also had a window. He's twice gone to the window near his team's cubicles and twice had to listen to Shane offer some kind of irritating comment about not trusting that they're all working or "yep, the outside world still exists, dude." From anyone else, the term, "dude," doesn't bother him, but from Shane, it's like a cheese grater running down his back. For his next snowfall check, he chooses a window far away from Shane.

As he gazes through the glass—the snow has stopped and started, which adds to his uncertainty rather than offer him a solid read on how the weather will be at the end of the day—Justin also considers he hasn't yet heard directly from Caleb about his return. It strips away a level of self-confidence. Justin's transition into his new position hadn't been smooth and Caleb has surely heard about the mistakes. Justin's handling of each mistake, however, has been commendable. Experience tells him that bad news travels faster than good, and negativity easier to believe than positivity.

Shortly after returning to his office, Austin stops by. "Justin? Can I talk to you for a second?"

Justin nods and Austin shuts the door behind him and sits in front of Justin's desk. Justin doesn't say anything, because Austin is the one who requested to talk to him. Austin also doesn't say anything.

After seeing Austin start to fidget, Justin asks, "What did you want to talk to me about?"

"So, well, I think I saw something that I wasn't meant to see, but I'm also happy I saw it. Well, not exactly happy, but probably it's good that I saw it? Except I'm not sure what to do about it, but I also thought you should know."

"Are you asking me a question?"

Austin shifts in his chair. "I don't know. Maybe?"

Justin concentrates on each of Austin's statements. "You saw something that may or may not be good. Yes?"

"It's not good, but I think it's good that I saw it."

"Okay. Do I need to know what you saw? Is that what I should know?"

Austin breathes out a deep sigh and nods. "Yes, I think you definitely do."

Justin is a patient person, but with the way his day has gone so far, he has an urge to shake Austin into making his point or request or whatever this is. *This*, Justin thinks to himself, *is why Caleb is worried.* Justin has little to no experience in managing people. Caleb would have figured out already what was going on.

"How am to know if you don't give me more information?"

"Yeah," Austin nods. "Fair, sorry. I'm nervous because ... okay, see, I know I've kind of been an asshole towards you in the past and gone along with things, even when it didn't always feel right, you know?"

"Yes."

"I'm pretty sure this thing is worse, but also ... maybe it could be bad in some way, if I tell you, too."

"Austin. Get to the point."

Austin's words come out fast and all run together. "Yasmin got an email from Shane that said, 'Hope you like being Justin's bitch.'"

Knots immediately form in Justin's stomach and something must change in his expression because Austin continues to speak quickly. "Right? And I asked her about it, wondering if I read it right, and she said it was nothing. That Shane kept sending her messages like that to see if he could rattle her and that it was stupid—"

"He's sent more than one of this kind of message?"

"That's what she said, but I don't know what was in the other messages and she made it sound like it wasn't a big deal. Except, maybe it is? It's different for women than it is for men, right?"

"It's not different, but you are correct, that it is a big deal. Thank you for telling me about it. I will figure out what to do next."

"Okay." Austin taps his fists on top of the chair arms. "Good. That sounds good."

Justin waits, expecting Austin to leave. Instead, Austin remains, now tapping his fingers on the chair arms.

"Is there something else I should know?" Justin asks.

"I'm sorry."

"For telling me about the email messages?"

"No. For everything else."

Justin wants to believe he knows what 'everything else' is. That it's for all the times Austin has 'gone along' with things. For joining in on pranks. For laughing at Justin during the times he didn't catch a joke that everyone else did. He learned long ago to never assume good intentions.

And if Justin is right after all, then he deserves to hear Austin be explicit about what his apology refers to. "Go on."

"I've been an immature prick to you and I'm sorry for all the stupid practical jokes. I'm sorry for not showing you and Caleb that I want to learn from you. I thought Shane could teach me stuff, but the way you do it makes me remember how much I love the powerful intricacies of code. I hope you'll keep teaching me."

It's more than Justin expected. A part of him doubts the full sincerity of Austin's words since he might only be trying to distance himself from the current situation. Yet Austin is young—about ten years Justin's junior—and most people Austin's age don't offer these kinds of confessions. He decides to take Austin at face value.

"Thank you for the apology, Austin. Yes, I'll keep teaching you."

When Austin finally leaves, Justin faces the problem of Shane's harassing emails to Yasmin. He told Austin he'd figure out what to do when in reality, he has no idea of how to start. He considers checking in with HR, but where has that ever gotten him in the past? He's filed numerous reports to them about Shane, and nothing has been done. All Justin needs is evidence, and he has access to their servers, including the email server, so he can find it himself.

He starts there, doing a search for all messages from Shane to Yasmin, then narrows them down to ones originating from Shane. Of those, he discovers around a dozen messages that disparage her ethnicity, gender, and in some cases, crudely insinuate a sexual relationship between her and Justin. With each message he reads, his anxiety increases, but anger joins alongside it. He prints all the messages, despite the bile that creeps up his throat at giving the words a hard-copy showcase. It will be a pleasure to shred them later.

A pinprick in the back of his mind tries to reason with him

to wait, but his rage towards Shane overshadows it. He walks out of his office and straight to Shane's cubicle.

"I believe in due process, so I will offer you one chance to explain yourself." Justin slaps the stack of printed emails next to Shane's keyboard.

Shane looks at the top paper on the stack and laughs.

Justin's blood pressure jumps so rapidly, he knows he's close to his personal danger zone. He doesn't care. He is done with Shane. And Shane is about to be done with All Choice Care.

"That's your explanation?" Justin asks, his voice low and even. "Laughter?"

"Yep. What are you going to do about it? Ignore me and walk away?"

"You're fired, Shane. You may leave now and schedule a time to return for your personal items, or you can take ten minutes now to gather them and then leave for good." Justin doesn't know if ten minutes is a proper amount of time or not, not having looked up any All Choice policies, which sends a red flag from that pinprick of reason he'd ignored earlier. He just knows he won't be able to stand any longer than that to look at this asshole of a human being. Douchebag. Jerk. Dirtbag. Creep. Scum.

Shane jumps to his feet, sending his chair spinning and banging into the desk. "You can't fire me. Only Caleb can do that since he hired me."

Could this be true? Justin worries. The red flag moves forward in his consciousness as it occurs to him that in his haste to gather evidence, he's failed to consider a careful review of any company policies and procedures about what he can and cannot do. Or what he is supposed to do. He let his emotions skip over all the necessary steps to effectively remove an employee and now he will look incompetent. He works to take a slow breath in and out, pushing away the low buzz that starts in his head.

"Which option, Shane? Take everything with you now? Or leave and make an appointment for collecting your items later?"

"This is fucking bullshit. I did all the work and this fucking diversity hire gets all the credit?"

The buzz increases in volume and a tingling travels through Justin's limbs. He manages to tell Austin to call building security before the fog in his head grows thicker. He's done things in the wrong order. Skipped steps he should have known to do.

"Put your badge and keys on your desk and leave, now," Justin says. Or he thinks he says that. He's losing a full awareness of his surroundings and needs to get away. His hands clench and he taps them on the sides of his thighs as though to force his legs to move, but he remains rooted in place. He hums, wanting to cover the sound of the buzz in his ears.

There are more people standing near them. Justin can't distinguish the voices. They are fuzzy and fading into the background.

"... *are you doing?*"

"*Firing your ass ...* "

"... *security ...* ?"

"... *robot's broken.*"

"What is *wrong with him?*"

And then, finally, somehow, he is moving. As they walk away from the crowd, a voice near his ear says, "It's okay, Justin. You're going to be okay. You're going to be okay."

40

LIZZIE

"I'm so sorry about the mix-up last Friday regarding dinner," Paula said when I got to her house. "I didn't realize I forgot to tell you about Simon bringing food home."

For a moment, I'd considered not mentioning how rude Simon had been when he came home. Calling out others has been my downfall more than once. Then I remembered Sebastian's reaction to the rapid changeover and tried for a diplomatic response with an allowance that Simon also probably felt the stress and chaos of a schedule shift.

"Yeah," I said. "It was not a great transition for any of us and was hardest on Sebastian."

Paula sighed. "He's always had a tough time with last minute changes. Lately it seems like it's every little change, though. This past weekend has been exhausting. He's spent much of today in the fort you set up last week."

"It's a safe, low-sensory zone for him."

"A what?"

"A place with no distractions that might normally overload his senses."

Paula nodded, but I wasn't sure she was really paying close

attention anymore as she moved around to pack an oversized purse with shoes, a bottle of water, and snacks, then put on her boots and coat.

"Okay. I only have paperwork waiting for me at the office today, and Simon's last surgery should be over by now, so I expect we'll both be home a little earlier than usual if post-op goes smoothly."

Well, at least I didn't lose my temper, despite some lingering annoyance. I said goodbye and searched for Sebastian. I stopped at his bedroom entrance. My first thought: chaos. No wonder he'd been living in his fort. His room had toys, knickknacks, and a few clothes strewn everywhere on the floor. A couple of spots looked to be toys in some stage of play. The rest of the room had the markings of tantrum or meltdown.

I navigated to Sebastian's fort and lied down on my stomach, propping myself up on my arms and peeking through the fort's door. Sebastian sat with a camping-type lantern, building a structure with magnet tiles. Construction was one of his favorite things to do. His creations often were homes for pigs with ramps to upper levels since it was easier for pigs than steps.

"Sebastian, my friend. How are you today?"

"Okay. My room is messy, so I'm in here."

"Makes sense. I'd want to do the same thing."

"You can come in, too."

A sweet offer, inviting me into his private sanctuary. I scooted myself forward on my stomach. It wasn't quite tall enough for me to sit inside comfortably, so the upper half of my body would have to do.

"Mami says if I make the mess, I have to clean it up."

"Yep, that sounds about right."

"It's ginormous."

I grinned at the word. Accurate. "I can help you."

"Mami helped, but stopped."

"Why did she stop?"

"She said I have to clean, too."

Teasing out stories like this from kids—all kids—took patience. I made a guess. "When I see a big mess, sometimes I feel overwhelmed. Do you know what 'overwhelmed' means?"

He shook his head.

"It's when something is ginormous and you don't know how to start. We'll clean your room in small steps. But first, tell me about what you're building."

He gave me all the details of his maze for pigs, and then we tackled the cleaning. We didn't finish, because it really was quite a lot, but we organized different sections for him to work on later. We watched an episode of Peppa Pig as a reward, and afterward, Sebastian told me all about the dinner they were going to have. Simon was going to make spaghetti and Sebastian liked having spaghetti at home because they all got to put on their own sauce, which meant they could put it on their own way and exactly the right amount. They would have breadsticks, too.

Unfortunately, Simon came home with yet another different dinner plan. He'd texted to say he was running behind because of the weather, but would only be a few minutes late. He didn't tell me about the change of dinner plans, which he wouldn't, of course, because dinner wasn't part of my shift. And if Sebastian hadn't told me all about what he'd expected, it might not have bothered me so much when Simon breezed in with a pizza box in his hands.

Or used all the names for Sebastian that he didn't like.

"Hey, Seb, buddy! Look what I brought home for dinner tonight! One of your favorites, cheese pizza!"

"Are we having that and spaghetti with garlic breadsticks?" Sebastian asked, his eyes wide with surprise.

Simon laughed as he toed off his shoes and set the box on the kitchen table. "That would be a lot of food, buddy. No, I'm too tired to cook tonight, so pizza it is!"

Sebastian slid off the couch to approach his dad. "Sebastian," I called to him, hoping I wasn't too late to divert what was about to happen next. "Let's figure things out in your fort. We can—"

"You said we were having spaghetti and garlic breadsticks today! Not pizza." Already Sebastian's volume had increased.

"I know, buddy, but—"

"NO THANK YOU, BUDDY."

"Seb...astian, yelling a nice word doesn't make it nice anymore."

Points to Simon for keeping himself calm, so far. Except then Sebastian looked at the pizza box and yelled again. "It's the wrong color. This isn't the pizza I like." He grabbed the box and slammed it to the floor.

That's when Simon lost his cool. I didn't really blame him. It's hard to keep it together in the face of a kid who challenged you, especially after a long work day. "Sebastian, enough. Return the pizza box to the table and then go take a time out."

I moved to stand a little behind Sebastian, readying for his tirade to sweep things off tables and shelves, in case we couldn't turn this around. I wished we had his stuffed pig nearby, but I didn't have time to grab it.

Sebastian flapped his arms and stomped his feet with the words, "you said spaghetti," on repeat.

"What's the real name of the Metallica pig, Sebastian?" I asked.

"Pick up the box and go take a time out, Sebastian."

"The pig's name isn't really Metallica, like your aunt Nuria says, is it?"

"Sebastian, you heard me."

"No," I told Simon. "He doesn't hear either of us right now. He's in a spiral. Can you go grab his stuffed pig?"

Simon growled in frustration. "And reward him for his behavior?"

"Would you rather he knocked everything off shelves and tables? The different pig noise might cut through the static he's hearing right now."

He tightened his jaw and said through clenched teeth, "Fine. Where is it?"

"In his fort, in his room."

I tried soothing tones and pig facts I remembered Sebastian sharing with me until Simon returned with the pig. He pressed the button and when Sebastian didn't stop, I asked Simon to do it again. Sebastian's behavior wasn't escalating, so this intervention had a chance of success. By the third time Simon pressed the button, Sebastian quieted and reached for the stuffed pig. Simon held it just beyond Sebastian's reach.

"What do you say?"

Sebastian stared blankly at his dad, arms outstretched. We were about to have a next level meltdown. *For fuck's sake.* I yanked the pig from Simon and handed it to Sebastian, who hugged it tightly and dropped to sitting on the floor right where he'd stood. He rocked with his pig and pressed the button. I wanted to scoop him up and hide us both away in his calming fort.

Looking at Simon, I almost went there myself. He was livid. A part of me knew I had crossed a line. The rest of me didn't care.

"You are here to help us out when we can't be here for our child," Simon said, speaking in sharp-edged word enunciation. "Not to act like a child yourself."

"My concern is for Sebastian, first and foremost, so I'll do what I need to in order to help him," I said, my words equally clipped.

"He needs to learn appropriate behavior and instead you modeled highly inappropriate behavior. That does *not* help him."

"He's not going to remember most of what happened because *you* didn't encourage or support him with anything from the second you stepped through that door upending his whole sense of order and expectation."

Simon blew out a long, slow breath and looked away, then down at the pizza box on the floor. I closed my eyes for a moment, searching for grace. Sebastian's behaviors were surely not new, but Simon was tired, and it was hard to find patience for something you expected to go over well.

"I don't understand why he has to make everything so hard," Simon said. "Why can't he act like other normal kids?"

I could have forgiven him for being angry with the way I snatched the pig from his hands. I could have forgiven him for his frustration at one of his son's favorite foods not getting the hoped-for response. With the use of the words, "normal kids," however, I nearly watched my grace tumble away. I reeled it back in and chose my words carefully.

"Everything he does is normal. It's normal for *him*. He's not trying to 'make things hard.' He is simply attempting to make sense of his world. If you can't take the time to learn this about him, then all he will keep learning is that he doesn't fit and if you think that is hard for you, a grown-ass adult who understands how to navigate life, imagine how it all is on your five-year-old son." Well, maybe the use of "grown-ass" wasn't totally grace-filled, but I didn't regret any of the other words.

"Do you have children?" he asked.

What a nonsensical question. "No."

"I think we're done here."

Done for today? Done forever? I didn't know. If I was going to lose this job, at least I hadn't gotten anyone injured this time and I spoke my truth.

41

LIZZIE

Nuria had texted earlier to cancel our plans tonight as she forgot about agreeing to help her mom with a project. It was just as well since I didn't know how she'd take me telling off her brother-in-law and wanting to do the same with her sister. I sat in my car in a store parking lot near Sebastian's house, watching my windshield wipers move back and forth, slowly developing a light layer of slushy ice.

I'd told Justin I wasn't coming home right away because I wasn't ready to talk. I still wasn't, at least not about the whole Elizabeth-Isabel thing. And I didn't want to admit to him that I might have lost yet another job, but the certainty that he would understand and not judge me beckoned me to return to his place. To home.

I texted him to let him know I would be around for dinner after all, but he didn't have to change any plans. I'd eat whatever.

I added on, *The roads aren't too bad, but lmk if you want me to pick you up.*

Given that the last time I drove in snowy weather I'd almost killed us both, the offer might not have been helpful. I hopped out of the car to clear away the windshield wiper buildup and hoped for the best back at home. If I had to face Justin with all the other stuff when I returned ... well, I guessed I'd simply have to do it.

❄

I WAS STILL SHAKING off snow as I walked down the hall to the apartment. I unlocked the door and pushed it open, pausing for a moment to look at Reign's door, my shoulders drooping forward slightly in disappointment that they were gone. Reign would have made for a great buffer. When I turned back to slip inside Justin's place, I felt and then saw Crash fly past my legs and disappear around the corner in the hall. I heaved out a sigh and then cursed when I didn't see any lights on inside the apartment, meaning I would have to try to fetch the little heathen on my own. I pocketed my keys, but quickly shed my coat and bag. I kept my boots and gloves on, the latter for self-protection.

I followed in the direction she darted, and as I rounded the corner, I almost ran into some guy who looked up from his phone and said, "hey, is that your cat I just saw go into the stairwell?"

"Yeah, did you see if she went up? Or down?"

He shrugged, looked at his phone again, and continued walking.

Right. No wonder Justin didn't like any of our neighbors.

I went into the stairwell and called out for Crash. I heard the faint meow and my heart sank, already knowing where she was. I crouched down to the broken maintenance wall plate, shone my phone flashlight in and, as expected, encountered two yellow eyes staring back at me.

Meow.

"Oh, Crash. Why?" I fell back against the wall and rested my head on top of my raised knees. Thinking of the last time I had to hunt her down, she probably dashed out of the apartment in search of Justin. He wasn't home during a time she expected. Justin likely headed to Amelia's after work. Still, it wasn't like him not to text back.

I tilted my head to the side and checked my phone. Six-thirty. He'd been working later in the past few weeks and if he was commuting now to Amelia's, it would take him a bit with the weather, especially since he took side roads when driving through snow. His logic argued there was less unpredictable traffic on side streets versus my argument that well-traveled and earlier plowed main roads made for safer travel.

Regardless, my throat grew tight at the realization that it was up to me to retrieve Crash. My first plan was to grab her treats from the apartment, except I was worried she'd decide to get out on her own after all and find somewhere else to hide before I returned. It would likely be a fruitless attempt, anyhow, as she'd never come to me before when offering treats.

I can do this, I told myself. I had my flashlight so it wouldn't be completely dark and all I had to do was reach in far enough to grab the scruff of Crash's neck. *Easy peasy.* I didn't exactly have claustrophobia, because I was fine in elevators and small spaces, but the combination of dark and the potential for no easy escape produced anxiety. I had no intention of squeezing myself fully into the tiny access space.

I set my phone just inside the narrow opening and closed my eyes to visualize the interior as open and spacious. I took slow breaths in and out and when I opened my eyes again, my heart ignored everything my brain said and raced into a full gallop. I shivered when Crash gave a tiny, plaintive, meow.

"Okay, girl, it's okay. I'm sorry I'm not your person, but I'm his sister, so that means we're all family." Family. It was true. Justin was the most important person in my life. Always had been, and with how much Justin loved this witchy cat, I loved her too. Begrudgingly, but I did. I took that knowledge with me as I inserted myself a few inches into the maintenance space.

My breathing shallowed and suddenly, all I heard was the rush of wind in my ears. We weren't in an exterior wall and it didn't feel like a wind tunnel, but as I reached toward Crash and said, "C'mon, girl, crawl towards me, okay?" my chest and lungs also seized as I heard Justin's voice so many years ago.

We're gonna crawl through the window, okay? Watch for broken glass and follow me so you go the right way. Away from the water.

What about Mommy? Is Beth already out there?

Just c'mon, okay?

I yanked myself out of the crawl space quickly and gasped in the warm air from the stairwell. *Oh, Beth,* I thought, and my eyes stung from the crawlspace dust and the sharp memory. *And poor Issy,* I also thought, as I put my hands to my face to wipe away tears for my young self who had no idea what truly lay ahead for me after escaping the car.

Two amazing aunts-turned-mothers, that's what. They never gave us any impression that we were an unasked-for burden. And despite my doubts about myself and all to come in my life, it always included a brother who was there for me in all the ways I needed him. I might not have been meant for teaching, but Justin kept reminding me that I remained an unapologetic advocate for kids who needed adults to understand and believe in them.

A low rumble sounded near me as soft paws pressed against my thighs while I knelt in front of the crawlspace, my face still in my hands. I moved my hands away to see Crash's tri-colored face nosing up at me. She gave a tiny meow. I scooped her into my arms and snuggled her into my face and neck, sinking into her softness and the comforting rhythm of her purr.

"Thank you, Crash. Thank you for seeing me."

42

JUSTIN

Justin sees Yasmin in a chair near the door when the fog lifts, and he pauses his pacing. She sits with her legs crossed, arms also loosely crossed over her knee. She holds her phone in such a way that suggests a readiness to use it, but not actively doing so.

"Have you been taking video of me?" Justin asks, his voice quiet and uncertain.

"What? No, of course not." She taps on her phone and turns to show her camera app to Justin, then taps to show her files. "Clear."

"Thank you for showing me. You didn't have to do that."

"I definitely did. I know I'd want someone to prove it to me." She tips her head towards the door. "And just so you know, I heard Nihal demanding everyone give him their phones as soon as he got back out there after escorting you here."

Justin collapses into another chair and rubs a hand along his jaw. "I don't know if I would have thought to do that." He remembers the addition to their handbook about the policy, stating no videos of any All Choice Care employees may be recorded on the premises or at any company-related event unless it is for authorized, promotional purposes. It is Nihal, in fact, who added it, among several other policies related to social media and privacy issues.

Yasmin shrugs. "Me neither. Then again, I wouldn't have done an email scrape without HR oversight."

Justin can't tell whether she's pointing out his action out of approval, disapproval, or simply stating a fact. "Will you elaborate on that statement, please?"

"I would have appreciated a heads-up about what you were going to do."

"Why?"

Yasmin doesn't answer right away. Justin wishes she would move her chair back over by his desk. Positioned like she is at the door, he feels as though he's under guarded watch, which he supposes he is, and that scratches at long ago wounds of being locked in his room, left to his own devices to work out why everything spiraled out of control.

"Look," Yasmin says. "I know Austin went straight to you after he saw the email I got from Shane. Then an hour later you come out and fire him. I put two and two together, and I think since it involved me, I should have had a say in how it got handled."

It's Justin's turn to pause before answering. "Shane's actions directly violated company policies and expectations. It's the supervisor's responsibility to take appropriate action."

"But it could have been in the privacy of your office instead of in front of everyone while he yelled out insults about me."

Justin ducks his head down and focuses on more deep breaths. Justin had been so angry, so fed up with the extent of Shane's offensive behaviors, that he hadn't taken the time to work through any sort of plan or process at all.

He raises his head again. "You're right. I'm sorry. What I did ... how I ... it's not how I usually work through a problem."

Yasmin nods. "Thank you. I appreciate you really hearing

what I said." She tilts her head slightly and fiddles with one of her small hoop earrings. "From what I've seen, axing Shane was probably a long time coming. It's not like I'm sad to see him go."

"Why didn't you come to me with what was happening?"

She laughs, but it doesn't sound to Justin like a genuine laugh. It sounds like the kind of laugh he gets when he says or asks something, indicating he's missed a joke. His body compresses and his mind pulls closed metaphorical doors as he bows his head down once more. He doesn't have the energy to deal with any more landmines.

"Shit, Justin," Yasmin says as she moves her chair closer to Justin. "I'm sorry, too, because I know now I could have come to you. I'm only still getting to know you and I haven't really been able to trust past supervisors with this kind of thing. IT can be a pretty shitty environment for women."

"Yes, that's true," Justin agrees. "What's happening out there? Am I being fired, too? Is that why you're keeping watch over me?" It occurs to him that of the many things he didn't think through, making sure Shane no longer had access to any All Choice files and accounts should have been taken care of. Maybe this is why Yasmin was sitting by the door inside his office. Making sure Justin doesn't access anything.

Someone knocks on the door.

"Would someone knock and wait for permission to enter if you were being fired?" Yasmin asks, smiling, and the smile does more to ease Justin's mind than anything else.

Justin gets up and opens the door to Nihal.

"May I?" Nihal gestures to enter.

"Yes, of course."

Nihal comes in, thanks Yasmin for making sure Justin was okay, then suggests she take the next day off as comp time.

"I'll bank that one for later, if you don't mind," Yasmin says.

"Honestly, it will be a breath of fresh air working tomorrow without Shane. See you tomorrow, bosses."

Nihal closes the door behind her and turns to Justin. "Tell me. How are *you* doing?"

"I'm feeling a bit like a mental hospital patient about now. I'm fine. I'm sorry you had to come in and take over for the mess I was in."

Nihal sits in the chair Yasmin had occupied. He raises an ankle to rest on his opposite knee. "I don't mean to treat you like you're fragile, Justin, but to be honest, it *was* a mess, and you definitely were not doing well. I'd like you to take my concern for what it is. I care about how you're doing."

Justin appreciates the honest assessment, despite it exposing a part of him he's always worked so hard at hiding. "Meltdowns haven't been a regular part of my life for a long time and it hasn't happened at work in years." It's been concerning how often he's reached this point in recent weeks. He should have scheduled an extra appointment with Alonso. He strokes his jaw and offers his own current evaluation for Nihal. "The work situation these past few weeks has been stressful at times."

"Well, that sounds like a vast understatement. I'm guessing you haven't had to fire anyone before."

"No."

Nihal nods and gives a slight smile. "My offer to you is the same as it was to Yasmin. Take tomorrow off."

"Thank you, but I'd rather face everyone sooner rather than later." Justin doesn't add that he already fears the damage has been done. That he's come across as unstable and incompetent. He might be okay with his team, but he's not so sure about the others.

Nihal moves his leg back to the floor and leans forward. "I'm going to share a little secret with you."

"I'd rather not be privy to any more secrets."

"No, don't worry. This one will probably make you feel better. And it's not really a secret. The first time I ever managed a team of people, I was absolutely terrible at it. I messed up a huge order and when it became clear that it was my fault, I cried. In front of my boss and in front of almost my entire team. It was humiliating."

Somehow, Nihal's story does not help Justin feel better. What happened to Nihal sounds awful. Worse than what happened to Justin, although when he examines that thought, he realizes what Nihal is trying to do.

"The good news," Nihal continues, "is that they fired me on the spot."

"How was that good news?"

"I didn't have to come back the next day and face everyone, which would have been truly awful, especially since I'd cost the company a lot of money. I would have fired me, too."

This man, Justin thinks, *is baffling*. Nihal must notice Justin's expression and silence because he bursts out into loud laughter. "I am the worst at figuring out how to talk to you, aren't I? My point is that what happened with you is not as bad as you think. What people are really going to remember and appreciate is that *you* did the firing of someone who needed to go. What you did was for all the right reasons, even if it got a bit bungled in the execution. Take tomorrow off or don't. Either way, I have every confidence you're going to come out ahead in the long run."

There's another knock on the door and Nihal stands. "We'll debrief tomorrow, yeah?" He opens the door to leave and Justin's heart skips upon seeing Amelia.

"Amelia? What are you doing here?"

Nihal sends a huge smile Justin's way and gives him two thumbs up after he moves past Amelia. "Or Wednesday if you decide to take tomorrow off after all."

"Your sister and I have been worried sick about you." Amelia comes in and puts her hands around Justin's face. "And here you are, still just at work."

Justin reaches into his pocket for his phone, only to find it empty. He glances around quickly and sees it resting on his desk. When he grabs it, he lets out a soft, "Oh." There are so many messages from both Amelia and his sister. Not a "Justin" amount, but for them, a lot. Warmth fills him knowing his sister is home and waiting for him while at the same time nervousness builds up over how he's worried her. Lizzie's text about the roads and snow suddenly hit him in the gut. He shoots off several texts in a row.

I'm sorry for not replying.

I'm okay.

Work blew up. (Not literally.)

Amelia's here. I'll be home soon.

We can make pizza.

Exhaustion slams into him, and he realizes he's not okay, though. He stares at the phone, waiting for his sister to text back, which she does moments later.

I'm glad you're safe. Let's save pizza for tomorrow.

His body sags in relief at her suggestion, but mostly for the fact that she will still be there.

Amelia's arm slides around his back, and he leans gently into her.

"Work was pretty terrible today," he tells her.

"I'm so sorry. Let's get you home."

❄

THE DRIVE HOME IS QUIET. Amelia doesn't talk to him or ask him any questions. She seems to understand the need for silence, and Justin is deeply grateful. He's maxed-out on input and for as much as he wants to talk with his sister when he gets home, he knows he's in no condition for it.

Amelia pulls up to the front door of the apartment complex instead of parking, but he invites her up, anyway.

"I didn't pack an overnight bag and you'll need me to pick you up tomorrow morning to swim and then get you to work, right?" she says.

He leans over to cup his hand around the back of her head and neck, kisses her, then rests his forehead against hers. "Thank you."

"Get some good rest tonight, my sweet bear."

When he gets inside his apartment, most of the lights are out except for a lamp in the living room. His sister lies on the couch, asleep, and curled up next to her is Crash. He smiles as he strips off his coat, scarf, gloves, and shoes, then walks over to his sleeping family. He crouches down and pets Crash, who immediately purrs in response.

"That's my girl," he tells her. "I knew you would love her, eventually."

"That's me," his sister's sleepy voice says. "The girl everyone will love ... eventually."

He's about to explain himself until he sees her smile.

"Work was shit for me," she says. "You?"

"Same."

"I told off my best friend's brother-in-law. Not sure if I still have that job anymore."

"I had a meltdown in front of everyone in the office. Not sure I have anyone's respect anymore."

"Dinner tomorrow?" she asks.

"Dinner tomorrow."

He stands. Before he goes to take a shower and then sink into his bed, he tells her, "You did the right thing."

"You too. Also, there's nothing wrong with you. At all."

Justin isn't sure how she always knows the exact right moments he needs to hear those words, but he's grateful. He nods and heads toward his room, Crash following behind him.

43

LIZZIE

Paula left me a voicemail during my shift at the gas station sharing that Simon's mother was coming to town for a few days to help with Sebastian and I wouldn't be needed. "It will offer us some time to re-group."

"Re-group" sounded a whole lot like "find a new nanny." I was sad to not work with Sebastian anymore and hoped for smoother times ahead for all of them. I had more worry over whether or not Nuria would be upset with me.

I also didn't want to lose Nuria the way I lost Monica. I hadn't faced her honestly like I should have. I texted Nuria.

Hey, I had a sort of confrontation thing with Simon yesterday. I'm hoping you'll let me tell you about it.

And if so, there's also so much more I want to tell you. A lot has happened recently.

Mac had texted to see if Justin and I had talked about everything yet. Both of my moms had sent a lot of hearts, love, and way too many "you've got this" animated gifs. Apparently, they'd been taking texting lessons from Justin.

Nuria replied to my texts a few minutes after I sent them.

YES! I have so much to tell you, too! NBD about whatever happened with Simon. *This family does NOT hide news. I would have heard about it if it were something big or awful.*

Hiking later this week?

I agreed, grateful for the cheerful text, though I wondered if plans would change if and when she found out the whole story with Paula, Simon, and Sebastian.

❄

MY NEWEST FRIEND, Crash, dashed off the stool and over to the door when she heard Justin's key in the lock. Up until then, she and I had been chatting amicably in the kitchen while I set up ingredients for the pizza Justin and I were going to make together for dinner. I'd almost suggested we cook something else, having had my fill of leftover homemade pizza for lunch and dinner the past couple of days, except Amelia told me he'd been making it daily, especially for me. A reconciliation gesture, as well as one of love.

Crash shared her own sign of love as she sat on her back legs and lifted her front paws up, waiting for Justin to finally pick her up.

"Hey," I called out.

I got a "hey" back, but Justin's focus quickly shifted to give all the attention to Crash. I didn't mind. He and I still had a lot of heavy baggage between us and Crash offered a slower transition to it.

He set her down, and she followed him into his bedroom where he'd change out of his suit. I fiddled with the cutting board, the knife, and the bowls that awaited the sliced and diced versions of the vegetables in front of me. It didn't seem right to begin dinner prep until Justin was ready. No sense throwing him off of this routine of him taking the lead and me being his sous chef.

Justin came out of his bedroom in khaki-style pants and a

lightweight, dark green sweater. Crash trotted along beside him and leaped up onto the same stool she'd been sitting on before Justin arrived home.

"No hissing," Justin said. "Does this mean you and Crash are still friends?"

"We are. She and I were having a nice chat as I got things ready in here."

Justin put on an apron. "She's a good listener."

Justin started in on the dough for the crust, and I began chopping the vegetables. "How did it go today? Were people weird with you?"

"Claire from HR was a little weird. My team was fine, though. Most everyone else thinks I'm an asshole, so it was all business as usual with them."

I wondered how true his statement was. Part of me jumped to the conclusion that his colleagues were the assholes by assuming things about him, but then I thought, what do I know? There's a whole different side to Justin I normally don't see.

"What happened yesterday?" I asked.

"I can't tell you some parts because of confidentiality, but I can tell you most of it." He launched into his day, starting with his swim, a doorknob prank from Shane—what a complete tool—then worrying about the snow and traveling to Amelia's, Austin telling him about something he found out about Shane, firing Shane—

"Hallelujah!" I cheered before he continued. His smile was small and brief before he finished with how that final bit triggered a meltdown.

"It might have been okay if Shane hadn't started yelling. Or if I'd done it in the privacy of my office instead of in front of everyone."

"That sucks, JT. I think it's good that you had witnesses to you firing him, though. If he'd accused you of not having the authority while sitting in your office, he might not have left."

He rolled out the dough and did his impressive toss of it into the air.

"Following protocol would have been best overall," Justin said.

"Okay, yeah, but it's not nearly as good of a story for you or for everyone who saw it. They all went home and said to their friends and family, 'You know that douchebag I've told you about? His boss came out and fired him in front of everyone. It was awesome!'"

"And then they continued with how the boss fell apart afterwards."

I slid the chopped green pepper from the cutting board into a bowl. "Exactly. That was all the most exciting drama an IT department has seen since Facebook came out with sad and angry emojis."

Justin smiled. The microwave beeped, and he took out a small dish of melted butter, which he then brushed over the crust before popping the pizza stone into the oven for a couple of minutes.

"Your turn," he said. "What happened with Sebastian? Do you still have the nannying job?"

I gave him my rundown of the issues I had been running into with Paula and Simon, as well as the fiasco from the day before. "I don't know if I still have that job. I suspect I don't due to the 'let's regroup' statement."

"Regroup. Reorganize. Reform. Restructure. But also recover. Recuperate."

"You think they're using one of those last two possible definitions?"

"Why not?" He pulled the pizza stone out of the oven and set it atop a folded towel on the countertop, readying it for sauce and toppings.

He made it sound so easy.

"Do you want to hear the real reason things went totally south at Meadowfields?" I asked.

"It's not because you feel responsible for that one girl's accident?"

"I feel responsible because I *was* responsible for it."

The fourth grade field trip to the zoo had mostly gone okay, despite the frustration of supporting a small group that included two children—Skylar and a boy named Rory—who triggered one another on a loop. Rory had no impulse control and reached out to grab anything that dangled, including scarves, hat bobbles, and the knit "plates" that stuck up along the spine of Skylar's pink stegosaurus hat.

Rory would pluck at Skylar's hat, Skylar would roar at him like a T-Rex, and Rory would yell back with "Mean! Mean! Mean!" which would then cause Skylar to run away. Most of the time she wouldn't go far, and we'd easily catch up to her as our group meandered from one exhibit to the next. And the other kids in the group were patient as I gave most of my attention to keeping Rory busy with fidget toys and offer fun challenges such as "Who can find the white spot on the big snake?" and "How many bats can you see?"

But sometimes Skylar would hide. And sometimes Rory would yank too hard on a scarf. Sometimes one of the other kids ran out of patience. By the time we gathered for the busses to go home, I was exhausted from being on high alert all day. The Triple As, along with several of the parents, stood apart from most of the students, drinking coffee. Ashley caught my eye and held up an extra cup.

Skylar was pacing on the periphery with a pop-it toy, but the rest of the kids were getting antsy and loud as they waited for the busses to arrive. Rory weaved in and around everyone, bopping heads like a game of Duck, Duck, Gray Duck, but it didn't seem to bother kids among their own building chaos.

Against better judgment, I walked over to grab the coffee from Ashley.

"And then," I said, putting my knife down as my self-directed anger and disgust escalated, "I took some fucking selfies with her and the others, like we were some stupid, fancy influencers or something. Like I was nineteen and thought I was being so fucking cool and popular."

What I didn't say was that I'd been so easily won over by one of the Triple As thinking enough of me for once to have gotten a coffee for me. I'd felt special. That is, until Ashley told me as she handed me the cup that they'd messed up her order and gave her the mistake for free. I'd gone along with the selfie to help laugh off the story and shed my embarrassing moment of self-importance.

"A familiar roar from Skylar interrupted us," I continued. "I looked over to see Rory holding Skylar's stegosaurus hat above his head with other kids laughing and one of them shouting for Rory to throw the hat to them. But Rory had terrible aim, and it shot past the curb, into the parking lot. And well, you know the rest of that part of the story."

"Why didn't Ashley bring the extra coffee over to you?" Justin asked.

My memories of the screaming children and Skylar in a tiny, tangled heap on the icy pavement came to a halt at Justin's question. "What do you mean?" I asked, although Justin's point slowly crept up to me.

"She should have brought the coffee to you since the kids still needed supervision."

How had I never considered this angle? I'd been frustrated that the teachers and parents weren't helping with the kids, but for some reason, I never connected it to the idea of Ashley at least joining me instead of beckoning me away.

"It doesn't absolve me from stepping away, though. I knew things were escalating."

Justin nods and it soothes me to know he doesn't lie to me—won't lie to me—to make me feel better. His observation about Ashley is an assurance and his agreement about my responsibility is an understanding. It made the next part of the story easier to tell him. I didn't hold on to any guilt about the aftermath, yet it also wasn't something I was very proud of.

We continued the pizza preparation as I went on with the story. "The next morning, during the emergency staff meeting, when our principal began with the words, 'unfortunate accident,' I stood and yelled at him and at those teachers for negligence and for valuing their social media following more than kids. That was why I took a one week leave at first. When I returned, my principal forced me into a meeting with him and the fourth grade teachers from the field trip and I apologized. I wasn't allowed to work one-on-one with kids anymore and only under the supervision of the special ed staff because I was unpredictable and some teachers were suddenly 'scared' of me."

Carrie, my former para-friend-turned teacher seemed especially fond of "checking in with me" to make sure I was okay and not in danger of having another mental breakdown because "she knew what it was like" to be in my position. The Triple As, of course, were the only teachers who were supposedly scared of me, but when they didn't get as much support from other teachers about this attitude, they followed Carrie's lead and turned it around into a fake concern for my mental health.

It was true not everyone blamed me for what happened to Skylar. Since the ones who did had my principal's ear, regardless of the special education director supporting me, blame and incompetence weighed heavier on me than any argument about circumstance and shared responsibility. Besides, didn't I turn around and blame everyone else the day after the accident?

Fiona's comment to me about it being difficult to stay somewhere that has caused harm hit me from two sides. Meadowfields had caused me harm in multiple ways, but I was complicit.

"I'm sorry all of that happened," Justin said. "I'm also glad you yelled at everyone. They probably needed to hear what you had to say, regardless of how you said it."

"Loudly and obnoxiously?"

He smiled and some of the tightness in my chest loosened. It gave me the courage to ask the next question. "Isn't that who I was when I was little? You know ... before?"

"Loud and obnoxious?"

"Yeah. I mean, I don't remember Beth ever yelling and she always seemed to figure out how to make you feel better. She knew what to do."

"You did, too," he said as he spread mozzarella cheese over the pizza.

I dumped some grated parmesan into a bowl and handed it to him with a spoon. He didn't like shaking it on from the canister, complaining it came out too unevenly. Sprinkling it with a spoon gave an even, proportional layer.

I didn't know what to say next. I hadn't been an overly affectionate child, so I doubted I'd ever brought Justin his favorite toys or tried to snuggle with him. More fuzzy memories came to me of Beth tucked into bed with Justin. There hadn't seemed like there was enough room for me.

Justin spoke again instead. "You always put things in order for me in the ways I liked it. Plates, glasses, napkins folded in half like a rectangle, then forks, then knives. Food according to how I put it on my plate. Drink containers last. I think Beth used to assume you changed everything around to bother me, but really you were helping me."

I shook my head. "I probably did it so you wouldn't scream or make Mom and Dad mad." I only remembered our dad as impatient and mean. His frustration with Justin overpowered any affection he felt for the rest of us. Our mom was unpredictable.

"Maybe that's true," Justin said. "But you still knew the right order. And you always asked me if you could hug me before you did it. You cleaned the toothpaste tube after you and Beth used it."

"Even if I did all of those things, how do you know it wasn't because I was always doing it to prevent you from yelling and screaming and ruining things?"

"So what if you did? I did ruin things sometimes. I still do."

"You didn't. You don't. You can't ruin things by just being yourself."

"Of course we can."

Well, he had me there. Obviously, I ruined things by being who I was. All incarnations of myself.

"Why do you insist upon assuming the worst about yourself?" Justin asked.

I stifled the urge to respond as I always had inside my head, that my sister was clearly the one he liked better because she was the good one. Except I couldn't use that excuse anymore, whether or not it was true. I had to live as myself.

"I think ... survivor's guilt?" I ventured. "And a way to remember what I wanted to about Beth. Regardless of details, my heart remembers how close you two were. For so long, I've been scared that one day you'd realize I'm not the one who you turned to back when you had a choice between us. It's hard reconciling your knowledge of the truth all this time and not knowing if you've come to me because you didn't have Beth, or if you've chosen to lean on me."

"I've relied on you most of our lives. Does it matter why?"

"Yes." I wished it didn't, but I couldn't let go of the fears. Maybe therapy would change that. For now, I needed the validation one way or another.

Justin slid the pizza stone back into the oven and set the timer. He turned to me and leaned against the counter. "Okay. Here are all the facts. Beth did have an instinct with me and I latched onto it because no one else understood my extreme emotions, not even me. It probably helped that she didn't know how everyone at school looked at me differently and treated me differently. You both were too young for that reality. Also, she never yelled at me."

"I yelled at you, though?"

"Sometimes, yes. I'm not saying I didn't deserve it, but on days when it seemed everyone was yelling at me, I took refuge with Beth. You want to know if I would have kept doing that with her if she didn't die and I can't answer that. I'm terrible at guessing how *living* people will act so to guess how four-year-old Beth would have been as she got older? I don't know."

"Next fact," he continued. "Beth died, you didn't. I can't remember why I said, 'she was supposed to be the good one' and I hate how something I did made you believe you haven't always been the very best person I know. You are the good one."

Truth bombs all around. Heat built up behind my eyelids and my voice came out thickly. "If I'm the good one, I have you to thank for it. You are the best person I know, too."

"Last fact," he said, then reached for my hand and held it in his own. "I choose you. Always."

My tears broke through and my chin fell to my chest. He squeezed my hand and added, "I love you, Lizzie-IssyBeth-Isabel. I'm really glad you didn't leave me alone in this world."

"I love you, too, JT." I choked out through my crying. "Thank you for saving me. Twenty-five years ago, now, and all the years in-between."

He pulled me into him, the kind of hug to remind me that he was always my home, no matter what and no matter who I thought I was.

"Will it irritate you if I change my name again?" I asked.

"It's never irritated me. Until recently, I just never understood it. I know names are important, but I also know our names are not everything we are." He released me and cleaned up the counter. "If they were, my nickname from Hugh would imply I would have to be a boy band pop star or emulate one."

I laughed. "There's still time."

"No, thank you. Do you have a new name picked out?"

"I was thinking Izzy. I know Isabel is my real name, and you used to call me Issy, but..."

"Izzy is an ideal name."

I smiled, appreciating the very *Justin* word for it. Not a "great" name or "perfect" name, but *ideal*. And while my name might not be everything I was, Justin's endorsement of it felt pretty close.

44

JUSTIN

"All Choice owes you an apology, Justin," Nihal says.

Caleb, who returned at the end of the week as Claire from HR indicated he would, has joined Justin in Nihal's office. It's the end of a long week, although one where he has learned a lot.

Caleb nods at Nihal's suggestion about an apology.

Justin also agrees with the suggestion, but isn't sure he, Nihal, and Caleb will agree about what the apology is for. "How so?"

"When Caleb took his unexpected leave of absence, we left you to your own devices to figure everything out. It wasn't the kind of transition it should have been."

Caleb puts his foot on the floor and leans forward. "I should have put a pin in your promotion and had some of the other department heads cover for me until I could come back and train you."

"That's not exactly what I—" Nihal starts, but Caleb keeps going.

"I didn't realize it at the time, but when I found out you had autism, suddenly everything made sense."

Nihal's eyes widen and Justin wonders if it's because he has some kind of lightbulb moment, too. "Caleb, what are—" Nihal begins again, but this time Justin interrupts.

"I don't understand. What is it exactly that suddenly made sense?"

Caleb nods and smiles and holds his hand out as he says, "Yes, that! You need me to be explicit. All the jokes you don't get are because you are one hundred percent literal. You don't like change." Caleb's voice changes pitch and he uses both hands to help with his enthusiastic lesson. "You need directions in clear, distinct steps. You're often rude, but who cares because you're super good with numbers and code."

"Caleb, wow," Nihal inserts himself more firmly. "You are really out of line right now."

"Which blog did you read all of that from?" Justin asks. He's not upset by all the stereotypes Caleb spilled out as Justin has heard and read them all before. He's watched the terrible representations of autistic people on TV or in movies. Hearing Caleb use the stereotypes to describe Justin specifically, however, hurts him more than he wants it to. He'd considered Caleb a friend. Not a close one, but at least a work friend. He thought Caleb knew him, yet Caleb has just whittled him down to a list of "symptoms."

Justin is hurt, yes. And also angry.

"First," Justin says, "I have never disclosed to anyone here about autism. Second, I have implemented countless updates and numerous new programs and initiatives with no need for your hand-holding."

Caleb sits back again. "Well, yeah, now that you mention it, I guess that's probably—"

"Third—yes, it is rude to interrupt, but that seems the norm we are following in our discussion right now—I didn't need you to train me in this new position. Although extra guidance in some nuances of a leadership role might have proved useful, I've done quite well as Project Manager. I've hired an exceptional software analyst, and our team, despite an initial setback, has rolled out significant upgrades with positive data to support calling them a success. Fourth, the issue has never been me or my promotion. It's been the insistence of keeping an under-qualified, immature, prejudiced, and misogynistic employee on our payroll in disregard of the numerous harassment reports against him."

"Those are some pretty heavy accusations, Justin." Caleb says. "I know you and Shane haven't been the best of friends, but your reports—"

"Caleb," Nihal says. "Justin's reports, which I've read and am shocked nothing has been done about them in all this time, are not the only ones filed against Shane. Two others recently came forward from the IT support team. Claire did some investigating for me and it would seem my predecessor convinced HR to dismiss the reports as not worth full investigation. That you and your counterpart with IT support deemed the complaints as 'petty pranks.' After talking with our president, it appears you are not the only one joining Shane in losing your job this week."

Justin has never been one for a dramatic reaction, but Nihal's casual news of "you're fired" to Caleb nearly has Justin dropping his jaw in shock. Instead, he strokes his jawline, thinking he can hold his mouth closed if necessary while organizing his thoughts.

"What?" Caleb asks.

"I think you'll find it a fair and generous severance package. We'll talk more later this morning, but for the moment, I need to speak with Justin individually."

"I don't understand," Caleb says.

Justin resists the urge to ask Caleb if he needs clear, distinct directions.

"That's part of the problem," Nihal says. "Now, if you'll excuse us?"

"I ... yes, okay." Caleb stands, and without looking at Justin, leaves Nihal's office.

"Well, then," Nihal says. "I'd like to back up to how I began this conversation before Caleb took us in the wrong direction. All Choice owes you an apology for allowing the continued harassment against you. Shane should have been let go far sooner and your decisive action to do it shows your team they can trust you to do what's best not only for the company, but more crucially, for them."

Some of Justin's anxiety slips away at the validation. He holds no regret over firing Shane. Aside from the initial uncertainty of how people would treat Justin after his work meltdown, he's enjoyed coming to the office more than he ever has. It's a reminder to him to never underestimate the importance of a safe work environment.

"Thank you," Justin says.

Nihal offers a small smile. "I think you can stop worrying about a team-building ice breaker after that grand gesture."

"I probably still need something for when I hire his replacement."

Nihal nods. "Perhaps you're right. And about that ... you're going to need two new analysts."

"Two? You want us to expand the team?"

"No, but I assume you'll want to promote either Austin or Yasmin to Project Manager, since that position will be open once you agree to the promotion to Systems Management Director."

Justin's heart rate spikes and his breathing shallows. He closes his eyes and works to slow everything down. He hears a rustle and then there's a hand on his shoulder and Justin opens his eyes again. Nihal sits where Caleb had.

"Too much all at once?" Nihal asks gently.

"This meeting has been, to quote my sister, 'A Lot.' But I'm okay, thank you."

Nihal laughs and sits back in his chair. "That it has. Look," he pauses, and the smile disappears. "I owe you an apology, too. When Caleb took his leave of absence, I should have stepped in sooner to make sure you were okay with the transition. To help with those nuances you mentioned. When I joined this company a few months ago, I didn't realize so much of my time would be spent on clean-up. What happened with the early launch of the new client portal wasn't just Shane's fault. It turns out Caleb let a few other things slide and the web team had some issues, too. I'm sorry I didn't communicate those issues to you."

Justin's never had a supervisor apologize to him before. Problems have always been waved off and sometimes circularly blamed on him for being too sensitive or narrow-minded. Or "too literal." His chest loosens and his shoulders relax as his body sinks into the back of the chair.

"I appreciate you saying that," Justin says. It feels too formal, but he also doesn't want to fall into a response that minimizes the moment, since he deserves the apology. *Always know your worth*, his sister tells him, has told him all of his life. He also knows he deserves the promotion Nihal offers. Even with the recent messiness, Justin knows he can handle the higher level responsibilities, especially with Yasmin as Project Manager. He has a few ideas for how both positions should take shape.

"What do you say about the promotion, then?" Nihal asks.

"Yes," Justin says. "I accept—with a few adjustments."

Nihal holds out his hand to shake Justin's. "I look forward to the negotiation."

45

IZZY

Nuria might have initially said "no big deal" regarding my blow-up with Simon, but I wasn't sure she'd feel the same way a few days later, after she would have surely heard more of the story from Paula. Yet, here we were at Hyland Lake Park for a snowshoe hike, with Nuria still waving off her sister's vague voicemail.

We trekked under a mostly cloudy sky, though the forecast didn't call for more snow. For the first time in weeks, the temperature remained above freezing without the icy wind, and that was almost a worthy trade for the sun.

I told Nuria all about the past couple of nannying sessions with Sebastian, the confrontations with Simon, and even my difficulties with Paula not really listening to me or her son. It had been a few days since everything happened, and I'd talked over the situation in more detail with Justin—and Amelia—as well as with Mac and LiLi. While some of Simon's behavior remained problematic, I was working on seeing the bigger picture from his and Paula's perspective, so I was able to offer Nuria a softer version of the story than I'd originally shared with Justin.

I was practicing grace.

"They'll come around," Nuria said. "To be honest, Simon can be a bit of an entitled, egotistical idiot that I've learned is sometimes just part of being a surgeon. I see it in Paula occasionally, too. I also know how much Simon loves Sebastian."

I knew this was true. I'd seen the way Simon's expression lit up when he came home to see his kid and the efforts to bring home things Sebastian would like. I also knew I wasn't ever seeing Simon or Paula at their best. They'd been going from a full-time daycare to adapting schedules around a part-time nanny.

Grace, I thought to myself again.

We came to a fork in the trail and looked at the map. "Longer way or shorter way?" Nuria asked.

"Longer. We have a lot to catch up on."

"Perfect." We headed along the path to our left. "The other thing is," Nuria went on, and I assumed we were still talking about nannying. "I basically knew you'd help them see that Sebastian needed different things. You told me you weren't 'qualified' or whatever to make a diagnosis, which I understand. Still, you effectively did that for Sebastian, and they're going to figure it out. I predict you get a phone call this weekend. I think you should ask for a raise."

I laughed at her last comment. "More money, more credibility?"

She nodded with a grin. "Ya sabes. Definitely."

I smiled. "They pay me pretty well already, but I'll keep that in mind." A raise would probably be the thing that would allow me to move out of Justin's place and live on my own again. Somehow, that idea didn't sound as appealing as it would have a few weeks ago.

I loosened my scarf—another Reign creation—to release some of the heat building up from our workout. Mid-thirties temperatures after a cold streak felt like hot weather in comparison. I also might have been feeling nervous about revealing the other recent events in my life, specifically the stuff about me, Justin, and my sister. It wasn't that I was ashamed of any of it. It was just still hard to talk about it. Justin said talking about hard things got easier the more we did it.

He was right, and I trusted Nuria, unlike the Triple As, who would have turned my painful past into a TikTok challenge.

"Do you remember when I told you about the car accident where I lost my sister and my mother?" I asked.

Nuria stopped, reached out to take my hand and squeezed it. "Yeah, I do." She let go, and we started walking again and I told her my story. Already, by this third time through, the words came out less jumbled, breathing was easier, and tears were less prolific. We reached the top of a hill and Nuria turned to me, her eyes glistening.

"Can I hug you?" Nuria's question came out shaky and I nodded, unable to trust my voice.

She lunged at me with her arms flung out and I did my best to hold on to her, except my snowshoes tangled into hers and soon we'd let go of each other as we fell into the snow. Our tears rapidly changed to laughter, lying on our backs, bodies slanting down the hill and our legs every which way. We'd gotten so much snow over the past several days that we'd sunk deep into it and as we tried to roll ourselves up and out of it from the incline, we laughed harder at the efforts to get upright again, which only made it more difficult.

After considerable rolling, rocking, and pulling at each other, we finally managed to stand and catch our breaths.

"Oh my god, I needed that so much," I said, my stomach aching from both laughter and the recovery effort.

"Snowshoes are great if you stay on your feet," Nuria said. "Absolutely worthless if you're literally ass deep into a snowbank. For real, though. Thank you for trusting me with your story. And I'm with Justin. You can't possibly have pulled off pretending to be someone else based upon a messed up memory from four-years-old."

"Yeah. You're right. But it feels like I've been pretending, and that's where I remain messed up. I'm working on it."

"Well, you don't have to work on it alone." She pointed down the trail. "C'mon, we're almost back."

"Your turn. I've monopolized enough of our time together. I want to hear your news."

Nuria threw out her arms, looked up at the sky, and said dramatically, "Finally, it can be all about me."

I bowed with a flourish towards her. "The floor is all yours, my queen."

"Well, while you've been off 'finding yourself'—" she smiled to show me she wasn't serious about the air quotes—"I've been trudging through volunteer shifts at my mom's clinic because she kept insisting they were short-staffed and desperately needed my help."

"I'm guessing they weren't in dire need after all?"

"Not really. It's not like I had nothing to do, but it was definitely my mom's way of getting me to reconsider my career path. Which I did, just not in the way she hoped and planned."

"And?"

"I'm going back to school. For game art and development through a school in New Hampshire. They have an online program and since my schedule is so flexible at the salon, I can easily make the job and classes work."

"Nuria, that's so great. I'm extra happy that it's an online program because I don't think I have it in me to find another best friend."

"Best haircut I ever gave."

"Among other things," I nudged her with a knowing smile. "Seriously, I'm so excited for you. Your art is absolutely amazing. I can't wait to play all the games you help create."

"Thanks. Can you bring that confidence with you when I take you with me to tell my mom?"

"She doesn't know?"

"I only just got the acceptance letter this morning, and I already sent them my deposit before I could chicken out!"

I whooped in appreciation. "Yesssss! I'd tackle hug you, but we know how that will end up."

She laughed. "Yeah, with our ends up."

We reached the end of our trail, full circle to where we'd started. "I will definitely be there for moral support if you need it when you tell your mom. I'll bring all the research stats about how much money you can make and the international popularity of solid game design. I'll bring her *Tomorrow and Tomorrow and Tomorrow* by Gabrielle Zevin! Those characters were wildly successful with their gaming business."

"And were in a pretty dysfunctional relationship. You're the best, but I was thinking I'd go with the 'this will make me happy' argument."

I grabbed onto Nuria's shoulder as I popped off each of my snowshoes. "I suppose if you want to be all authentic or whatever, that's one way to go. When do you start classes?"

"Summer. I'm just starting with one intro class. Fundamentals of Design."

"That is so cool. Your mom will come around. I know it. I bet all she wants is for you to get a degree to give you more options in the future."

Nuria shrugged. "I hope so."

I shook my head. I'd had a really great talk with Mama LiLi and Mama Mac the day before, who finally admitted the "options" part was all they ever wanted for me. I'd been so close to graduating and they'd always wanted me to simply finish the final semester's worth of credits. They helped me dig into what I did and didn't like about working in a school as well as what I'd always enjoyed about PCA work. LiLi came up with the possibility that clicked.

"I've decided to go back to school, too," I told Nuria as we got into her car.

"Yeah? Gonna finish up the teaching degree and be Sebastian's teacher next?"

"Not exactly. An occupational therapist. I'll be able to keep working with kids like Sebastian. Some OTs work in schools, but many don't. I'd get to work with families who understand their kids' needs and help with developing social and self-regulatory skills."

"That's so cool. We'll be study buddies!"

I high-fived her. "I can't wait."

Nuria put the car in gear, and as she drove out of the parking lot she asked, "Wanna get coffee?"

"I do, but can we do a drive-through for it? There's something else I want to do today, and I'm hoping you can help me with it."

46

IZZY

Not only did Paula and Simon "come around" like Nuria said they would, but they also increased my hours and pay, allowing me to reduce my hours at the gas station and still earn enough to keep saving for school and eventually move out of Justin's place. Paula, Simon, and I had a good, honest talk about Sebastian's needs and their boundaries for me. They appreciated the kinds of help I could offer and how I always put Sebastian first. We agreed to take time daily to share with each other more details about Sebastian's day so we could all contribute to his routine and prepare Sebastian for last minute changes to plans.

For the first time in months, I looked forward to my jobs again, and I was excited to do both of them right, even the Gas-n-Guzzle. Fiona stopped by the gas station weekly with Skylar, and I joined Fiona separately one day for coffee. It felt good to be developing a potential new friendship and doing it as the truest *me* that I hadn't been for a long time.

It was Thursday, one of the two days per week I took care of Sebastian all day. We were walking through a parking lot towards the Panera entrance, each holding an item under one arm and holding hands with the other. Sebastian would only hold hands if he wore mittens or gloves, which he did today as we traipsed through the slushy lot of a warmer, sunny March day, though still not yet forty degrees outside.

"I like the rainbow sticker on that car because it's a rainbow. I don't like the color of that car because I don't like the color green." Sebastian was in a stage of stating all of his likes and dislikes, probably because Simon sat with him earlier in the week, talking with him about how he and his mom needed to understand why he liked or didn't like certain things. While Sebastian did this in the way Simon and Paula expected sometimes—like when he said a shirt felt too itchy—he also did it with everything else, without always having a clear reason to offer for the like or dislike.

"I don't like his jeans because they have holes," Sebastian said as we passed a couple who might have been father and son.

Of course, we were also working on when it was polite or impolite to express those opinions.

The man laughed. "I don't either, kiddo. Thanks for being on my side."

For the record, Sebastian liked my hair, striped sweater, jeans, boots, and hat. He didn't like my gauges, nose ring, or my jacket. Almost all valuations were based upon color choices, except for the nose ring, but he said it looked like it would be itchy.

We were meeting Justin for lunch. We were a substitute for Amelia, who he normally ate lunch with every Thursday. She had an appointment and the night before, Justin invited me, saying it might be fun to meet Sebastian if he was up for it. For me, it was perfect timing because of the package under my arm —I'd gotten the notification early in the morning that it was ready.

I let Sebastian do the ordering on the touchscreen kiosk and by the time we sat at a corner table, Justin had arrived. He'd ordered ahead, grabbed his food from the pickup shelf, and joined us at the table as Sebastian unpacked his lunch bag. We'd looked at the menu ahead of time and though Sebastian liked grilled cheese sandwiches, he'd never tried one from this restaurant before and opted to go with his own, tried-and-true choices.

I introduced Justin and Sebastian to one another.

"I don't like your shirt because it's green," Sebastian said. With anyone other than Justin, this might have signaled an inauspicious beginning. It was my brother, though, and his response reinforced why I didn't need to worry.

"I understand. I don't really like this shirt, either," Justin said.

I laughed. "Why are you wearing it, then?"

"Because Amelia bought it for me. She likes me in green. She forgot about my preference for a higher cotton blend."

"You probably at least should have worn it when she'd see you in it, though."

"Well, she did see me for a few minutes after swimming this morning. She also told me I could give this shirt away after today."

I loved Amelia and hoped she'd reminded him to be straight with her about such things in the future.

"I like your coat because it's black," Sebastian inserted himself again.

"Thank you. I like your mittens because I like the pigs on them," Justin replied.

"Thank you. I like my mittens, too."

"Let's be all done with what you like and don't like for a few minutes, okay?" I interjected before this ran down a never-ending path. "You can share more after we leave the restaurant."

My food came, and suddenly I was too nervous to eat it.

"What's wrong?" Justin asked after a bit when he noticed I had barely touched my sandwich or chips.

"I brought you something, but now I'm kind of worried it's maybe a little silly and not as cool as I originally thought."

"Is it an eighty percent polyester blend dress shirt?"

"Rude."

He smiled.

"No, but, whatever, here you go." I gave him the flat, brown-paper-wrapped present.

Justin tore away one side of the paper and slid out the framed artwork. After my hike with Nuria a week ago, we'd gone back to her place, and I told her I'd wanted to do something for Justin. I'd wanted to find a way to show him how much he meant to me, and I wasn't especially artistic. I thought I could compromise by using a website to create a cool design of all the words I associated with Justin.

Nuria gave the idea an extra boost after hearing about our imaginative exploits as kids. She created a pencil drawing backdrop of a castle—our Gramsie-Graham Castle—and in the center, in larger, block lettering, was the word "brother." I filled the page with words and their synonyms for ideas like "giving," "creative," "kind," "caretaker," and "funny."

Justin's voice was quiet. "Oh, this is *fantastic*. Fabulous. Outstanding. Remarkable. Also, did you come up with all of these words on your own?"

"Most of them, but you know, it wouldn't be really a *you* gift if it didn't have more obscure words, too." Such as "tutelary" and "paladin."

"Am I holding you in this photo?" he asked of the picture our moms had sent me to fill the "O" in "brother." It was of Justin, age four, holding me, or maybe my sister, as a baby.

"Honestly? I don't know. Our moms weren't sure, either, but I figured it didn't matter. I'm kind of surprised you don't know." I had been a little worried he would remember and that it would have been Beth and not me. But then I decided I didn't care.

Justin had been my brother back then, just as he still was now. A photo didn't change that.

"Thank you, Izzy. I like it because I love it."

"All done what we like and don't like until we leave the restaurant," Sebastian reminded Justin.

"Correct," Justin said. "Izzy, I've been working on something, too, for you."

"What? Why?"

"Why not? Except we've been hitting dead ends."

"What do you mean?"

Justin still had his eyes on the framed poster, probably reading every single word on it. "Me and moms are trying to change the death certificate. To change the name to Elizabeth, but we need evidence to support it and since you were identical twins, DNA won't help. We were trying to track down Dad, but we can't find him."

Whoa. I sat back, a little stunned by the offer. By the possibility. I hadn't seen the death certificate, but I wonder if I had, or saw it now ... how would I feel about seeing the name—my name—Isabel on it? My throat closed up for a moment as I envisioned it, then the feeling passed and I swallowed once more without issue.

"Once we found him," Justin went on, looking up at me now, "we were going to ask you about it, making sure it's something you would want. Is it something you want? Will it help?"

My heart burst for the deeply thoughtful gesture. "Wow, Justin. That is ... I don't know if it's something I need or want." Part of me had the urge to say I didn't want it. Honesty with myself, authenticity, was my work-in-progress and my truth signaled the importance of a remedied death certificate, so I nodded. "Yeah, actually. It would help. If we can do it. Thank you."

Justin's eyes went back to the frame, and I saw the moment

his eyes caught it. The last word in the frame, ever-so-slightly bigger and almost like a signature.

JustIzz.

Justin's voice remained low, but now turned rough with emotion. "It's like IssyBeth, but us."

"Do you li—" I stopped myself from saying "like," not wanting Sebastian to interrupt the moment. "Does it work?"

He smiled. "It's ideal."

I wiped away a tear that escaped my eye and sank into Justin's approval. I didn't always know how to nurture Justin and I'd never know if my sister would have remained the "good one" over me had she survived the accident. Justin could be irritating, obtuse, and ridiculously finicky about shoes on his carpet. Yet, together, we'd always figured out all the important ways to be each other's refuge. Each other's home.

"Sebastian," I said. "Let's talk about our likes and dislikes again. I like my brother because he's my best friend."

"And I like my sister because she won't be upset when I say I have to get back to work." He stood to put on his coat. Sebastian jumped in immediately with his opinions, starting with his cheese sandwich. As he prattled on, Justin leaned over to kiss me on top of my head and added, "And she's my best friend, too. JustIzz rules the castle."

He grabbed his present and waved to Sebastian, who paid him no attention and merely continued with his list of opinions about his drink, his crackers, the chair he sat on, the different people he'd seen throughout our lunch. I could only grin, loving how lucky I was to be me, Izzy, and every person I had been to bring me to this point.

I didn't know if I'd ever find the perfect closure to all my questions about me and my sister or about her and Justin. The only answer I needed right now was about Justin and Izzy. *JustIzz.*

I loved everything we were together. We were ideal.

ACKNOWLEDGMENTS

Not a single book I write is done in isolation, and none of them could reach your hands, my fabulous reader, without the support (help, assistance, advocacy, care, championship) of others in my writing community. The least I can do is try to name them all, yes?

I started writing this book almost ten years ago. Ten! Usually people say it takes that long to write their first novel, and this is my third to publish, so that gives you an idea of how hard I worked (endeavored, labored, strove, toiled, struggled) to make this book what it needed to be. The siblings were always at the core, but thanks to Jen Escue for listening to the much more eyebrow-raising ideas I originally had for this story back while we explored Puerto Rico. Or perhaps it was during an off-travel year when we met somewhere between Minnesota and Tennessee. And thanks to her for reading a completely different novel between then and when I was finally able to come back to this one. And later for giving it a read-through on the way to Colombia and talking through the prologue, especially.

I seriously don't know when this novel ever would have been finished had it not been for my critique partners, Lynn Haraldson and Densie Webb. Thank you for motivating (urging, driving, pushing, prompting, impelling) me to finish and for all of the other ways you've made this story stronger and your patience with me and Lizzie. I'm grateful to you both for taking me across this finish line.

There are several others who have contributed to (collaborated, participated, clarified, added to, fostered) the development and betterment of this story in both small and larger ways. Thank you to Elena Mikalsen, Carolyn Morain, David Herbst, Melisa Rivera, Jeff Taylor, Mitch Saice, Phyllis Book, Nancy Ostrom, Andy Rundquist, Di Ann Rundquist.

Thank you to Ann's Badass Basement Babes (best writing group name ever) and WFWA - especially our Tuesday night Write-In crew. We are few, but we are stalwart (resolute, committed, dedicated, tenacious, true).

Thank you to Claire Smith and BookSmith Design for the beautiful cover that captures the story perfectly and to Charlie Rundquist (Dawn Sky Web Design) for my beautiful website which has all kinds of extras on it and you should definitely check it out.

Thank you to my husband, who always champions my dreams, no matter what they are, and to my kids. Once again, I'm sorry that this still isn't the Cloud Stories book. Then again, maybe you don't care anymore, although I still plan to get those out into the world, too.

I have a continuing, deep gratitude for an amazing community of family and friends who have always, *always* supported me and my writing. Not everyone has this kind of support. I know how lucky I am. And if you don't have this support, I hope you still write. And even if you don't write, I hope each and every one of you gives time to do the thing you love no matter what it is. Passions don't have to be profitable to be what brings you joy.

Finally, and most importantly, thank YOU, my dear readers. Always.

READER'S GUIDE QUESTIONS

this isn't everything you are

1. How does the winter season and weather affect each of Justin and Lizzie's trauma responses?
2. Justin at one point considers that he's been experiencing near meltdowns and actual meltdowns more frequently than usual. What is happening to trigger them? Do you think Justin suspects why it's happening? Or is he in denial? For someone who is "almost always completely honest," why might he not be facing this honesty about himself?
3. If Lizzie had chosen to move in with her moms instead of Justin, how might Lizzie's path have been different? How would it have affected her relationship with Justin?
4. There are references throughout the story to Hugh, Lizzie and Justin's cousin and Justin's best friend. How has his death affected each of them?
5. During Lizzie and Justin's drive in the winter storm, Lizzie accuses Justin of playing the victim and hiding behind his autism. Why does she feel he's doing this? Do you agree with her?

6. While Lizzie is definitely "lost" throughout the story and figuring out who she is and what she wants, Justin also concludes she is sad. What does he see and recognize to come to this conclusion?
7. Justin struggles with routine disruptions and unpredictable behaviors from others. What kinds of things on a regular basis cause you to struggle? How does your build-up of struggles differ from Justin's? How do his reactions and yours (or others like you) differ?
8. Is Lizzie to blame for Skylar's accident? Why or why not?
9. How do you live with uncertain truths or fuzzy memories? How have Lizzie and Justin dealt with their unknown past? How might they work through it, moving forward?

WHAT'S NEXT?

One of the great ways to support an author is to leave a review or rating of their books. It can just be a rating or even a single line opinion. Any review helps readers find authors' books. Goodreads, Amazon, Barnes & Noble, BookBub, StoryGraph... wherever else. They all help! Thank you for considering!

Want to keep up with what's coming? Where I'll be (in-person and virtually)? Tidbits about life and stuff? Book recommendations? Extra stuff about my books and characters? Sign up for my newsletter! I'd love to see you there.

https://jmarierundquist.com

Turn the page for a sneak peek at the opening chapter of my next book, *When I Leave You* - a story about love, loss, transition, and forged family

WHEN I LEAVE YOU

2015-*Before*

"My mother, of all people, found me a personal trainer to hire for the salon." Corrina tells me on the speaker phone as I pull into my garage. "And he's transgender!"

"Your mother contains multitudes," I say, turning off the engine, but leave the keys in the ignition so I can still talk to my best friend in hands-free mode.

"I begrudgingly accept the truth of that statement. He's pretty hot, too, but I refuse to date someone my mother has recommended, no matter how much she is evolving."

I laugh. "Fair. Look, I'm home and I gotta get inside for dinner. Are you coming over for Sunday brunch?" Sunday brunch is a resurrection of a tradition she, my daughter, Melanie, and I used to have for years. When I started dating my husband, Tim, the tradition became more sporadic, and then in the past year or so, dropped off completely. The foundation of our lives crumbled like a building caught too near a fault line after an earthquake. Corrina was thrown out of the debris while I remained buried within it.

And yet, it's as though I dug myself out, tossing rocks aside that landed on her instead. She caught all of those rocks and used them to lay a new ground for me, Melanie, and Tim, then took the rest to build something else: her new venture into the salon and fitness business aimed at serving the LGBTQ community as well as any other underserved populations.

Corrina's amazing and I'd let myself forget that she is my cornerstone. We are back to daily phone conversations, Sunday brunches, girls' nights out, and soon, I hope I will learn about the shadows I occasionally spot behind her cheerful disposition.

"I will definitely be at brunch with a tasty, pastry treat. Love you, Ellie."

"Love you, too."

When I walk through the mudroom and into the kitchen, I expect to be hit with appetizing dinner aromas. Tim always makes it home before I do and usually cooks dinner, and I clean up. Instead, I see him staring into the fridge and Melanie, my seventeen-year-old daughter, slouching at the kitchen table staring into her phone.

"Eat out or eat in?" I ask.

"Eat out," Tim replies, closing the refrigerator door decisively. "We deserve it."

"I think we should go to El Loro," Melanie says from the table.

"Definitely," I reply.

Tim's hand snakes around mine and Melanie puts away her phone with an exclamation of "Awesome!" I tilt my head up to Tim's and kiss him. His other hand cradles my neck and face to hold me there just a smidgen longer. It's easy to relax into this kiss, and I feel anticipation for later that night. Tim's kisses have that effect on me pretty much every single time.

It's late March, and the sun still lights the sky, the temperature hovers close to sixty, and the snow melts away like crazy as we enter the tail end of a long, cold, Minnesota winter. Mel doesn't have that much homework, and I don't have any papers to grade that can't be saved for the next day. A dinner out to celebrate nothing other than a fresh new season blooming ahead draws us in easily, especially after too many impossibly difficult months.

Tim drives, and on the way to El Loro Mel talks about prom. I worry for a moment she'll be upset she doesn't have a date for this all-important high school milestone. I'd understand if she were unhappy. It's her senior year and she broke up with her boyfriend recently. Instead, she chatters on about the plans she has with her friends, unless one of them ends up having a date after all, but even then, that friend probably won't go because everyone is still so lame about same-sex prom couples at her school.

"Why can't our school be like some of those others where they're voting for transgender homecoming kings and queens?"

"You guys have been trying, Mel. Sometimes progress moves at glacial speed," I tell her, then pivot in my seat so I can see her better in the back. "What about an alternative prom?"

"We talked about that, but then we figured how much work it would be to set up. And where would we even hold it? Besides, now there's not enough time to pull it off."

Tim looks at me, eyebrows raised. I give him a little shrug and an expression that indicates, why not? He nods with a smile and chimes in. "We could host something at our house for you and your friends. Maybe the backyard?"

"Some of those fancier summer Christmas-type lights would make the yard look festive. We can make some fancy snacks and mocktails," I say.

The idea excites me. I latch onto it, clinging to this connection with my daughter who has hidden so many parts of herself from me lately. "I bet we'd easily convince Corrina to stop by and be a photographer." I say we can "convince" her, but she'll be all over this entire plan like glitter on, well, everything.

"No offense, Mom, but like, can my friends and I just get a hotel room?"

"Oh." I swivel to face forward again, telling myself to ignore her stinging tone, the return of teenage rejection. My instinct is to reject Mel's request out-of-hand. I tamp down the urge to exert total control over the decision and put my trust in Tim to offer what I know will be a much more measured and fair response. Our therapist would be proud.

"Let's talk more about the hotel room option over dinner," Tim says.

"Okay."

The easy agreement from Mel reinforces my efforts to let go of my tight hold over my little girl, who is obviously not so little anymore. I can't quite put my finger on it, but something within her seemed to change after she broke up with her boyfriend after being with him for almost a year. She's stronger, which both surprises me and makes me incredibly proud of her. I shouldn't take her rebuff about my prom day idea as an insult. She's simply reminding me that it isn't her thing.

When we arrive at the restaurant, Tim, with a limp that may never completely go away despite all the physical therapy since the accident ten months ago, meets me on my side of the car, like he always does, even after seven years of marriage. I step out onto the pavement and run my hand down his arm as he closes the door after me. We walk, the three of us, happy, hopeful.

Tim's soft, warm hand holds mine securely as we cross the parking lot to the restaurant. Though the sun sits low in the sky, the remnants of its presence throughout the day settle deep inside me. Glimpses of spring in Minnesota are enough to cheer anyone, including my angsty teenager, who challenges Tim to a hot pepper eating contest. He readily agrees, since Mel usually loses. After all, Timoteo Rivera has many more years of spicy food behind him.

We are all different, yet Mel still seems the one most distant from me. As a family, we have been through the wringer. Mel, however, has something in her eyes that hint at a hidden secret. Perhaps it isn't a secret, but I don't know what it is. I want so much to carry this moment forward, to propel us along the right track. I'm no stranger to hard work. I will keep at it. After all, she has willingly joined us. We are all together, still a family.

I turn my head to smile at Tim.

And then, everything happens.

ABOUT THE AUTHOR

J. Marie Rundquist believes a day isn't complete without time spent reading. Stories she loves best–to read and to write–feature characters from all walks of life who learn from one another. When she isn't writing, you'll find J. Marie exploring all the K-12 public education world has to offer through teaching, learning, and supporting others in their educational roles.

In spite of trying to live in other parts of the U.S., J. Marie accepted her fate and now embraces six-month winters in Minnesota, showing off photos of hiking in sub-zero temperatures. She lives in the Twin Cities with her family, two cats, and a never-ending supply of Dr. Pepper.

Photo credit: Kate Ann Photography

- facebook.com/JMarieRundquist
- instagram.com/ProfeJMarie
- bookbub.com/profile/j-marie-rundquist
- threads.net/@profejmarie